SECOND VIOLIN

SECOND VIOLIN

John Lawton

Weidenfeld & Nicolson
LONDON

First published in Great Britain in 2007
by Weidenfeld & Nicolson

1 3 5 7 9 10 8 6 4 2

© 2007 John Lawton

A CIP catalogue record for this book
is available from the British Library.

ISBN-13: 978 0 297 851 967
ISBN-10: 0 297 851 969

Typeset by Input Data Services Ltd, Frome

Printed in Great Britain by Clays Ltd, St Ives plc

Weidenfeld & Nicolson

The Orion Publishing Group Ltd
Orion House
5 Upper Saint Martin's Lane
London, WC2H 9EA

www.orionbooks.co.uk

for
Ion Trewin

Britain became bomb-conscious: trenches were dug; many Londoners went to earth in the country; hardly had the trenches become water-logged and the earths abandoned than it was all to do again. After that many new fashions came in; windows were crisscrossed with tape; gas masks were carried about and left in cinemas and on blackberry bushes, bags of sand lay on pavements, rotted, sprouted, and burst asunder; through Cimmerian blackness torches were flashed, annoying drivers; women went into trousers, civilians into fire, ambulance and wardens' stations, older men into the Home Guard; young men and women were put into the forces and factories, enemy aliens (hostile and friendly) into camps, British Fascists and others into gaol, policemen into tin hats. Cars crashed all night into street refuges, pedestrians, and each other; the warning banshee wailed by night and day; people left their beds and sat in shelters ... where a cheerful, if at times malicious, envious and quarrelsome social life throve ... Conversation was for some months on catastrophic lines; key-words were *siren* (by the less well instructed pronounced *sireen*), *all clear, bomb, under the table, a fine mess in blank street, a nice shelter in dash street,* and *blitz* ... [later] conversation tended to turn on ... food: what was permitted, what was to be had, what was not permitted and where this was to be had and at what cost, what was not to be had at all and how so-and-so had had it ... food talk often beat bomb talk. So, later, did clothes coupons talk (those who said *sireen* said *cyoopons*). Standards of smartness depreciated, to the relief of those who found them tedious or inaccessible. Bare legs became a feminine summer fashion; men, more sartorially conservative, clung to such socks as they had. Evening dress was seldom seen. Life was less decorative and less social; but human gregariousness found, as always, its outlets. For many, indeed, it became more communal than before; uniformed men and women were assembled for military or civil defence, and, in the intervals of their duties, played, ate and drank together; it was a life which tended to resolve class distinctions; taxi-drivers, dustmen, window-cleaners ... shop assistants, hairdressers, and young ladies and gentlemen from expensive schools and universities, met and played and worked on level terms, addressing each other by nicknames. English social life is ... moving a few steps nearer that democracy for which we say we are fighting and have never yet had ... and whether these will be retraced or continued when the solvent furnace of war dies down ... we cannot yet know.

Rose Macaulay, *Life Among the English,* 1942

Thought I heard the thunder rumbling in the sky;
It was Hitler over Europe, saying: 'They must die';
We were in his mind, my dear, we were in his mind.

Saw a poodle in a jacket fastened with a pin,
Saw a door opened and a cat let in:
But they weren't German Jews, my dear, but they weren't German Jews.
W.H. AUDEN *from* REFUGEE BLUES 1939

'Do you think this war will rid us of cellophane?
I speak feelingly, having just tried to get at
the interior of a box of cigars.
A world without cellophane or petrol – as in my youth!
What a dream of bliss'
H.M. HARWOOD, *from a letter to* SAM BEHRMAN
19 SEPTEMBER 1939

'If ever there was a time when one should wear
life like a loose garment, this is it'
U.S. GENERAL RAYMOND LEE,
The London Observer Diaries
15 SEPTEMBER 1940

I

Red Vienna

At 451 °F paper burns.
At 900 °F glass melts.
At 536 °F flesh will burst into flames.
At −40 °F Fahrenheit and Centigrade meet.

§

Under moonlight
a madman dances.

§ I

12 March 1938
Hampstead, London

Yellow.

It was going to be a yellow day.

The nameless bird trilling in the tree outside his window told him that. He had learnt too little of the taxonomy of English flora and fauna to be at all certain what the bird was. A Golden Grebe? A Mustard Bustard? He took its song as both criticism and compliment – 'cheek, cheek, cheek'.

Fine, he thought, if there's one thing I have in spades it's cheek. Do I need a bird to tell me that?

He watched its head bobbing, heard again the rapid chirp – now more 'tseek' than 'cheek', and was wondering if he had a yellow tie somewhere for this yellow day and whether it might sit remotely well with his suit, when Polly the housemaid came in.

'My dear, tell me . . . what is this bird in the tree here?'

'Boss . . . there's bigger fish to fry than some tom tit–'

He cut her short.

'There, do you see? In the cherry tree. The one with the yellow breast.'

'Boss . . . I'm a Londoner. Born, bred and never been further than Southend. Sparrers is me limit. Just call it a yeller wotsit and listen to me.'

He turned. It was typical of her to be so casual in her dealings with him, untypical of her to find anything so urgent. It was as though she'd seized him by his lapels.

'Yes?'

''Itler's invaded Austria. It was on the wireless just now. The missis sent me to to tell you.'

The missis was his wife. Time there was, and not that long ago, when he would have learnt of such things not by his wife sending in the maid, but by a phone call from his Fleet Street office at whatever time of day or night, deskside or bedside. On his seventy-fifth birthday he had told his editors, 'History can now wait for me.' Usually history waited until he had his first cup of coffee in his hand.

'Do you want me to turn the set on in here, Boss?'

'Yes, my dear. Please do that.'

It was indeed a yellow day. What other colour has cowardice ever had? It was all too, too predictable. Hitler had signalled his punches like a feinting boxer. He had had his editorial ready for a month now, ever since Hitler and Schuschnigg had met at Berchtesgaden in the middle of February for Schuschnigg's ritual humiliation – 'I am the greatest German that ever lived!' . . . so much for Goethe, so much for Schiller, for Luther and Charlemagne, for Beethoven and Bach. He'd listen to the next bulletin on the wireless, and if nothing forced a change upon him, and he doubted that it would, he'd take the editorial out of his desk drawer and have a cab take it to Fleet Street for the evening edition. All it needed was his signature . . . a rapid flourish of the pen and, in the near-cyrillic of his handwriting, the words 'Alexei Troy'.

§ 2

14 March
Vienna

The Führer took his triumphant time getting to Vienna. There was his hometown of Linz to be visited, embraced, captured on the road to Vienna. The town from which, as he put it himself, Providence had called him. He drove through streets gaily decked out with the National Socialist flag – red and black can be so striking in its simplicity – past cheering citizens, gaily decked out in green jackets and lederhosen.

In the second car SD Standartenführer Wolfgang Stahl, a fellow Austrian, wondered where they got it all from. As though some wily rag-and-bone man had been round the week before with a job lot of old coats and leather britches. It seemed to him to be parody, to be bad taste, to be Austria's joke at its own expense. All this, all of it, would be at Austria's expense. It was simply that Austria didn't know it.

It was past lunchtime on the following day before the entourage rolled into Vienna. Hitler was in a foul mood. The motorcade had broken down. Not just the one vehicle but dozens had ground to a halt with mechanical failure. It looked half-arsed. And the trick to invading without a shot fired, to taking a country that was all too willing to capitulate, was to look wholly-arsed, as though you could have taken them by force if you so desired. The Wehrmacht was untested in the field. Any failure now sent out the wrong signal to the fair-weather friends of Austria and Czechoslovakia. The world was watching. That nincompoop Chamberlain was watching. Entering Vienna, they crossed a bridge that had been mined. Schellenberg had inspected the device personally, taken a gamble with their lives, thought better of telling this to Hitler, and mentioned it to Stahl only as a problem solved. It was just as well. The bad mood did not lift. Hitler accepted the adulation of the crowds in the Heldenplatz, scowled through the reception at the Hofburg Palace and flew on to Munich the next morning. Country captured, country visited, Secret Police installed. Next.

Stahl stayed. The SS was already rounding up suspects, tormenting Jews and murdering discreetly as a preamble to murdering indiscreetly. Neither was his job. Himmler and Schellenberg had flown in ahead of the convoy at first light. Heydrich, flash as ever, had flown in in his own private plane, meditating on his plans for Austria's first concentration camp. They had gilded thugs aplenty, thugs in oak leaves, thugs in lightning, thugs in black and silver. Stahl was just an ornament. He'd been invited to Vienna, his native city, merely as part of the Führer's sense of triumphalism. He'd been presented to the Viennese as a prodigal son, someone not quite called by Providence, which only had room for one, but touched by it. The hand of fate that had grabbed Adolf Hitler, had brushed the sleeve of Wolfgang Stahl. Others stayed on simply because the pickings were too rich – not simply what could be stolen, but what could be bought. The department stores of Vienna were so much better stocked than those in Berlin. Stahl had in his pocket a hand-written note from Hermann Göring – 'Could you get me a dozen winter woollen underpants from Gerngross's, waist 130 cm?'

Stahl stayed because Vienna fixed him, fixed him and transfixed him as surely as if it had struck out, stabbed him and pinned him to the wall. He could not help Vienna in her suffering, and at the same time he could not resist watching as she suffered.

§ 3

14 March
Berlin

TELEGRAMME : TROYTOWNLON

TO : TROYTOWNBER

ATT: ROD TROY

MY BOY, DO YOU NOT THINK IT TIME YOU CAME HOME?

THIS IS, DARE I SAY, A JACKBOOT TOO FAR.

DO NOT WAIT FOR WAR. COME BACK NOW.

COME BACK TO YOUR WIFE AND YOUR FAMILY.

YOUR LOVING FATHER,

ALEX TROY.

Rod showed the telegramme to Hugh Greene in Kranzler's restaurant at lunchtime.

'I can't say I'm always getting them. But it's not the first and it won't be the last. Thing is ... the old man never wanted me to come out in the first place.'

In 1933, when the Nazis had taken power, Rod had been just short of his twenty-fifth birthday and had been three years a parliamentary correspondent on his father's *Sunday Post*. He begged his father for the Berlin posting. In the September the old man had finally agreed and Rod had presented himself to the Press Office of the National Socialist

6

Workers' Party and the British Embassy as the new Berlin Correspondent for the Troy Press. The Germans had looked askance at his authentication, but said nothing. The embassy had said in one of those subtle walls-have-ears tones, 'You're taking one hell of a risk, old boy.'

Greene echoed the line now, 'Your father has a point. You don't have the protection I have.'

Greene had come to Berlin, via Munich, for the *Daily Telegraph* the February after Rod. He was younger than Rod by nearly three years, and taller by more than three inches. They had been 'absolute beginners' together, often sharing what they knew. Rod revelled in the languid mischief that Greene seemed to exude, the nascent wickedness of the man. It reminded him more than somewhat of his younger brother. Much as he was loth to admit it, there were times when he missed his brother. Even more he mised his wife. She had joined him a few weeks after the posting and, like the colonial wife in Nigeria or Sierra Leone, she had returned home for the birth of their first child in 1936, and was home now expecting the second.

'If I have to weigh that one up every time Hitler pushes the country to the brink, I might as well go home and become the gardening columnist reporting on outbreaks of honey fungus and the private life of the roving vole.'

'Questing vole, surely?' said Greene. '"Something something through the plashy fens goes the questing vole".'

Rod ignored this.

'What matters, what matters now is that I should be here. My father doesn't see that. I should be here. So should you.'

'Quite. Except, of course, that we should both be in Vienna.'

§4

15 March
Berggasse, Vienna

Martha showed every courtesy to the SS thugs who had burst into her dining room. Gesturing to the table, where she had piled up her housekeeping money, she invited them to 'help themselves' as though it were a plate of sandwiches and they guests for afternoon tea. They stuffed their pockets like beggars at a banquet. Then they stared. They had probably never been in an apartment quite like this in their lives.

Could they feel the burden of dreams?

Martha's daughter, Anna, sensing that they would not be satisfied with the best part of a week's housekeeping, knowing that they undoubtedly subscribed to the Nazi notion that all Jews were misers and slept on mattresses stuffed with banknotes, went into the other room, beckoned for them to follow and opened the safe for them. 'Help yourselves, gentlemen' – to six thousand schillings.

Even this was not enough. They hesitated at the door to her father's study – she would have little choice but to step between them and block the way with her own body – when the door opened and a diminutive, white-haired, white-bearded man appeared before them, glaring at them silently with the eyes of Moses, the eyes of Isaiah, the eyes of Elijah. Behind him they could see row upon row of books, wall to wall and floor to ceiling, more books than they had ever thought existed. The old man said nothing. He was a good foot shorter than the biggest of the SS men, and still he stared at them. Did they know these eyes saw into the depths of man?

'We'll be back,' they said. And left.

Could they feel the burden of dreams?

§ 5

The next day Professor Nicholas Lockett, of King's College, London, a lanky Englishman so English his furled umbrella remained furled in the worst of weathers, a man possessed of size 12 and a half feet, a man passionate about his subject, arrived in Berggasse expressly charged by the Psychoanalytic Society of Great Britain to impress upon Sigmund the necessity of leaving. Sigmund needed impressing.

He stretched back on the wide, red chenille-covered couch reserved for his patients, stared at the ceiling and said.

'My dear Lockett, I am too . . . old.'

'Nonsense . . . you are . . .'

'. . . Incapable of kicking my leg high enough to get into bed in a wagon-lit!'

'You are Psychoanalysis. Where you are . . . it is. The Society is a moveable feast.'

'Alas, Vienna is not. It is quite securely fixed to the banks of the Danube. I've lived here since I was four. If at all possible, I'd like to die here. To leave now would be . . . like a soldier deserting from the ranks.'

Lockett did not hesitate to be blunt. Perhaps it was the prone, patient-like position that Sigmund had adopted.

'More aptly . . . to remain would be like being the last officer on the Titanic. If you stay, that end may come quicker than you might think.'

'Quicker than I desire?'

'I don't know. How fondly do you desire death?'

'One does not need to desire what is inevitable. It is a waste of desire. Desire what is possible, desire what is merely likely.'

'Very neat. Is that original or is it Marcus Aurelius?'

'Need you ask? I am desire's biographer.'

'But you'll come?'

'Where? The French will admit me, as long as I agree not to be a burden on the state and starve to death. The English . . .'

'. . . Will let you in.'

'The English have closed their gates on Europe.'

'No we haven't. It's not at all like that.'

'What are you saying, Lockett? That the indifference of the English is an aberration, a temporary aberration?'

'Yes. That's exactly what I'm saying.'

'Fine. Get me out. Get us all out.'

A dismissive wave of a hand in the air.

Now Lockett had cause to hesitate. It was not simply that the old man's assertion was unconvincing – he was far from impressed yet – there were the flaws in his own insistence too.

'It's not entirely straightforward. It's possible. It's most certainly possible. I'd even say it was likely. It's really a matter of who you know.'

'Was it not ever thus? When was it not thus?'

'I mean – who you know in England. Who you know who might be ... well, who ... who ... who might be in *Who's Who*?'

'My dear Lockett, you sound like an owl.'

'A few names I could approach on your behalf, perhaps?'

'Do you know Alexei Troy?'

'You mean Sir Alex Troy – the newspaper chap?'

'The same.'

'Where on earth did you –'

'A patient. You will understand, Lockett, that this is strictly between ourselves. You have read my 'The Case of the Immaculate Thief'?'

'Naturally.'

'That was Alex Troy.'

Lockett was silent – all he could think was 'Good Bloody Grief!'

'The Alex Troy of 1907–8. He had not been long in Vienna. He had landed up here after his flight from Russia. Or, to be exact, from the 1907 Anarchist Conference in The Hague. He turned up on my doorstep the day after it finished. I treated him all that winter. Indeed, he lay on this very couch. Shortly afterwards he moved to Paris, and I believe from Paris to London, where, as they say at the end of tuppenny novellettes, he prospered.'

Prospered, Lockett thought, was hardly precise. Troy was, and there was no other phrase for it, filthy rich. But then he had begun as a thief, as Freud would have it, an immaculate and far from filthy thief. One to whom not a speck of dirt could stick, either to the clothing or the conscience, it would seem.

'We did not keep in touch. Merely the odd letter from time to time – more often than not when an English translation of something or other of mine came out. His German was never good, after all. But I think I can safely say he is unlikely to have forgotten me.'

'Quite,' said Lockett.

'Will he do?'

'Well, he knows everyone. That's undeniable. I doubt there's a politician in England that would not take a telephone call from Alex Troy.'

§ 6

19 March
Leopoldstadt, Vienna

Krugstrasse was a street of tailors. Beckermann's shop stood next to Bemmelmann's, Bemmelmann's stood next to Hirschel's, Hirschel's next to Hummel's. The shop beyond Hummel's had stood empty for nearly a year now. Ever since old Schuster had packed his bag and caught a train to Paris. He'd tried to sell the shop, but the offers were derisory. From Paris he wrote to Hummel: 'Take the stock, Joe, take all you want. Take the shop, it's yours. I'd rather see it burn than sell it to some Jew-hating usurer for a pittance.'

Not that he knew it but Schuster would almost have his way. It would be Hummel who watched the shop burn.

The following week Schuster wrote, 'Forget the shop, Joe. Leave Leopoldstadt. Leave Vienna. Leave Austria. How long can it be safe for any Jew?'

The day before the German annexation the local Austrian SA had rampaged carelessly down the street of tailors, smashed Hirschel's windows and beaten up Beckermann's grandson, who was unfortunate enough or stupid enough to be out in the street at the time. Most people had more sense. Had the SA been less than careless they could have taken out every window in the street and looted what they wished. No one would have stopped them, but the rampage had its own momentum and, once it had gathered speed, roared on from one target to the next, glancing off whatever was in the way. Hummel and Beckermann's grandson helped Hirschel board up his window.

'Is there any point?' Hirschel had said. 'They'll be back.'

But a week had passed, a week in which many Jews had been robbed of all they possessed, some Jews had fled the city and some Jews had taken their own lives, but the mob had not returned.

At first light on the morning of the 19th, a German infantryman banged on the doors all along the street with his rifle butt.

Bemmelmann was first to answer.

'You want a suit?' he said blearily.

'Don't get comical with me grandad! How many people live here?'

'Just me and my wife.'

'Then get a bucket and a scrubbing brush and follow me.'

Then he came up to Hummel, shadowed in the doorway of his shop. Hummel had not been able to sleep and was already dressed in his best black suit.

'Going somewhere, were we?'

Hummel said, 'It's the Sabbath.'

'No – it's just another Saturday. Get a bucket, follow me!'

By the time he got back from the scullery every tailor in the street was standing with a bucket of water in his hand. Old men, and most of them were; not-so-young men, and Hummel was most certainly the youngest at thirty-one; men in their best suits, pressed and pristine; men in their working suits, waistcoats shiny with pinheads, smeared with chalk; men with their trousers hastily pulled on, and their nightshirts tucked into the waistband.

The German lined them up like soldiers on parade. He strutted up and down in mock-inspection, smirking and grinning and then laughing irrepressibly.

'What a shower, what a fuckin' shower. The long and the short and the tall. The fat, the ugly and the kike! Left turn!'

Most of the older men had seen service in one war or another and knew how to drill. Beckermann had even pinned his 1914–18 campaign medals to his coat as though trying to make a point. Those that knew turned methodically. Those that didn't bumped into one another, dropped buckets, spilt water and reduced the German to hysterics. Well, Hummel thought, at least he's laughing. Not punching, not kicking. Laughing.

He led them to the end of the street, to a five-point crossroads, where the side streets met the main thoroughfare, Wilhelminastrasse. In the middle of the star was a long-parched water fountain, topped by a statue of a long-forgotten eighteenth-century burgomaster. Someone had painted a toothbrush moustache on the statue – it was unfortunate that the burgomaster had been represented in the first place with his right arm upraised – and around the base in red paint were the words 'Hitler has a dinky dick!'

'Right, you Jew-boys. Start scrubbin'!'

They scrubbed.

When they had finished the message was still more than faintly visible. Gloss paint did not scrub so well. And they'd none of them been able to reach the moustache.

The tailors stood up, their knees wet, their trousers soggy.

'We can scrub no more off,' Hummel said as politely as he could.

'Who said anything about any more scrubbin'?' said the German.

He took a dozen paces back and raised his rifle. Bemmelmann sagged against Hummel's chest in a dead faint. Hummel heard the gentle hiss as Beckermann pissed himself. Heard Hirschel muttering a prayer.

But the rifle carried on upwards, drawing a bead on the statue's head, then the crack as it fired and chips of stone showered down on Hummel. The second crack and the stone head split open and two chunks of rock heavy enough to stove in a man's skull bounced off the cobbles behind him and rolled away.

'Right,' said the German. 'Pick your feet up Jew-boys. And follow me.'

Hummel roused Bemmelmann.

'Where am I?' the old man said.

'In hell,' Hummel replied.

§7

Hummel had no difficulty seeing himself and his neighbours as Vienna saw them from the early-morning doors and windows, in the eyes of women shaking tablecloths and in the eyes of unshaven men still munching on their breakfast roll, clutching their first cup of coffee. A raggle-taggle bunch of damp and dusty Jewish tailors led by a bantam-cock of a soldier, strutting while they straggled – a recognisably barmy army.

Every so often the German would try to kick a little higher, but, clearly, the goose step was not as easy as it looked and needed more practice than the man had given it, and was all but impossible whilst turning around every couple of minutes to urge on his charges. It might have been better to herd them like pigs or cattle, but Hummel could see the thrill of leadership in the way the man stuck out his chest and kicked out his legs. He'd probably never led anything in his life before. He shouted, they shuffled. Down to the river, across the Aspern Bridge, along Franz Josef's Kai and into the ancient heart of Vienna.

The German yelled 'Halt'.

Hummel was wondering why he could not just yell 'stop' – as though there was any particular military relevance to a word like 'halt' – when he realised where they were. Outside the Ruprechtskirche. Probably the oldest church in the city – some said it had stood twelve hundred years already. It was a small church. A simple, almost plain exterior. Not a touch of grandiosity in its conception or its accretions. What desecration now? Of course, the final desecration would be if this idiot, this tinpot Boney at the front, were to marshal them inside. Hummel had never been in this or any other Christian church.

A crowd had their backs to them. The German parted a way with his rifle and Hummel found himself on his knees once more, his bucket and brush set down before him, facing a large bright blue letter 'H'. Beckermann plumped down next to him, the bucket obscuring the letter. Hummel looked to his left wanting, for reasons that were inaccessible to him, to know what word he was obliterating now. The man next to him was hunched over, scrubbing vigorously, the letter already half-erased. Hummel knew him. He could not see his face, but he knew him. He looked at the blue wide-pinstripe of the man's back, and he knew the suit. He had made it himself not two months ago for a young violinist named Turli Cantor.

Cantor did not turn. Hummel dunked the brush, gazed outward at the mob and bent his head to scrub. They had an audience – a crowd of onlookers who seemed to Hummel to be neither gloating nor commiserating. He had heard that the mobs could be as vicious as the SA, jeering and kicking as rabbis were dragged from their homes to clean public lavatories. This lot showed no inclination. They were watching with the casual half-attention of a crowd watching a street entertainer who they found just distracting enough to pause for, but who would be off the minute the hat was passed. So that was what they were? Street entertainment The Famous Scrubbing Jews of Vienna. Roll up, roll up and watch the kikes on their knees on the steps of a Christian church. He looked again. They were blank, expressionless faces. Perhaps they had no more wish to be there than he had himself. The troops standing between the Jews and the mob weren't ordinary soldiers like the one who had led him here. They were black-uniformed, jackbooted German SS.

Hummel was making good progress with his 'H' when he felt a change in the mood of the mob. He risked an upward glance. The SS were all standing stiffly upright – perhaps this was what was meant by 'at attention'? – and the crowd had parted to let through an officer in black and silver.

From his left he heard Cantor whisper, 'My God. Wolfgang Stahl!'

For the first time his eyes met Cantor's. 'I have known Wolf all my life,' Cantor said, his voice beginning to rise above a whisper, 'Surely he will save us?'

Cantor stood, clumsily, one foot all but slipping from under him on the wet stone flag and uttered the single syllable, 'Wolf.'

An SS trooper shot him through the forehead.

The crowd scattered, screaming. This was not what they had paid to see. Hummel rose – afterwards he assigned the word 'instinctively' to his action – only to feel the pressure of a hand on his shoulder, forcing him back down, and the sound of the German soldier's voice saying, 'Don't be a fool. You can't help him. You can only get yourself killed. You and all your mates.'

Hummel saw a boot push Cantor's body over, saw the black hole between Cantor's eyes, saw the click of the heels as the same boot came together with its mate and saluted the officer. Then he twisted his head slightly, enough to make the German tighten his grip, and saw the black leather of the officer's gloves drawn tight across his knuckles. Then one hand rose – the salute returned. The man turned and all Hummel saw was his retreating back and the movement of SS troopers across the steps, and then a voice was shouting 'Show's over', and someone he could not see at all was dragging Cantor's body away.

They scrubbed until the graffiti was washed away. They scrubbed until the blood was washed away.

Slouching home Hummel asked Hirschel what the word had been.

'Schuschnigg,' Hirschel replied. 'And it may be the only memorial our chancellor ever gets.'

§ 8

Death notwithstanding, it felt a little like a kindergarten outing. The German saw them all the way back to Krugstrasse. It was a curiously paternal attention. He'd even slowed the pace of the march to the weary shuffle of old tailors wholly unaccustomed to walking four or five miles in the course of a day. When Beckermann had dropped his bucket and declared that he could not go on – 'Shoot me now. It would be a blessing' – the German had picked up the bucket and urged him on with 'Don't make me waste my bullets, Grandad.' Now, he stood in the alley as Hummel unlatched his door, waiting.

'Yes,' said Hummel. 'There was something else?'

'Too bleedin' right there is. I saved your life today. You damn near got yourself shot.'

'You are surely not standing there waiting for me to say "thank you"?'

'I ain't waitin' for nothin'.'

And he turned and walked off, and Hummel could not help the feeling that the slouch of his shoulders, the bantam-strut of morning long since worn out, was partly of his own making, that his ingratitude had caused it. But he could not find it in him to feel blame.

The next day Bemmelmann called early to tell him that Hirschel had slit his own throat in the night.

§ 9

'Kings and Tyrants come and go, Rothschilds go on forever.' If that is not the motto of the Rothschild family, it should be. An empty Rothschild palace – empty of Rothschilds that is, a few dark spaces on the walls where paintings had been removed, but otherwise full of Rothschild furniture, Rothschild crockery, Rothschild opulence – had been seized by the Germans for the exclusive use of the SS.

By the time Stahl got there, his comrades-in-arms had achieved a remarkable semblance of normality, of continuity. White-jacketed waiters served black-uniformed officers, silver platters and soft shoes, scarcely raising their voices above a whisper, aiming for that servile pretence of invisibility, while the SS roared and guffawed and preened – plain as jackdaws, vain as peacocks, all twinkling buttons and buffed leather. But for the unseemly loudness of the members, it struck Stahl as being less the Munich bierkeller that had spawned these vultures than a bad parody of some London club. The sort of thing he'd read about in the works of P.G. Wodehouse.

'I'm going back to Berlin in the morning. I have seen enough,' he told Schellenberg.

'No matter – we have everything under control. You must try this lemon torte. It's simply delicious. Matches the Earl Grey like peaches to cream.'

'Really.'

'The apricot's good too. Except, of course, the apricots can hardly be fresh at this time of year. You know, the Viennese make exceedingly good cakes.'

'Then perhaps it would be a good idea to keep the patissier out of the camps until after the apricots fruit in August?'

Schellenberg paused mid-bite, swallowed with a slow, saurian gulp of the throat and said, 'Do you really think he might be Jewish?'

'I was joking, Walter.'

Schellenberg laughed, a soft little schoolboy giggle. Tucked into his tart again.

That was the problem with Nazis, Stahl thought, no sense of humour.

§ 10

20 March
Hampstead, London

It was going to be a green day. He'd no idea why. It was just the way it felt. The green of leaf unfurling, the green of sap rising. He had a fat, and as it happened green, anthology of English verse on his desk and was trying to find the line about 'a green thought in a green shade' . . . but clearly it was not the first line of anything and he couldn't remember the name of the bugger who'd written it or even in what century he had written it. Was it Donne or some bugger like Donne?

Alex caught sight of his younger son passing the door, pulling on his jacket, a slice of toast clenched between his teeth.

'Frederick?'

Troy took two steps back, took the toast from his mouth and said, 'I'm due at work, Dad.'

'Work? I don't understand. Where is your uniform?'

'I'm a detective now. Remember? About six weeks ago? I joined CID?'

'Of course,' Alex said. 'CID. Plain clothes. No more boots.'

'No more boots. Exactly. But I am in a tearing hurry, so if you could just . . .'

'A green thought in a green shade?'

'Marvell. Andrew Marvell.'

'Ah . . . not Donne then?'

'No, not Donne. Not even the same generation.'

'What does it mean?'

'Could I tell you later?'

Alex went back to his anthology, to Quiller-Couch's index of authors and found 'Marvell, Andrew, 1621–78' . . . and from that the lines he had half-heard in the ear of the mind:

> The mind, that ocean where each kind
> Does straight its own resemblance find;
> Yet it creates, transcending these,
> Far other worlds, and other seas,
> Annihilating all that's made
> To a green thought in a green shade.

Oh fuck – what did that mean?

His son would tell him the next time they met. Alex thought he had more insight into the English mind than most foreigners might manage, but his son had the distinct advantage of being English.

Then the phone rang.

'Good Morning. I wonder if I might speak to Sir Alexei Troy?'

'Speaking,' Alex said.

'Nicholas Lockett here, King's College, London. We've never met but we have a mutual friend in Sigmund Freud.'

'A friend I have not seen in many a year. How is he? Indeed, where is he?'

'He's still in Vienna. And actually that does bring me rather quickly to the point. I'm trying to get him out.'

'I cannot help but wonder that he did not leave the sooner. The writing has been upon the wall these last five years and more.'

'Quite. It's all a bit last minute. But the upshot is the Nazis won't dare touch him yet. In fact, they'll let him go. There's been some quite remarkable behind-the-scenes pressure. President Roosevelt has been kept informed and there's even a rumour that Mussolini has spoken directly to Hitler about Freud. The problem I have is not getting him out, it's getting him in – in here, I mean.'

'I understand. I understand also the urgency. The Nazis are still responsive to the notion of world opinion. That cannot last. Freud must leave while the door is open. I take it you're lobbying?'

'I'm pulling every damn string I can find. And, of course, you're one of them, almost needless to say. I'll speak to the Home Secretary myself, I've met him socially – I was wondering if you couldn't write a leader or if there weren't some prominent politicians you could call?'

'Of course,' Alex said, making a mental list, reaching for a pad and pencil. 'How about . . .'

§ I I

'Were you out bricklaying?'

'Painting. But I am happy to be distracted . . . everything today is too . . . green,' said Churchill. 'Besides, I have all the time in the world to paint. I may do nothing else for the rest of my life. I shall watch governments tumble like ninepins from the safety of my easel. To say nothing of the obscurity.'

Out of office might, on one of his black dog days, seem an obscurity tantamount to invisibility to Churchill. Alex saw it as self-pity. The man's profile was as high as that of any cabinet minister. He had his 'Focus

Group', a cross-party gathering of the rebels, and he had the freedom no minister had to write for any newspaper that would publish him – as well as a regular column in the *Evening Standard*. The country knew what Winston thought because Winston told them. Alex would publish the man himself given the chance. But he wasn't. 'Obscurity' was lavish self-pity.

'One of those days, eh?'

'As I said, Alex, too green by a yard and a half. One craves a little red or pink. Now, what can I do for you?'

'Freud.'

'Freud?'

'As in Sigmund.'

'Ah . . . the trick-cyclist.'

Alex had met so few English prepared to reap the benefits of psychoanalysis. All enquiry into the mind was a matter less of explanation or enquiry than of pathology as far as they were concerned. You ignored the mind until it was sick. First you tried cold showers and laxative, and then you consigned it to the mercies of the psychiatrist – usually referred to, as Churchill would have it, as the 'trick-cyclist'. Alex did not feel it within his powers to explain to Winston the difference between a psychoanalyst and a psychiatrist. That Winston had heard of Freud was the best he could hope for.

He elaborated the case Lockett had put to him. When he had finished, Churchill said, 'Do we *need* him?'

An odd choice of word, but one Alex understood.

'That is not my point. He is old, I fear he may well be ill . . . he will hardly be a vital force in our culture, but his symbolic value cannot be exaggerated. If the Nazis keep him, there is . . . there is what I can only think of as a propaganda coup. If he stays, and I gather he has taken some persuading to leave, that propaganda value would be irredeemable. No, we do not *need* to have him, but we need the Nazis *not* to have him.'

'Yet the buggers will let him leave?'

'For now, yes . . . in a year or perhaps less, who knows? When their contempt for the rest of us reaches its zenith, who knows?'

'Then we shall rescue your trick-cyclist. I shall call anyone who'll still listen to an old backbench has-been like me and do what I can for you.'

'Has-been? Surely–'

'Alex, how many MPs did you call before you called me?'

This was no time for white lies and spared feelings.

'Six.'

'Good Lord . . . you mean I made the first eleven?'

§ 12

28 March
Berlin

They met late in the afternoon, over coffee and cream cakes in a noisy café off the Ku'damm.

'I'm going to Vienna.'

'How did you wangle that?'

'Didn't. The Nazis did it for me. They've kicked our man out. Someone has to stand in for a week or two. I drew the short straw.'

Rod raised an eyebrow at this.

'What do you mean "short"? I thought you wanted to be where the action was?'

Greene shrugged.

'Quite. I mean to say, they've taken Vienna haven't they? They've got Vienna. What more is there to say? The point is to be where it's going to happen next.'

'Well . . . you could always ask for a posting to Tirana to cover King Zog's wedding.'

'Zog . . . nog . . . bog. I'm immune to sarcasm, Rod. Besides, I was thinking more along the lines of . . . well . . . Warsaw.'

'Hugh, I won't argue about Warsaw. Warsaw's not an "if" it's a "when". But if you think it's all over in Vienna you're very much mistaken.'

'Oh . . . I don't think I meant that at all. I mean . . . it's not over till it's over is it?'

§ 13

5 April
Leopoldstadt, Vienna

It was about two weeks later. Whilst every day brought fresh outrage, Hummel was coming to the conclusion that now the radicals and toffs among Vienna's Jewry were under lock and key, Leopoldstadt was being left largely to its own devices. True, all Jewish assets at the banks were frozen, but Hummel did not come from a class that kept money in banks, he came from a class that kept it under the mattress – yet the kosher butchers remained open, and the Jewish cafés and restaurants were still doing a lively trade. And he still had his shop window – albeit now somewhat obscured by the word 'Jude' in yellow letters a foot high. It was, he thought, an odd normality. As if to prove him wrong a bang on the door at dusk, some half-hour or more after he had shut up shop, gave him that hubristic shiver down the spine. Less speaking too soon, than thinking too soon. He opened the door wide. Better to let them walk in than have them smash it in.

In the street stood the German, the infantryman whose beat Krugstrasse seemed to be.

'Can I help you?'

'I want to get measured for a suit.'

'You have the wrong address. It was Bemmelmann asked you if you wanted a suit. Two doors down.'

'Nah. I heard you're the best. I want a suit from you.'

Hummel beckoned to the man to come inside. Fine, he was going to let the man steal a suit. So what?

The infantryman said little as Hummel measured him up. When Hummel had finished and was jotting down figures on a notepad, he said 'How long?'

'Three days. If you can wait.'

'I can wait.'

'And the material?'

'Eh?'

'You haven't chosen the swatch.'

The German looked confused. Out of his depth. Hummel pointed to the wall of swatched cloth behind him. The German turned, peered at the ends of rolls in the dim light and said, 'What's . . . respectable?'

'You want respectable?'

'Yeah. Nothing flash, just . . . respectable.'

'Blue. Blue is respectable.'

'OK. You pick me a blue then.'

Hummel approached the shelves with a 'This one might . . .' bursting on his lips, but the German said, 'No. Just pick one and make it up.'

Hummel showed him to the door.

The man breathed in the night air, shouldered his rifle, turned to Hummel and said, 'I never owned a suit before.' Then he strolled off as though he and Hummel had conducted a perfectly customary business transaction.

Three days later he was back, knocking on the door at the same time of day.

Hummel handed him the finished suit in a blue worsted, and waited while he dressed. The man stood in front of the full-length mirror. A stocky brick-shithouse of a man, exuding a mixture of pride, pleasure and nervousness.

'I never wore a suit before.'

'Of course not,' Hummel said. 'If you never owned one . . . you never wore one . . . except for your uniform, of course.'

The man gazed at his own arse in the mirror and seemed not to hear the jibe in Hummel's voice.

'Good,' he said. 'It's good. Good to be in something that ain't grey.'

Another twirl to look at his barrel chest under the double-breasted jacket.

Then he said, 'What do I owe you?'

'I'm sorry?' Hummel said.

'How much?'

'You mean you want to pay?'

Hummel knew he had not kept the utter incredulity he felt out of his voice.

'Course I wanna pay. Or did you think I was a thief?'

'You will understand,' Hummel said, 'if I say that there are those among us who might think that you are all thieves.'

The soldier had to think about this. Hummel thought about it too,

23

hoping that it was too subtle, too shot through with conditionals, to be taken for an insult. Far be it from Hummel to point out that robbing Jews was legal – trading with them wasn't.

'Mind,' the man said at last, 'a trade discount wouldn't come amiss. What's your usual price?'

'For a suit like this? Seventy-five schilling.'

'Sixty-five?' the man ventured.

Hummel had been about to say fifty-seven-fifty.

'Done,' he said softly. 'What name?'

'Trager. Joe Trager. I'm a Joe just like you.'

Hummel doubted that the word 'like' could ever reasonably be used to compare the two of them but said, 'How do you know my name is Joe? Do you have records on us all?'

'Records? O' course we got records. We got files a foot thick. But they don't get shown to the likes of me. I'm just a regular Fritz, I am. A professional soldier. Never been more than a private and I shouldn't think I ever will be. No, I seen it over your shop – "Josef Hummel & Son".'

'Ah,' said Hummel. 'Josef Hummel was my father. I am merely "& Son".'

Trager laughed as though Hummel had just told him the funniest thing he'd heard since the Anschluss. He was still laughing when Hummel handed him his receipt, still laughing as he slipped his uniform back on and went out into the night with his blue suit in a brown paper parcel tied up with string. The notion of hubris left Hummel. It was indeed an odd normality.

§ 14

25 April
Leopoldstadt

The normal came to claim him with a calendrical regularity. Passover. The first under the iron heel.

Hummel had the merest adherence to faith. He had endured his *bar mitzvah* out of loyalty to his father, a man not long widowed, but once it was done the old man had not pressured him, nor even expected him to attend the synagogue. If Hummel went, as on occasion he did, it was for the merely aesthetic pleasure of chanting and architecture, much as he might go to the theatre. Indeed, that was how he thought of services in a synagogue, second-rate theatre − second-rate but free. Passover brought obligations. Krugstrasse could not cope with an atheist, hence his neighbours ignored Hummel's lack of faith, any faith, and thought of him merely as neglected, inattentive, and were it not for his industrious tailoring, lazy. Hummel was not allowed to escape the feast days that mattered nothing to him by those to whom they did matter − and, out of nothing more than good manners, he accepted invitations from most of the families in the street in the years following his father's death. A Passover tradition is to invite a stranger into a family occasion. So it was that at Passover 1938 he found himself at Beckermann's for the family *seder,* presided over by old Beckermann in a dining room crammed with his descendants . . . sons, daughters and grandchildren . . . fourteen people seated in a room that might have served Baron Rothschild as a broom closet.

Hummel had always liked the room. After his mother's death, house-keeping in the Hummel household had been no more than perfunctory. If something other than the functional wore out, it was thrown away and not replaced. It was worth going to a *seder* just to eat off a tablecloth, since, left to themselves, neither he nor his father would have bothered. It gave Hummel a pleasure that was wholly secular to sit in the overplush, nineteenth-century velvet drape and tassel clutter of the first-floor front room over Beckermann's shop. Portraits, single and group − scarcely a space on the wall to hang one more − more beards, more Franz-Josef moustaches, and a Darwinian likeness between them all that came close in Hummel's mind to abolishing notions of individuality. It was a visit to ur-Beckermann, to an amorphousness, that beckoned, swallowed and failed to consume. It was the kind of room he had lived in for the first ten years of his life, while his mother lived and a woman's touch had turned the plain boxiness of the room into a magician's cube, a chinese box, far from plain, layer upon layer of memory and history. The tangibility of trivia. Every photograph a name, every name a story. It was a journey to the public places of the heart, back into childhood. And childhood was a place well worth visiting − once in while.

For once the elder's prayer struck Hummel as being more acute than the mereness of analogy. For once it had teeth and it bit. Holding up a tray of *matzohs*, old Beckermann recited in Aramaic the prayer of deliverance: 'This is bread of affliction, that our fathers ate in Egypt. Those who are hungry, let them come and eat; those who are needy let them come and celebrate Passover with us. We are here now, in the year to come we may be in Israel. We are slaves now – in the year to come we may be free.'

Fat chance, Hummel thought.

Beckermann turned to the youngest in the room, his grandson, eleven-year-old Jonny – younger brother of Adam, the one who had been beaten up by the SA just before the Nazi conquest, and who still bore a livid blue scar across his forehead.

'Jonathan – the four questions.'

The boy knew what was required of him. He'd done this since he was seven. At that age Hummel too had been often called on to ask the same four questions. All he had to do was ask about the oddness of the meal, the things on the silver *seder* plate in the middle of the table – herbs and *matzohs*, chicken bones and a mish-mash of apple and walnut that Hummel always thought looked like a Waldorf salad gone wrong. The questions served as prompts for the old man to bang on again about slavery and Egypt and deliverance . . . lest we forget. Hummel had long ago concluded that the point of being a Jew was that you were never allowed to forget anything.

Jonny said, 'Zayde . . . why have we not risen up and kicked out the Nazis?'

The boy's mother whispered none too softly in his ear.

The boy replied loudly, 'I know, I know. Didn't you hear me last year? I know the answers to the four questions. Zayde was kind enough to tell me then. Now there are new questions.'

Beckermann was flummoxed – he had the routine off pat and was all but incapable of improvising. There were no new questions. It had been done this way for the best part of three thousand years. Beckermann's daughter-in-law was angry – her son also had it off pat, and it was not something that required thought or criticism. Beckermann's grandson was, however, resolute.

'Will God deliver us from this evil, Zayde, as he did in Egypt? I only ask because if he takes as long as he did in Egypt there may be none of us left to be safely led into the land of milk and honey.'

A vein in Beckermann's forehead had turned purple-ish and was beginning to throb. But he said nothing. His daughter-in-law, all of sixteen stone, grabbed the boy, well under five feet tall and less than six stone, and bundled him out. Silence reigned. Hummel thought Beckermann was only seconds away from weeping. Still he did not speak. Then Adam Beckermann, seventeen, tall and skinny, got up from his seat, slipped off his *yarmulke* and spoke.

'Grandfather, I can no longer pray for our deliverance, prayer is pointless. God has gone deaf, either that or he is dead . . . I can no longer pray for our deliverance, but I'll fight for it.'

The *yarmulke* thrown down landed on the *seder* plate, knocking over the chopped parsley and bitter herbs. Adam's father, Beckermann's third son, Arthur, shot bolt upright from his seat and bellowed the one word 'Adam!' But the boy was gone. Beckermann wept. Hummel slipped out quietly, unnoticed he hoped, from the ruins of the *seder*. It was not the last he was ever invited to, but it was the last he ever went to.

§ 15

2 June
Berggasse

The Freuds were travelling light. Sigmund, Martha, their children, his sister-in-law, two maids and a doctor, the dog – and the furniture. The furniture was travelling separately. The furniture included some three thousand Greek and Roman figurines and sixteen hundred books. The furniture was leaving first.

It was sod's law that on the day the men arrived to clear Sigmund's study – an event that could have been calculated to turn his head and heart as topsy-turvy as the room itself – 'would you let a strange man rummage through your trousers?' – the Nazi Commissar of Vienna, one Dr Sauerwald, should also arrive, just as two aproned removal men were struggling down the stairs with the patients' couch. Having no choice but to invite him in – a courtesy they were able to avoid extending to his SA escort – Sigmund asked, 'To what do I owe the honour?' and realised at once that the man was taking the terms of the question literally.

'A simple matter of paperwork,' the Doctor replied.

Sigmund took the single sheet of paper from its envelope and read.

'Since the Anschluss ... blah, blah, blah ... I have been treated ... blahdey-blah ... with all the respect due to my reputation ... blah, blah, blah ... and could live and work in full freedom, if I so desired ... blah, blah, blahdey-blah ...'

Sigmund looked at Sauerwald. As the name implied, the man was humourless. Perhaps that was the key to Nazism ... no sense of humour. It was the funniest thing he'd read in weeks, but he was the only one laughing, and even then laughing only on the inside.

'Of course,' he said. 'But you are too modest. Would you mind if I added an endorsement?'

'Endorsement? Er ... certainly.'

Sigmund scribbled 'I can heartily recommend the Gestapo to anyone', added a spidery 'S. Freud' by way of signature and handed it back.

Sauerwald looked at it. He didn't get this joke either. It was the sort of thing you found on the side of brown, ribbed bottles of patent medicines, cures for indigestion or piles, general tonics and spurious pick-me-ups – the sugared water sold by rogues to rubes in *Huckleberry Finn*.

'Most kind,' he said. 'And if I can be of any ... er ... assistance to you and your family ...? I have long been an admirer ...'

Sigmund stopped listening. The only place to air stuff like this was on the couch. He would have loved to get this one on the couch, but alas the couch had gone out as he came in.

After lunch Sigmund took a slow stroll in the summer sun, an old man's stroll from bench to bench, resting as often as was possible. It would be so hot in the apartment while his daughter burnt his papers.

§ 16

Saturday, 4 June
Vienna Westbahnhof

Two days later, late in the evening, the Freuds boarded the sleeper train to Paris.

Regardless of what he had told Lockett, Sigmund would kick his leg high enough to reach the bed in the wagon-lit. It might kill him, but he'd do it.

As they emerged from the corridor that connected the palatial white-stone frontage of the station with the glass and iron engine shed at the back, a young man of thirty or so approached the Freuds, set down his attaché case, doffed his trilby and introduced himself.

'My name is Smith, sir. From the United States Embassy. I'll be with you as far as Paris.'

'Interesting,' Sigmund said. 'Are all spies called Smith in the United States?'

'Most of us are, sir. But I have several colleagues with a preference for Jones and one or two favour Brown.'

Freud was curious about most things. An occupational hazard. He asked to look at the engine – a squat-bodied, high-domed monster more evocative of the empire than of Hitler's Vienna – and he gazed one last time at the great glass roof. He'd made a career in symbols. There was no point in dodging them. But when the train pulled out of the station, past the twin towers at the end of the engine shed, he did not look back. Instead he quizzed Smith, a dozen quick questions – but Smith was adept at dodging them.

§ 17

Sunday, 5 June 1938
Leopoldstadt

It was a pleasant summer's afternoon, a Sunday in early June. Hummel had surrendered to the normality and pushed the oddness of it to one side, onto a mental shelf for the afternoon. He had accepted an invitation from Bemmelmann and his wife to take tea with them – a weak, black Darjeeling with feather-light flaked almond pastries Frau Bemmelmann made freshly that day – and afterwards to walk in the Prater, the vast, hilly park on the eastern edge of Leopoldstadt that housed the city's funfairs and, since the World's Fair some forty years ago, the world's biggest Ferris wheel. The views over Vienna were unequalled. Hummel made a point of going up at least once a year. He valued the perspective. Whatever his own troubles, to see the world writ large and humanity writ small – ants, as he thought of them – always sent him away calmer and more sanguine than when he arrived.

They would not be going up today. Frau Bemmelmann had no head for heights. They would walk the lanes, slowly climb the hills, no more than that. They were tailors – on Sunday afternoons mannequins for their own wares. It was June and still Bemmelmann carried gloves and a rolled umbrella.

They had no warning, just the clatter of boots and the sudden surge in the volume of everything. Voices raised, birds put to flight, women screaming. Then the Germans were everywhere, herding the Jews with rifle butts and steering them towards a clump of trees.

Hummel raised his hands in surrender. Bemmelmann raised one arm, and embraced his wife with the other. For five minutes nothing happened. The Germans laughed and chatted amongst themselves, aimed their rifles almost casually in the direction of the Jews. When they had about thirty penned, the Germans moved among them pulling out the men and telling them to kneel.

Bemmelmann whispered to Hummel, 'Is this it, Joe? Is this how it all ends? On our knees with a bullet in the back of the head?'

Hummel looked at the Germans, still laughing, still not really aiming at anyone.

'No,' he said. 'They're having too much fun, it's just a game.'

A big, sweaty corporal spoke to them in a voice that could be heard in Budapest.

'Right, Jew-boys. Get 'em off!'

No one moved, because no one knew what he meant.

'Strip, you buggers, strip. Take off your keks! Take off every last stitch! Now!'

Hummel tugged at his tie. Bemmelmann still hadn't moved.

'Do it, Herr Bemmelmann. Please.'

'I can't Joe ... the women. The women can see. I have not been naked in front of a woman for twenty years. Not even in front of my wife.'

'Don't think of the women. Just do it.'

A dozen Jews discarded their best summer clothes and stood naked in front of half a dozen German soldiers and twenty-odd women of all ages, women who'd seen naked men and women who probably never had. The Germans pissed themselves laughing. One went from man to man, a cigarette dangling from his lips, lifting up the cocks with the end of his rifle, delicately, displaying them like prize fish to his fellows, helpless with laughter. Another German produced a box camera and snapped away as though they were all one big happy family at a beach resort.

'Right you dickless wonders. On yer knees again.'

They dropped to their knees.

'Now eat!'

'Eat?' a lone voice queried.

'Eat, my little piggies. Eat grass!'

They chewed grass.

Hummel felt he could read Bemmelmann's mind. The old man was thinking that this was bad but if it was all they had in mind he would live through it. Hummel knew better. The show wasn't over yet. From nowhere the Germans produced a couple of ladders which they propped against the bole of a vast, spreading chestnut tree with boughs thicker than a man's thigh.

'Now ... while the piggies eat ... the birds can sing!'

A woman was prodded to the foot of the ladder and made to climb into the tree. One by one the Germans forced seventeen women up the tree. Frau Bemmelmann was next to last, weeping and protesting, plead-ing and begging. A young woman ahead of her took her hand. A young woman below her pushed bravely at her backside, until the old lady found herself perched on a branch twenty feet off the ground.

'Little birdies go cheep, cheep, cheep.'

Only the sound of women weeping.

The Germans pointed their rifles at the tree. One woman softly said, 'cheep', and the others joined in . . . a pathetic chorus of 'cheep, cheep, cheep'.

'Cheep, you birdies!'

And to the men, 'Eat you pigs!'

The women chirped, the men chewed. The Germans hooted with laughter.

'All the little birdies go cheep, cheep, cheep! All the little piggies go chomp, chomp, chomp!'

They lowered their rifles and doubled up in spasms of near hysteria.

And then they left. As suddenly as they had arrived.

Hummel found himself naked, a cool summer breeze on his buttocks, an awful taste in his mouth, as though he had awoken from the archetypal Freudian dream of public nudity to find it was real after all. He had been briefly acquainted with the mind of the Nazi, the merest insight into the dark pit that passed for mind, and felt it a lesson learnt at a high price – part of the tragedy of the Nazi, he felt, pulling on his trousers, was that to the Nazi the world must be a terrifying place, being, as it was, full of kikes and niggers.

§ 18

Smith had left them in Paris. At Victoria Station, London, the Freuds were met by their eldest two children, Martin and Mathilde, by the Superintendent of the Southern Railway and by the Station Master of Victoria – a man privileged to wear the highest top hat in Britain. Freud would have loved to ask him about the phallic symbolism involved in wearing a hat more than eighteen inches high, wearing one's cock on one's head as it were, but Lockett had arrived with his motor car to whisk them away. Past crowds of reporters and well-wishers, out into the strange freedom of a country that, whilst he had never chosen it, finally seemed to have chosen him.

'The short way or the pretty way?' Lockett asked.

Freud already had his *Bartholomew's Street Map of London* and his *Baedeker* open in front of him.

'Oh, I think the pretty way ... the long way ... I would like to see Piccadilly Circus ... and Regent Street ... and the BBC ... and ...'

Lockett slipped the car into gear and headed off in the direction of Buckingham Palace.

§ 19

It was a light night in the middle of August Bemmelmann knocked on Hummel's door and said, 'We are leaving. Come with us.'

'Leaving how?'

'Downriver. By boat. A boat that will take us down the Danube, out into the Black Sea and then on to Palestine.'

'What about the Germans?'

'What about the Germans?'

'How will you get past them?'

'Trager will help us.'

'Trager?'

'Our German.'

'*Our* German? We have a German?'

'The one who patrols the street, Joe. His name is Trager.'

'I know. I've just never thought of him as being *ours*. Why would he help you?'

'The Germans want us to leave. They have established an office of Jewish Emigration.'

'Herr Bemmelmann, I have heard of this office of Jewish Emigration, we have all heard of it. It's a front for bribery. There are wags who call it Adolf Eichmann's Piggy Bank.'

'There are even representatives from Palestine here to assist us to leave.'

'Jews from Palestine? Zionists? In Vienna? How do you know this?'

'Rabbi Lippmann at the Leopoldstraße synagogue told me so.'

'Yet, Herr Bemmelmann,' Hummel plodded on. 'The Germans demand we apply for exit permits, for which they charge all our jewellery, all our savings and even our furniture – and if they aren't demanding exit permits, how many countries do not have an entry visa requirement? Schuster is even now stuck in Paris waiting for his British visa. Herr Bemmelmann, this is so risky.'

'You said it yourself that day in the Prater, Joe. They're having fun. They want us all to go. They'd be happy if we all went to live in Palestine and complicated life for the British instead. Meanwhile, it amuses them to make us jump through hoops. We fill out their forms, we pay their bribes, we sit in the trees and we chirp like birds.'

'So you jumped? You have an exit permit? You have a passport?'

'Of course not. Why would an old Jew like me have a passport? I have never been out of Vienna in my life. That is why we go by night, on a boat. That is why Trager will escort us across the city. With him in uniform the night patrols will leave us alone. If anyone asks he will say he has arrested us.'

'And how much has Trager asked for this service?'

'Nothing,' he said.

'Yet,' said Hummel. 'Yet.'

'Come with us, Joe. Joe, I have known you all your life. I spent the night of your birth sitting up with your father. I was present at your *bris*, at your *bar mitzvah*. Your father asked me to watch over you the day before he died. I am too old to do that now. Come with us, Joe, you can watch over us.'

It was a neat inversion. The most subtle form of blackmail. Hummel smiled at the old man's wiliness.

'And the shop, Herr Bemmelmann, what about the shop?'

'Ach, I sold it this morning.'

'You were able to find a buyer?'

'A gentile . . . ten pfenigs on the mark . . . he'd buy you out too at the drop of a Nazi hat.'

Hummel knew this to be true. The miracle, small though it was, was that he, Bemmelmann and the rest of the street were still in business. All over the city Jews had been forced to sell their businesses at pitiful prices to demanding gentiles – Aryans as they saw fit to term themselves. In the tailors' alley Schuster's old shop was boarded up, as was the widow Hirschel's – although the old lady still lived behind the boards and broken glass – the rest carried on a scrappy trade, but then it had never been much better than scrappy. Vienna had too much of everything . . . too many photographers . . . too many painters . . . too many composers . . . too many psychiatrists . . . too many tailors.

§ 20

It was a long walk. Hummel was surprised Frau Bemmelmann had the strength – across Leopoldstadt, zig-zagging through the side-streets along Praterstraße, in what Hummel thought to be a daft attempt at being unobtrusive on Trager's part, to the broad avenue that led straight to the banks of the Danube, at which point Trager abandoned his plan and ushered them along in the open. Hummel carried the bags. Trager walked behind them, carrying nothing but his rifle.

'Why would I be carryin' bags for Jews – be sensible.'

'They are old, Joe. Perhaps we could catch a tram to the river?'

Now that is askin' to get nicked. We walk, just like I'd collared you lot. Now, just trust me, will you?'

They reached the railway line that ran along the banks of the Danube, ducked under it to the riverside, and emerged on a stone quay a few yards from the Reichsbrücke. Hummel stared unbelieving at the unbroken darkness of the other bank of the Danube, so dark he could almost believe it wasn't there. He'd never been there. It wasn't Vienna, at least not his Vienna. He'd heard it was still farms and fields, and Hummel had never been to the country and never felt the desire to go to the country. This was as far east as he'd ever been.

They descended by steps to the water's edge, Frau Bemmelmann wheezing all the way, and ducked under the shadow of the bridge. Two more German soldiers waited for them, visible at first only by the glow of their cigarettes. No money changed hands. Hummel could only assume that Trager had taken care of all this beforehand.

Then he saw the boat. He grabbed Trager by the sleeve of his jacket. The look Trager gave him was enough to make him relax his grip and take a step backwards. There were ways to behave when they were alone and ways to behave when there were other Germans around. He'd just broken the cardinal rule. He'd touched a German. He thought for a moment that Trager might carry the pretence of protocol to the point of hitting him just to save face in front of the Germans. He didn't, he snarled, 'What?'

Hummel took a few steps closer to the river and pointed down.

'The boat is not a boat. It's a raft.'

Trager looked.

'Nothin' I can do about that.'

'Herr Trager, it is a couple of dozen logs and planks and old car tyres lashed together, with a makeshift rudder at one end and a dog kennel for a cabin. Frau Bemmelmann is supposed to live in a dog kennel? On this they are supposed to reach the Black Sea?'

One of the Germans called out, 'What's the problem, Joe?'

Trager yelled back, 'You know kikes. Nothing's good enough for the chosen race!'

Bemmelmann said, 'Joe, it doesn't matter. It floats. We will go. Anything is better than staying. Now, I urge you one last time . . . come with us.'

A piece of his life, a piece of his childhood was breaking off in front of him.

'I cannot.'

Bemmelmann hugged him silently.

Hummel watched as they drifted out into the flow. Herr Bemmelmann struggling with the rudder, Frau Bemmelmann sitting on the bags. Lost and awkward, miserable and terrified. Weeping. And the two Germans hooting with laughter. Hummel watched until they were lost in mist and darkness and all he could hear was the occasional splash, soon smothered by the night.

'C'mon, Jew-boy. Back the way you came.'

Trager prodded him in the small of the back with the barrel of his rifle. Hummel went up the steps, turned, looked downstream one last time and could see nothing and hear nothing of the Bemmelmanns. The Germans' laughter echoed in his mind, but not half so loud as the weeping of Frau Bemmelmann. Schuster was gone, Hirschel was dead. Now Bemmelmann had gone. There was only him and Beckermann left of the old street. Another piece of his childhood had broken off and drifted away – off into the night and the fog.

Out of sight of his comrades, Trager shouldered his rifle, said 'Fuckem' and strode out for Leopoldstadt.

§21

Walking back it seemed to Hummel that they must look an odd couple to anyone they passed, but it was as if they passed no one. Vienna had become a city in which everyone averted their eyes and made no contact. Trager and Hummel walking side by side, a miscegenous version of Laurel and Hardy. Hummel the lanky Jew, much the taller; Trager the brick shithouse of a soldier, dumpy in his grey uniform, his rifle slung from his shoulder as casually as a fishing rod. What they did not look like was captor and captive.

Neither spoke. Only when they reached Hummel's shop did Trager have anything to say.

'You should have gone with the old boy, Joe.'

§22

30 September 1938

Informed by his office that the Prime Minister, Neville Chamberlain – the first Prime Minister to fly to a foreign conference, and thus, arguably, the inventor of shuttle diplomacy – had arrived back from Munich, from a meeting with Hitler which had carved up Czechoslovakia without so much as a word from any Czech, as none had been invited to the meeting, and was now waving bits of paper in the air and bleating about peace and honour, Alex Troy decided to break the habit of many months and to hear the idiot in person. He had the chauffeur drop him in Horse Guards Parade, walked the back way into Downing Street, stood behind a crowd of hacks and listened.

'We, the German Führer and Chancellor, and the British Prime Minister, have had a further meeting today and are agreed in recognising

37

that the question of Anglo–German relations is of the first importance for our two countries and for Europe.'

The man looked, as an odd but fetching English phrase had it, 'like death warmed up'.

'We regard the agreement signed last night and the Anglo–German Naval Agreement as symbolic of the desire of our two peoples never to go to war with one another again.

We are resolved that the method of consultation shall be the method adopted to deal with any other questions that may concern our two countries, and we are determined to continue our efforts to remove possible sources of difference, and thus to contribute to assure the peace of Europe.'

Alex thought this to be bollocks. We had just sold yet another small country up the river. But, Chamberlain was not finished.

'My good friends, for the second time in our history, a British Prime Minister has returned from Germany bringing peace with honour. I believe it is peace for our time ... Go home and get a nice quiet sleep.'

Alex walked out into Whitehall. His chauffeur pulled the Rolls up at the kerb and asked simply, 'Where to, Boss, office or home?'

'Home. I have been told to get a good night's sleep.'

Sleep? Nice? Quiet? Alex would be up most of the night, and most of the next, writing his editorial for the following Sunday. 'Peace for our Time'? How long did the man take our time to be? Peace until our time chanced and changed into the next entity? It was a slogan for the next five minutes and no more.

§23

The Sunday Post
2 October 1938

Like most of my readers I am an Englishman. Unlike most of my readers, I chose to be an Englishman. I doubt what little remains to me before I shuffle off this mortal coil will alter my accent one jot, but I have long since ceased to be incomprehensible to London cabbies, and when they ask 'Where to Al?', I do not flinch at the curt improbability of the abbreviation, I wear the badge of Englishness with pride. No doubt there are some among you who feel that I have not yet earned the right to lecture you on the matter of Englishness. Tough – I am about to do just that.

Patriotism, as Dr Johnson so famously observed, is the last refuge of a scoundrel. It can be evoked as excuse without apology, but this should not blind us to the possibility of virtue inherent in what a nation stands for. As simply as I can put it, Englishness has, since Magna Carta, meant the rule of law and the notion of constitutional law. In that document lie the foundations of democracy. We tinker with it at our peril – indeed we should no more tinker with it than America would tinker with the Bill of Rights – for much the same reason – it is the chief constraint on tyranny.

All too easily Germany has become a tyranny. Herr Hitler shows no respect for the rule of law, either domestic or international. What Germanness (if such a concept can be said to exist at all) stands for is the rule of the jackboot. Might is now right. Mr Churchill has been at pains to point this out to us for some time. I fear he has been a voice in the wilderness. But I say now, and I say it unequivocally, that Mr Churchill has been right about Hitler all along. Mr Chamberlain's aerodrome diplomacy, his abject shuttling back and forth this summer between England and Germany, has given us the worst of compromises, it has given us – to steal from whichever German minister uttered the phrase at the start of the last war – another 'scrap of paper' (contempt all but oozes from the words, you will agree) for Hitler to tear up at some not-so-distant date.

The agreement at Munich is not peace with honour, it is not peace for our time – it is a post-dated cheque written in the blood of Europe's young men. It cannot surely be long before the word Munich has the same ominous ring to it that Sarajevo has had these twenty-five years. It is time to pray for peace, gear for war and ignore all ideas that the former is rendered hypocritical by the latter. It is not. It is the key to our survival as a nation. Ask me what virtue of Englishness I admire most at the moment and

I would answer 'our guarded optimism' – and, dear reader, I mean the adjective as much as I mean the possessive plural.

Alexei Troy

Later that evening a telegramme arrived at Church Row addressed to Alex Troy. It read:

A HEARTY THANK YOU FROM AN OLD HAS-BEEN.
WINSTON SPENCER-HASBEEN.

As they sat down to dinner Alex showed both the leader and the telegramme to his son.

'Fine,' said Troy. 'Do you want me to give you a list of all the tyrants England has thrown up since Magna Carta?'

Alex tucked a corner of his napkin between the buttons of his waistcoat and reached for the soup spoon.

'Perhaps later,' he said.

§ 24

One pleasant, sunny Monday morning in early November – the 7th to be precise, and this is a matter of precision – the moment, one of those moments, when small acts, in themselves of little significance, precipitate greater – a young German Jew, only seventeen years old, of Polish parentage, bought himself a five-shot hammerless revolver in a Parisian backstreet in the 10th arrondissement, caught the Metro to the Boulevard St Germain and walked the last few yards to the German Embassy in the Rue de Lille with the intention of shooting the Reich Ambassador Count Johannes von Welczeck. Welczeck passed the young man as he set off for his morning walk. Instead, Herschel Grynszpan shot one Ernst vom Rath, a third secretary at the embassy, not quite the nonentity Grynszpan was himself, but not much more. He fired all five bullets at vom Rath and hit him twice in the abdomen. On hearing the news, Hitler immediately promoted vom Rath to the rank of counsellor and dispatched two physicians to Paris. Vom Rath took almost three days to

40

die, but by then Grynszpan, a boy thought by those who knew him to be an indolent non-achiever, had written both himself and his victim into history as surely as Gavrilo Princip had done almost a quarter of a century before. The motive? The Reich had just indulged in a pogrom, rounding up non-German Jews and forcibly repatriating them. Most of Grynszpan's family had been dumped at the Polish border and told to walk home.

Hitler was celebrating the fifteenth anniversary of the failed putsch of 9 November 1923 in the Rathaussaal in Munich when the news that vom Rath had died reached him. It is unclear whether he said anything at all – but the most telling report is of him saying 'Let the SA have their fling.'

Several hours later, closer to one in the morning, it fell, as so many things did, to Reinhard Heydrich, head of the Sicherheitsdienst, the Reich security service, to cross the Ts and dot the Is. The spontaneous nature of what was about to happen needed to be choreographed.

Heydrich was not to be found in any bierkeller, he was propping up the bar in the Four Seasons Hotel, a few streets away in Munich, sampling the bartender's skills with the cocktail shaker, in the company of his deputy, Wolfgang Stahl. They had the place to themselves. It would be a brave bartender who told an SS General he was closing up. Neither Heydrich nor Stahl had been party members in 1923 – indeed, Stahl had been nothing more than a schoolboy in Vienna. Neither of them could quite share the street fighting, beer-swilling pleasures that seemed to have given such simple gratification to the pioneer brownshirts. Stahl had done this a thousand times. Heydrich sampled drinks in the same way he sampled women. Given the choice – and saying no was hardly possible – Stahl preferred the nights when they hit the bars and boozed to the nights when the Obergruppenführer wanted to lurch from one high-class brothel to the next. If they couldn't share a taste in women, occasionally they shared a taste in music. Heydrich wasn't a bad violinist, Stahl was even better on the piano. Together they played Mozart, which was to Stahl's taste; and Haydn, which was very much to Heydrich's. As Nazis went they might be considered sophisticates – each respected the other's intelligence, talent and taste, and privately despised his foibles, fads and paranoias. They kept files on everyone – they had files on each other and, unknown to the man himself, they even had secret files on Hitler, although of what use they might be within the Reich Stahl could not imagine – their uses outside the Reich he considered limitless.

Stahl pushed his whisky sour to Heydrich. Heydrich pushed back a Manhattan in exchange.

'As the English say, not my cup of tea.'

Stahl opened his briefcase and slid a few sheets of paper across to Heydrich.

'One of our men brought me this earlier today. He thinks it might be important.'

Heydrich fanned the papers out and looked at the first page.

After a minute or so he turned it over and looked less carefully at the second. His reading of the third and fourth was no more than cursory.

'Do you think it's important?' he said at last.

'If it's real, if it's authentic . . . yes. Just about.'

'Where was it found?'

'In the home of a retired Professor of Music. A man in his seventies. A critic of the Reich whose criticism finally came back to him today. We packed him off to review Dachau for us, from the inside. It appears that this was among his father's papers when he died about thirty years ago. The good professor has had it ever since.'

'I suppose things like this turn up from time to time.'

'They do.'

'Is it any good?'

'That's a different matter.'

Stahl pointed to the arcane symbols on the paper. Meaningless if you didn't know the code, perhaps meaningless if you did.

'Look at the left hand . . . all those turgid minims and semi-breves. It's as though someone had doped Debussy with a horse tranquilliser and slowed him down to a crawl. It's leaden stuff, plod, thump, plod.'

'It's better when the violin chips in.'

'Perhaps. I think the only thing to be said for it is "historical import-ance" – you no more have to play it or listen to it than you'd pay attention to a war memorial in a suburban cemetery. It's hand-written, untitled, but at least he signed it . . . F. Nietzsche, 9 May 1888. About a year before he went bonkers, I should think.'

'Can I take it you don't *want* to play it, then?'

Stahl burst out laughing, Heydrich joined in – an unpleasant, high-pitched nasal whine. Only the bartender setting a house phone in front of Heydrich stopped them degenerating into schoolboy giggles.

'For you, Obergruppenführer.'

Heydrich spoke his name, listened for ten seconds, said 'Ja.'

Then, to Stahl, 'Find that useless sod Bruhns and get us a staff car. We're wanted at Äussere Prinzregentenstrasse.'

§ 25

Stahl had never been to Hitler's Munich flat. It seemed odd that he should have one at all – as though he were some sort of national deputy maintaining a home of political convenience in a remote provincial constituency rather than the absolute ruler of millions of Germans. Berchtesgaden he could understand – the Eagle's Nest spoke of the self-aggrandisement, the colossal ego that was Hitler . . . from flophouse to Bauhaus – a flat in Munich didn't.

He sat in an outer room while Heydrich talked to Hitler, Himmler and Goebbels. There were those at the same level as Stahl – that is, noticeable and acknowledged, without being 'one of us' – who took every opportunity to string along to meetings with the Führer. Stahl waited until he was invited. Something about Hitler, something he thought ought to be obvious to anyone who met him, made his flesh creep. And the thought of Hitler, Goebbels and Himmler all together was like a freak show – the club-footed, demented dwarf, the bespectacled, bourgeois owl and the Charlie Chaplin doppelgänger.

Heydrich emerged, tense and holding in his anger.

'We're here to structure chaos,' he said softly. 'The demented dwarf appears to have taken control of the public response to vom Rath's death. And that amounts to no control at all. He's turning the SA loose. Himmler's nose is severely out of joint.'

'There'll be a bloodbath,' Stahl said.

Heydrich said, 'Let us then consider that prospect. Do you have pen and paper?'

Stahl took Nietzsche's sheet music out of his briefcase, flipped the top off his fountain pen, and turned the music over. He could write almost as fast as Heydrich could speak, and to improvise aloud, fingers pressed to his high forehead, was one of the Obergruppenführer's preferred ways to work. Twenty minutes later he was reading his notes back to Heydrich. Himmler emerged from the inner room, threw them a Heil Hitler to which neither responded, and left a strained silence in his wake.

'What exactly are we saying?' Heydrich asked.

'Smash everything. Round up the rich, kill those who resist. But we must not seem to be involved, indeed we must appear to be the hand of restraint.'

'Restrain the SA? We recruited the buggers to be thugs.'

'If they go completely berserk, there are consequences . . . once they've sacked the synagogues and the department stores . . . we must stop them looting. I don't care that they will want furs and jewellery and God knows what for themselves. I don't give a damn how many Jews they rob. But if they are seen as looters . . . well, the world will judge us on that . . but we can gain valuable information, files, names, addresses . . . that alone is reason to stop them looting.'

'The world will be watching.'

Stahl heard the irony in Heydrich's tone, but responded to the literal truth in what he said.

'Exactly. We cannot harm any foreigners . . . Jews included. We haven't kicked out the foreign press yet.'

'What do you suggest?'

'Put the Criminal Police on the streets. Let them be seen to intervene to stop looting. Of course . . . once a synagogue is ablaze . . .'

'Quite. And the press?'

'Police escort. Entirely for their own safety . . . of course.'

'Of course.'

By the time they had finished, the list of instructions and the veil of restraints that couched them covered all but one page of Nietzsche's manuscript in unsubtle ambiguities. Heydrich lay back on the sofa, stretched out his arms and cracked the joints in his fingers. Stahl slipped the sheet music back in his briefcase.

'I'll get this to a teleprinter.'

As Stahl opened the door, Heydrich turned his head and spoke.

'Tell me . . . which side of that document do you think will really be of "historical importance", which will go down in history and which will be your suburban monument?'

Stahl didn't care – all he knew was that he might just have saved a few hundred Jewish lives . . . if one cop, one kripo in a hundred, bothered to play by the rules they had set. And it was as though Heydrich had read his mind.

'You know, in the end we'll have to kill them all.'

'I know,' Stahl said, stating for the first time what had been obvious to him for ten years.

'There won't be enough bullets in the world to do the job.'

Stahl could only guess at what the Obergruppenführer meant by this.

§ 26

Rod Troy had finally prevailed upon his father to let him go to Vienna. After the September riots the *Post*'s Vienna stringer, one Stan Burkinshaw, citizen of Sheffield, had boarded a train to Paris and simply refused to go back: 'They're worse than the bloody Germans. It's as though they'd got the copyright on anti-Semitism. I'd sooner be covering pigeon-racing in Sheffield.' Alex obliged and assigned him to a local paper in his home town, where he duly reported on amateur dramatics and burgeoning steel production as well as pigeon-racing, and continued to think Sheffield more interesting than Vienna.

His last report, and Rod had read all his reports, had been to state the risk that Vienna posed. Vienna had long since been home to most Austrian Jews – ninety per cent of them. Since 1933, numbers had swelled as German Jews had left the Reich in search of safety. It was a city ticking like a time bomb. They had, Burkinshaw wrote, leapt from frying pan to fire.

The vacancy created as Burkinshaw leapt from frying pan to pigeon loft remained unfilled. Rod had put it to his father that he could and would fill the gap until a new man was hired. Alex had argued for three weeks but the day before Herschel Grynszpan shot vom Rath he had relented. Rod had arrived in Vienna, checked into the Meissl und Schadn hotel on Kärntnerstrasse – because Hugh Greene had told him it would be stuffed with the Nazi hierarchy – rather than his father's recommended Imperial, to find the place buzzing with the assassination of a complete nonentity who wasn't even dead yet.

On the evening of the ninth – or, to continue to be precise, the small hours of the tenth – he sat in the bar, alone, quiet, eavesdropping, and heard the news that the nonentity had finally expired. He had a street map of Vienna and spread it out on the table in front of him. So far he'd reported nothing back to London. While his father might think it appropriate to talk to the new rulers of Vienna, Rod didn't. He had walked the city centre for a couple of days, taken a tram ride out to the Prater and viewed Vienna from the wheel, got, as he told himself, a bit of a feel for the place, found it evoked no memory, dunked no cake, and was now feeling a bit stumped. Whatever was going to happen could happen anywhere. All he wanted was a bit of a clue. Where to go and who to follow. Something was going to happen. The sheer glee with which the Germans spoke of the death of Ernst vom Rath told him that. It was a godsend, the very excuse the buggers had been waiting for for just one more rampage.

He was just thinking that perhaps he should not wait for news of any disturbance, and that he should actively go out and seek it, when he saw a waiter pointing in his direction, and a small man in a grubby macintosh and a grubby trilby, looking very different from the customary clientele of the Meissl bar, came over to him.

'Herr Troy?'

'Yes ... I don't believe I've had the pleasure ... ?'

The little man opened a small leather wallet he had been clutching in the palm of his hand, held it up just long enough for Rod to read, and said, 'Oskar Siebert, Detective-Sergeant, Vienna HQ.'

So, the little scruff was a copper. Certainly looked like a copper.

'Am I under arrest?'

Siebert smiled, pulled out a chair uninvited and sat down.

'Far from it, Herr Troy. I'm here to protect you.'

'Protect me?'

Rod could not help feeling that if the Vienna police wanted him protected they would have sent someone bigger.

'Surely you have heard?'

'Of course I've heard. I'd be a pretty poor excuse for a journalist if I hadn't.'

'We – that is the Kripo – fear there may be consequences beyond our control. Naturally you, as a reporter, will wish to see whatever happens tonight. And, as I said, I am here to ...'

'See, that I don't see.'

'As I said ... to protect you.'

'I think I get the message.'

Siebert gave Rod a nervous little smile, picked up a book of hotel matches from the ashtray, fished around in his pockets and pulled out a crushed packet of Astas. He held it out to Rod, Rod declined and he lit up a bent cigarette and inhaled deeply. For the first time Rod noticed the deep nicotine stains on the fingers of his right hand – the hand waved the match out, wafting across his words as he did so.

'Herr Troy, I am just a simple police sergeant.' Siebert paused, lowered his voice to the not-quite-confidential-but-the-certainly-discreet, 'We're not all Nazis you know.'

Was this deliberately disingenuous? Greene had told him for a fact that most of the Vienna police *were* Nazis.

'My brother's a police detective.'

'Then perhaps we have something in common?'

'I doubt that, and the purpose of me telling you is that while there might be such a thing as a simple copper – and trust me, I come from a village in the English Home Counties and they're full of simple coppers – I don't think there's such a thing as a simple detective.'

Siebert shrugged a little – the nervousness of his smile broadened into a grin.

'I suppose I should be flattered. But tell me ... it's almost two in the morning. You have waited up in anticipation. Knowing it or not you were waiting for me and we are neither of us destined for an early night or even an early morn, so tell me ... what are you are plans?'

Rod knew he'd never be able to shake this bloke off. He even thought that the man might be telling the truth – that he was here to protect him, and if he was ... why not take advantage of the fact?

'I was thinking that perhaps I should be in the Jewish quarter, across the canal. I think I'll just roll up the map and get in a cab.'

'Not tonight you won't. There's such a thing as cabman's instinct. I doubt you'll find a cab on the streets tonight for love nor money. They're all staying home. However ... I have my car outside, or I should say I have a car, my own does not have Polizei written on each door ... but tonight will hardly be a night when discretion pays. Shall we go?'

Outside in the Kärntnerstrasse Siebert led the way to a big, black Opel Super Six. Rod slipped in next to him. It was old and smelly and the springs in the seat were shot, and it was deathly cold.

'I found it in the car pool,' Siebert said, almost by way of apology. 'Regret to say the heater does not work, but we'll be fine.'

Rod did not think they'd be fine. It was a clear starlit night. They'd probably freeze to death.

§ 27

They crossed over the Danube Canal at the Franzens Bridge. Siebert had been right to choose a marked police car. The bridge was packed with SA men marching into Leopoldstadt by burning torchlight, all brown shirts and black boots – so many Rod began to wonder if fascism hadn't been started by an enterprising bloke in the clothing trade to shift several million rolls of brown cloth. Faces flickering in the fractured light, half-glimpsed as though half-formed, hiding in the half-darkness. A few banged on the roof of the car – most thought better of getting in the way of the police.

'It's bigger than I thought,' Siebert said. 'There'll be some dead Jews by morning.'

Rod found his matter-of-factness alarming. But, then, coppers could be like that, and whilst he had refuted the notion that Siebert and his little brother might have a common bond in being coppers, he had seen just the same near-amoral detachment in Frederick Troy. Not a blasé acceptance that such things happen, or that they cannot be prevented, but an apartness, a degree or more of separation, a distinct lack of 'there but for the grace of God . . .'

Siebert swung the car into a side street only a hundred yards or so past the bridge. Pulled up outside a small, brightly lit café – Bordoni Fratelli.

'We'll be alright here. They're open all night, and only an illiterate would think it was a Jewish-run place.'

Rod thought it highly likely that the average Brownshirt – if anything like the ones he'd come across in Berlin – probably was close to illiterate. Instead, he said, 'Why do we need to be anywhere off the street? That's where the action will be.'

Siebert pushed the glass door open and Rod followed. A man in a stiff off-white apron waved at him from behind the counter as though to a regular customer.

'I mean . . . we have only to follow one of these gangs of –'

'Trust me . . . you want action, you will get action.'

Rod was troubled by the simple truth buried in the statement.

'Of course I don't want action. I just –'

'You just want to be there if . . .'

'If what?'

'Whatever. You want to see Jews beaten up? You will. You want to see shops looted in the name of politics? You will. Cheap thuggery dressed up as moral force? You will.'

'I . . . I . . .'

'Giuseppe . . . an espresso and a glass of Pellegrino for me. And for my friend?'

'The same. Look, I feel I'm not making myself clear.'

Siebert had his hands cupped to his face lighting up another Asta. He waved out the match.

'Now, Giuseppe here . . .'

The proprietor looked up from his hissing coffee machine – a gentle smile beneath the comic-book moustache.

'Giuseppe here, he comes from a country in which fascism sees its first priority as being to make the trains run on time. What was wrong with Italian trains under the monarchy, I have no idea. But this is what one hears about Italy. Until Abyssinia it was all one heard about Italy. Il Duce makes the trains run on time. No doubt he sees to this personally.'

Siebert had the old Italian smiling broadly now.

'We, on the other hand . . . we Austrians . . . no I shall let Austria off the hook . . . we Viennese . . . it is a Viennese affair after all . . . have other priorities. What do our fascists do? . . . they take the German disease of anti-Semitism and they nurture the virus like a beloved family pet, and, once the cage is opened by Anschluss, they let loose a beast that has teeth and claws to terrify even Germany. Don't worry Herr Troy – tonight the gutters of Leopoldstadt will run with Jewish blood. It is what we Viennese do best, we torment and we torture Jews. All you have to do is listen for the first clap of doom. And do not let your conscience trouble you. We are both of us merely doing our job.'

At last Rod had found out what it was that united coppers across continents. An unflagging talent for razor sarcasm.

'Tell me, Herr Troy. Shall we reach a gentleman's agreement not to despise one another, and not to despise each other's professions? Would that be "cricket"?'

Siebert accepted his coffee, slapped down a couple of coins on the counter and took a tentative sip. Sipped, dragged on his Asta, sipped. Blew smoke with all the self-evident pleasure of a self-confessed addict. Sip, drag, sip.

'Mmmm . . . good. You should try it. Do not let it go to waste.'

Rod picked up his cup. Drinking coffee – and he had to admit that it was the best he'd had since his last meal in Soho, sharper than the Viennese taste – seemed like an appropriate diversion. A good enough way of not answering a question he rather thought Siebert did not much expect an answer to in the first place.

'Listen, you said. Listen for what?'

A boom like thunder rattled the coffee cups and blew the door open. A poltergeist had entered the room.

'That,' said Siebert.

§ 28

Hummel's mother had died when he was ten in the great flu pandemic that swept Europe towards the close of the Great War. His father had been a good father, a gentle spirit who had never laid a hand on the young Hummel, but whose vocabulary was severely limited, both verbally and emotionally. He would have bought the boy anything he wanted, anything his young heart desired, but the boy had to ask for it first – Old Hummel had not the imagination to know what a child might want without asking. Hence Hummel had found the nurture he lacked at his father's hand in books. He had been a word-child, forever with his nose in a book when other boys were out in the alley bouncing a ball off the back wall. He had, in so short a time, come to prefer the company of fictional characters to real ones. Hence, while his verbal vocabulary greatly exceeded his father's – so much so that neighbours used to joke that the boy had 'swallowed a dictionary' – his emotional vocabulary was as constrained as his father's, a world of love and pain bent double, hairpinned into restraint, straitjacketed in a tailored suit of good manners and long words and convoluted sentences. When the novels of adolescence had lost their fascination for him – he had ripped through Tolstoy and Stendhal and Balzac, but found most pleasure in the work of Theodore Fontane, if only because he was reading the author's work in the original German – he had turned to philosophy. As a young man in his twenties he would while away long winter nights with

Schopenhauer or Spinoza, subjects on which he could converse with no one.

In November 1933, about ten months after the accession to power of Adolf Hitler, Old Hummel had died, leaving young Hummel alone in the world, in full possession of a tailor's shop that thrived or not as the tide of tailoring ebbed or flowed, and the skills to run it. Social skills he had few, and, as Bemmelmann had remarked on his departure, young Hummel had been watched over by his neighbours, his father's contemporaries – each one baffled by the gangling, big-eared youth.

His father's last words had been, 'Joe, whatever will become of us?' Hummel had taken this to be more a reference to the fate of Jews in general than to the tiny tribe of Hummel.

So it was that each November, on the morning of the 10th, Hummel would go at first light to the Jewish cemetery on the far side of the Prater and sit at his father's grave. It was a ritual that began the night before. Hummel would take his father's best suit from the wardrobe, his father's best brown shoes and his father's best grey herringbone woollen overcoat. The only item that fitted remotely well were the shoes – the suit and the overcoat were far too big, and he looked, at thirty-one, as he had at eighteen, a boy masquerading as a man – a scrawny youth in the baggy clothes of a long-dead father. Dressed in mourning.

He sat that evening, and into the small hours, cocooned in his father's overcoat, gently rocking in his father's rocking chair, re-reading Descartes, weighing up for the fourth or fifth time that everything is mathematics and struggling to understand how Descartes could reach this conclusion and remain a deist. He had not read a newspaper of any kind for a week or more – he was no more aware that Ernst vom Rath had just died than he was aware that Ernst vom Rath had ever lived. Had he been aware he might not have ventured out when, a few hours before dawn, listening to the creaking silence of night, he had heard the biggest bang of his life. It rattled the windows, it shook dust down from the ceiling. A poltergeist had walked into the room and it appeared to have come from the direction of Leopoldstrasse.

He slipped out of the door. The street was deserted, the curfew observed. But from the same direction came the sound of smaller explosions, and a red glare above the rooftops. He walked to the end of the street. He'd been ready to break the curfew to sneak across the park to the cemetery, what would a peek into Leopoldstrasse matter? At the sound of running feet, he pressed his back against the wall, and, invisible in the darkness of the alley, watched as three men of his own age, one in his nightshirt, ran past pursued by half a dozen Brownshirts.

He looked down Leopoldstrasse. Several buildings were on fire. He walked on – no more running, no more shouting, jeering Brownshirts. A small crowd had gathered. He approached their backs, almost certain of what he would see. They'd been torching synagogues for weeks now. He rather thought this was the first time they'd blown one up with dynamite. And in so doing they had wrecked the houses to either side.

He found himself standing behind an old couple in dressing gowns and carpet slippers. They wept, the man no less loudly than the woman. The air seemed full of confetti, dancing in the heat and dust like autumn leaves caught in a breeze. Hummel held out one hand and a fragment settled – it reminded him of a game he had used to play with his father at just this time of year in the park. His father would walk several paces behind him. The young Hummel would spot a crisp, brown autumn leaf swirling to earth and run ahead to catch it, cup it in his hands. His father would say, 'Well done, Josef' – that had been his contribution to the game.

It was not a leaf, it was a piece of the Torah. The holy word of the God of his ancestors, looted from the ark, shredded like yesterday's newsprint.

The text was still legible, three words of Hebrew clear and distinct upon the scorched paper – a quotation Hummel recognised from Genesis, 'brimstone and fire', and he knew how it ended . . . 'brimstone and fire from the Lord out of heaven' . . . and the destruction of Sodom followed. He thought it singularly inappropriate. This was Vienna not Sodom. This was the work of man not God. He looked up, as though searching for someone with whom to share the thought. He was alone. All around had fled, and down the street came the same bunch of Brownshirts he had missed going the other way. They had lost their quarry and were now lumbering up to him. Hummel's first reaction to the cry of 'Jew-boy!' was a silent 'Who me?' And his second was to run.

Hummel ran, great flat feet slapping, the great grey overcoat flapping. Down Leopoldstrasse, around the next corner.

'Get-'im-catch-'im-rip-'is-bollocks-off!'

The cries pursued him round the corner, through an alley and into the next main street. A man standing in a doorway took off after him, and for a second Hummel thought he was caught, but a backward glance told him it was just another Jew in the same plight. Hummel turned left into another alley. The man ran straight on and the Brownshirts followed him instead of Hummel. Hummel emerged at the other end of the alley – suddenly it was almost quiet. No noises on the street, but off the street, high up in the apartments, he could hear the shouts and the crashes as the boot of the new civilisation met the flesh and culture of the old. He stepped back into a shop doorway as windows on a third floor burst outwards showering the street in broken glass. A woman screamed, and just as suddenly stopped. Then Hummel heard grunts of exhortation and something very large appeared on the window ledge. A tallboy? A wardrobe? Hummel heard a jangling, a discordant music, as though a cat had just run across the keyboard of a piano. Then he realised. It was a piano. A full-sized concert grand was pushed out and dropped into the street below. It seemed to Hummel to land like some outsized creature in one of those American Disney cartoons he had occasionally seen at the cinema. The legs splayed like an elephant on ice, the belly of the beast hit the cobbles, the lid shot up and the keyboard exploded in a roman candle of ebony and ivory.

Brownshirts appeared at the window, jostling each other for a view and laughing. They soon tired of the joke, their heads pulled back and the screams from within began again. Hummel emerged from the shadows. The piano seemed to be humming rather like an aeolian harp, the wind across its strings. Hummel crept closer. The humming seemed less like an instrument and more human. He stood on the remains of the lid and peeked in. There, on the metal frame of the piano, lay a short man of sixty or so – crucified ... strapped down, tied into place with piano wire. He was naked, he was drenched in blood, his chest was punctured where a rib protruded through the flesh, and he was indeed humming. One note might be groaning. Three was humming. It was not a tune Hummel knew.

His eyes opened, he looked at Hummel and spoke.

'Oh my God ...' he said, and died.

A blow to the kidneys doubled Hummel up, he felt his knees give way, beery breath upon his face, and a voice in his ear.

'Right, Jew-boy ... you'll get yours next.'

Hummel sank to the cobblestones. They kicked him in both legs until the pain of the blows was worse than the pain in his back and then he struggled to his feet. There were six of them, the same six he'd shaken off only minutes before. Two hoisted him upright, a third punched him in the face, and he found himself frog-marched, half-conscious and tasting blood, off down the street to he knew not where. His feet slithered on the stone, the Brownshirts heaved and his father's shoes slipped from his feet – they dragged him on, over rubble, through puddles ... he felt the searing pain of bashed toes and, when the pain subsided, he felt the cold and damp begin to seep through his socks.

A couple of hundred yards on they lugged him like a sack of spuds up a long staircase, kicked open a door and dumped him on the floor.

Someone was shouting. Hummel looked up, found himself staring at the high ceiling and the old black hammerbeams and slowly recognised where he was – in the upstairs dining hall of the Guild of Master Silversmiths. He'd been here every year as a boy for the spring flower show, when all the window-box gardeners in Leopoldstadt paraded the bulbs they had overwintered into blossom. Whoever it was shouting, they were not shouting at him. He sat up. There were about twenty Brownshirts in the hall, all much of a muchness, confirming what Hummel had always thought about them – that they were the fat and the lazy, nature's idlers, who bizarrely yearned for life in uniform, for the physical grace that eluded them and the physical fitness they'd never work for – office clerks and Sunday soldiers who in any other country would end up as scoutmasters dunning mindless patriotism into the young and gullible. And there were countless Jewish men – men of all ages, fit young men with broad shoulders, old men, old men stooped and white-bearded. They were doing knee-bends – up down, up down, hands behind their head. An old man fell over – two Brownshirts immmediately kicked him in the ribs until he forced himself up again.

At a cry of 'Up, you fuckers, up!' a young man answered back and was smashed in the nose with a truncheon.

Someone prodded Hummel with the toe of his boot. At least it was a prod, not a kick.

'You too, Big Ears, or did you think you were going to sit there till Kingdom come?'

Hummel stood, winced at the pain in the small of his back, locked his hands behind his head and began the rhythmic squatting and rising.

'Down, you fuckers, down, up, you fuckers, up.'

He'd done no more than a dozen, when the command changed to, 'Press-ups, you fuckers. Let's see what you kikes are made of.'

Hummel had no more strength in his arms than a skinny schoolgirl. He had spent his working life at the meticulous task of sewing, not the bicep-building tasks of a labourer. One good push up and he was spent.

He looked around at his fellow prisoners. Most were flat on the floor exhausted. One or two younger men were valiantly responding to the cry ... 'Push, you fuckers, push.' A few more pushes and they too hit the floor and groaned.

'What now?' Hummel thought. 'You can't flog a dead horse.'

A few seconds in a huddle of whispers and a bunch of Brownshirts took off at a run across the prone bodies, using them as stepping stones, and stamping on them with every ounce of their strength, jumping on them like kids upon a mattress.

Men screamed, men writhed, and, seeing the approaching boots, one old man rose to his feet, summoned the last of his resources, ran for the leaded window and crashed through it head first.

He was silent as he fell – all Hummel heard was the distant thud as his body hit the street below and the fountain tinkle of glass falling.

Every Brownshirt in the room ran to the window to look out.

'Bloody hell.'

Hummel looked around. Behind him was a closet door. He turned the handle and stepped inside. With all eyes on the window, no one had noticed. He crouched down and put an eye to the keyhole. The novelty of suicide had passed in an instant. Now they waded into the herded Jews with truncheons, smashing noses and cracking skulls, until the floor was red with blood, until they had found the perfect target – a rabbi, a man in his eighties, it seemed to Hummel, hiding at the back of the room not far from where Hummel had been standing. They forced the old man to his knees. One of the Brownshirts held a scroll of the Torah, no doubt one of dozens looted from the synagogues, tore off a piece and shoved it into the old man's mouth. Then he struck a match and set fire to it. The rabbi could not scream with his mouth full – all he could do was writhe in agony as his beard and eyebrows went up in flames. Another Brownshirt whacked him on the back of the head with his stick and the rabbi fell face down, flames out, face scorched, acrid, pungent smoke wafting off him.

Hummel could look no more. He turned his back, and in so doing noticed a tiny shaft of light at the back of the closet. He went up to it and looked through. It was the keyhole of another door. He was, he realised, in a closet that connected two rooms. The other room was smaller. It looked empty. He put his ear to the keyhole, just to be certain, heard nothing and gently turned the handle. The door wasn't locked. He stepped into the room and tiptoed across to the main door. That too was unlocked. He inched it open and found himself looking out onto a staircase – not the one he had been brought up and not one in frequent use from the amount of dust and cobwebs. At the bottom of the stairs he found a door, apparently a fire escape door, held shut only by a push bar. He pushed. The door opened an inch or two. He pushed harder and heard the clang as a couple of dustbins rolled away. Then he stepped out and found himself in a deserted narrow channel at the back of the Silversmith's Hall – the sort of place only ever visited by criminals, illicit lovers and dustmen.

Hummel ran, great flat feet slapping, the great grey overcoat flapping.

§ 29

At each street corner Hummel would slow to a walk, glance round the corner and enter only if the street was empty of Brownshirts. If there were people around – ordinary citizens, if that phrase meant anything any more – he would walk past them, hoping they would not notice he was barefoot, and begin to run again only when well clear.

He wondered what it was the fascists had against pianos. In the length of four or five streets he had passed half a dozen smashed pianos, and only half a mile or so back he had narrowly escaped a sense of déjà vu when another piano came crashing down from a top-floor apartment. He had resisted looking inside and walked on as though it rained pianos every day in this part of Vienna.

At the corner of Lindenstrasse he leaned out and peered into Waldenstrasse. It wasn't empty, there was a bunch of kids dawdling in front of the smouldering shell of a row of shops – but kids were kids, they weren't Brownshirts. Hummel pressed on. He'd run as soon as running became practical. The next thing he knew a boy of six or seven was stamping on his toes.

'Big Ears got no shoes!'

It was a call to battle. Before Hummel could stride out on his long legs and escape the little pest, the rest had joined in, stamping his toes, kicking his shins – 'Big Ears! Big Ears! Big Ears!'

Big Ears ran, great flat feet slapping, the great grey overcoat flapping.

He outran the little monsters, turned one corner and then another – but it was no time for complacency – to conclude he'd shaken them off would be rash.

Around another corner, and a horde of Brownshirts were waiting. A volte-face. He'd rather run a gauntlet of kids than a gauntlet of Brownshirts.

Retracing his steps he saw the approaching kids just as he reached a narrow channel that cut between two streets. He dashed down it and, as he emerged the other side, felt arms grip both of his and heard another beery voice say, 'What's the hurry, Jew-boy?' And a knee to the testicles doubled him up.

It occurred to Hummel through the haze of pain that seemed to start with his bruised toes, shoot upwards via bruised balls to his bruised skull, that they'd probably take him back to the Silversmith's hall and the whole bloody cycle would begin again. But clearly he was dealing with a better class of Nazi – this lot had their own van. They threw him in the back – the man Hummel landed on groaned and, as he groped around, Hummel felt at least a dozen different bodies under him. He touched an ankle, a thigh, withdrew at once ... reached out again and touched a potato. They were in the back of a greengrocer's van.

Hummel counted the number of turns, and the stops. No more bodies were piled in, and he concluded when the van stopped and the doors were flung open that they had been driven about two miles, and he was almost certain they'd crossed a bridge back into the city centre.

It was getting light. Hummel found himself in a group of about fifteen, moaning, but otherwise silent, Jews in front of a pair of high, black gates.

A truncheon in the back prodded him forward. The gates swung open, and Hummel knew at once where they were. The high brick walls, the sandy oval track around the perimeter – they were in the Police Academy Riding School.

'Well ... don't just stand there – run!'

Hummel stared. There were dozens of Brownshirts lining the track, and twenty or so Jews attempting the circuit, running till they staggered, staggering till they fell and, if they fell, kicked and trampled and left to bleed into the sand.

Another prod in the back. Hummel did not wait for a third. The man in front had set off and Hummel followed. The Nazis were armed with everything from bamboo canes to stout cudgels. The faster you ran, the more blows you escaped. The man in front of Hummel caught a blow in the face from a cane, lost his stride and backed into Hummel. Hummel side-stepped him, took a blow to the chest from a leather whip and ran on. It was like any other race. The only point was to win, and as he kicked out his long legs the Brownshirts cheered him on.

'Come on, Big Ears. Come on, Big Ears!'

Big Ears ran, great flat feet slapping, the great grey overcoat flapping. Big Ears ran, overtook the fat little Jew in his fifties, overtook the two lanky teenagers, the young rabbi . . . overtook everyone until the Brownshirts gave up hitting him and simply cheered . . . and cheered and cheered. They had got what they wanted from the night's carnage, pure entertainment . . . better than a dancing bear, or a fighting dog . . . they had . . . a performing Jew . . . a shoeless big-eared Jew flapping around in his father's best overcoat . . . a running Jew, fit to leave Jesse Owens standing.

They gave Hummel laurels in the form of a lavatory seat around his neck, gave him one last kick and shoved him indoors. The indoor riding track was the best part of forty feet high, with windows set close to the ceiling. From each window ledge hung a red and black swastika that reached almost to the floor – the two biggest framed a twenty-foot-high portrait of Hitler. It was a makeshift temple, Hummel thought. A place of worship for the Beast of Braunau. And if he had thought the Silversmith's hall had been crammed with Jews, this scene defied counting . . . there were thousands of Jews. Hummel wandered among them, a lost soul himself. And it occurred to him that the only comparable scene was a painting, or perhaps every painting, by the Dutchman Hieronymus Bosch . . . the catholic vision of hell in all its gore. Every Jew nursed a wound . . . so many broken noses . . . so many split lips and torn ears. So many bodies in the sand. Hummel wandered, exhausted from his running, but unable to sit. To sit would be to settle, to seep away into the sand and die. He thought he recognised faces in the sea of blood, but no one seemed to recognise him. Was that not Herr Freleng the butcher? Was that not Herr Schenckmann the actuary? Was that not Herr Adler, his old history teacher? He felt as though he had become suddenly invisible.

Time passed. Daylight streaked in through the windows. The doors opened and a voice shouted . . . 'Run . . . all of you run . . . go back to your stinking hovels . . . run . . . because if we catch you we'll do it all over again. Run!'

A surge of the able-bodied ran for the door. The rest lay in the sand. Big Ears ran, great flat feet slapping, the great grey overcoat flapping.

§ 30

Hummel shuffled across the Franzens Bridge. It was teeming with people. Most of them crossing the other way, most of them too weary or too burdened with loot after a night's pillage to bother much about a raggedy, bloody scarecrow of a man who might or might not be Jewish.

A young 'aryan' couple, evidently man and wife, pushed a handcart onto which they had managed to manoeuvre a four-seater leather sofa. A Brownshirt waddled along, his pockets so full of cutlery that he rattled like Harpo Marx in a classic Hollywood sketch and even, although oblivious to it, shed the odd knife or fork as he made his way home. Two children staggered along clutching a large wireless set, cord and plug trailing behind them. The smaller child dropped his end. The wireless hit the stones, split its wooden casing, shattered its tuning screen. One more bit of broken glass. The child bawled. The bigger child clipped him round the ear and walked on.

Hummel aimed at being invisible and almost succeeded.

He had reached the far end of the bridge, the Leopoldstadt side at the corner of Schüttelstrasse, half a mile from home, when he spotted a bunch of kids approaching. The same bunch of kids he had escaped only a couple of hours earlier.

'Oh shit,' he said. 'Oh shit, shit, shit.'

§ 31

Rod Troy and Oskar Siebert were sharing Rod's hip flask. Siebert had lit up his twentieth Asta of the night and was alternating the pleasure of tobacco with the pleasure of a rather nice Armagnac. They were standing in a shop doorway on the Leopoldstrasse a couple of hundred yards from the remains of the synagogue. It seemed to Rod that the night was running past him like a newsreel in one of those all-day news cinemas in central London – life on the loop. They'd circled the district three or four times in Siebert's car – Siebert had let Rod choose when they stopped and so far had not made any attempt to get between him and the 'action'. They'd seen 'action'. Now they were taking a breather. Every so often, a bunch of thugs would swagger down the street – one of them, the self-appointed leader – usually, Rod thought, both fat *and* ugly – might spot the two of them and approach with a snarl of assumed authority in his voice. Siebert would flash his warrant card and tell the the Brownshirt to 'Fuck off' – if this didn't work, he'd open his coat and show him the automatic pistol tucked into his shoulder holster. There'd been three or four encounters so far – Siebert had not once had to draw the gun. Better still, he'd managed to restrain the Englishman from behaving like St George and tackling any dragons. It had been a night of incident, it was always going to be a night of incident, but without the incident he most feared.

'Tell me, Herr Troy ... did you go to one of those private English schools where they beat you black and blue and roasted your arse by a roaring fire?'

Rod didn't get it for a second, then he realised Siebert was referring to *Tom Brown's Schooldays*, one of those English 'classics' Rod had never bothered to read, but whose plot seemed to be part of the general knowledge of English culture – books you never had to read as long as you knew the odd bit of plot and could fill in the author's name in answer to a crossword clue. But then that, Rod had long ago concluded, was the purpose of English culture – to enable one to do the crossword on the back page of a newspaper.

'As a matter of fact I did ...'

12 down.

'... And I think you mean a bloke called Flashman. The school bully.'

'Imagine, if you will, that the school bullies take over the school, and then, not content with the schools, the city ... the nation ... half Europe.'

3 across.

'The Brownshirts?'

'Schoolyard bullies given a whole city to play with.'

7 down.

'In England ... they wear black.'

'Really? It would be so much easier if all the fascists would wear the same outfit. Imagine visiting abroad and not being able to tell a Nazi thug from a postman.'

Rod began to giggle. A failing he had long since given up trying to control.

'One might think that the Führer would have opened an account for them all at the same department store – "Oh, joining the fascists are you sir? ... then you want the Hitler list ... Mr Hitler was in the other day and picked out the shirts personally ... he'll be back for the trousers next week. Right now he's favouring something in green corduroy, but we can't be sure he'll stick to it once he sees the cavalry twill" ...'

Rod laughed out loud. Siebert smirked a little at his own wit and swigged once more on the brandy.

'"The good news, sir, is that the Führer has chosen something in tasteful brown for the shirt – a shade we in the trade call 'dung'."'

A man ran past them in a huge grey overcoat and stockinged feet. He was pursued by a mob of children all chanting 'Run, Big Ears, run!'

Big Ears ran, great flat feet slapping, the great grey overcoat flapping. By now it was an encumbrance – Hummel sloughed it off and let it fall in the street behind him. With any luck one or two of the little bastards might trip over it. One child did, and another ran straight into him, and then another shunted the first two and they fell in a pile. Hummel made it to the next corner. Brownshirts heading towards him. He swung around, a pirouette on one foot, and charged into the mob of kids. One or two went flying, the rest kept chanting 'Run, Big Ears, run'. And two little shits grabbed hold of his right leg. Much to Hummel's surprise either they were weightless or the flight/fright boost of adrenaline had given him strength he never knew he had. He picked up his left leg and plonked it down, he picked up his right with the two kids attached and plonked that down – fee fi fo fum – one more step and he was running, the kids slamming down onto the cobbles and screaming.

When he saw Hummel turn and charge the mob of kids like a lone nutcase going over the top at the Somme, Rod Troy dashed from the shop doorway, flailing at the kids as he did so in a fruitless attempt at discipline – some utterly erroneous instinct that told him children did what grown-ups told them as long as one was firm with them.

'Stop it! Stop it at once! Stop it and go home to your parents.'

He was behaving less like St George, more like the most ineffectual schoolmaster in the world – and he looked to Siebert like the worst traffic cop in the world. He thought the Englishman would be lucky to escape alive.

'Oh shit,' he muttered to himself, just as the Brownshirts caught up with the kids, ran between him and Troy and sent him flying. He spun to earth, dropped the hip flask, reached for his gun, and a blow to the head sent the world bright green for a minute or more . . . and when his head cleared the street had cleared and he found himself sitting on the cobbles alone. No kids, no Brownshirts, no big-eared Jew . . . and no Englishman.

'Oh shit,' he said. 'Oh shit, shit, shit.'

§ 32

Hummel staggered into Krugstrasse. Leaned a moment on the cold brick wall, hearing only the beating of his own heart and the roar of blood in his ears. Then he turned the corner to face the row of tailors' shops and heard for the first time the commotion at the end of the street. They'd stormed the city by the light of burning torches. Now the torches were out, and with the sun behind them, he saw the outline of another bunch of Brownshirts. They were everywhere, a universal stain upon the fabric of the city. His best hope seemed to him to be a dash for home. He made it to his own doorstep, fumbled in his pocket for the house key, and realising that it had been not in his trouser pocket but in the pocket of his father's overcoat, stuck his hand through the letter box to grab the string from which the spare key had always hung. Which was when they grabbed him. Yanked him to his feet by the scruff of his neck.

'My, my,' said a voice behind him. 'We've caught ourselves a big one this time.'

'If you please, sir,' Hummel said. 'You have caught me once this night already and chose to let me go. I have served my time, and have already had my beating, thank you, sir.'

Another punch in the kidneys brought Hummel to his knees again.

The same voice said, 'This your shop then, Jew-boy?'

And a very familiar voice answered, 'Who wants to know?'

The man holding Hummel let him fall. Hummel counted up the feet. Eight pairs including one pair of German Army boots.

'Who the fuck are you?'

'Oberschütze Trager, Infantry. Or did you think field grey was fancy dress? This is a *real* uniform. Grey, not the shit brown of you part-timers. And *this* is my patrol. My beat. Has been since we came and liberated you dozy Ostfuckers.'

'Then why don't you take a hike and come back in ten minutes?'

Hummel looked up. Glanced quickly around. The SA all had what looked to be pick-axe handles. The one doing the talking, a stout man with a jagged red scar down one cheek, clutched a very old pre-war revolver. Trager had unslung his rifle and was holding it across his chest, barrel up, stock down, in a way that suggested he could point and aim at the drop of a hat.

'I ain't going nowhere. You've had your fun. Now bugger off.'

Scarface turned as though about to say something funny to his mates, but the voice Hummel heard was that of Beckermann's grandson, Adam.

'Pigs, pigs, pigs!'

The boy was in front of his grandfather's shop holding a blunderbuss – the sort of gun Hummel had seen only in story books when he was a child. The logical part of his mind wondered where the boy could have found anything to load it with. Young Beckermann cocked the hammer, aimed at the mob of Brownshirts, producing a communal flinching as he did so, pulled jerkily on the trigger . . . and nothing happened. He pulled again, and before he could try a third time they were on him, all seven of them, beating him to a bloody mess with their pick-axe handles.

Hummel did not wait to see young Beckermann die. He ran, head down, feet and heart pounding, back down the alley and straight into the chest of a man at least as tall as himself and twice as wide. The man spun with the impact sending Hummel skidding across the cobbles to land at the feet of a Brownshirt coming the other way – one more pair of black leather jackboots.

Young Beckermann was dead – he had to be or they would not have stopped. Hummel backed away from the Nazi coming down the alley, bumped gently into the back of the big man in the black overcoat who'd sent him spinning. As the rest of them advanced the big man gently steered Hummel to the imagined safety of the space between himself and the wall – physically blocking the way between Hummel and the Nazis. One against eight. Perhaps one against nine. Who could tell which side Trager was on?

Scarface approached.

'Who the fuck are you?'

The big man flourished a piece of paper in his face – a piece of paper bearing enough swastikas to give Scarface cause to pause.

'*Presse aus* London,' the big man said in accented, Berlinish German. 'I have papers signed personally by Dr Goebbels.'

Scarface stared at the paper as though he'd never learnt to read. Hummel wondered if his rescuer was bluffing, but Scarface moved no closer, no more certain than Hummel was himself.

'So what? Is this your kike then? Your personal, private kike? The English love their kikes so much they have 'em as pets? Is that it? He's your kike is he?'

With one hand the Englishman pocketed his papers, with the other he gestured protectively towards Hummel.

'Not quite . . . he is God's kike. And God has sent me to protect him.'

The Brownshirts split their sides laughing at this. If there hadn't been the new arrival in the alley, Hummel would have chosen this moment to run for it.

Scarface recovered his breath, tears of laughter streaming down his face.

'Marvellous. Absolutely fucking marvellous. And who has God sent to protect you?'

And out of nowhere a voice said, 'Me.'

The latecomer jerked forward, prodded by a gun barrel in the small of his back. Enough sense to raise his hands.

Hummel watched as a small man in a grubby raincoat and a battered trilby came out of the darkness, pushing the Brownshirt forward with the end of his automatic pistol. Hummel could say this for Scarface, he didn't scare easily.

'Not another one. Now, who the fuck are you?'

It seemed to be his catchphrase.

The shabby little man held up a card in a small leather wallet. Perhaps Scarface could read after all. Perhaps he'd merely been arrested enough times to know the signs. He turned to the gang and said, 'Would you believe it . . . never one around when you need one . . . always one when you don't. He's a copper, boys! A common Viennese flatfoot!'

'The party's over. Go and trash some other street.'

'No . . . you're wrong there copper . . . it's over when I say it's over.'

Scarface had stood clutching his revolver at his side. Now he aimed it vaguely in the direction of the policeman. The policeman shoved the latecomer forward and aimed his gun at Scarface's head.

'You touch the Englishman, you're dead. I don't care about the Jew, but you take one step closer to the Englishman and I'll blow your brains out.'

'Then tell your Englishman to move.'

Nobody moved. Nobody spoke. Hummel saw Scarface's hand wave unsteadily. He had the gun at arm's length. The policeman was using both hands, one on the gun, the other supporting his elbow – his arm didn't wave and the barrel of his gun stayed unerringly aimed at Scarface's head.

Scarface lowered his gun, turned to the mob and said, 'Hans ... the bottle.'

A young Brownshirt, a boy no older than young Beckermann, stuck a bottle in his hand, a bottle with a dirty rag stuffed in the neck. Then the young man flicked a cigarette lighter and the rag burst into flame and Hummel realised it was what was known as a Molotov cocktail, a bottleful of sand and petrol.

'You don't care about the kike?'

The policeman said nothing.

'Cos if you don't care about the kike ... you won't give a toss about his shop neither ... will you?'

Scarface holstered his pistol, strode towards Hummel's shop, raised his arm. Hummel screamed, 'Noooooo!!!', charged past the Englishman only to find the Englishman's arms around his neck and his voice saying, 'Don't be a bloody fool.'

Hummel squirmed. The Englishman tightened his grip.

Scarface lowered his arm.

'You,' he said to Trager. 'You do it.'

Trager? Hummel had almost forgotten Trager was there.

'No,' Trager said softly.

'You do it, soldier boy. Just for us. You've done your bit for the kike here. We all heard your little speech. We all want to see you do something this night. Something for the real Germans, something for the Reich, something for ... the boys in shit-brown.'

Trager looked at Scarface, looked from Scarface to Hummel, back to Scarface and then he smashed a hole in the front window of the shop with the butt of his rifle, took the blazing bottle and hurled it through the hole. The workshop behind erupted into blue and orange flames.

Hummel screamed. But for the Englishman's grip he would have sunk to his knees. The Brownshirts cheered and jeered. Then, as if by some secret signal, they stormed off down the alley trampling young Beckermann's body as they went.

The Englishman let go of Hummel. Hummel flopped to earth, raised his head to look at Trager. Trager did not meet his look, shouldered his rifle and walked off in the opposite direction to the Nazis.

The glass on the shop front pinged and shattered – a crystal rain around Hummel. He felt a hand on his shoulder, heard the Englishman saying, 'You can't stay here.'

Then the copper: 'Yes he can. It's you who must leave.'

The shop was well ablaze, the heat blasting out across the cobblestones.

'Troy. For God's sake. We must go now.'

Hummel felt the Englishman finally let go, heard the clatter of feet as the policeman bundled him off down the alley. Then he was alone. He curled into a foetal ball and wished for the world to end, for the earth to open up and swallow him like Jonah into the belly of the whale. Down the street a dog was barking, but all the noise of the night now seemed so far away. As though he had lived this night in another place and another time. He felt as though he could sleep now, in the cold early light of morning, exactly where he was on the cold, cold stone, under the hot, hot breath of his burning shop.

A soft sound, near at hand, nearer than the wretched dog, crept into his senses. Somewhere a man was weeping. Hummel opened one eye, at ground level. Down the street old Beckermann was hunched over the broken body of his grandson, the pool of blood seeping outward, ever nearer Hummel. The boy's words at Passover came back to Hummel.

'God has gone deaf. Either that or he is dead.'

Down the street a dog was barking.

§ 33

Siebert was hunched over the basin in the bathroom of Rod's suite at the Meissl und Schadn, rinsing the blood out of the matted hair on the back of his head.

Rod looked at the wound, said, 'Doesn't need stitching. It's quite a lump though. You were lucky you weren't out cold.'

'I was,' Siebert said, his face still in the basin. 'Did you think I'd let you escape if I were conscious?'

'Come through when you're ready. I ordered lunch as soon as we got in.'

Rod went back into the sitting room.

'Lunch? What happened to breakfast?'

Rod called back, 'The night ran away with you ... it's past noon.'

Rod lifted up the silver domes to look at the meal. Siebert came in, head buried in a hotel towel, rubbing at the wound on his skull. The sound of a cork popping made him flip up the towel and look.

'Champagne?'

'Champagne, blue trout, black truffles.'

'Good God, do you always eat like this?'

'If at all possible. Otherwise what's the point of staying in a joint like this?'

Siebert dropped the towel and accepted the glass of champagne.

'Well ... it can hardly be the company.'

'The Germans stay here for the food ... makes it the right place to eavesdrop. Bad company, good food. Let's eat.'

Siebert was surprised, pleasantly, at how hungry he was. They ate and chatted. Afterwards he realised he'd kill for a fag, only to find that the Englishman had read his mind and flipped a napkin off an unopened packet of Astas.

'My God ... you think of everything. Tell me, have you thought what you're going to write about the night's ... what shall I call them ... happenings ...?'

A waiter with a pot of coffee interrupted any answer for a moment or two, but when the Englishman sat down it was obvious to Siebert that he was going to answer.

'Yes. Of course. In fact I think I'm going to write two pieces at rather differing speeds. One I'll get down to as soon as we're through here, and it'll be in the morning edition tomorrow if I can get it out. In black and white ... everything we saw. I'll file from Berlin. I'm leaving on the sleeper tonight. The other ... something for the *Sunday Post*. More of an essay ... something on the nature of mob mentality ... the instinct to survive ... to survive by destroying ... to pass on the humiliation. That's what kikes and niggers are for ... the whole point of such notions of the alien ... to make damn sure there's some poor bugger who's worse off than you are yourself. Some poor bugger who can be blamed for all your ills. It's sort of what makes the world go round.'

Siebert had no facial reaction to this. No shrugs, no twist in the lips to say it was beyond him. He simply sat back with his brauner – a strong cup of coffee with a thick head of cream – stuck a cigarette between his lips, lit up once more – drag, sip, drag – and said, 'Could you leave me out? Whichever one I might be in, could you just leave me out?'

§ 34

Little had burnt. Little but enough. The packed swatches of cloth, dense and heavy, had resisted flame in much the way the pages of a telephone directory would if one tried to light the inch thick edge. They had scorched and smouldered but not burnt. His sewing machine in contrast was a train-wreck. A small tortured sculpture in twisted iron and steel. Hummel could still make out the word 'Singer' on the frame, stripped of its black and gold. For all his adult life and much of his childhood the old Singer, which had been his father's before it was his, had seemed like an extension of Hummel himself. His big flat feet rhythmically worked the treadle, and through the treadle Hummel connected to the earth, the universe, the everything and the all. The small Antaeus of the sewing machine. As a boy he had sat and pedalled, no cloth no thread, and stared at nothing and found it easy enough to think of nothing, almost mesmerised by the motion. His father would come in and tell him how the sun was shining and that he should go out and play. A limb had been severed. Two arms, two legs, but treadleless. It was a moment to weep and had Hummel been a weeping man he might well have wept.

He became aware of someone standing behind him in the skewed frame of the shop doorway. It had to be Trager.

Without turning Hummel said, 'Why, Joe, why?'

Trager shuffled forward kicking up fine, flying black ash with the toecaps of his boots.

'You just don't get it, do you?'

'What's to get?'

'It had to be me. That's what you don't get. 'Cos if it wasn't me it wouldn't have been one of them. It would have been all of them. The whole fuckin' lot. Do you honestly think one Viennese copper, some stupid English twat who'd got himself lost and me . . . Little Joe Trager . . . could have held off that lot?'

Hummel said nothing.

'It's not even as if they were Germans. That was your lot. Austrians, Viennese . . . for all I know people you've known all your life.'

'I'd never seen any of them before. They might as well have been Germans for all I know.'

'Fine. Have it your own fuckin' way. Germans, Austrians, whatever *they* were, but Joe, if you stay maybe *they*'ll kill you.'

'*They?*' said Hummel with all the irony he could cram into one syllable.

'We . . . then . . . we . . . fuck it, Joe, maybe *I*'ll have to kill you?'

'But you'd only be following orders.'

He'd finally got to Trager. Trager had turned red in the face, risen to his full short height, all but loomed over Hummel. Hummel expected foul-mouthed rage, perhaps a blow from his fist.

'Jesus Christ, Joe. Jesus Christ.'

He had spoken so softly it was neither oath nor curse. A heartfelt whisper. Then he hoisted his rifle, turned and left. Hummel did not see him again until it was dark.

He thought better of sleeping in the flat over the shop. The floor might give way, and 'they' might return. Instead he went round to Shkolnik's Kosher Butcher's two streets away and asked Old Shkolnik for four steel meathooks. Shkolnik was standing in the remains of his shop, shuffling around on a carpet of broken glass making no attempt to clean up anything.

'Take as many as you like. I'm out of business. The buggers stole everything. You might not even find a meathook. I'm filth. I'm scum. We're all scum. Dirty bunch of Juden. Funny how my meat's clean enough to be worth stealing and cooking.'

Hummel found the four hooks he wanted amongst the rubble and took them home. There was nothing he could say to Shkolnik, nothing he could say to anybody. Shkolnik had pointed out that there had been Shkolniks in the shop for five generations. On the way home Kostiner at the corner café said there had been Kostiners for three generations, and Linsky at the drapers said it had been four. Hummel was not counting. As far as he knew there had been Hummels in Vienna since the original Hummel disembarked from Noah's ark with a pair of unicorns and caught the first passing tram into Leopoldstadt.

He kicked about for a while in the ash and soot of the shop and found unscathed, a roll of grey Hessian, as heavy as sackcloth and closer in the weave. Then he hand-sewed a meathook to each corner of a long strip of the cloth, doubled over for strength, and with each hook thrown over a rafter in the shed, he had himself an improvised hammock. He felt safe in the shed. 'They' wouldn't look in the shed. 'They', in the form of 'he', dropped by about nine in the evening. Dark and cold and wet. Hummel was in his hammock, buried under several eiderdowns, reading by candlelight. The door opened and Trager stuck his head in.

'Wot yer doing?'

'What does it look like?'

Trager shone his bullseye torch on the book, mouthing and mangling what he saw on the spine.

'Renn Dezcartiz?'

'René Descartes,' Hummel said trying to keep his voice chatty. '*The Discourse on Method.*'

'What method?'

'The method of reason and mathematics.'

'Oh. I prefer a good yarn meself.'

'Oh it's that alright.'

'I see you made yourself cosy then?'

It was not the word Hummel would have chosen.

'Needs must,' he said simply.

'I been thinking. About you leaving.'

'Who said I was leaving?'

'I told you this morning . . .'

'It's OK, Joe. This morning you convinced me. I just don't know how. I have no visa for any foreign country. I'm on no one's quota. And, as of last night, I have nothing Herr Eichmann could possibly want in exchange for my freedom. Perhaps you were right. I should have gone with the Bemmelmanns. Did I tell you I got a letter from Palestine last week? They are on a *kibbutz* near Haifa.'

'They was lucky. Lots o'folk drowned in the Danube. One poor couple got stuck on an island between one of them there Balkan states and whatever country's got the other bank, and neither one'd let 'em in.'

'Now you tell me. All the same, Joe, I would leave if I knew how.'

Trager had been thinking. He had that smug hint of self-regard of the man who knows he has had a good idea, if perhaps for the first and only time in his life.

'I got this mate. Patrols the marshalling yard next to the railway station.'

'Which station?'

'Does it matter?'

'Of course it matters. I'm not getting on a train to Russia. That would be frying pan to Nebuchadnezzar's furnace.'

'It's the Westbahnhof. You know ... trains to Germany, France ... Belgium.'

No, Hummel thought, trains to England.

'And he can get me on a train?'

'Sort of.'

'How sort of?'

'He can get you on a goods wagon. Maybe. Like a boxcar.'

'Surely they – I mean you – surely German troops have enough sense to search the boxcars?'

Trager saw his idea crashing down around him in flames as fast as the Hindenburg in New Jersey.

'Dunno. I'll have to ask him.'

'Fine. And when you do, ask him for the measurements between axles on a small wagon.'

'How the hell are we supposed to find out that?'

'To the nearest pace will do. Half a metre either way. Put your jackboots to good use for once. Pace it out from wheel to wheel.'

Trager went away puzzled but willing. Hummel felt for the first time a hint of the gratitude he had always resisted extending towards Trager and anything Trager did. He had had a good idea too, and it beat the hell out of anything Trager could come up with.

§35

Two days later Trager reappeared at Hummel's shed. Another dark, cold, wet night.

My mate reckons he can get you in a boxcar. Reckons he can bury you under something, so as you won't get noticed.'

Bury me is right, thought Hummel.

'And the distance between axles?'

'Four metres, give or take . . . but it's all a risk, d'ye see?'

'Risk. Yes. I see.'

Drawing breath had been a risk from the day the Germans rolled in.

'He can't . . . like . . . do it for free and for nothing.'

'Of course not, Joe. Everything has its price.'

Trager was almost immune to sarcasm, it drifted by him.

'Too bloody right. And it's too far to walk. I'll have to bung something to the bloke with the staff car.'

'Fine. I understand. But how do you come by a staff car?'

Trager tapped the side of his nose.

'When there ain't no "staff" around . . . make it a hundred apiece.'

At the back of the shed Hummel dug out the spare sewing machine that got used only if the workhorse machine needed to be repaired. It was old, and very heavy, and Hummel could not quite remember when he had last used it, but it worked. Another length of Hessian, slightly over four metres, got hemmed and reinforced at the corners. An offcut about 200 mm wide and a metre long got turned into a money belt. Upstairs, in the back bedroom, Hummel looked at his skinny frame in a full-length mirror, wanting to know that beneath his overcoat, his jacket and his cardigan, the belt, now full of notes, did not reveal itself as a bulge. It didn't. And the immediate satisfaction gave way at once to the thought, 'Have I used a sewing machine for the last time? Is this the last garment I will ever make?' A thought that Hummel, with some difficulty, set aside. He took off coat, jacket and cardigan, wound the four metres of Hessian around and dressed again. He'd be lucky. He looked portly. But to someone who'd never met him? The contents of his small leather case, still bearing his father's initials in faded gold, were as innocuous as he could make them – a safety razor (with blade), a flannel, a toothbrush, a change of socks, shirt and underpants, a copy of *Baedeker's Guide to Paris* (published in Leipzig in 1907 and disguised with the dust jacket from a German translation of *Le Juif Errant* by Eugène Sue) and four meat hooks (there was not much he could do about those, a meat hook was a meat hook), and four cheese sandwiches.

The next night, Trager called for him close to midnight. Looked at Hummel, wrapped up for winter. Black coat. A bit stout around the tum.

'You sure about this?'

'Joe, you've been nagging me to go ever since the Bemmelmanns left.'

'OK. Same routine. Anybody sees us you're under arrest. I'll be in the back with me rifle, you'll be in front . . . you just look . . .'

'What, Joe? Look what?'

'Look nicked . . . look scared.'

'I will have no problem looking scared.'

They walked to the end of the street, the ridiculous couple once more, the short and the tall, the German and the Jew. Hummel did not turn around, thought of the story of Lot's wife and kept on walking.

The staff car was an open-topped Opel six-seater, driven by 'my mate Gus'. The wind cut into them as they tore down the Ring, and two hundred yards from the station in Mariahilferstrasse Hummel's hat flew off and he tried to see no symbol in it.

At the gate of the marshalling yard, the car stopped and they all got out, Trager loosely holding his gun at waist height, loosely and unconvincingly pointing it at Hummel. Then he winked. Hummel took the cue, reached into his pocket and handed Gus a roll of notes. Gus said nothing – but he had not spoken at all as they had crossed the city centre – looked both ways in the hammiest pretence of caution and pocketed his money.

They found 'my mate Erik' by the waving of his lantern, down a dark alley created by long, long trains of goods wagons.

Erik had a gift for the obvious, 'This 'im?'

'Course it's 'im.'

'Worth savin' is he?'

Trager said nothing to this. Erik rolled back the door of a boxcar, shone his light inside to show a wall of square packing cases stacked like toy building blocks in the nursery.

'See where the bottom one's out? You get in there. We push it back and you got about half a metre clear on the far side. You'll be snug as a bug in a rug. Gettit?'

'Yes. I gettit. But I need to know. Where is the train going?'

'Five o'clock tomorrow morning, it'll pull out for Munich. Munich's first stop. Half the train'll uncouple there. This bit goes on to Stuttgart. After that you're on your own. Plenty o'trains cross the border from there. You just have to find one.'

Hummel looked at Trager. This wasn't what he wanted, but it was pretty much what he had expected. Another wink from Trager and he paid off Erik. Erik went off down the line, swinging his lantern.

'I'll tuck you in,' Trager said, inadvertently maternal, and as he and Hummel squatted down in front of the gap in the wall of packing cases, Hummel took another roll of notes from his pocket and held it out. Trager looked at it by the light of his torch.

'It's not about money.'

'Of course not. All the same you'll take it?'

Trager hesitated, took the bankroll and said, 'Get inside now.'

Hummel slid in, felt a moment's passing panic as the last box was pushed in behind him cutting off the torchlight, and said, 'Goodbye Joe. And thank you.'

The last words he ever heard from Trager, half-muffled by the boxes, were, 'I didn't do it for the money.'

§ 36

Hummel gave it about an hour, decided it was close to 2 a.m., and pushed at the loose box. It slid out as easily as it had slid in. He tried the sliding door, found it was not locked, slid the box back into place and jumped down to the tracks.

There was moonlight overhead, but the shadows from the trains left it too dark to see what was written on the side of the car. He took the risk, pulled out a pocket torch, cupped his hand around the beam and found the word 'Stuttgart' chalked just to the left of the door. The same word was written on the cars coupled at either end. He chose the right-hand car and crawled underneath. He took off his coat, jacket and cardigan, unwound the long stretch of Hessian, inserted a meat hook at each corner, and slung his new hammock between the axles of the boxcar. Lying in it, case clutched to his chest, money-belt feeling lumpy round his middle, he found he was well clear of the ground – Trager had got the measurement right – but he'd still be visible to anyone searching underneath. If they searched underneath.

He heard an engine in the distance, building up steam. Then the slow, rhythmical throb, the inhalation and exhalation, as it drew nearer. The bump as it touched buffers, sending every car into temporary motion, one after the other, a metal ripple, like a giant's card trick. When the train pulled out he could feel the jolting in every bone in his body and began to wonder if he might not rattle to pieces long before Stuttgart, but once the train gathered speed, the roughness evened out and he began to think that it might even be possible to sleep in his hammock, to lose the sense of the ground beneath him rushing so rapidly past.

The train stopped well short of Munich. From the time they'd travelled Hummel thought they could be no further than Linz. It was light, and it was cold, and it was damp. Morning in mid-November. There was shouting, and there were boots running up and down almost level with his eyes. Then he heard a door slide open. Not the car above him, the car he had been in, it sounded like. The sound of the packing cases being torn down, and a voice saying, '*Niemand!*'

Three pairs of boots gathered right in front of him.

'Wankers,' a voice said. 'Total wankers, just wastin' our fuckin' time!'

'We could search the lot,' a second voice added.

'Don't be so fuckin' stupid. One yid in a haystack? . . . I ask you is it worth it?'

The train moved on.

'Erik?' Hummel wondered. 'Gus? Just so long as it wasn't Trager.'

§ 37

It was three days later – eating nothing after he had finished his cheese sandwiches on the second day, drinking out of firebuckets – that Hummel found himself at Strasbourg in France, a town that found itself in

Germany or in France from one time to another, depending on who was winning. At Strasbourg, speaking no French, he simply uttered the word 'Paree' at the ticket office and, in response to words he did not understand but whose meaning had to be obvious, put down all the francs he had. Even he could understand when the clerk told him with words and grimaces that it was not enough. And when he wrote down the figure on a piece of paper Hummel pulled out more than the equivalent in Austrian schilling and proffered them. The look on the clerk's face was part of Hummel's immediate education in the ways of the French nation. The way the man rubbed the thumb of his right hand against his first two fingers spoke more than words. Was this a country in which one could bribe one's way? That, thought Hummel, might well be to the advantage of a man with no papers and a fat wodge of foreign currency. Hummel offered the price of the ticket again. The clerk grinned, swept the bribe quickly off the counter and punched out a ticket. And a world of new possibilities began to open up for Hummel.

On the train, acutely conscious of what he looked like, he shaved, washed, cleaned his teeth, changed his shirt, combed his hair and did his best to knock the mud off his overcoat and trousers.

A few hours later, looking almost respectable – somewhat worse for wear than the customary railway passenger, he thought, but hardly a tramp – he stepped off a train at the Gare de L'Est ... wreathed in steam and smoke at his ankles, an urban hubbub of foreign syllables lapping at his ears – into a city of dreams, a city that spun dreams and consumed dreams, a city of which so many had dreamt – but Hummel had not been one of them. All his life, it seemed to Hummel, he had dreamt of Vienna. And now that was what remained of Vienna – a dream.

§ 38

Sigmund dreamt. He was back in Vienna. Not the Vienna he had left only months before, nor the Vienna of his youth, but the city around the year 1900, the Vienna of Empire, the Vienna of Franz-Josef ... Vienna before the war. Vienna before Sigmund was 'Freud' in the one-word way Picasso was 'Picasso' or Shakespeare 'Shakespeare'.

In his dream he was sitting in a café he could not name. A fine spring day, the trees in the square outside the window in bud, sunlight glinting on the cutlery at his table. He was thinking about the book he was writing, *The Interpretation of Dreams*, and with the hindsight of the dreamer knew that he had already finished this book, that it had run to eight or nine editions, had been translated into half a dozen languages. The waiter took his cup away and replaced it with one twice the size, and when Sigmund had finished that, one yet bigger. Soon he was drinking coffee out of a cup the size of a bucket – and found he could drink no more. The cup once raised to his lips tipped coffee down his shirtfront. He looked at the waiter, waiting. He was not alone, a dozen waiters stood in line behind him. The man in the square was ringing a handbell and shouting something Sigmund could not understand . . . and it was Autumn, leaves tumbling down around him, a wind blowing them flat against the glass. And suddenly he was alone, the sole customer at the sole table . . . no cup . . . no cutlery . . . no tablecloth . . . just the man with the handbell outside the window.

He opened his eyes. He was in his study in Hampstead, stretched out on the chaise longue reserved for the analysands. His daughter, Anna, was standing over him.

'The telephone?' he said.

'Made it through to the dream, eh? Yes, it was Alex Troy returning your call.'

'You should have woken me. I would have taken the call. I have been trying to meet him since we got here. Somehow we always seem to miss one another.'

'Plenty of time,' said Anna. 'Would you like to tell me about your dream?'

'My dream told me there was not plenty of time. I saw the grim reaper. He had a bell rather than a scythe but I knew him all the same. I saw myself go from anonymity to fame to oblivion in the course of a rather large cup of coffee.'

'Chastening.'

'Quite.'

§ 39

Hummel walked as far as the Île St Louis without opening his Baedeker. It pleased him to drift without words, without guidance, albeit in the right direction. On the Pont St Louis that linked the small island to the larger Île de la Cité, he opened his case and took out the Baedeker, looking for the address from which Schuster had written to him – Rue Mouffetard in the 5th arrondisement.

He unfolded the maps, turned the book this way and that to find the Quartier Latin. He must have stood too long. By the time he found the Rue Mouffetard on the pink map he realised that he had been caught by a street artist. A man wearing a cloth cap back to front, a blue canvas jacket stained with pastels, sitting on a folding stool by the bridge wall, was rapidly sketching him in charcoal. By the time Hummel had folded the maps back in and was ready to set off again, the man had leapt from the stool to offer the portrait to him.

It was accurate, Hummel knew. It was chilling. The man had caught the way he felt. The way he knew himself to be. The gauntness, the hollow cheeks, only emphasised by the big ears, the lines etched into his face by the months since the Germans marched in, the cold light of grief that had lingered in his eyes like impending rain since the death of his father. And to crown it all, shaving and washing and brushing had not prevented him from doing up the buttons on his overcoat wrongly. He looked like an overgrown child, clutching his case too tightly as comfort. He looked an oddity, big ears, big feet, wrong buttons. He looked like what he felt he was – another *Juif Errant*.

Honesty earned its reward. Hummel gave the artist a couple of schilling and took the portrait. He'd never had a portrait before, not so much as a snapshot from a box camera since he was a child – but if he had to have one he wanted one that was honest.

§ 40

Hummel found the apartment Schuster lodged in. Halfway down the Mouffetard, up a staircase, above a *bouchier chevaline.* He'd passed two or three on his walk down the street, along with fishmongers, wine merchants, coffee shops and greengrocers. It was a street of bustle. In total contrast to the street of tailors he and Schuster used to live in. There, silence had not so much reigned as ruled. Noise was unwelcome. Whole days passed without the sound of a voice, the background burble of a wireless — often as not just the rattle of the treadles on the sewing machines. He rather thought Schuster must enjoy the contrast.

Confronted by the landlady he kicked himself. What folly had led him to presume that Schuster would lodge with Jews? That he would be able to get by on the lingua franca of Yiddish? This woman — short, late-forties, dark hair done up in a greying bun — was about as Jewish as the pope. Madame Birotteau, that much he could grasp, and all she seemed to grasp of his was the word 'Schuster'.

She encouraged him inside, rattled off a few sentences of bafflement, and, seeing his incomprehension, picked a photograph off the sideboard and pointed. Herself and a teenage boy.

'*Mon fils*, Charles!'

Hummel deduced that he was her son. Easy. What he didn't deduce was that she was telling him the boy would be home from college in an hour and spoke German. He accepted a cup of coffee, took off his coat, sat silent and nervous on a straight-back chair and waited for he knew not what.

Shortly after five o'clock, a tall, pretty young man bounded up the stairs, dropped his books on the floor, threw his cap at the peg on the wall and began a fulsome account of everything that had happened to him since breakfast; the bus ride, the lecture, who he had chatted to over lunch . . . before noticing Hummel.

Hummel stood, held out a hand and said, 'Hummel. *Aus Wien.*'

And the boy understood at once.

'You've come all this way to see Manny?'

'I've come all this way to escape the Nazis,' Hummel said.

The boy sat down, pulled up a chair, closer to Hummel, reassured his mother with a smile.

'Herr Hummel, Manny Schuster has already moved on. He has been in London since September.'

Hummel's heart sank. Another presumption, for which he could kick himself. He'd counted on – felt as though he had staked his life upon – Schuster being here.

'But,' the boy went on, 'his room is still empty. I could talk to my mother. Perhaps you could stay here, at least until we can make contact with Manny.'

'I have money,' Hummel said. 'I can pay. It must be dangerous to take in Jews.'

'Not yet. Jews are not popular. Foreigners are not popular in a country flooded with refugees. But I cannot yet say that it is dangerous to take in a Jew.'

'All the same . . . I can pay.'

'It isn't about money, Herr Hummel.'

§41

Madame Birotteau let Schuster's old room to Hummel without hesitation. Charles Birotteau showed him up to the attic. A single white-painted iron bedstead, big enough for Schuster but short for Hummel, a hand-sewn cover in blue and white, a jug and bowl on a tiny deal table, a view over the rooftops towards the Panthéon and the Jardins du Luxembourg.

'It's a chilly room,' Charles said, 'but an hour before bedtime we could light the paraffin stove and warm the room.'

Hummel wanted to tell the boy that for a week he had slept in a shed and for three nights had been suspended beneath a goods train. Chilly did not matter – clean and dry mattered. To be safe mattered. To be still mattered. For the whole world to stop moving around him mattered. But he found he could say none of this. He found that the power of speech had dwindled to almost perfunctory answers to questions. His capacity to initiate conversation seemed to have been abandoned in Vienna along with everything else.

At ten o'clock, after a meal of haddock, cabbage and potatoes that left Hummel both silent and grateful, Charles lit the stove for Hummel and said, 'Don't let the bedbugs bite.'

Hummel looked shocked, but said nothing.

'A joke, Herr Hummel. A joke! Bedbugs in my mother's house?'

'*Ja*,' said Hummel. 'Joke.'

As though he had forgotten the meaning of the word.

The boy wished him goodnight. Hummel heard his feet banging down the stairs, then silence – only the odd sounds of the city wafting up from the street below.

He looked around once more. Bed, chair, table, bowl, jug, window – noticed for the first time the chamber pot under the bed – noticed how in its simplicity the room was like a van Gogh. It was his room. Didn't matter for how long, it was his. Bed, chair, table, bowl, jug, window, chamber pot. They none of them moved. In the wall by the crucifix over the bed was a drawing pin. Hummel removed it, pinned up the sketch of himself next to Christ, thought better of it and moved it to the opposite wall. He would get used to living with this stranger, the man he had become.

He lay in bed, light out, wishing he had really brought a novel with him not just a dust jacket. Tomorrow he would change money, find a foreign language bookshop and buy something. Told himself he had never been able to sleep without reading. Then slept.

§ 42

Charles warned Hummel that the black market in currency would cheat him, but what else could a man with no papers do? He said he could introduce him to half a dozen men who would give him francs for schillings, but that each would be as bad as the other. The rate of exchange would be lousy.

The rate of exchange was lousy and Hummel took it.

Charles said that perhaps they should go home now and write to Schuster in London. Hummel said perhaps they could go to a book shop first, preferably one with some German stock, and Charles led him to the Boulevard St Germain, to where La Hune Bookshop sat between the Café aux Deux Magots and the Café Flore. While Charles sat in the Deux Magots hoping for a glimpse of someone famous or literary or both, Hummel found the shop's German section and bought a first edition of *Der Steppenwolf* (S. Fischer Verlag A.G., Berlin, 1927) by a writer he had never heard of called Hermann Hesse.

When they got home Hummel wrote to Schuster.

A week passed. Hummel walked the streets of the Quartier Latin, once ventured as far as the Champs de Mars and saw the legs of the Eiffel Tower vanish topless into mist, visited La Hune every other day and bought another novel, and, being a quick learner, acquired some basic French.

Schuster wrote:

11a White Horse Lane
Stepney
London E1
30th November 1938

Dear Joe,

So you finally took my advice and got out of Austria? Try to forget Austria, Joe, it is not so much a country now, more a memory. You will be very happy with Gabrielle and Charlie – a good woman and a nice boy – you may be very happy in France, but I am going to egg you on still more.

I have a job here with a tailor in the East End of London, a Jewish firm set up by Poles after one of the pogroms. Kind people – I lodge with them too. The master, Billy, has landed a government contract for uniforms. Maybe the British are getting ready to fight after all? Who knows? But Billy says he can take you on, and maybe get the paperwork sorted to get you into England. You would be classed as an essential worker. What you have to do is get yourself out of France. You didn't come in by the front door did you? I thought not. Then you will have to

get some sort of paperwork. And with this I
cannot help you. Charlie can. I will say no
more. Talk to Charlie, Joe. Meanwhile Billy will
set wheels in motion.

   Your father's old friend and yours too,
   Emmanuel Schuster

§43

'Of course we can get you papers,' Charles said. 'It will cost, everything does.'

'Who do I bribe?' Hummel asked.

'Two people. An Inspector of Police, and his brother-in-law at the Prefecture. That's how we did it for Manny.'

'What does it gain me?'

'A French visa, which would protect you from the round-ups the cops occasionally indulge in . . .'

'Round-ups?'

'They seem to hit each arrondissement with some sort of quota to fill. Find refugees without visas. Deport them. When they fulfil their quota they forget about refugees for a while.'

'Deport them where? England?'

'No such luck. Usually Belgium. They drive them to the border and dump them. Then the Belgians will jail them all for not having Belgian visas, and sooner or later they'll all be shoved across the Dutch border in a giant game of pass the parcel.'

Hummel nodded, quietly appalled.

'And of course,' Charles went on. 'Manny had a passport. You don't, do you?'

'No.'

'Then there'll be a bit extra for a Nansen passport.'

'But they are for the stateless, are they not? For people from all those countries that seemed to disappear off the map during the last war. I'm Austrian.'

The boy said nothing, waiting for Hummel to say it.

83

'And, of course, Austria has disappeared now. Not so much a country more a memory.'

'Joe, however much that hurts you as an Austrian, it doesn't matter at the level of French bureaucrats and French paperwork. The visa will be real, the Nansen will be fake. Look at it this way, you won't really be stateless on a fake passport.'

§ 44

Alex had fallen asleep. To fall asleep after lunch annoyed him. It reminded him too much of the old man he was and freely admitted to being to his family, but privately denied to himself.

He could have sworn he had heard the telephone ring. It would pay him to fall asleep at his desk and not in the morning room in an armchair.

The door opened noiselessly, Polly the housemaid peeped in.

'Sorry, boss, I thought you was 'avin' another one of your kips.'

'Another' – Good God, was he making a habit of it?

'I thought I heard the telephone.'

'You did, but like I said I thought you was 'avin' a kip. So I told 'em you weren't in.'

'Who?'

'Some bloke with a German accent. Name like Frood or Fried.'

'Freud?'

'Yeah, that was it.'

Bugger.

§45

Schuster was late. Hummel sat with two dozen others on a long wooden bench in a cold corridor, in a cold, cold February, in a cold, cold, cold 1939.

He had gained weight in the last two months, run through most of his money, learnt some French, and thanks to Charles Birotteau's facility with languages, a little elementary English that went some way beyond 'please' and 'thank you', but not far enough to let him understand what was happening to him now.

Schuster had insisted — do not sail into Dover or any of the coastal ports ... 'they have the refugee business down pat, you could find yourself in gaol or worse, on a boat back to Calais, before Billy and I have waved the right pieces of paper in front of them.' So it was a devious route out of Boulogne on a freighter and into Tilbury in the Thames estuary. Hummel and two dozen ragamuffins, clinging to their respectability as tightly as to their suitcases.

The man in the blue uniform stood at a high-legged desk at the end of the corridor, like the head clerk in a counting house, called out 'Wixstein', pronounced with a W not a V, a stain not a stein, and the man sitting next to Herr Wixstein had to nudge the old man to recognise his own name. He got up and before he reached the desk and the official, another man in a blue uniform had called 'Hummel' — and there were no two ways to pronounce Hummel.

'Yes, sir,' Hummel said, hoping nothing in his inflexion sounded impolite.

The man was leafing through the eighteen crisp pages of Hummel's Nansen. Hummel knew the cover by heart, so much had he treasured it like a love letter since the day he had received it. He looked at the cover now, held up in front of him.

'*France — Passeport Nansen — Gratuit.*'

Now there was a joke, the Nansen had been far from 'free' — it had cost him a week's wages.

'*No. AS4424 — nom Hummel — prenom Josef — Certificat d'identité et de voyage.*'

And that had been the beauty, the wonder of this fake — the word '*voyage*' had almost moved him to tears the day Charles had brought the passport home in a slip of cellophane. *Voyage,* quite possibly the most beautiful word in any language that day.

The official pulled out the visas·Hummel had folded into the passport; a British Entry Visa that Schuster and his boss Billy had posted to him, and the French Residency Visa that he and Charlie had paid for with bribes. Neither was a fake, but he took more time over these than he had over the passport, but, then, apart from Hummel's name, the passport was blank. He hadn't been anywhere to get it stamped.

'There are two men outside who have come to vouch for you,' said the official. 'They appear to be offering work and accommodation. So you're in. One of the lucky ones. If I had my way you'd all be on a boat back to Yidland at dawn. But I don't make the rules. I just enforce 'em. On yer way . . . you're just what England needs right now . . . another Jew.'

Fortunately Hummel understood not a word of this.

§ 46

If one knew at any given moment the significance of that moment, would one behave differently or merely take notes?

Confronted by the sight of two short men, one of whom he knew well, the other he had never met before, Hummel took notes. One look at Billy Jacks, master tailor of Stepney Green, and he knew. This was one of the moments that changed lives. And his changed.

'Billy Jacks,' said the scowly, fat-faced little man in the homburg hat. 'We been waitin' for yer.'

His was accented Yiddish, but perfectly comprehensible to Hummel. Hummel did what he had done in Paris, stuck out a hand and said, 'Hummel. *Aus Wien.*'

The grip was tight, a big, muscular hand on the little man that went with the broad shoulders and the barrel chest. The scowl, which Hummel took to be merely the natural lack of upward inflexion in the facial muscles and the preponderance of five o'clock shadow, broke into something like a smile and the troubling hint of brutality vanished from his face.

'Yeah, well. Billy Jacks. *Aus* Stepney. And the sooner we drum some English into you the better. My wife won't understand a bleedin' word you say!'

Left to himself Hummel would have embraced Schuster. He had known Schuster all his life. It seemed at once natural and impossible.

'So, Joe, you made it. This is England.'

This England in February was bleak. The night wrapped itself around them. The Thames seemed to suck every last ounce of warmth out of the air, and the view across the river seemed to Hummel like an infinity of darkness, broken only by a few pinpoints of light on the Kentish shore. Again, he wanted to embrace Schuster, but Billy Jacks was anxious to move off.

'Brass monkeys. We'll freeze if yer hang about. You two have yer chinwag on the way back, why don't yer.'

Schuster looked older, but then he was. Nearly seventy, Hummel thought. But the warmth in his smile, the brightness in his eyes made him seem younger than anyone he'd left behind. The lights in Vienna might still be on, the light in the Viennese had been snuffed out.

'*Ja*, Joe. In the car we shall talk. Billy has a car. Better still, a car with a heater.'

§ 47

He had not dreamt of it. If he had, it could so easily have been everything he had dreamt of. The all-enveloping womb of family life, from the gust of heat, the faint soot-tang of an open coal fire as the front door was thrust open . . . the swish as the heavy curtain was drawn back across the door on its iron rail . . . shutting out night and fog and cold . . . to the patter of a child's feet in the room above . . . and the smell of cooking from the kitchen. It picked up Hummel and wrapped him in sensations he had forgotten. Sensations scarcely remembered, they had stopped with his mother's death. At thirty-odd he felt like a child, a willing child wanting the Jacks' household to pick him up, to adopt him, to feed him and tuck him up in bed. It was not the opposite of the freedom he had felt in Paris – 'my own room, mine' – it was the complimentary sensation

... the house of Jacks, its larder stocked, its fires lit, its curtains drawn ... everything you might want in a place you might find it ... from the scissors hanging by the mantelpiece to the roller towel on the back of the scullery door. It was a created world, a maintained world. A world someone cared enough to make. His world, and his father's too, had been one of easy neglect. And the nagging voice of guilt told him that perhaps that was why it had been so easily taken away from him ... because he had neglected it.

'Hello, I'm Judy.'

With one hand she pulled her pinafore over her head and dropped it onto a chairback, then she leaned over, pecked Hummel on the cheek and said, 'You must be Joe. We been hearin' so much about you. Old Manny, he's talked of little else since he heard you got away from 'Itler.'

Schuster whispered in his ear, 'Mrs Jacks does not speak Yiddish, Joe. In fact she isn't Jewish.'

He was not prepared for a 'mixed' marriage, in fact he'd never come across one before, but he had prepared a stock phrase for just this occasion.

'How very please to meet you. I am ... *sharmed*.'

The blonde, blue-eyed vision smiled, turned to her husband and said, 'I don't care what you think, Billy Jacks. For that he gets another smacker.'

And she kissed him again.

Jacks said in Yiddish to Hummel, 'The missis, my Judy. Gets a bit sentimental y'know.'

And in English, to himself, 'And the rest of the time you could cut diamonds with her.'

Hummel said nothing.

§48

It was a big house. Five storeys, rooms below ground level, rising high into the eaves where Schuster had an attic very like the one Hummel had had in Paris. He had given Hummel the larger attic room, saying he found he needed so little of anything these days, less space, less sleep – even less money, so long as he had just enough.

Hummel pinned his portrait to the attic wall.

At breakfast Hummel met the family. Sallie, who made a point of holding up fingers to show him she was nine years old; Lena who told him through her father that she was twenty and worked 'up West . . . in Liberty's . . . that's posh that is'; and he became acquainted with the prospect of Danny, who had come in after Hummel had gone to bed and gone out before Hummel had got up. All Hummel learnt was that Danny was seventeen. Billy seemed disinclined to say any more about the boy.

'We got two families,' Judy said, Billy translating and scowling simultaneously. 'I had Lena when I was only eighteen, and Sallie when I was twenty-nine. She's our little mistake. A lovely weekend at Walton-on-the-Naze, summer of 1929, wasn't it, Bill?'

Billy stopped translating.

'I ain't tellin 'im that. Why should I tell 'im that? Why would he want to know that?'

'Am I a mistake?' Sallie asked.

'See what you done? You want to answer that? I bleedin don't!'

Judy ducked the question and ducked into the kitchen. Schuster smiled away the tension.

'So long since we either of us lived with women, eh Joe?'

Judy came back with plates for the men, ranged along her forearm like a practised waiter.

'Eat up, you lot . . . before somebody rations it!'

Hummel had not grown up in a kosher household – who could run to two sinks and all the extra crockery? – but he had been made aware of the abominations of Leviticus and had never been served bacon in his life.

He watched as Billy made a mountain of fried bread, crispy bacon and fried egg. The tomato Billy left disdainfully on the side. Then he saw Billy stretch his jaws to the limit, bite into the mountain, catch a dribble of egg yolk with his finger tip and heard him mutter, 'loverly'. To his amazement Schuster did the same, and after his first mouthful said, 'Trust me, Joe, it's delicious. An English delicacy.'

Judy said, 'You tuck in, Joe. Use your knife and fork if you want. You don't have to eat like a pig, just 'cos they do.'

But no one translated.

Hummel ate bacon. A bland taste he thought, but a delightful texture. The crisper the better, he concluded. And he thought his host wrong to ignore the fried tomato. When he thought he had finished, Judy stretched out a hand for his plate and uttered a single syllable he had no difficulty understanding.

'More?' she said.

''Ere,' said Billy. 'You ain't offered me seconds!'

'Oh you're such a kid. He's our guest, Billy.'

'He's our guest till we get to the workshop. And when we get back, he's just another lodger!'

'Sure – but right now he gets seconds. Look at him for Gawd's sake. He's as thin as a runner bean.'

§ 49

Minsky was dead, to begin with.

Billy's workshop was a short walk away. On the Mile End Road, only yards from Stepney Green. One flight up from street level, a long low room with a wall of windows front and back, and row upon row of overhead lights in dirty metal shades. Over the door was a peeling painted sign much like the one over Hummel's shopfront in Vienna: 'Abel Jakobson & Son. Est 1902' – and beneath that in gold lettering so faded it would soon be invisible: 'Formerly Minsky & Jakobson'. But Minsky was dead, to begin with.

'Abel. He was my dad,' Billy said, pointing at the sign. 'I'm just "and son".'

'Me too,' said Hummel.

'And Jakobson got dropped years back – I never been anybody 'cept Billy Jacks.'

Billy's War Office order was blue. Several different shades of blue. He was, he explained to Hummel, never told what branch of the forces they were destined for – that was a secret and all insignia were added later by others. Jakobson & Son made, as it were, blank uniforms.

'But light blue's RAF, stands to reason, navy blue's the Navy – obviously – the really dark blue's Civil Defence and the blue that's black – well, you look at it . . . they call it blue but it's black init? – that's coppers out in Suffolk, the Suffolk Constabulary. That's a different order altogether that is. We do the blouses and the trousers. That's all. Unnerstand?'

What was not to understand? Compared to making a bespoke suit it was basic tailoring, but as Schuster whispered in his ear, 'It's still our trade . . . and it's a living.'

Hummel had no argument with this.

Hummel cut cloth – duck to water.

Mid-morning Billy muttered something along the lines of 'See a man about a dog', and went out.

Schuster said, 'I know what you're thinking.'

Hummel wasn't thinking anything.

'But he's a good man. A rough diamond, as they say here. And Judy's a good woman. She and Billy, well they have their . . .'

Schuster put down his scissors, levelled his hand mid-air and tilted it this way and that to illustrate the equivocation.

§ 50

The following Sunday, the Jacks ate a late breakfast. It was Billy's one lie-in of the week – a day on which he slept till eight. On Saturdays they worked a half day, which meant no lie-in but an afternoon off – mostly, Schuster opined, to let working Londoners attend a football match if they chose . . . teams with odd names like the Arsenal or Leyton Orient or Tottenham Hotspur. Schuster knew there was a place called Tottenham, although he'd never been there, but he doubted the existence of places called Arsenal or Orient.

Breakfast was the same – it never varied in that nothing was missing from the plate but on a Sunday something might be added. So this Sunday Hummel faced two novelties – the pork sausage, and the errant son, Danny putting in his first appearance. Each looked as odd as the other. The former cooked to the point where burnt might be a better word, and the latter stuck at the end of the table still in his overcoat, with a scarf pulled up to his nose, which was only lowered to insert food.

He seemed to have no inclination to speak to his father.

'You was in late last night,' Billy said to the boy.

'Meeting,' Danny muttered.

Hummel gently tapped his sausage on the plate to see if it flexed. It didn't. Judy looked up from her tea at the sound and said, smiling, 'Billy likes 'em that way. Says what's a banger if you can't bang it?'

Schuster conveyed her meaning to Hummel.

'Izzat all you do?' Billy went on through a mouthful of sausage, 'Just go to yer party meetings? When I was your age I wanted a bit of fun in me life.'

Danny said nothing. Hummel bit into his sausage and chewed. He concluded that the British banger might be kosher – as he couldn't be at all certain it contained any pork.

'And,' Billy blathered, 'if I went to a party it wouldn't be the bleedin' Labour party!'

'Oh for Christ's sake, Bill,' Judy said. 'Leave the boy alone.'

'Leave 'im alone. How can I? He's an embarrassment to the family. My son the Red . . .'

'That's Commies, Dad, not us,' said Danny.

'Same difference. You think I count for nuffin', don't yer? Well I got standin' in this community. How do you think it looks, me a lifelong Tory with a son who goes out canvassing for pinkoes?'

Danny pulled up his scarf and retreated. Blue eyes and spiky hair visible above the scarfline.

'You?' Judy said. 'A lifelong Tory? When did you ever bother to vote? I never known you to vote Tory or anythin' else. You ain't even on the roll. Lifelong selfish git would be better way of puttin' it. All you've ever done is look after number one!'

'So? What's wrong with that? Yeah, I've looked after number one, but lookin' after number one's what puts the grub on the table. There's women in this street out skivvyin' and cleanin' – you've never had to do that. So don't knock it. Lookin' after number one's what comes naturally.'

Danny got up. Muttered, 'Stick another record on, Dad.' And slammed out of the door to Billy's cry of, 'You ungrateful little gobshite! – and you, Manny, don't bother to translate that!'

Hummel watched the room dissolve. Billy to sturdy, unpleasurable trencherwork at his plate, Schuster to a judicious silence, Judy to a loud kitchen display of pot and plate rattling.

The previous day, the Saturday, he'd persuaded Schuster to take him 'up West' – they'd visited a dozen bookshops in the Charing Cross Road. He'd bought a couple of English novels and an English-German/German-English dictionary. If he didn't understand the Jacks' rows, at least he might learn enough English to ask to start the day with coffee rather than tea.

At teatime Billy found him at the table, hunched over *David Copperfield*, dictionary splayed, humming softly to himself.

'Ere, Manny. Just listen. Joe's away in birdland hummin' to hisself.'

Schuster looked up from his place in an armchair by the fire, where he had dozed lightly while pretending to read a newspaper.

'*Ja*, Billy. He always hummed when he was a boy in Vienna. Usually when he was reading, but then he was always reading. I think it means he is happy.'

'Happy? After what he's been through?'

'Why not? Why not be happy? A free afternoon. A stolen moment. The worst may be yet to come.'

§ 51

Each Saturday that spring and summer, when he had a free afternoon, Hummel went back to the Charing Cross Road and visited Foyle's bookshop, where he would steal a volume of the German edition of the *Collected Works of Sigmund Freud* – an edition that had been appearing at intervals ever since 1925 – until he'd got the lot. He wasn't wholly sure why he did this. He felt the need of a gesture of defiance – even a gesture only he would ever know about. Nor was it stealing merely for the sake of stealing – he read the books.

On his third venture, having just stuffed *Studies on Hysteria* into a specially sewn pocket inside his overcoat, he crossed the road and set off south towards Cambridge Circus and another book shop, one of his favourites, at 84 Charing Cross Road – prop. Marks & Co.

He peered in through the window. There was always a bentwood chair by the counter. Often elderly customers would sit and chat, or sit and wait while Marks's staff found a book for them. The man sitting there on the second Saturday in March was a familiar face, one he had seen on odd occasions in the streets of Vienna – Professor Freud.

Hummel took the coincidence as sanction. On two subsequent occasions, having pinched more volumes of the *Collected Freud*, he stopped by Marks's to see Professor Freud sitting there. He did not go in, but walked on, clutching his book and humming to himself.

§ 52

After Hitler took Prague, as easily as moving a bishop across a chess board, in the March of 1939, Alex and Churchill met in Alex's London club, the Garrick. Churchill knocked back his customary whiskies and soda – the man's capacious liver never failed to surprise Alex – and quite soon the conversation dwindled to mutual 'I told you so's'. Indeed, each had told the other and both had told the nation. Round about glass five Churchill said, 'Of course, this is bound to make the Prime Minister shape up. I think we can safely conclude that appeasement is dead. This has got to be the point at which Neville stops being a mouse and becomes a man.'

Alex said, 'Mice don't shape up, they just get eaten.'

§ 53

May 1939
Berlin

They had forsaken Kranzler's for the Taverne. Less private – half the foreign correspondents in Berlin drank there, traded stories, boasted. Less private – half the Berlin Gestapo seemed to be there, trying to be unobtrusive, trying to listen in. As Rod put it in his schoolboy manner,

94

'they ear'ole everything and understand bugger all. And as for inconspicuous they might just as well have "nark" tattooed across the forehead.'

He looked around, saw heads turn away and shoulders hunch over glasses of beer. Those three chaps at the next table, surely they didn't think they hadn't been spotted? Hugh Greene was looking at him, waiting for a pause in the prattle to say something that clearly burnt at the tip of the tongue.

'Spit it out.'

'Spit what out?'

'Hugh, you're dying to tell me something.'

'I was just wondering . . . you're not in *Who's Who* are you?'

Rod always thought the title of that famous register of English toffs could not be uttered without sounding like the mating call of a barn owl.

'Of course not. At my age? I'm only thirty for Christ's sake.'

'I'm twenty-eight.'

The penny dropped.

'You've had the form?'

'Indeed I have . . . mother's maiden name, education, hobbies, clubs . . . in that order.'

'Congratulations,' Rod said flatly.

'It's a bit of a coup, isn't it?'

'I suppose it is,' Rod replied.

'You know, I thought I'd . . . well . . . made it . . . when I got a pay rise to twenty quid a week. The magic figure . . . thousand a year man . . . smacks of hand-made shoes and an account with a decent tailor . . . sort of thing makes you want to dance around the room . . .'

'I'm on twelve-fifty,' Rod said just as flatly.

'Bastard,' said Hugh.

But Rod was no longer listening. He was staring at the doorway, to where more Gestapo had entered, this time without any subterfuge – full uniform, leather coats for the underlings, black jacket, lightning and silver skulls for the bloke in charge.

Hugh squirmed in his seat to follow Rod's gaze.

'Bugger me, that's Wolfgang Stahl. He's never seen in public. What on earth does he want here?'

'Us,' said Rod. 'He hasn't looked at anyone else.'

'Stahl wouldn't know either of us from Adam.'

'Hugh, after that mickey-take you published on Goebbels I doubt there's a member of the Gestapo who hasn't got your phizzog imprinted on his brain.'

'Oh crikey – he's coming over.'

Rod's first reaction was that it was odd that Stahl was the hidden face of the SD, so rarely seen, so rarely photographed – they were missing a publicity stunt. Too dark – saturnine might be the word – for the Aryan ideal, nonetheless he was tall and he was handsome … an advertisement for the Reich – which was more than could be said for Stahl's SD superior Reinhard Heydrich, and much more than could be said for Propaganda Minister Josef Goebbels. Stahl looked good on parade, Stahl looked good just picking his way through the room to their table.

'Herr Greene, Herr Troy.'

No Heil Hitler. No salute. No Prussian clicking of the heels.

'Will you be joining us, Standartenführer?'

'Not today, Herr Troy. Nor any other day. You will be leaving shortly. Both of you.'

Stahl put two folded foolscap sheets in front of them. Neither moved to pick them up.

'Expulsion?' Rod asked.

'Yes. Try not to take it personally. Half the people in this room will be in the same boat, metaphorically if not literally.'

'I'm sure you're right,' Rod went on. 'However, we do seem to be the only ones receiving orders of expulsion … as it were … personally.'

'Consider it an honour.'

'And where might we be expected to go?' asked Hugh.

'You, Herr Greene, can go where you like as long as it is outside the Reich. You, Herr Troy? Alas not. I shall be putting you on a plane to London myself. Go home and pack. Your plane leaves at midnight.'

'Midnight,' Hugh protested. 'Good God man. I've got family here, I can't just –'

'*You* have three weeks, Herr Greene. Pack up your suitcases, ship your furniture. We are not unreasonable people. Three weeks should be enough. But Mr Troy has until midnight. I shall leave an escort to assist you, and I shall see you this evening at Tempelhof. Good day to you both.'

Stahl left. Again no salute, no Heil Hitler. Hugh looked at Rod and said, 'And you think I've blotted my copybook. What on earth have you done to upset the buggers?'

But Rod wasn't giving any mind to what he had done. He was wondering what his father might have done to finally prise him out of Berlin.

§ 54

Politely and firmly Rod was put into an armoured car and driven out to Tempelhof. The Gestapo man assigned to guard him had said next to nothing, answered all Rod's questions minimally, and seemed to be the sort of bloke who could wear a leather coat in May without breaking into a sweat. He had scarcely left Rod's side since Stahl had set him the task. Back in his apartment, Rod had paused in packing to take a pee, peeped through the keyhole to find the man not three feet from the door – not listening or looking, merely guarding, doing exactly what had been asked of him to the letter.

Out at the airport he had walked Rod up to a wooden hut somewhat isolated from the rest of the buildings, knocked on the door, and opened it. He stood, waiting for Rod to move.

'In here?'

'*Hinein.*'

Rod peered in. It was empty but for a couple of bentwood chairs of the sort he'd so often seen between the thighs of lusciously decadent singers in Berlin cabaret. One chair was empty, and on the other was Wolfgang Stahl, long legs outstretched, eyes closed, fingers locked behind his head, the scattered pages of the banal *Beobachter* and the almost-as-banal *12-Uhr Blatt* at his feet. Rod stepped into the room, heard the door close behind him, turned quickly to find that the man had not followed him in. Stahl's eyes opened. He took his hands down, glanced at his wristwatch. No standing to attention, no Heil Hitler.

'So – we have ten minutes in hand.'

He waved the hand at the chair, motioned Rod to sit.

'Ten minutes,' Rod said. 'Just enough time for an interview, if you have a mind to it, Standartenführer.'

'Fine, then I shall interview you.'

'I meant –'

'I know what you meant, Herr Troy. Do you never think that your cleverness might on occasion be a failing?'

'Ah, I see. Was it something I said ... or rather something I wrote?'

'The expulsion you mean? No. It has nothing to do with your reporting. In fact it's a simple piece of tit for tat. One of ours is being expelled from London, so we send five or six of you packing in retaliation. Greene was top of the list. The man has a natural talent for making mischief. Indeed, I'm sure he will go far in his profession – if he lives. You were a good second. But your prose has nothing to do with it. You take risks in what you say. I would hardly expect otherwise. But the biggest risk you took was Vienna.'

'You mean the piece I did on Leopoldstadt?'

'No. I read that. You may well have been accurate in your account. God knows. I couldn't care less. The risk was not what you wrote, it was in going there.'

This gave Rod pause for thought.

'That's what Greene said,' he said.

'Good advice. You should have taken it.'

'I felt like seeing Vienna.'

Stahl shook his head.

'No, no, Herr Troy. Far too casual. A very lazy lie. You have been angling, cajoling, pleading and wheedling to see Vienna since last April. I have read all your exchanges with your father. It has been ... what shall I say ... a compulsion on your part.'

'And on yours, what? You didn't have to go back to your home town looking like a conqueror as part of Hitler's entourage. But you did.'

Stahl spoke as though explaining the obvious to an exasperatingly literal child. 'Unlike you, Herr Troy, I live in a country that lives by a chain of command, by orders and by obedience to orders. I was doing my job.'

'You know, Standartenführer, when all this is over in ten or twenty years and your thousand-year Reich is dust and bad memories, I wouldn't rely on "I was only following orders" as my defence.'

'Perhaps I'll take your advice. In the meantime let me give you some. Europe is ours now. We live in a world which demands clear ethnic and national distinctions. And in such a world people such as you blur the lines. That is not a safe or healthy position to be in.'

'Blurred ethnic lines? In a country led by a man of dubious parentage and racial origin?'

For a second Rod thought Stahl was going to hit him. But he had risen from his chair, stretched in a lazy-cat fashion, muttered 'Jesus Christ' a couple of times, sat back down, leaned close to Rod and lowered his voice to a stagey whisper.

'Good God man – that's the Führer you're speaking of. You know, if you'd said that to Heydrich or Himmler they'd have had you taken out back and had you kicked till your balls were black and blue. Take my advice, if it is a touch of Vienna that you crave ... there are now so many Viennese in London I rather think you will find enough of the old city to sate your craving. Give them enough time and they'll have Little Viennas popping up everywhere. Now, go home to your wife and family and never come back.'

Stahl already had his hand on the doorknob, his back to Rod, when Rod said, 'You know Standartenführer, there's a story doing the rounds of Berlin that Heydrich came home one night and shot his own reflection in the mirror. I wonder ... who do you see when you look in the ...'

It was as smooth as a Hopalong Cassidy or Tom Mix in a Hollywood two-reeler – Stahl had turned, drawn and levelled his Luger at Rod's head so swiftly it took his breath away.

'This is Berlin, Herr Troy. I could shoot you now and no one would ever know. Your father would phone the embassy, telegraph von Ribbentrop, demand the lists for Sachsenhausen and Dachau and no one would know a damn thing. You would have vanished into *Nacht und Nebel*.'

§ 55

7 July 1939
Belgravia, London

A time there was when London seemed to have been dominated by women like Daffy Carfax. Alex wondered when that time might come to an end. It had, after all, lasted the duration of his life in London, and that was close to thirty years. Paris wasn't like this. New York was, but in its own way – London, after all, ignored the notion of new money, and to elevate and integrate took time as well as money. Beerage into peerage. Daffy had money, and Daffy had breeding – the youngest daughter of a viscount, several of the right schools, in most of which she had behaved very badly, a year in Switzerland, a quick curtsey to Queen Alexandra on her coming out in 1902, a whirl of courtships by eligible young men, all of whom she had rejected for Sir Mungo Carfax bt., an entomologist many years her senior who was guaranteed to prefer pinning his dead moths to inflicting his carnal attentions on her, and she, as Lady Carfax, was installed as one of London's leading society hostesses. Her dinners and luncheons were legendary. Few, if any, ever turned down an invitation from Daffy. At fifty-three she looked thirty-five and was, a broken nose (result of a climbing accident in the Alps) notwithstanding, an eye-catching beauty – mixed a thorough knowledge of politics and the arts with a dash of mild flirtation and had the young bucks and old dogs of London eating out of her hand. Mungo hardly, if ever, attended. His wish to further the work of Darwin and Mendel, to do for moths what they had done for tortoises and peas, might be no more than a dream, but it was one that walled him up happily in a library and a world of his own. Alex never said no to Daffy . . . nor did Churchill.

Alex found him getting out of a cab in Chesham Place. He could have walked here from his London flat, just the other side of Victoria railway station, but Churchill hardly walked anywhere.

'I hear we have a treat in store,' Alex said.

Churchill was fumbling in his trousers pocket for change. Alex handed the cabman a florin, told him to keep the change and smiled at Churchill.

Churchill smiled back. 'I seem to have a pocketful of ha'pennies,' he said. 'The grand summation of my career. Stuck for the right change. Days there are when I feel I could turn my pockets inside out like elephants' ears and not hear one farthing clink against another.'

'That sounds like the opening line of a very rude joke.'

'It is, and one I only perform when very drunk. The treat, by the way, is another of Daffy's continentals . . . no idea who, but doubtless some bugger she's got over to lecture us all on the Balkanisation of this and that or the Arab question.'

'What is the Arab question?'

'How do you castrate a camel?'

'No idea.'

'Well, you get two bricks . . .'

As if by magic the front door of the Carfax house opened and Churchill abandoned his music hall routine. Daffy greeted them in the hallway, effusive, calling them both darling, and before the door could close again a young man – short, forty-ish, undistinguished – bounded up the steps and in.

'Victor, darling!'

And Daffy glided between the two old men to embrace the younger. Churchill stalked off. Alex waited for a friendly handshake from Victor Cazalet, then followed Churchill.

One of the delights of Daffy's luncheons was that she would throw together a mixture; differing politics, differing generations. It was a chance to meet those whom one might not otherwise meet. Alex had met Cazalet once or twice and thought him interesting. He had, for a while, been in the same business – running an unsuccessful arts magazine called *Night and Day* (Alex had no idea if it was named after the Cole Porter song or if this was just coincidence). He had attended the magazine's launch, thought it extravagant, given it less than a year and watched it fold in six months. In that brief interval it had given employment to the young novelist Graham Greene, whom he rather thought might be related to the journalist of the same surname with whom Rod knocked around Berlin. What he did not like about Cazalet was his support for the Spanish dictator Franco. It was as though fascism appealed to some dusty pocket in the English mind that craved uniforms and order and was capable of turning a blind eye to the brutality by which that order was bought. Mussolini had English fans among the most respectable and intelligent of people – something Hitler had been unable to achieve outside of a bunch of black-shirted tearaways and demagogic, messianic crackpots – and a nation devoted to railways (W. Heath Robinson had his finger on the political pulse here) and proud of making them run on time always seemed to admire any nation and any political system that would emulate them in this. He'd had rows with his old friend H.G. Wells about the fascists ever since the Twenties, and was inclined to accept this English quirk without being able to tolerate it. Churchill had not been notable in his opposition to Franco. It might have been what he and Cazalet had first had in common. Now, Alex wondered what the young man had done to incur Winston's grumpy silence. It need not have been much.

If Churchill no longer cared for Cazalet's company, Alex found him in Daffy's morning room in *company* he surely cared for even less. All but buttonholed by Wells – a man with an opinion on everything under the sun and quite a lot of things beyond it – a man who had imagined life on Mars and the Moon . . . the shape of things to come . . . and the start of World War II (and that he had played as comedy, as it happens, in a railway station). He was expressing many of those opinions to Churchill at speed, in a high, slightly strangulated voice. Something about the fate of mankind, and the inevitability of extinction, how no dominant species had ever been succeeded by its own descendants . . . but then he'd been banging on about this for forty years, his novels full of trolls and crabs and thingies that ruled the earth after us. '*Homo sapiens* has failed . . . we have not developed the right brain . . . we have less than a thousand years left.' Alex doubted whether Churchill was bothering to take any of it in. He doubted that Churchill had ever read *The War of the Worlds* or *The Time Machine*. Yet, years ago, about the time he and Wells had met, in the long Edwardian summer, every literate left-thinking person seemed to have read Wells's fascist vision *Anticipations*, much as these days everyone seemed to have read the latest P.G. Wodehouse or J.B. Priestley. And as the cast assembled – Victor Cazalet MP, Winston Churchill MP, Harold Nicolson MP, Duff Cooper MP, Harold Macmillan MP, Alex wondered that he and Wells might be there simply because neither of them had a seat in parliament, that they were, as it occurred to him, the yeast in the Westminster loaf.

He found himself standing next to a dishevelled old man wearing what appeared to be cricket whites, a man well prepared for lunch as half of yesterday's seemed still to be drying on his shirt and trousers, which trousers, Alex surmised, were held up by a knotted old Harrovian tie. It was Mungo. A scotch and water in one hand, a specimen dead moth in the other.

'It's a Clifden Nonpareil,' Mungo said without introduction. 'You can tell it by the blue hindwings.'

Alex plumped for the obvious response, 'Rare, is it?'

'Caught two in Kent in '36. Not seen another until last night when this little chap tapped on me windowpane. Attracted by the poplars in the street, I suppose. There are several British *Catocala,* the red and crimson Underwings, for example, but this isn't one you'd ordinarily regard as anything but a migrant . . . a sort of stray dog of the moth world.'

Mungo looked at Alex for the first time. They'd met dozens of times, but Alex was fairly certain that all of Daffy's men blurred into one from the husband's point-of-view.

'I suppose you're here to put the world to rights?'

'When am I not?' said Alex.

'Well, now's your chance … the wife's new specimen has arrived … another bloody stray.'

Alex followed the old boy's gaze and saw a man in the doorway, about Cazalet's age and about the same height – but less handsome, a hint of brutality in the broad, flat face, a severity in the close-cropped hair – without a monocle or a duelling scar and in a civilian suit of tasteless brown, still so obviously a German officer of some sort – a man born to horseback and military service.

Alex turned back, but Mungo had vanished into his study and Daffy was introducing, word for word and at length, the Graf Lieutenant-Colonel Gerhard von Schwerin to the room.

He greeted Alex by saying that he had long been an admirer, and Alex replied, 'Of what are you a Lieutenant-Colonel, Count von Schwerin? From what pack have you strayed to London?'

'I … er … don't understand.'

'Oh ignore him, Count,' Daffy cut in. 'He's been talking to Mungo. I'd be prepared to swear he has. It's one of Mungo's thingies, one of his ill-chosen words. All Alex means is "what's your unit?" and as you're here incognito, my dear, feel no obligation to tell him.'

But von Schwerin said, 'My unit, Sir Alex? The Abwehr. I work for Admiral Canaris, of whom you have surely heard? A stray dog of the highest order.'

And Alex looked at Churchill and Churchill looked back at Alex, the both of them realising that when Daffy had said 'treat' she had meant it.

At lunch Alex was seated next to their hostess, with Cazalet on his right, and Wells on her left. Von Schwerin was placed where he could be of most use, between Churchill and Macmillan. Alex was, he knew, here to observe rather than participate. And he hoped Wells would shut up long enough for them to hear what von Schwerin had come five hundred miles to tell them all.

'It is the gravest crisis Europe has seen these twenty years. More – I would say, without implied respect, that Hitler will plunge us all into war the way Napoleon did. And what were the wars of Napoleon but a world war for which we did not yet have the name?'

Churchill was slow off the mark, left too long a pause for Wells to nip in.

'Is it not inevitable? The inevitable end of mankind in an armageddon of its own making. Our destiny since we crawled out of the primeval slime?'

'I'm sorry, Mr Wells? Inevitable? There is nothing inevitable about Adolf Hitler. I cannot see the force of destiny in the rise of an Austrian corporal . . . a tyrant who grew out of your ill-conceived treaties and our politics . . . not from our "natural evolution" . . . indeed, if he is destiny why then were we given so many opportunities to stop him?'

'The Rhineland,' Churchill muttered.

'Austria,' said Macmillan.

'Czechoslovakia,' said Cazalet.

'Bert,' Alex cut in. 'How long would you like the list to be? A dozen violations of international treaties. They are political moments – mostly ones we missed – not strata in the rocks.'

If they'd been alone, Alex knew, Wells would have come back at him with a lunchtime thesis as long as a French loaf. But with Daffy doubtless pinching him under the table, he deferred with uncharacteristic modesty and said, 'And what's next on Hitler's list, Count?'

'Need you ask? He means to take the Polish corridor, to reclaim Danzig and link up with the rump of East Prussia.'

'What,' said Macmillan, 'about this proposal for an extraterritorial road?'

'It is nonsense,' von Schwerin replied. 'There is no plan for a road of any kind. Hitler saying there is merely lulls the Poles into thinking he will negotiate. The truth is he will negotiate nothing.'

'Surely,' Cazalet said, 'surely he realises that would mean war?'

'War with whom?'

It was pretty much the last retort any of them had expected of von Schwerin, and von Schwerin knew it. As Cazalet almost gasped for breath at the audacity of it, von Schwerin slowly turned his head to take in everyone in the room and be certain that his bluntness had hit home.

'With us! With the British!' Cazalet said too late.

Von Schwerin could not be made to feel the urgency Cazalet had put into his words. But 'we shall fight' was becoming such a worn and shabby phrase. 'We', as von Schwerin had pointed out, had passed many stages at which it might have been deemed prudent or honourable to fight, and we hadn't.

'Mr Cazalet, I was with Hitler last autumn. I cannot remember who said what to provoke the remark, but I distinctly heard him say, "I saw the British at Munich ... they are sheep." Now, you are in the Reserve are you not?'

'Yes, but how did you know that?'

'I'm in the Abwehr – shall we say it's my job to know? If I were you, Mr Cazalet, I'd dust off my khaki and get ready for war.'

This stilled the table into silence for a few moments, and silence gave way if not to small talk then to smaller talk.

Alex found he could see himself in the words of future diarists, the chronicles-to-come ... half the men at table (and Daffy was the only woman) most certainly kept diaries. He knew Nicolson did, he knew Duff Cooper did and he'd be willing to bet Cazalet did. He doubted Churchill could find the time and equally doubted Wells would bother, but Wells and he were pretty well contemporaries ... it was what the younger men wrote that momentarily flashed through his mind: 'Lunch at Daffy's ... found myself sitting next to Alex Troy. My God, he's looking old. And he's not really on the ball any more. Didn't seem to understand the German situation at all.' So that was his fate ... to be an entry in someone's diary published twenty or thirty years hence. His father had ended up as a footnote or an index reference in lives of Tolstoy and Kropotkin. Tolstoy's first biographers had provoked the old man to a restrained form of rage, and a flurry of letters dashed off to the literary editors of the national newspapers, some of which even printed them – in particular, the *Observer* had seemed delighted with his witless reworking of Twain's 'reports of my death have been greatly exaggerated'.

'Do you keep a diary, Daffy?'

'There are many ladies who would think that an impertinent question, Alex. But I am not one of them, and it so happens I do.'

'Hmm ... am I in it?'

'Alex, darling, we've known each other twenty-five years or more. Of course you're in it. And no one should be recording today's little chat – not in their diaries and certainly not in their newspapers. Now, change the subject.'

The woman had a point. How did men like von Schwerin get away with this in a nation where the disaffected could vanish overnight? Von Schwerin was by no means the first of Admiral Canaris's casual envoys – unlike the others he seemed to be taken seriously. The risk was enormous. How would this man survive if a word of what he was saying leaked out?

It was, it seemed, a remarkable act of trust in the British . . . the sceptical, unbelieving, hesitant, appeasing British.

Cazalet returned to the subject with coffee. 'What else might we do to prepare for war, Count. My khaki has been dusted off a while now.'

Von Schwerin smiled at this, turned to Churchill, turned back to look at Cazalet.

'Well . . . you might persuade the man on my right to rejoin the cabinet.'

Churchill looked up, smiling modestly at the obvious truth in von Schwerin's words.

'Really, Count. Do you think I'm that frightening?'

This brought smiles and laughter from everyone.

'Well, you scare the hell out of me.'

'This brought guffaws, table slapping mirth, that enabled Daffy to rise and end the meal on a high.

Out in the street, Alex's car waited, the chauffeur holding the back door open.

'Are you and Winston going to the House?' Alex asked Cazalet. 'I'm driving right past.'

'I am. And I'm sure Winston is. But I doubt he will consent to ride with me.'

Alex looked back to the open doorway. Churchill was still deep in conversation with von Schwerin. Two men clutching hats and making wild gestures.

'Then let us leave him to it.'

Cazalet followed Alex into the back seat of the Rolls. When the door closed and the car moved off he said, 'One cannot doubt the wisdom of Count von Schwerin's remark . . .'

'Even if it is merely an echo of the British popular press.'

'Quite. And what neither the papers nor von Schwerin seem to grasp is the speed with which Winston makes enemies, and the tenacity with which he holds on to them.'

'You?'

'Oh Alex, it's not just me. You saw Harold Macmillan in there. There's a whole generation willing to sit at his feet and do his bidding . . . but if we deviate from his line . . . if we contest him on things that are minor in comparison to the prospect of war . . .'

'Such as?'

'Well . . . it doesn't pay to have a good word for the Soviet Union.'

'Not many of you have.'

'And India. That's why he cuts me, because I am in favour of India's independence. And that is anathema to Winston. Yet, much as I endorse it and he opposes it, it is a mere inkblot on the greater picture. It should not divide us over Germany. But he lets it do just that. You know, I think that German came here with the notion that there is a Churchill faction. He may be right, but the chief obstacle to that faction cohering around Winston and acting as one and speaking with one voice is Winston himself. Take Austria, for example. I have first-hand knowledge. I was in Vienna only a few weeks after the Anschluss. I could have painted a vivid picture for him of what the Germans are doing there. He wouldn't listen to a word I said.'

'And?'

'And what?'

'I lived a while in Vienna. For a while Vienna was home. I have not been there these thirty years. So tell me, how was Vienna? I'm listening even if Winston isn't.'

Cazalet sighed, 'I suppose it all comes down to the looks on people's faces. The middle-aged know they're done for. No one over thirty-five smiles any more. The Jews know they're done for, the aristocrats know they're done for – I had at least half a dozen people begging me to get them jobs in England. A Jewish doctor wanted to be my gardener. A count von somewhere or other said he'd valet for me! Alex, Vienna was desperate.'

Dropping Cazalet in Parliament Square, Alex found Vienna would not leave his thoughts. He could see streets of cobblestones and coffee houses. He could almost taste the coffee. And so he went in search of Vienna. To a meeting to which he had long been invited, and which for reasons he would surely be told later, he had as long put off.

§ 56

The Rolls pulled up in front of a vast Edwardian villa, 20 Maresfield Gardens, Hampstead, NW3 – almost walking distance from Alex's own Hampstead house. He'd had opportunity, if not occasion, aplenty to walk over. He never had. But doubtless the man inside would be able to tell him why.

The maid asked, 'Who shall I say is calling?'

'Alex Troy.'

There was a bustle from within as she announced his name, as though something had been knocked over. Then he bustled out into the lobby, stood before him, a tiny white-bearded man in a baggy cardigan, looking startled, as though awakened from an after-lunch nap, hastily putting on his round tortoiseshell spectacles, seizing Alex's right hand in both of his

'Alex!'

'Professor Freud.'

'Ach ... we are both too old for titles. Call me Sigmund. Come ... come ... everything is pretty much as it was.'

And it was. Stepping into Freud's library was to step back into the Vienna of forty years ago. A room heavy with the weight of a gilded age. The burden of dreams. The same paintings on the wall – the tell-tale Oedipus and the Sphinx – a portrait Alex had never asked about but which he assumed to represent Moses – the same books on the shelves: Goethe and the complete Shakespeare in individual German volumes.

'Of course I could not leave with everything. But there is nothing like a putsch to make you have a purge.'

Alex looked at the desk and the nest of tables crammed full of classical figurines. He remembered the day he'd asked Freud about collecting them. He'd never grace his own study with the word 'collection' – Alex didn't collect he just hoarded – and Freud's answer, that these figurines had only survived, and survived unchanging, because they'd been walled up in tombs for years. It was a metaphor for the unconscious – the unconscious scarcely changed because it was entombed.

Freud led the way from the library to the consulting room at the back of the house. The couch was the same couch – the analysands' couch from Berggasse, draped in a heavy, geometric-patterned red Persian rug. And at the end of the couch, out of sight of anyone reclining, the green velvet tub chair where Freud himself had sat – the disembodied voice.

To have lain down, to have stretched out would have been bliss – bliss and a bridge too far. They took armchairs and faced each other. Equals.

'Tell me,' Freud began eagerly, '... tell me about London. I can get out so rarely these days. It is what it always was to me ... a city I know through books. Tell me, what you have seen, what you have done lately.'

'Well ... today I breakfasted with my younger son, who has become, of all things, a policeman. You may imagine what qualms this caused me. However, they were long ago. I am reconciled. And I lunched with one of our London society hostesses of whom you have surely never heard – Daffy Carfax.'

'Indeed . . . I have never heard of her.'

'And among the guests was Wells.'

'H.G.?'

'Is there another?'

'The young one, the one in America who convinced them only last year that we were being invaded by Mars.'

'I must have slept through that one. No, it was H.G., the same old H.G. Wells who first brought me to England thirty years ago. Well, thirty all but a few weeks.'

'Wells, Wells. What I wouldn't give to get the bugger on that couch. And how was he?'

'Full of doom and gloom. The fate of *Homo sapiens* . . . mankind is . . . what was his phrase . . . "at the end if its tether" . . . it's time is over . . . we must now give way to other, if not actually superior, beings. It's nothing more than a new variation on his old song. He predicts. He always has. It's the trade he's in. You know he actually called an anthology of his stuff *Predictions and Prophecies* . . . or perhaps it was the other way round? He predicts the worst most of the time and most of the time he's wrong. But he's onto his third reprint of his latest, so he's happy. A quick survey of civilisation, a bit of a bash at the Jews . . .'

'Anything new?'

'No . . . same old stuff, even quotes that rather corny clerihew that goes "How odd of God to choose the Jews." You have to say it properly. I can never quite get the rhythm.'

'What's a clerihew?'

'Not really sure, but it's something English. Something like a limerick that isn't a limerick.'

'And what does he have to say about Nazis?'

'Oh he's unequivocal about that. Hitler is a nutcase. And then he goes on to warn us about how focussed complete nutcases can be.'

'Do you think he's read any of my stuff . . . you know . . . *Civilisation and its Discontents*?'

'I'd be quite prepared to bet he hasn't.'

'You know . . . I don't have much more in me. I've almost finished a new book . . . quite possibly my last . . . it will be translated into English as soon as I do finish ... *Moses and Monotheism* ... I have put the book aside so many times these last few years ... so many false starts.'

'What's it about?' Alex asked in much the same tone of voice with which one asked of a Hollywood film 'who's in it?'

'Moses.'

'Yeees.'

'And death.'

'Moses' death? How did he die?'

'The Jews killed him.'

'And ...?'

'And then they invented the faith to contain their guilt.'

'Interesting,' said Alex. 'You're going to upset a lot of people.'

'I already have. I have received ... what would you say? ... overtures? Overtures urging me not to publish. A personal visit from Professor Yehuda. Letters to the press would not surprise me.'

'I'll let you know if I get anything.'

'But it is ... personal to me ... a meditation on death, by one who feels its hand upon him.'

'I feel death's hand every day. And all I get asked about is sodding politics. Why does no one ask me about death?'

'Everybody asks me about sex.'

'I've done politics. I've done sex. Shall we now do death?'

'I don't see why not. Take the couch, Alex. Put your feet up. Politics, sex and death are the three most interesting things on earth. High time we tackled the last.'

Alex sat tentatively on the couch, felt history under each buttock.

'Please, please. I shall take my old seat too.'

Alex swung his legs up onto the couch. Freud disappeared into the green chair behind him.

'God – this takes me back. Vienna ... 1908.'

'1907.'

'If you say so ... now ... where were we?'

'We were dying,' Freud replied.

An hour or so later two men in their eighties shook hands on the threshhold.

Freud said, over the handshake, 'A favour if you would ... please ask Wells to come and see me. I fear he needs my services more than you do.'

§ 57

Daffy Carfax held luncheon in much the same way the football league played soccer. Tranmere Rovers v. Accrington Stanley – Accrington Stanley v. Tranmere Rovers … there would always be a return match. Alex was not in the least surprised when she phoned him up a couple of weeks later and told him she had 'some really, really interesting people you really, really should meet', and was surprised only at the extremity of Daffy's choice. Left, Right he was used to, but it was rarely Alex sat down to break bread with someone he thought of as an outright fascist, and certainly rare this close to the inevitable war.

He was not seated next to Daffy, he found himself next to the spare, wolfish figure of the Marquess of Fermanagh, an old-school Tory, thoroughly anti-Churchill, almost as thoroughly anti-Chamberlain, a man whose power to blackball had been formidable in its day but whose powers were now waning. He'd flirted with fascism – who hadn't? the friends of Oswald Mosley were legion – had been briefly quite impressed by the young Mosley and now gave the impression of being impressed by no one. The seat on his other side was empty. Beyond that sat Humphrey Rogerson, a humpty-dumpty, right-wing economic theorist who opposed the theories of John Maynard Keynes with the simple idea that there was nothing one could do about economics therefore one should do nothing. The remarkable thing was that he earned a living saying this at inordinate length. Next to him was one of the young turks of British politics, Geoffrey Trench MP – a man whose membership of the Conservative Party must have been baffling to many conservatives as he was an outspoken fascist. Alex occasionally wondered why they didn't just boot him out, but he would in all probability merely stand again in his own seat and win and, of course, no one wanted to see a fascist elected to the House and thus legitimised. Trench was better for the Tories in their own margin – but it was, Alex thought, such a wide, such a loud margin. And beyond him, Arnold Palfrey-Greeve, leader writer on the *Daily Mail*, a man who had tried his utmost to rally the nation to the cause of British Fascism until Lord Rothermere had tired of all the street-fighting and finally relented on his headline of 'Hurrah for the Blackshirts'. A deeply unpleasant man, Alex thought, but … if asked by Rothermere, Palfrey-Greeve would write headlines calling for the appointment of a turnip as Minister of Transport.

Given the nature of this motley, Alex could not have been more surprised when the vacant seat was taken by Daffy's husband, Mungo. Mungo didn't lunch.

'You again?' Mungo said jocularly.

'The bad penny,' Alex replied.

Mungo leaned in confidentially, 'They're all bad pennies, Alex. The old girl seems attracted by the odd buggers in life, but I'll tell you ... this lot take the biscuit.'

Mungo slurped into his consommé. Alex looked around the table, heard Rogerson holding forth, saw Daffy smiling inanely as though she understood, and decided Mungo was right. Daffy collected oddities – and he was surely one himself – but this lot were the oddest of all.

Alex had long thought it a mistake to dismiss fascism as merely rabble-rousing. That its practice degenerated so rapidly to mob violence and street-fighting was inherent, but its politics were as diverse as the people who supported them – most not for long – and as varied as the nations that spawned them in the wake of the Great War. For years it seemed Britain had been striving to evolve a fascism that was 'British', for almost as long the model had been Italian – far, far more people, looked to Mussolini as an exemplar than would ever look to Hitler – H.G. Wells had been an admirer for a while, so had Churchill. Then Franco had seemed to elicit an absurd level of British support from many respectable, intelligent people – Victor Cazalet was one – who had found something admirable in his blatantly anti-democratic usurpation of Spain. Of late the German model had prevailed, but then that had begun with mob violence and street-fighting. Along the way, Oswald Mosley had moved from Conservative to being loosely allied to the Liberals, to sitting in the house for Labour as Chancellor of the Duchy of Lancaster, and, in the end, to being the leader of the British Union of Fascists. Along that way – and this was easy to forget – he had uttered statements, written papers, on economic matters, that had been taken seriously, been respected and discussed as a means to ending mass unemployment and ultimately ignored. The problem with fascism, the scary thing about fascism, as Mosley's career exmplified, was that it touched most other ideologies – sooner or later something in its ragbag ideology overlapped with what you believed yourself or what the party of your choice purported to believe.

Thank God, Alex thought, for the likes of Geoffrey Trench – a thirty-five-year-old demagogue with whom it was impossible to find a square inch of common ground. He was a successful young man – Eton and Oxford, elected to the House of Commons in a by-election before he was thirty – handsome, tall, letting a stubby moustache brutalise an otherwise pleasing face. And he was just what the occasion called for – the complete fascist bastard one could despise without conscience.

'Can anyone still doubt,' Trench was saying, 'that the greatest conspiracy of modern times is the international movement – the rise and the spread of Communism? The international conspiracy between Russia and world Jewry to spread this despicable idea, this farcical pretence of a common humanity, across the world? What other race could do this? What other race is international? A country that harbours Jews nurtures the real Fifth Column, the only Fifth Column that matters. A race without nation, that feels loyalty to no nation. A race that knows only one loyalty – that of Jew to Jew, that of Jew to the Jewish idea – Communism!'

They were on the meat course. Lamb, mint sauce, roast potatoes, a pleasing hint of rosemary, and a bellyfull of hatred.

'Why, why would a man as obviously intelligent as Hitler root out from the population so many who might otherwise contribute their labour or their capital at a time of the rebuilding of Germany? Can we imagine that such a decision was taken lightly, was taken arbitrarily? Did he want half Europe howling at him over the Jews? Of course not. Hitler recognises the enemy within. And so must we. We must expose the conspiracy of organised Jewry. And first and foremost we must rid the Conservative Party of its pernicious influence.'

Trench had stunned the table into silence. Not so much with what he was saying – for all Alex knew he might well be the only one who disagreed with young Trench – as the force with which he said it. Alex had thin tolerance for politicians who treated any gathering as an audience, made speeches rather than conversed. Daffy clearly had more, or she would not have invited the little prick, or any of the other little pricks who had failed at the simple task of gracing her table over the years, but she flashed her beaming smile at everyone only to find most eyes fixed downward. Alex had stopped eating, Mungo was picking at his lamb as though wondering what it was. Fermanagh, however, spoke.

'All I can say, young man, is "words, words, words".'

'You have a plan for action?'

It was a prick's remark when uttered to any man who had seen combat in war – and Fermanagh was, famously in his day, a veteran of the battle of Omdurman.

'Fine,' the old man said, 'you want a plan of action, I'll give you one.'

Fermanagh pointed his fork straight at Trench's chest.

'Try this on for size. Others have tried this and failed, so here's your chance. Get rid of the Minister of War. D'ye understand me? Get rid of the Minister of War! Get up on your hind legs in the House and call for Hore-Belisha to resign. He's in the cabinet. He's completely bloody useless in my opinion. And it so happens . . . he's a Jew.'

The last three words were uttered as though throwaway rather than the point of the argument. Fermanagh wasn't even looking at Trench as he spoke them. The fork withdrew to the plate. The knife sliced up another mouthful of lamb. If Fermanagh thought he'd thrown down the gauntlet in such a way that Trench would have to commit himself to doing something, he was wrong. The challenge brought forth more words, words, words.

'There is no place for the Jew in the Conservative Party, there is no place for the Jew in British politics . . . there is no place for the Jew in Britain. We must drive them from office, from power and ultimately we must drive them from Britain.'

Mungo set down his knife and fork, turned to Alex, no longer the confidential half-whisper, but a voice that everyone in the room could hear.

'Y'know, old boy, I seem to have lost me appetite. But, God help me, I just can't eat and listen to a man talk such utter shite.'

So saying, he rose from his seat. One hand seized Trench by his collar, the other twisted his right arm behind his back. Mungo then bellowed for a footman, steered his captive into the hallway and, as the footman pulled back the front door, placed one foot against his backside and booted him down the steps and into the street.

Mungo looked back through the open doors into the dining room. His gaze fixed coolly on his wife.

'Daphne, my dear, a word if you would be so kind.'

'I . . . er . . . er . . . darling . . . my guests . . .'

'Daphne!!!'

Without a word she followed him into his study, the footman closed the doors behind her. Her guests looked at one another in a silence broken only by the roar of Mungo's rage.

'When will you ever learn that you cannot decide British Foreign Policy at the dining table?'

'Mungo!'

'No Daphne ... for once just shut up and listen. I have put up for years with the idiots you amuse yourself with. But enough is enough. You cannot ...'

A door closed somewhere in the house and Mungo's tirade was reduced to a distant murmur.

Palfrey-Greeve threw down his napkin and got up to leave. Rogerson followed. Neither spoke. Left alone, Fermanagh looked at Alex and said, 'Lamb's too bloody good to waste. That Mungo's trouble. I'd never let a little shit like Trench put me off me fodder.'

Alex ate a mouthful and floated an idea: 'Of course it may be that the Minister for War will resign, whether Trench calls for it or not.'

'Then I set the little shit an easy enough task.'

Fermanagh took a bite of lamb. A moment's appreciative chewing, a small ripple of satisfaction spreading on his vulpine face.

'Or did you really think we'd get ourselves into another German war with a Jew in charge of the army?'

'I never know what you people think,' Alex said. 'And I have spent half a lifetime trying to fathom you. I come from a country that set the gold standard for anti-Semitism and still you people amaze me.'

§ 58

On 23 August Germany and the Soviet Union signed a non-aggression pact. Alex did not save his leader for the Sunday edition, but published it the following day.

The Post
Thursday, 24 August 1939

Surely you were expecting to hear from me today? Fear not, I shall be brief. This is hardly a time for lectures, it is a time for the licking of wounds.

Our relationship with the Soviet Union has been troubled and tricky since the bloody birth of that vast nation some twenty-two years ago. Of late it has seemed to me to resemble an engagement between unlikely suitors in a Victorian music hall. 'She wouldn't say yes, she wouldn't say no', and which of us was left standing at the altar? No matter – that would be hindsight, the raking over of what cannot be mended.

We are at war – it is simply that we do not know it. We have been at war since the first German plane dropped the first German bomb on Spain more than three years ago. It is a war in which we lack allies, a war in which our greatest potential ally has just signed a non-aggression pact with the enemy. And, inevitably, this has brought forth howling cries of anguish from those who have said all along that there was no deal to be done with the Godless Bolsheviks of Russia, that they too are the enemy. I will say now that the Nazi-Soviet Pact is an action which shocks me – I saw it coming – indeed, it seems to me to have been the writing on the wall since the day Mr Litvinov was relieved of his duties as Soviet Foreign Minister – and still it shocks me. But the Soviet Union is a nation only twenty-two years old. What is twenty-two years? It is youth, it is adolescence, it is mere infancy. I say to my readers now that this is far from final, and that this is not the action on which to judge a nation so newly born. It is a time for the licking of wounds, it is, to quote I forget whom – my children would know – a time of the breaking of nations.

Alexei Troy

§ 59

On odd days Alex still went into his office. Often enough to demonstrate that he was still the boss. Never with any regularity or predictability. He was in his study in Church Row, standing by the desk, checking his pockets, patting himself down and muttering 'glasses, watch, wallet ...' when the phone rang.

'Alex, we must meet at once.'

'Of course, Winston. I have a car outside right now, I could be with you in twenty minutes or so. Your flat or the Commons?'

'Neither,' Churchill said. 'Meet me at Daffy's.'

He knew what this meant. It meant firstly that Churchill wanted neutral territory, which meant that either one of them, like would-be lovers on a blind date, could leave at will. And secondly that he wanted their meeting unobserved. There were always reporters at the House of Commons, and more often than not there'd be the odd one hanging about outside Churchill's flat.

As he stepped from the car in Chesham Place the door of the house two doors down opened, and its owner walked to the curb, glanced at his pocket watch, looked down the street in search of a cab, looked up at the summer sky, summer-struck for a moment, looked the other way down the street and finally caught sight of Alex looking at him.

Alex had not set eyes on Lord Carsington in more than two years. Who had? He had shot his bolt with British Fascism in 1936. But that was what Carsington did. He left things. He had left the Liberal Party in 1920, the Conservative Party in 1929 and had drifted into Mosleyite politics. He had spoken outrageously and provocatively at BUF rallies, and suddenly, after the 'Battle' of Cable Street had all but withdrawn from public life. Silence, the odd letter to the newspapers notwithstanding, had not diminished his role as a bogeyman to the Left. Alex had attacked him in leaders. They had both risked being thrown out of the Savoy after a public row just before Christmas 1936. And now there was not a hint of acknowledgement in his face. Carsington was looking straight through him. Part of Alex − the journalist − wished he would come right up and speak − he had a ready question after all, 'Why? Why would anyone withdraw from public life so completely at the age of fifty? What had happened?' And part of him − the diplomat − wanted no conflict, wanted simply to keep the appointment with Churchill. That would be conflict enough.

Carsington's arm shot up, a cab cruised past Alex to stop outside number 426. Carsington climbed into the cab without looking back. Relieved, Alex pulled on the bell of Daffy's house, only to find Churchill already at the door.

'They're all out,' he said gruffly. 'Mungo's out netting more bugs, and the servants have their half day. Daphne has left us to our own devices.'

'Did you know Carsington lived only two doors along?'

'I did. One cannot choose one's neighbours. I had thought, however, that one could choose one's friends.'

Churchill had fired the opening salvo. He turned and led off into Daffy's morning room. Back to the cold fireplace, he blazed.

'What were you thinking of? What possessed you? What do you think Russia is up to?'

Alex lowered himself into an armchair. Churchill could have a stand-up row if he liked, he was going to sit.

'I am keeping an issue, an argument, alive. At a moment when there is a rush to judgement, I merely stated that it is too soon to judge.'

'You are putting spokes in the wheel of history!'

Alex had the feeling that Churchill had thought this phrase up well in advance, but answered in kind.

'Then perhaps the wheel might roll at last. We do seem to have suffered years of inaction.'

'The Nazis are the ones rolling. Rolling across half of Europe.'

'And meanwhile we fall out amongst ourselves. We argue. We snipe at one another. The Rhineland is occupied, and we merely squabble, Germany re-arms and we bicker. Austria and Czechoslovakia tumble and we reject every overture the Russians make to us. What has happened in the last few years? What has happened as a result of our inaction, of our endless mistrust of one another? . . . Hitler has turned an *opéra bouffe* into a fighting machine. In 1933 he was stoppable, in 1936 he was stoppable. He might even have been stoppable in 1938. Now? God only knows how we shall stop him. What do I think Russia is up to? I think Stalin is buying time, with lies and dishonour and deceit he is buying time. He is supping with the longest spoon in history . . . but if it buys him time to restore the Red Army . . .?'

'If? If? Alex, do you have an inkling as to the nature of the man we are discussing?'

Now, he might just surprise Churchill.

'I met Stalin. In the first young years of the century I met him several times. He was living in a doss-house just off the Mile End Road. But I don't know the man, and anyone who says he does is, in the words of an English cliché, either a liar or a self-deluding fool.'

Puffed up with his own rage, Churchill puffed still further, one final face-reddenning inflation of his righteousness.

'Then hear this from this fool . . . re-arm or not re-arm, with the time he has bought he means to dismember Europe. Bugger the spoon, it's about sharper cutlery than bloody spoons. Hitler will stick in the fork from one side and Stalin the knife from the other. And between them they will carve up Europe like Gilray's pudding. That is the man you declared for in the *Post* this morning!'

§ 60

Alex felt an unbearable sadness. A sense of 'over'. It would be easy to head for home and lick his wounds. Instead he told the chauffeur to carry on to Fleet Street and decided to sit in his office for a while as he had intended – answer his mail *in situ* rather than wait for it to be sent up to Hampstead.

It had been weeks since he had been there. His appearance put his staff into a flurry, but he said, 'Just bring me a pot of tea and the day's post.'

He was sitting at his desk, eyes closed, listening to the murmur of traffic in the street below, when his secretary set a tea tray and two letters before him.

'My dear, is this all?'

'I assume you meant the stuff with your name on it, boss, not the stuff that just says "editor". That goes to Mr Glendinning as a matter of course.'

'Of course. Just the letters addressed to me personally.'

Only two. They wouldn't occupy his mind for as many minutes. But if he'd asked for the letters to the editor there would be dozens if not hundreds, and Glendinning's nose would be out of joint. He'd wished he could have handed over to Rod – but Rod had not wanted the job, and preferred to work on a memoir of his time in Germany.

The letters were the same size. Each envelope smudgily typed with his title, name and the paper's address. Two correspondents who had not noticed that he'd handed over the helm some time ago. He took one in each hand, weighing them up literally as well as figuratively. Did it matter a damn which he opened first?

He took the one in his left hand.

Sir,

At a time when virulent Jew-baiting has become a continental sport can it be wise for anyone in this country to be publishing works that, however scholarly, carry in them the inherent possibility of nurturing the cause of Nazism and anti-Semitism? We refer to the impending publication of the book *Moses and Monotheism* by Prof. Sigmund Freud, the Austrian psychoanalyst, currently residing in London.

We have the highest regard for Prof. Freud, as a doctor and as a Jew, but it cannot be wise to publish a study that strikes at the very foundations of the Jewish faith in an hour as dark as this. There may come a time for the publication of this book, but that time is not now, and we call upon His Majesty's Government to use their powers to prevent publication.

It was signed by every member of the Jewish Board of Deputies, and it was a stinker. Freud had warned him about this possibility. Alex needed it like he needed an extra belly button. He was contemplating phoning Freud when the telephone rang and his secretary said, 'Are you taking calls, boss?'

'Who?'

'Denys Quilty at the Ministry of Information.'

'Put him on.'

The last Alex had heard of Quilty he had been at the Home Office. He thought the term Ministry of Information something of an oxymoron.

'Alex?'

'Denys ... you are so lucky to find me here.'

'Taking chances ... I'd already tried you at home ... it is sort of urgent.'

'How so?'

'Have you opened your post?'

'I am doing so even now.'

'You'll find you have a letter that every editor of every major daily has received.'

'I will?'

'Signed by rabbis.'

'Ah!'

'You've read it?'

'Seconds ago. I was wondering what to do with it.'

'Don't publish it. I've asked everyone not to publish in the national interest.'

'Would that be in the national interest?'

'I'm afraid it would.'

'I wonder what Freud will say.'

'Freud? I'm sorry Alex, I don't quite follow . . .?'

'It's his book. Years of work. I rather think he will relish any response even one as prematurely negative as this.'

'Alex, are we talking about the same letter?'

'I have it in front of me . . . signed by the Board of Deputies.'

'No . . . That's not it. I was referring to a letter from a bunch of East End rabbis.'

Alex tore open the second letter, said, 'One moment, Denys.'


```
Sir,
War cannot now be far away. Anyone who has
experienced the disruption and conflict created
by British fascism in recent years, as we, the
Rabbis of Stepney, have, will surely agree with
us that it is now time to imprison our home-
grown Nazis? We call upon His Majesty's
Government to wait no longer on the outbreak of
war and imprison these men forthwith:
  Sir Oswald Mosley, Archibald Ramsay MP, Oliver
Gilbert, Victor Rowe, Roland Rollason, Lord
Carsington, Major Harold Haward-Pyke, Professor
Charles Lockett, Sir Michael Redburn, Viscount
Blackwall, Geoffrey Trench MP.
  Yrs Faithfully,
  Daniel Shoval
  Isaiah Borg
  Aaron Adelson
  Moses Friedland
  Elishah Nader
```

David Cohen
Jacob Kossoff.

Coincidence was a small world. You could fit it onto the head of a pin and still have room for all those angels. No sight or mention of Carsington for years and now twice in one day.

'I've read it, Denys. Explain the national interest to me.'

'It's simply too provocative.'

'The men so named need no provocation.'

'And, of course, there's the possibility of libel.'

'Denys, I think I've been sued for libel half a dozen times in the last thirty years. I've won with costs every time. Libel is not a consideration. I have had no chance to talk to our solicitor and I will not even bother. Everyone on this list has spoken against Jews. Everyone on this list has spoken for Nazis. They are our undeclared enemy. I see no reason not to treat them as such.'

'I agree – in principle.'

'In principle?'

'Well . . . we're not at war yet.'

'Only a matter of time.'

'And we've no law under which we could lock them up.'

'But you're getting one ready to put on the statute books?'

Quilty was silent too long.

'Denys?'

'It's imminent.'

'When?'

'Actually . . . later today. Second reading tomorrow. With any luck it'll be law by midnight on Saturday. But it'll take days before it filters down to enforcement level as rules and regulations.'

'So when will you lock them up . . . in a matter of days?'

'Doubtful.'

'On the outbreak of war?'

'Doubtful . . . we'd still need a reason.'

'War is not reason enough?'

'Alright – we'd need an excuse – and we're looking for one. It's all in the wording, and between you and me what's going through tonight isn't quite the blank cheque one would need to bang up any Tom, Dick or Oswald.'

'Then what will it do?'

'Well . . . it'll tell you which end to open your boiled egg at breakfast. And give a jobsworth in a tin hat the power to fine you fifty quid if you bash the wrong end with your teaspoon.'

'You're kidding?'

'Kidding, yes. Exaggerating, no. If it were up to me it would be a law that locked these buggers up post-haste. I think it's necessary. But that in itself is one reason not to publish. It would be, shall I say, tipping our hand? Why give the buggers any warning? They'll probably not think the law applies to them, and I'd rather they stayed complacent.'

'One reason you say – you mean there's more than one?'

'The Herschel Grynszpan factor.'

Alex could not find the name in his memory.

'Remind me.'

'He's the boy who shot the Third Under-Secretary or whatever in Paris and set off Kristallnacht. I don't want to give our homegrown fascists any warning – equally I don't want to give them any excuse to go after more Jews with one of their rent-a-mobs.'

Alex sighed.

'Denys – I won't publish this. And I hope I never regret it.'

§61

Alex spread out the two letters side by side. He picked up the first, read it once more and called Freud at his home.

Freud's response was simple.

'Alex,' Freud said, 'publish. I shall. I can do no other. Let them speak. I have no other intention.'

'As you wish. Now, there is another matter. I have received another letter from a group of rabbis. None of them men of whom I have ever heard and I doubt you have either. Not a deputy among them. They all live and work in the East End and have written to me calling for the arrest of fascist rabble-rousers who go into the East End and spread anti-Semitism . . .'

'I say again, publish.'

Alex ignored this. Had no wish to explain to Freud the reasons why he would not publish.

'Among the fascist demagogues named is a Professor Lockett. Was it not a Professor Lockett who called me last year, who persuaded you to leave Vienna?'

'It was. Nicholas Lockett is the younger brother of the man you are thinking of. Charles Lockett, I believe?'

'Yes . . . Charles. I know the name and I know he speaks from time to time against the Jews. Apart from the mere fact of his anti-Semitism I know nothing about him.'

'Nicholas Lockett is a protégé of mine . . . if I were messianic I might even say disciple. Suffice it to say he is a psychoanalyst of the highest reputation. His scientific credentials could not be faulted. His brother, on the other hand, is the inheritor of another Viennese school of thought. It was current when you first came to me. Perhaps you came across a magazine called *Ostara* and its publisher von Liebenfels?'

'Ah . . . what did they call themselves . . .?'

'Ariosophists.'

'So they did.'

'New wine in old bottles. A dash of phrenology, a cup of eugenics, a splash of Zoroastrianism, a twist of Hindu myth . . . shake the bottle and you get a disgusting mess of pseudo-science more appropriate to the middle of the last century than the middle of this one. The justification of Aryan superiority by a patchwork of mysticism. That is what the elder Lockett practises. The gobbledegook of racial differences. Tell me, Alex, is it your intention to contact this man?'

'Probably not.'

'Just as well, I'm sure he would ask to feel your bumps.'

§62

Alex's younger son, Frederick, had rebelled against the way laid out for him. An exhibition to read history at Christ Church, Oxford, might have impressed his father, but it hadn't impressed him. He'd thought about it most of the summer of 1933, and late in the summer shortly after his eighteenth birthday he had appeared in his father's study about breakfast time and told him he didn't want to go to Oxford, or any other university for that matter.

Alex had taken the news well. Had asked merely, 'What would you prefer to do?'

Frederick Troy admitted that he did not know.

'Journalism?' Alex said hopefully, knowing full well how different his sons were.

'Maybe,' Troy said, 'but where does one begin?'

'When one's father owns the paper,' Alex said parodically, 'one begins where one wants. But if one is asking for a suggestion – Dickens began as a court reporter. You could do worse.'

Troy joined the *Post* as court reporter. He learnt shorthand, did the job for a year and in 1934 moved on to become a crime reporter, and after a year on crime appeared yet again in his father's study at breakfast to say: 'I know now. I'd like to be a policeman.'

In 1936 he passed out from Hendon, and took up his first assignment as a beat bobby in Stepney, astounded the locals with his accent, and came under the benign care of Station Sergeant George Bonham – a gentle giant of a man.

By the summer of 1939, Troy was a detective constable in Stepney. Bonham still ran the station, still presided over Troy with all the attentiveness of a nanny, but in every other respect accepted that Troy had gone where he could not follow, occasionally muttering something about 'seven league boots'.

'This just came in,' he said one Tuesday afternoon towards the end of August, and the end of Peace. 'You might want to take a look. You never know.'

Troy had got used to Bonham's 'you never know'. It was a mechanism that allowed for being surprised. What he liked about coppering was the moment when you did know, when you finally had all the pieces on the board and got the last one into place.

'Bethnal Green Underground Station. Bloke found dead at the bottom of the escalator. Probably an accident, but . . .'

'You never know,' Troy said.

'How did you know I was gonna say that?'

Troy took the piece of paper from Bonham's hand, looked at his watch.

'I'll drive over now. The poor bugger on the beat is probably holding a crowd at bay.'

Accidents happen – another Bonhamism – and only one thing about the bundled body at the bottom of the escalator surprised Troy. The hat, the coat and the beard. It was an Orthodox rabbi.

The beat bobby was even younger than Troy – white as a sheet, admitted he'd never seen a dead body before, did not admit that keeping a nosy crowd at bay had strained his tact and his coppering skills.

Troy simply and loudly said, 'If anyone saw him fall, speak up. If anyone knows him, speak up. If not, clear off.'

The crowd thinned. Only a small boy remained. Twelve or thirteen, Troy thought – blue blazer, grey shorts, tufts of curly hair, and a *yarmulke* pinned to the top of his head.

'Do you recognise him?'

The boy nodded his head.

'It's the rabbi.'

'I can see that.'

'I mean it's our rabbi. Teaches us in *shul*.'

'Tell me his name.'

'Rabbi Shoval. His real name's Daniel. But we always call him Digger.'

Troy bent down to look at the dead man's face. He'd never met Rabbi Shoval, he'd heard of him – most people who lived in the East End had heard of Daniel Shoval, a campaigner, a fighter – but he'd never met him and he hadn't recognised him from the dozens of photographs that had appeared over the years in the local papers. Nor did he know that small boys had stuck him with such an undignified nickname – but they would, wouldn't they?

Troy picked up the broken pieces of the rabbi's walking stick. It had snapped just like the man.

The boy was dictating his name and address to the constable – clearly and calmly. Cooler in the face of death than either of the policemen. Then he turned to Troy.

'An accident?' he said. 'It was an accident?'

§

Under moonlight,
infectious moonlight,
a madman dances.

§63

1 September 1939
Warsaw

'Hello. Hello. Does anyone speak English? (pause) Eeeenglisshh? (pause) No, I don't speak Polish, not a word!'

'You have reached the press office of the Foreign Ministry, sir. Is it the press office you wanted?'

'Damn right it is. Kulikowski. I wish to speak to Mr Kulikowski.'

Greene heard muffled voices as though a hand had been placed over the mouthpiece.

'This is Kulikowski. To whom am I speaking?'

'Hugh Greene. Warsaw Correspondent, *Daily Telegraph*, London. We met at ... dammit ... can't remember where ... doesn't matter .... Listen ... Katowice ...'

'Katowice? I thought you said Warsaw?'

'Of course I'm in Warsaw, I'm the Warsaw correspondent.'

'So? Why Katowice?'

Jesus wept.

'We have a stringer ...'

'A what?'

'A correspondent. We have a correspondent in Katowice, at the moment. A colleague. She just telephoned me ...'

'She?'

'She. The female of the species. Some of us are women. You know, the odd-looking chaps with bumps on their chests? Look, will you just listen? The Germans have attacked.'

'Attacked what?'

Jesus wept.

'Katowice!'

The muffled voices once more, the hand not quite masking the conversation. Polish could do that all on its own.

'Mr Greene, this is nonsense. We would be the first to know. We are still in negotiation with the Germans.'

'Not any more, you're not.'

'What are you trying to tell us, Mr Greene?'

'I think I'm trying to tell you that World War Two has just begun.'

With pantomime timing an air raid siren began its demented wail. Greene heard it twice, once through the open window, and again down the telephone line from the Ministry.

§ 64

3 September 1939
'The Day War Broke Out'

In the absence of anyone more senior Troy had an office. His immediate superior, Sergeant McKechnie, being a member of the reserve, had been called up some time ago. The station inspector, Malnick by name, and, as far as Troy was concerned, Malnick by practice, had transferred to the City Police – hence Troy – a mere detective constable – had an office, and had it to himself.

Station Sergeant George Bonham – a man who stood just shy of seven foot in boots and helmet – was backing in through the door with a large wooden cabinet in his hands.

'George, what are you doing?'

Bonham stuck the cabinet on Troy's desk – its perforated hardboard back facing Troy. He recognised it for what it was – a wet-cell wireless, sold as portable, which it was if you also owned a wheelbarrow.

'Prime Minister's supposed to be on any minute. Address to the nation or some such.'

'George, I hardly think we need . . .'

Bonham sat down and Troy was drowned out in a barrage of hisses and whistles as Bonham twiddled the knob in search of the Home Service. He found it just in time. Pip, pip, pip and a BBC epitome-of-reserve voice announced the address. Troy accepted he had lost and thought he'd sit it out in silence, but at the sound of those few words . . . 'And now the Prime Minister' . . . Bonham stood up at attention.

'George, for Christ's sake, it's only Neville Chamberlain. Not the King.'

Bonham looked at him quizzically but sat down, perched on the edge of the chair as though ready to spring to attention should the wireless demand it of him.

'I am speaking to you from the Cabinet Room at 10, Downing Street. This morning the British Ambassador in Berlin handed the German Government a final note stating that, unless we heard from them by 11 o'clock that they were prepared at once to withdraw their troops from Poland, a state of war would exist between us. I have to tell you now that no such undertaking has been received, and that consequently this country is at war with Germany.'

What struck Troy was not the gravity of the matter – what sentient being had expected anything other? – but the tone. Chamberlain seemed old, frail. Almost bird-like in delicacy, a butterfly about to be broken upon a wheel of his own making. It roused no sympathy in him.

'You can imagine what a bitter blow it is to me that all my long struggle to win peace has failed. Yet I cannot believe that there is . . .'

Troy reached over and turned off the set.

''Ere 'Old yer 'orses. He hasn't finished yet!'

'Do you really want to hear a list of excuses? If you do, you don't need Chamberlain. I could recite for you word for word what he's going to say next . . . he'll tell us how no one could be more hurt by this . . . how no one could have done more . . . how he hoped for peace until about three minutes ago . . . how he really believed it was possible to do business with Nazis . . . and what you won't hear is any reference to the shabby betrayals of Austria, of Czechoslovakia . . . of small faraway countries . . . of which, apparently, we knew nothing. All I can say is, thank God Hitler didn't have his sights set on Wales ... it qualifies in both categories.'

'Bloody hell, young Fred. What a bee! What a bonnet!'

Troy was saved from having to answer. The ululation of an air-raid siren sliced the air and changed the subject.

Bonham stood up and looked out of the window as though expecting to see a German bomber. Troy opened a folder and went back to his paperwork.

'We'd best get to the shelter, Freddie.'

'False alarm, George.'

'How do you know?'

Troy didn't bother to look up from his papers.

'Trust me.'

'You know the procedure ... how would it look to Joe Public if us coppers didn't stick to the drill?'

'George ... nobody's looking.'

'Course not ... they're running for the shelters. Take a look out the window. The street was full half a minute ago. Now ... they've just scattered like hens!'

'I say again, false alarm.'

Bonham dithered.

'At least one of us should turn off the gas. They tell you to turn off the gas.'

'And then they give you a gas mask, just in case.'

'It's not funny, Freddie.'

Troy still didn't look up.

'Of course not. But we've read all the bumf, haven't we?'

'Course.'

'And you taped up all the windows with sticky tape.'

'You saw me do it ... an' you didn't lift a finger to help.'

'And you've got a stirrup pump?'

'Yep.'

'And a bucket of sand?'

'We got lots o' buckets o' sand. I reckon we got six or seven scattered round the nick. I have to stop blokes from putting their fag ends out in 'em.'

'Well, George ... with a gas mask, a stirrup pump, seven buckets of sand and about five hundred feet of sticky brown tape across the windows I'd say we're close to impregnable. You go to the shelter if you like. I'm finishing this pile of bumf, then I'm nipping out for a spot of lunch, a bit of a stroll across the manor, and, if any Germans get past our wall of firebuckets and sticky brown tape, I'll let you know.'

§65

After lunch Troy stood a while in the Whitechapel Road opposite the Underground station. People-watching, which might be deemed second nature to a policeman, had become a pseudo-academic hobby of the Thirties, under the title 'Mass Observation'. All over the country hundreds of volunteers, 'observers', who might otherwise have been out youth-hostelling or playing mouth organs, had compiled reports on the state of the nation, from the results of nothing more scientific than people-watching. People had, as Bonham had declared, 'scattered like hens'. Now, it was as if Troy was watching the same film run backwards. Most people seemed to be coming from somewhere rather than going to somewhere – although Troy recognised that this was an entirely subjective point of view. The same people he saw coming up from the Underground – one of the sub-surface stations, hardly bombproof by any stretch – could be 'scattering' as surely as those that had fled. There was a zebra crossing a few yards east of the station, broad black and white bands painted on the tarmacadam, and a pair of belisha beacons – flashing globes of orange on striped poles that signalled safety to the pedestrian. When they had been introduced a few years earlier by Mr Hore-Belisha, the then Minister of Transport, after whom they were named – a man now stuck with the unenviable task of Minister for War, and the same man subject to the rantings of those who wanted Jews out of government – Troy had watched a drunk trying vainly to blow one out under the impression they were gaslit. The traffic was now stopped at the zebra stripes and the flashing beacons to let a stream of pedestrians pass. Last of all was an old woman pushing a perambulator – no baby, it was piled high with her possessions – splashing through the puddles left by last night's thunderstorm. Coming or going? No matter. What mattered was the pair of well-dressed gentlemen poised at the crossing in the front seat of a sleek, grey, convertible, three-and-a-half litre, six-cylinder Armstrong-Siddeley – top down, chatting to each other in the accents of received pronunciation. Everything about them said 'toff', the car, the clothes, the inevitable if accidental hauteur. Indeed, Troy had met both at his father's dinner table, although he knew damn well they would not recognise him out of that context in a thousand years – Harold Nicolson, MP for Leicester, and Victor Cazalet, MP for Chippenham, one National Labour, the other Conservative, thereby demonstrating how in English life class so readily superseded politics. They hadn't noticed Troy, nor had they noticed the old woman still crossing at her snail's pace. But she had noticed them. She left her pram and shuffled across to the driver's side, to harangue Cazalet.

''Ere. You. You lot. Toffs!'

Both heads turned.

'This bleedin' war. It's all your fault. You fink the poor ever started a neffin' war? What poor bloke ever started a neffin' war. Wars is toff fings, they is. It's all your neffin' fault. It's all the fault of the neffin' rich! You fink we wanna go through all that again –'

Cazalet cut her short, smiling politely all the time, slipped the car into gear and drove carefully around the pram.

The old woman pushed it to the edge of the road, up onto the pavement, banging into Troy as she did so. An arthritic hand, all bulging knuckles, beckoned him closer.

'I lorst me 'usband in Flanders, lorst my Johnnie I did. I lorst two o' me bruvvers an' all. And this bunch o' tosspots fink I'm gonna send me sons now. Fuckem, fuckem all. We could've seen this 'Itler bloke off in thirty-three!'

She did not wait for a reply. Troy had none ready. It was, he thought, a bit like hearing one of his father's editorials boiled down to the rub with a few choice foul words thrown in for good measure. If only his father had the succinct freedom to print 'fuckem'. If only she'd known to whom she had been speaking.

Troy looked up at the clear afternoon sky. It was cloudless, it was still summer. It was hard to imagine the sky darkened by bombers, yet every pundit in the land was predicting, and had done so for years, that London would be pounded to dust. It was the received wisdom of the times. He looked up – trying to get through his head the simple notion of being 'at war'. It didn't work. It just didn't work. Besides, he'd had high hopes of being out of Stepney before the balloon went up. He'd never expected to see this war through in Stepney.

§66

17 September 1939
The Day Russia Invaded Poland

A one-word Latin telegramme arrived at Church Row:

NUNC? CHURCHILL.

What now? It would be the last word they would ever exchange directly.

What now? Alex knew only too well what now, and in the evening summoned his entire family into his study. With the exception of his younger son, Frederick, the policeman, they all managed to be there. Rod, Rod's wife Lucinda, known as Cid, his twin daughters Sasha and Masha, their respective husbands – the Hon. Hugh Darbishire and Lawrence Stafford – his wife of forty-one years, Maria Mikhailovna, and his youngest brother Nikolai Rodyonovich, Professor Troitsky – the only other member of his family to cross to England with him, and the last one to cling to the old family name.

'I shall be retiring from public life – forthwith.'

There was a prolonged silence, a sigh from his wife that he took to be one of relief, and a little coughing from the sons-in-law. It was Lawrence who spoke first.

'Might we ask why?'

'Why? Because one lives with the consequences of one's own words and actions. Because I have made a fool of myself in public and will henceforth be a fool in private. If that were not enough . . . well . . . I am old . . . and we are at war.'

'Actually . . . y'know it's hardly even started yet . . . and there were these chaps in the club last night who reckoned it'll all be over by Christmas,' Hugh chipped in. And everyone in the room looked at him as though he were the fool.

§67

18 September 1939

It was an odd normality. As so many said, it didn't feel like being at war at all. There was something fake and phoney about it. No lurid patriotism, no vicious xenophobia. No raining death of shrapnel and cordite. It was, for want of a better phrase in Troy's mind, business as usual. What had changed, in odd ways, struck him as changed for the better. The city was darker, quieter, moonlit, almost enchanted. The nights suited him fine. To walk London after dark was to touch beauty, to immerse in ... in what? He hadn't found the word. He had merely found the vision. To sit in Piccadilly Circus, freed from the electric rain of advertising and look at London as none had looked at it since the 1880s – and even then they'd had gaslight. This embracing darkness, smothering night – surprised by a kiss – had not been seen in centuries.

It was a fortnight after the outbreak of war. Two weeks of apprehension and unreality. It was the day after Russia's invasion of Poland. The telephone on his desk rang.

'Stanley Onions,' said a northern voice at the other end.

Troy shifted a little in his seat at the sound of Onions' voice. A hint of sitting to attention. It had been ages since he'd heard that blunt Lancashire accent crackle down the wires from Scotland Yard. Onions outranked Troy in spades. A superintendent, and, at that, the superintendent in charge of the prestigious Murder Squad.

'You'll recall I said I'd be in touch?'

Not that Troy could forget, but that had been the best part of three years ago.

'I've been watching you. You've a few feathers in yer cap. A few scalps on yer belt.'

'I've been lucky,' Troy said with a modesty he did not much feel.

'Luck's got nowt to do wi' it. I said, I said back in thirty-six that when the time was right I'd want you for the Yard. Now's the time. You'll get a fortnight's leave to mek the move, but I want you here at the end o' the month.'

'Just like that?'

'Take it or leave it, lad, it's not a negotiation.'

'Then I take.'

'Good. 'Cos there's more. You'll be stepping up a rank. From the thirtieth you'll draw a sergeant's pay. I don't think for one moment you need it, but I've never yet met a man who'd turn down a pay rise.'

Of course he wouldn't. In fact his gratitude was inexpressible. Just as well. Onions rang off and left him no time to express it.

When the phone rang a second time, Troy had already made up his mind to sound a little more grateful, a touch more enthusiastic about a job he would have chopped off a leg to get. But it wasn't Onions, it was his father.

'My boy, do you have any holidays owing?'

'I'm twenty-four, Dad. I've left school. In the Police Force we call it leave. And as it happens, I've got a fortnight in hand. I'll need a couple days of that to sort a few things out ... so tell me what you have in mind.'

'Let us go abroad while we still can. Let us go to the Continent before Hitler's tanks roll over it. Let us go to France and Italy before the lights go out all over Europe again.'

Troy was acutely aware of how that sentence ended – Sir Edward Grey, Foreign Secretary in 1914: 'We shall not see them lit again in our lifetime'. It was, Troy thought, less the onset of war than awareness of his own age and mortality that motivated his father. It occurred to Troy that he did not even know how old his father was. But he was old. Possibly even over eighty.

'Not perhaps the grand tour, but France and Italy. Perhaps Le Touquet, and Paris and then on to Rome and Amalfi.'

'Not Le Touquet, Dad.'

'As you wish, but why not? Time was we would go *en famille* at least once a year.'

'That's precisely why not.'

Troy hoped his father would probe no further and he didn't. Troy had no wish to offend the old man by letting him know, if he did not know already, how bored he had been as a small boy on a French beach looking back at England, his parents conversing in multiple languages with decrepit strangers, the well-heeled, well-clothed, musty refugees of a revolution that, whilst it had happened in his lifetime, might as well have happened a thousand years ago to a boy of ten. Troy had long since lost track of, ceased to pay heed to, M. le Comte de Thisanthat or Prince Whateveroffsky, and their well-wrapped, lace-enfolded, big-bosomed wives, the latter of whom seemed far too willing to be enchanted by his pre-pubescent surliness.

'Why not choose your own itinerary, my boy?'

'Really?'

'Be my guest.'

'Paris ... of course, Paris. But I'd rather see Florence or Siena than Rome.'

Alex was thinking. Troy counted past ten before his father spoke again.

'Good, good,' he said. 'Paris it is, and Siena. September in Siena is still outdoor weather. Who would not sit in the campo gazing at the night sky with a Campari and soda in hand? But ... would you mind a substitution for Florence?'

'Try me,' said Troy.

'Monte.'

'Monte?'

'Monte Carlo.'

Bloody hell.

'I think you need a little vice if not in your soul then in your fingertips. I have not been to Monte in years and you never have. Stop being a policeman for two or three days and indulge in the sins.'

'Do I get a choice of sin?'

'Be my guest.'

§68

Troy's father had two *modi operandi* for breakfast when travelling. Silence behind a newspaper – the newspaper in any of four or five languages – and garrulousness with strangers he had only just met but to whose geopolitical wisdom and crackpot theories he would listen with unfeigned interest. Neither mode required him to talk to his son. Troy would either take breakfast in his room or sit in the dining room of the Georges V with a novel or a newspaper, ready to be distracted from it whenever his father decided to sum up what a night and a morning of incessant natter had gleaned for him. He'd read that morning's *Post* with a professional eye – the Old Bailey report on the conviction of two soldiers for the savage murder and necrophiliac rape of one 'Amaryllis', prostitute of Hindhead, Surrey; a case his new boss, Stanley Onions, had chosen to handle personally. Scarcely in a lighter vein he had chosen *Splendères et Misères des Courtesanes* by Balzac as his novel. Not possessing his father's facility with language – two was quite enough, and French made only two-and-a-half – he read a leaden Victorian translation. It seemed an appropriate book for Paris, and would last him well into Italy, if they ever got there.

'They're cocky,' his father said by way of summary. 'The French seem confident that the line will hold when the time comes, that the Germans will not roll over France as they did in 1871 or even a corner of it as they did in 1914. I keep hearing the same words, "impregnable", "impenetrable".'

'Sounds like morning assembly . . . "im-something, in-something . . . God Only Wise . . ." have they not noticed the German troops rolling over Poland right now? God knows what the Poles had thought beforehand. Impregnable?'

Alex shrugged.

'It remains, however, an untried army,' Troy added.

'Untried?'

'They fought no battle for Austria, none for Czechoslovakia. Are they fighting anything more than skirmishes in Poland?'

'All that means is that no one has called their bluff.'

'My point in a nutshell, Dad.'

'No one has called it . . . to find out that they're not bluffing.'

This was one of the things that made talking to his father awkward. The bugger had a way of trouncing you in two sentences.

'And you still want to go on to Monte Carlo and Italy?'

§69

Their next breakfast together was on the sleeper train heading for Monaco.

Alex had spent most of the previous evening in conversation with a party of Italians – in Italian. At breakfast he chose to eat with his son and switched to Russian, something he hardly ever did – he had embraced the English language with fervour – but when he did it meant he sought confidentiality.

'I have some business to attend to when we get to Monte Carlo,' he said, taking the top off his egg with a knife.

'But you're not going to tell me what?'

Alex shrugged.

'So it isn't a holiday after all?'

'Of course it is.'

'What am I supposed to do while you get involved in another of your conspiracies?'

'It is not a conspiracy. It is . . . an arranged meeting. And you will, as we agreed, have the opportunity to sin.'

'You mean gambling?'

Alex nodded

'I thought I got to pick the sin?'

'Then pick . . . chemin-de-fer, roulette . . . the choice is yours, just don't expect three-card brag or Glewstone Donkey . . . it's a far cry from the Snug in a London pub . . . land I can tell you now roulette is a mug's game, a mug's game of no perceptible skill.'

'Dad, they none of them hold the appeal of a cold omelette.'

'Indulge me, my boy. Indulge yourself. It will only be for one evening.'

'At least tell me who you're meeting.'

'I can't.'

Alex got stuck into his second egg, Troy pushed away his cold omelette. A rustle of skirts at their table and a black-haired beauty of a woman brushed past them, her backside all but perched on the edge of their table as she passed the waiter coming the other way. Troy turned to follow her trail down the car to an end table. She sat facing him, neat as ninepence in her black suit and matching hat, looked straight at him, smiled and vanished behind the menu.

'I told you you'd find another sin,' his father said in English. 'I admire your taste. She is a fine-looking woman.'

'Dad ... in the parlance of my generation, she's an absolute stunner. That's why I won't stand a cat in hell's chance.'

He turned again, stealing a last look. A tall, grey-haired man in his fifties was now taking the seat opposite her, a proprietorial touch of his hand on her arm as he did so, and she wasn't just smiling at him, she was beaming.

Fat chance.

§ 70

Troy was in a muddle with his bowtie.

'It's not essential, my boy.'

'You're wearing one.'

His father declined the jibe and stood behind Troy, much as he had done ten minutes before every formal occasion of Troy's childhood, and in a couple of swift motions had tied the tie with what he referred to as his 'bugger's grip'.

'And don't go in there with any sense of awe. It's all grandiose rather than grand. A mock-palace full of one-armed bandits much as you might find in a London pub – and at that managed by bank clerks and mechanics.'

Troy said, 'It looks intimidating. It looks awesome.'

'Before the war – the last war I mean – that might have been true. They still used coins in those days – gold Louis d'Or. In 1909 I saw an English ship's captain win a small fortune at roulette by putting down one of the shiny buttons off his jacket.'

'And they paid up?'

'Of course they paid. He staggered back to his ship with his pockets stuffed with gold. However, I have no such expectations of you. I'd be happy if you won the price of a good dinner for the two of us.'

§71

Troy wandered. He could see why his dad had warned him of the danger of 'awe', it would be easy and it would be a misperception. The casino made Versailles and Les Trianons look understated – tempting as it might be, awe did not strike. This was the lurid fantasy of a king layered with the even more lurid fantasies of commerce. It might look like a royal palace, but it was also, Troy felt, tacky. Tacky and unreal. As unreal as a film set. As unreal as the sets of the silent epics of his childhood, like *Ben-Hur* and dozens of others that had never lodged in his memory. It came almost as a surprise to pass through the doors and not find the struts and props that supported the papier-mâché façade. Inside it was overblown, grandiose to the hilt – too many columns, too much onyx, too much stained glass – and too many characters who looked like leftovers from Central Casting.

He watched roulette for a while. Indeed, gambling for the first time struck him as a spectator sport – as many people watching as playing. And he concluded his father was right. No skill was required and none possible. All the same, the looks of concentration and calculation on the faces of the players showed that they believed in some sort of system. A large woman, wearing a small fortune in diamonds – Troy's immediate mnemonic for her was Mrs van Hopper from *Rebecca* – repeatedly bet the same number and repeatedly lost. And no doubt she thought of it as her lucky number.

Troy moved on to chemin-de-fer. The game his dad had recommended. The old man had said 'it's like that English game you appear to have learnt furtively in your schooldays in some act of adolescent rebellion behind the bike sheds'. 'What,' Troy had replied, 'Conkers?' 'No,' said his father, 'Pontoon ... vingt-et-un, pay twenty-one ... whatever.' Only when Troy sat down at a chemin-de-fer table in one of the casino's inner rooms did he realise it wasn't exactly like pontoon, and that, really, he hadn't a clue what he was doing. And that now people were watching him.

The shoe was in the hands of an Englishman of about Troy's own age. Unlike Troy he seemed completely at his ease, drawing on a distinctive custom-made cigarette with three gold rings, gunmetal case and lighter set out like props on the table, staring back at his opponents with unflinching self-confidence, a lock of unruly hair curling over one eye like a comma – he looked to Troy like a raffish version of Hoagy Carmichael, an effect at once dispelled by the cruel twist of his lips as he mocked Troy openly for putting down a jack and an ace in the fond illusion that he had won.

'Learn the rules, old man,' he said. 'We're not playing for ha'pennies in a London pub. Face cards don't count.'

With that he passed the shoe, scooped up his winnings, tossed a hefty chip to the croupier and left. Troy was tempted to follow, give up and go to bed early with a good book. He'd still got most of the money his dad had given him – that alone would buy dinner for two. Just as he put a hand on the table to lever himself up, there was a swish of silk and the chair the Englishman had vacated was taken by a woman. It was the same woman he had seen on the train, the simple black suit replaced by an equally simple, but rather daring black dress, and the hair that had been so neatly tucked up into a pillbox hat now bouncing off her shoulders in thick black ringlets. She was a study in monochrome. A fantasy in black and white. And she was talking to him. Softly, leaning in to keep her words private.

'What a snob! Don't judge the English by him. We're not all Lord Muck, you know.'

'I am English,' Troy replied, and before he could explain further, the table was betting again. He wasn't even sure she had heard him.

'Five is the sticky point,' she whispered. 'Simple maths really. Every-thing comes down to numbers in the end. You're aiming for nine. Five and four make nine. Double figures, say sixteen, only count the last digit so really you've only got six, which is not much better than five. And what Snobby forgot to tell you is tens don't count either.'

Troy watched a painfully thin, deeply lined old man – so many old Englishmen seemed to end up looking like Ernest Thesiger in *The Bride of Frankenstein* – lose twice, and then heard the woman say '*Banco.* My friend will play.'

The young Arab – more Charles Boyer than Valentino – holding the shoe dealt two cards. The croupier scooped them up on his giant fish slice and set them in front of Troy. Then the banker dealt himself two, face up – an ace and a seven. More than enough to stick at. Troy looked at his own hand – the ten of clubs, the five of hearts. Five was what he had, all he had, if the woman's method of calculation was correct.

'I always ask for another card at five,' she whispered, 'because the bank will usually do the same. You're simply evening up the odds.'

'The bank already has eight,' Troy said.

'Just play,' she said.

The banker was looking at Troy. A hint of impatience. Troy hesitated. The banker had won twice in a row. The pot had tripled to two million francs. He had enough to cover the bet and no more. And he needed the maximum to win. Lose this and dinner would be brown bread and dripping.

'Remember,' she said, 'You bet the two million when you said *banco*.'

'I didn't say *banco*. You did.'

'You have, trust me, absolutely nothing to lose.'

'*Suivi*,' Troy said.

The banker slipped a card out of the shoe and turned it face up.

Four of diamonds. Troy hoped he wasn't smirking. More than that he hoped the woman, whoever she was, had got the rules right. One more put-down and he'd feel obliged to leave the table.

'*Huit à la banque. Neuf seulement,*' the croupier said.

Troy turned over his first two cards.

'Well done, M'sieur,' said the banker. 'I can only wish the same muse would whisper in my ear.'

Troy had now amassed in the region of four million. Almost, as he felt, inadvertently.

The woman spoke softly to him, less a whisper now than a confidence.

'Often as not the banker would pass the shoe now, but he can still play another round – if he has the funds that is.'

The banker spoke directly to her.

'Will Madame be playing? The seats are really meant for players not guardian angels.'

She smiled at him, a smile that would have disarmed the Mongol Horde, and tipped her purse out on the table.

'Quite,' she said 'I think our apprentice is *au fait* with the game now. Please, deal me in.'

Then she spoke to Troy again, 'Made quite a killing on the roulette wheel. Only came in with the price of a packet of crisps.'

'So much, he thought, for the mug's game.

The Arab lost with good grace. After the woman took another six million from him, he kissed her hand, thanked her for the pleasure of the game, passed the shoe to the monocled Frenchman on his left – a

Gallic Oliver Hardy as Troy saw him – and quit the table.

'I think we should follow, don't you,' she said to Troy. 'I don't believe in luck, and I don't believe in pushing it either.'

Coming up the steps to the *caisse* they encountered the Englishman who had been so rude to them – casually tapping another cigarette against the gunmetal case, with all the sang froid that Troy never seemed to be able to muster.

'If I'd known we had lady luck at the table, I'd've stayed for the second house,' he said, slightly sibilant on his s's – 'shecond houshe' – all but leering at the woman, utterly ignoring Troy.

'Bastard,' she said, kicked him on the shin, and left him hopping on one leg.

'Bastard, I know his sort. Sort of man who thinks you're just waiting to be tumbled into bed.'

Out on the front steps, beyond the papier-maché façade once more. A large wad of notes in his pocket, a larger one in her handbag.

She said, 'Where are you staying?'

'At the Paris, just across the square.'

'Me too. But of course ... I'm sharing a room.'

'I'm not. I have a suite to myself.'

'That settles it then, doesn't it?'

Crossing the square, she said, 'Did you notice the waxworks?'

'Waxworks?'

'All those people who looked like characters from the old silent films. As though the place preserved them and rolled them out on special occasions.'

'Yes. I noticed. What do you think the special occasion is?'

She slipped an arm through his. It was a small but startling gesture. It should not have been. She had taken possession nearly an hour ago. He looked. She was his height. The same black hair, the same dark eyes. A looking glass.

'Oh ...' she replied, 'I think we're both about to find out. Now, did you spot Fatty Arbuckle?'

'I thought he was Oliver Hardy?'

'Oh no ... far too jowly, and besides you never see Ollie without Stan.'

§ 72

One of the many things a boy is not taught in an English public school is what to do with a full condom. Or even how to do it. What is the post-coital protocol? Men buy condoms in an all-male-world – the barber shop. Once used they seemed to Troy to default to that all-male world. There seemed no place for a woman in an awkward moment or more made up of smelly latex and cooling semen. Does one discreetly head for the bathroom – always supposing there is one? Does one perch on the side of the bed, peel the damn thing off a detumescent member, knot it with one of the many knots learnt in the boy scouts and fling it carelessly to the floor with the air of a man-of-the-world who has sexual relations daily and doesn't care that the woman might be watching?

The woman was watching. One hand buried in the mass of black ringlets, her upper body weight on one elbow. Troy could see her out of the corner of his eye. The teat of the condom hung on his cock, opaque and glutinous like a strand of toadspawn.

'Am I your first?'

Troy said nothing.

'You can tell me, you know.'

'Did it feel that way?'

'Just a bit.'

Then the other hand snaked out, plucked the condom off him and let it drop. The hand regripped his cock.

'Everybody has to start somewhere.'

'You're not the first. Really you're not.'

The hand began to work life back into him.

'But there haven't been many?'

'No there haven't.'

'Well,' she said, 'let's get some practice in shall we?'

After the third bout, he was exhausted. There was nothing left to come, and he hoped she had wrought some pleasure out of him. He hoped even more she did not want a fourth.

Now she seemed coolly chatty. Not all passion spent perhaps, but all urgency gone from her voice. She lay on her side, stroking his thigh with one hand – it seemed perilously like affection – musing far from idly.

'Who was the old man you were sitting with on the train?'

'My father.'

'Oh ... I see ... well, I don't really ... what language was that the two of you were speaking?'

'Russian. My father's an emigré from an old revolution.'

'Ah, I get it ... he's sort of an Alex Troy figure.'

'No, not sort of.'

'How not sort of?'

'He *is* Alex Troy.'

She propped herself up on both elbows. Belief and disbelief competing for the expression in her eyes. A quick shake of her head as though clearing cobwebs from the mind, her hair brushing his chest, only to be swept back again with the upward jerk of her chin.

'You know I think I've been rather stupid.'

'How so?'

'Did you not recognise the man I'm travelling with?'

'No more than you recognised my father. I just assumed ...'

'Assumed what, Mr Troy? Assumed what?'

'That ...'

'That I was a gold-digger and he was my sugar daddy?'

'Yes, that's pretty well word for word what I thought.'

'Well, half-right, he is my sugar daddy. Of course, he is. It's just that I'm not digging for gold. And he's also my boss by-the-bye.'

'Boss of what?'

'He runs the low-temperature physics lab at Cambridge. I am, as you can readily deduce I'm sure, a low-temperature research physicist.'

'Chilled to the marrow already.'

'Quite. But there's more. He's also a whatnot to a politician.'

'Whatnot?'

'Advisor, consultant, expert. That sort of thing.'

'And his name?'

'Gustav Lindfors.'

Now Troy felt stupid. He should have recognised Lindfors as surely as she should have known his father.

'Ah, Churchill's expert on the price of chewing gum and the level of German jackboot production.'

'Quite. As you say, a bit of a Poo Ba ... a Lord-High-Everything-

Else. And we've both been stupid. Your father is here to meet Lindfors. And they got us both out of the way by giving us a tanner each and sending us to the flicks, didn't they?'

'Some flick. But as you say, there's more. They're not here to meet one another, they could have done that in London. On the train they ignored each other. It was as though they'd never met. No, they're here to meet a third party. And you and I are the cover.'

'Bloody hell. Wonder who? Not – !!?!?'

'Of course not . . . he's rather busy invading Poland.'

'Then who?'

'Do you really need to know?'

'Need be damned. I want to know. I thought I was going to Monte for a dirty weekend . . .'

'I think you'll find you're having that right now.'

'. . . Not to be his . . . his . . . fig-leaf.'

'Well, my dad's not leaving any clues.'

She flopped down on top of him. Hunger struck.

'I could eat a horse.'

'Don't ask. They'd probably serve you one,' Troy replied. 'But I have a better idea. An old favourite of my father's. Champagne with scrambled eggs and crisp bacon. Perfect after-midnight munching.'

'Sounds rather sybaritic to me.'

'Even more so when prepared by someone else and consumed in bed. Let me call room service.'

'OK. I believe you now. You have done this before.'

A quarter of an hour later there was a tap at the door. Troy answered it in his dressing gown – his, as yet, nameless lover discreet behind the bathroom door – and the waiter wheeled in a trolley. Veuve Clicquot in an ice bucket, bacon and eggs under silver hoods. Standing in the doorway to sign for the meal, Troy saw the next door down on the opposite side open. A small man in a grey suit emerged from his father's suite. The waiter and the stranger passed each other in the corridor, just as the woman, wrapped in a bath towel peeked over his shoulder.

'Don't dawdle – the smell's driving me wild.'

'Look,' said Troy, and she leaned out.

'Do you know him?'

'Not from the back I don't.'

'He just came out of my father's room.'

Then the door to his father's suite opened again, and Lindfors stood in the doorway, speaking softly to a face still hidden in the room, and she ducked back with a muttered, 'Oh hell . . . close the door.'

She dropped the towel and ran naked for the bed. Troy closed the door. She lay back like an Ingres odalisque, feet crossed at the ankle, one arm raised high across the pillow to set both breasts quivering.

'Indulge me, Mr Troy. Indulge me.'

Troy lifted the lids on the dorm feast.

'You like close shaves, don't you? You like danger.'

'Bloody hell. Who doesn't? Don't tell me you don't.'

'I'm . . . not indifferent . . . that's not the word . . . but I take it as an occupational hazard.'

'My God . . . I'd never have guessed. You're in the army!'

Troy shoved a piece of crisp, smoked bacon into her mouth.

'No comment.'

'Alright, then the RAF or the Navy . . .?'

Troy twisted the bottle of Veuve Clicquot and eased the cork out with a gentle hiss.

'Still no comment.'

§73

Troy and his father breakfasted together. He scarcely heard a word his father said for the roaring of last night's woman through his veins. She started off somewhere in his groin, sped to the head and all but deafened him to the outside world.

She passed him, almost as closely as she had done on the train, arm in arm with Lindfors. She did not acknowledge him, Lindfors and Alex ignored each other just as steadily. It was, Troy thought, just a bit farcical. But whilst he spoke not, he thought too soon.

As they left the dining room the other man, the 'Third Man' as Troy had come to think of him, was descending the staircase from the mezzanine. He was dressed outlandishly, like a parody of an English country gentleman, tweedy plus fours and a matching, far-from-fetching baggy jacket. The factotum behind him lugged a set of golf clubs. Alex and he passed without a word.

Now, Troy thought, they were even dressing for a farce.

§74

All farces involve a bedroom as a necessary setting. A farce is incomplete without one. If at all possible the protagonist should lose his trousers.

More scrambled eggs, more crispy bacon, more chilled Veuve Clicquot. No trousers. A second night together.

'You do realise I don't know your name?'

'You do realise you haven't asked? And besides, all I know is Troy, Mr Troy.'

Troy bit on the bullet. Toted the burden his parents had lumbered him with in a fit of madness one day in 1915. Felt her fingertips trail lazily down his chest.

'Frederick.'

Her hand stopped in its tracks.

'Frederick. You mean you're a Fred? I don't do it with Freds!'

'Quite. As an old school chum of mine put it, "You can ruin anything with the word Fred".'

'What's it to be then, Fred or Frederick?'

'At home I'm Freddie. Anywhere else I find Troy suffices. One syllable is quite enough. And you?'

She was toying with a strand of her hair, head down close to his chest, enunciating slowly, stringing out the word.

'Is . . . a . . . bella.'

Head up, eyes smiling. Mischief.

'Is that three or four syllables?'

'Four, I think, but you can call me Izzy.'

He knew she was lying, but he couldn't care less. Izzy it was. And Izzy Who really didn't matter.

'When are you going back to England?'

'As soon as Lindfors and your father are through. And you?'

'We're going on to Siena. I was wondering . . . when I get back . . . it would be nice to see you again.'

Izzy buried her face in the pillow. A muffled voice said, 'You're making plans. It's been nice. But for God's sake don't make plans.'

§75

Troy decided that he could probably, given the choice, spend every warm evening the calendar had to offer for the rest of his life sitting in the Campo in Siena, with a glass of rich, red Vino Nobile di Montepulciano in one hand – but, then, what choices was he not given? Given the head start in life of being the son of a wealthy man – none of whose children needed employment for its own sake, he had chosen to be a copper and live in the middle of London. In his other hand was *Il Giorno*, with which he struggled and failed. At least pictures, names and titles required no translation. The man on page two was captioned 'Count Ciano', husband of Edda Mussolini, son-in-law of Il Duce and Italian Foreign Minister. He was also the man Troy had seen emerging from his father's room in Monte Carlo. The man he'd seen setting out for the golf course the morning after.

His father was gazing at the palazzo tower on the southern side of the Campo, outlined in burnished gold against a sky so vividly blue Troy could not think of an appropriate shade to describe it. It was a reverie of sorts, the sort all the Troy men were prone to. It seemed a shame to break it, but he would do it all the same.

He put down the paper and tapped on Ciano's picture.

'You could have told me,' he said.

Alex only glanced at the photograph before resuming his gaze into the night sky, his Campari and soda untouched on the table.

'Knowledge of this kind can be a burden. I merely chose not to burden you.'

'I know anyway.'

'You spied on me?'

'He came out of your room about two in the morning. I didn't recognise him. And I saw him setting out the next morning, looking like an extra in *Laurel and Hardy Go Golfing*. I didn't recognise him then either.'

'Let us hope you were not alone in your ignorant condition, my boy. Golf was meant to be his . . . what is the word . . .?'

'Cover?'

'Cover? Quite. I was thinking of something a little more elaborate . . . the red herring . . . he is golf crazy and golf boring after all. Anyone who saw him in Monte might readily have concluded he was there for the golf. There is a British ex-pats' golf course just above the city, on the French side, just as there is in Rome.'

'Why not meet him here?'

'Then everybody would have recognised him.'

'And the real purpose? The real reason you and Lindfors met with him in secret?'

Alex looked at his son at the mention of Lindfors' name, but let it pass. A brief sigh, the merest hint of exasperation and Troy knew the old man was going to tell him.

'To talk. I saw no harm in talking one last time. The lack of talk is how we got into this mess after all. There is still a possibility Italy will stay out of the war. Ciano is not pro-war. Who knows, he may have some influence? He may persuade Mussolini to let Hitler go it alone. I can even see advantages for Hitler in going it alone.'

'Such as?'

'They would benefit from Italian neutrality . . . they would have a trading partner whose ships we would not sink, whose airfields we would not bomb. And as a bonus . . . he would not be called upon to bail out the Italians when they cock up their war – as they surely will.'

'But will Ciano persuade Mussolini not to invade his neighbours . . . to stay out of Greece and the Balkans? Invading Albania was a pretty poor precedent for peace . . . and hardly evidence for them cocking up their war.'

'That is where our talks broke down. But, I still say it was worth the attempt.'

'Hardly a pleasant experience – talking to a fascist, I mean.'

'"Jaw jaw is better than war war" as Winston is apt to say. But he is scarcely the exemplar of his own wisdom – he will not talk to Labour . . . they are little short of Bolsheviks . . . he will not talk to Russia . . . they *are* Bolsheviks . . . he will not talk to rebels in his own party if they do not agree with him almost word for word . . . and for whatever reason he would not talk to Ciano. He sent Lindfors. Whether he sent Lindfors because he knew I would be there, I did not ask. I have known Ciano since the Twenties. I've no idea whether Winston and Ciano have even met and I have not had the occasion to ask. He is not speaking to me and may not again.'

'Since when?'

'Since my editorial on Russia . . . but let us not ruin a beautiful sunset with talk of Mr Churchill. We will be hearing quite enough from him, however indirectly, in the months and years to come.'

'Do you really think this war will last years?'

Alex was gazing at the darkening sky again. He looked at his son, shot him an ancient mariner's fixing glance and said, 'Tomorrow will be beautiful. Why don't we stroll down to the botanical gardens before luncheon, and then perhaps a visit to the Duomo in the afternoon? I believe there is a Donatello of one saint or another.'

Whichever saint Donatello had carved for the cathedral in Siena, Troy never got to see. In the morning at breakfast Alex showed him a telegramme:

FREUD DEAD. FUNERAL TUESDAY. GOLDERS GREEN.

'Would you mind terribly if we missed Amalfi? I would like to be there. It is a chapter in my life. So many chapters lack a sense of an ending. I would like to be there when this one ends.'

Troy did not argue.

§

Under moonlight,
infectious moonlight,
a madman dances.
Smeared in excrement,
naked as nativity,
Lord Carsington dances.

An Interlude

§

March 1940 . . .
London, the Phoney War or thereabouts

While the British Expeditionary Force was still on the Continent, the blast of war seemed scarcely to touch England. The bureaucracy did. It was a time of organisation and regulation, a time of the amassing of paperwork – usually referred to as 'bum fodder' – a time of mass evacuation, of recruitment, of innovation and wild suggestion. Everyone had ideas to help with the war effort, from the shoolboy designing giant tank-carrying submarines on his school jotter, to the man who wrote to *The Times* suggesting that the way to be seen in the blackout was to carry a white Pekinese dog. Some suggestions were not so daft – growing one's own vegetables for instance.

Tite Street might be fashionable. It was once, fifty years earlier, home to Oscar Wilde and might therefore be notorious as well as fashionable. At the end of Tite Street is a small green Chelsea square, Tedworth Gardens. Shrubs, flowerbeds, a patch of grass, the odd tree, lots of railings, the unfortunate residue of visits by errant dogs . . . that sort of thing. One breezy afternoon late in the spring of 1940, a big man – not a fat man or a stout man or a portly man, at this stage merely a big man – was ripping up shrubs and breaking turf in Tedworth Gardens. His employer, home on leave and still in uniform, had come to the square in search of him, somewhat exasperated with his gentleman's gentleman. But, as he had long learnt, you get nowhere with this particular gentleman's gentleman by showing exasperation. So he asked simply, 'Busy, are you?'

'Wossit look like?'

'It looks to me as though you are a one-man pagan horde vandalising the flowerbeds and lawn of a rather pretty London square.'

'Bugger off, then.'

'No, honestly, what are you doing?'

'I'm teaching me Aunt Fanny how to knit balaclavas for fuzziwuzzis. Wossit look like I'm doing, yer berk? I'm getting a patch ready for me spuds. 'Cos tomorrow a bloke from Fullers' brewery is bringing me a load of horse's doins. Always pays to get yer spuds in before Good Friday. That's what my old dad used to say anyway. And as I means to grow King Edwards, the sooner they're underground the better. I got some nice second earlies too, Edzell Blue, as nice a tater as you've ever got yer choppers into.'

'Oh, I see,' said his employer not seeing, and wishing there was someone around to press trousers and iron shirts and generally get him back into civvies for a weekend as a free man.

The big man reached into the back pocket of his trousers, and thrust a Ministry of Food pamphlet into the man's hand.

'See for yourself.'

'"Dig for Victory with Potato Pete".'

'That's the little fellow, green hat, hobnail boots looks a bit like a spud with legs.'

'Yes, I can see that.'

'There's another bloke, he's based on a carrot he is. He's a laugh too. I don't know how they think 'em up.'

'Yes. It's alright. I get the picture. I meant . . . will you be long?'

'Why are you askin' me? Try askin' old Adolf. I shall be diggin' for victory for the duration of hossitilities. I won't be the only one neither. There's Lady Diana from Tite Street and an old codger, Admiral Wotsisface, from Radnor Walk, and me. Yours Truly. We's'll have a patch each and a hut between us. Come back in a fortnight you won't recognise the place.'

'Ah . . . quite . . . yes . . . I see . . . but . . . could you see your way clear to doing the odd bit of valeting before peace breaks out? At the moment I would appear to be a gentleman without a gentleman.'

'Course, old cock. Is it yer socks again? Just stick 'em on the pile. I'll be doin' a spot of darning once the nights start drawing in.'

'Nights drawing in? It's only March. You won't be planting potatoes until November?'

'No cock, by November I'll be feeding the peelings to the pig.'

'Pig? What pig?'

'That pig.'

He wasn't sure how he could have missed the pig, but once pointed out to him it was undeniable that a large white pig had fixed him with its beady eye from its chosen spot under a rose bush.

'You can't be serious. This is . . . this is . . . Chelsea.'

'Just watch me, old cock.'

The gentleman departed, doubtless to darn his own socks. We will not see him again. The gentleman's gentleman remained, back bent over his spade, digging, as he put it, for victory. Of him we shall hear more, but not for three or four years.

II

Little Vienna

§76

Onions, Troy had learnt, was not one to count his chickens. An arrest would often as not result in a 'Well done, lad' – or worse, if no confession was forthcoming, a 'D'ye think you can make it stick in court?' It was, Troy concluded, a modesty he would do well to share. He knew when he nicked Jack Seaton for the murder of his brother-in-law in the January of 1940 that he could make it stick, confession or not, and any tendency to smugness would always be wiped out with the judge's wearing of the black cap – which was no kind of cap, more like a black silk handkerchief – and the majesty of the law reduced to the ritual mechanics of death. Hence, after a morning court appearance one day early in June, the verdict 'guilty', the ritual so enacted, Troy, finding himself with no appetite for lunch, was in his office when Onions appeared in his doorway.

'I heard,' he said.

Troy said nothing.

''Nother feather in your cap.'

'Another one for Tom Pierrepoint to breathe whisky fumes over before he ties the noose. Another body in quicklime.'

Onions looked at him quizically, took the seat by the bleached and blackened bars of the gas fire – turned off by written instruction since the end of April and not on again until October, regardless of the English weather – took out his Woodbines and lit up a cigarette.

'I wouldn't have thought you'd be much bothered by that. He had it coming after all.'

'I don't think I am much bothered. I became part of the business of death the day you brought me to the Yard. But I'd be less than human if I didn't feel a sting at sending another man to his grave.'

Onions ignored the obvious and said, 'Business of Death? I reckon you read too many novels.'

Troy said nothing.

'Have you got your teeth into another case?'

'No,' Troy said. 'I hesitate to say this, but once I sling Seaton's file back in the cabinet there's not a lot on my desk.'

'Good,' said Onions. 'Good, good.'

He drew deeply on his cigarette and slowly exhaled a plume of smoke.

'How do you fancy a spell with the Branch?'

Troy didn't, but this was hardly the moment to say so. Special Branch were, in Troy's opinion, legalised thugs – door-kickers, head-crackers all – and to be in the Branch required no police skill other than a blind obedience to orders, which in the case of the Branch came not from Onions or the Metropolitan Police Commissioner but from MI5.

'I doubt I've any talents they'd want,' Troy said more in hope than expectation.

'Oh, but you do. Local knowledge.'

'They want me to police Hampstead?'

'Stepney.'

'Stepney?'

'The order's gone out. We're rounding up all the Category C aliens. C means mostly harmless buggers with the misfortune not to have their mitts on a British passport. Germans, Austrians, some Eyties . . . lots of 'em in the East End . . . lots of 'em Jewish, I shouldn't wonder. The view from on high is that rounding up the Bs last month was a bit of a pig's ear and it's thought best if we put men in charge who've been there, been around a bit, worn out a bit of shoe leather . . . rather than a paddy wagon full of Branch blokes bussed in for the raid.'

'In other words, you want me to go back to Stepney and nick innocent people whom I got to know as a beat bobby?'

One more drag and exhale, then the fag was stubbed out in the otherwise pristine ashtray sitting on the tiles in the hearth.

'I knew you'd get the picture. You'll be working to Ernest Steerforth. D'ye know him?'

'No.'

'He'll be the Chief Inspector in charge. You'll be working with another local. Inspector Stilton. Walter Stilton. D'ye know him?'

'Of course. He's an old pal of George Bonham's. Lives just around the corner from George. I know him . . . but I've not had much to do with him.'

'He's one of the best. Take it from me. You and Walter report to Steerforth tonight. Six o'clock, back at your old nick.'

§77

Out on the coast, in the seaside village of Burnham-on-Crouch, much the same conversation was taking place.

Squadron Leader Orlando Thesiger had the task of interrogating any refugees from occupied Europe who landed on the North Sea coast anywhere between Southend and Harwich. The short description of his job was 'Spycatcher'. In this he was assisted by both Military Intelligence in the shape of a lanky, laconic guards officer, Captain Charlie Leigh-Hunt, and by Special Branch in the shape of a rotund, robust trench-erman, Inspector Walter Stilton.

Walter Stilton prided himself on his German. It was the one positive thing he had salvaged from the Great War, an event otherwise viewed by him, as by so many of its veterans, as a fiasco. As a married man with children, Stilton would have been low on the list for conscription, but as a patriot he had answered Lord Kitchener's call to arms and volunteered for the London Rifle Brigade, the 5th Battalion, commonly known as the Queen's Westminster Rifles. In 1915 Lord Kitchener had needed him. It had seemed almost personal. In 1916 he was thrust into battle in the bloodiest baptism of all – the Somme. He had been lucky. He was one of the few who lived. A few scrapes and scratches, a minor flesh wound to the upper left arm that had missed both bone and artery and he was captured. Captured to sit out the rest of the war in Cottbus POW camp in Prussia – a *Kriegsgefangenenlager* fifty miles beyond Berlin, about as far from the Western front as he could be without actually being on the Eastern front. Cottbus had thrived. He had not felt harshly treated. He had enough to eat and joined an active Amateur Dramatic Society, playing Lady Bracknell in *The Importance of Being Earnest*. He had read more than at any other time in his life. But acting and reading alone could not fill the hours – so he had sat down with his guards, decent enough blokes, he thought, like himself that bit older than the average soldier, and learnt German from them. By the time of his repatriation at Christmas 1918, he was fluent. He had returned to his old job as a policeman, fathered more children, moved up the ranks at the Yard, transferred to the Special Branch – and found all but no use for his German. Until about six months ago, when the Branch had assigned him to be the hands and feet of Squadron Leader Thesiger in MI5. It seemed to be the perfect job. The arrest powers of a London bobby allied to a command of the German language. Who better to trail after spies? And who knew how many spies there were going to be in the wake of the fall of France? It had been low key, so far, almost inactive at times, but it was all in the preparation, Stilton thought, in being ready for the moment when the moment might come. And it was the perfect job.

Stilton wondered about the perks of the job. Might they in fact be just liberties? Thesiger hardly ever seemed to wear full uniform. When they had all set out for Burnham in the winter to set up the unit he had favoured green corduroy trousers, black wellingtons and his RAF blouse. Today, flaming June, was clearly the morning after the night before. Thesiger had been up to town, got back late and had worked through the morning in evening dress, bow tie hanging loose, studs popped. The concessions to uniform were, Stilton concluded, the scuffed RAF-issue shoes and the pale blue braces. The peaked cap sat in his in-tray – but Stilton had never seen him wear that.

Thesiger had sent for both Stilton and Leigh-Hunt and was tut-tutting to himself as he leafed through a sheaf of papers and they sat waiting – Stilton looking idly around the room, Leigh-Hunt even more idly jingling the coins in his pocket.

'I'm not happy about this, really I'm not.'

'Not happy about what, old man?'

Leigh-Hunt never used ranks. Not once had Stilton heard him address Thesiger as 'sir'.

'I have to let Walter go.'

'What?' Leigh-Hunt and Stilton said together.

'Don't panic, chaps. It isn't permanent. Better not be anyway. Just when I thought we'd got the team up and running . . . but the Branch want Walter back in the East End for a spell.'

Thesiger put the letter flat on his desk, looked straight at Stilton.

'You don't mind do you, Walter?'

'Mind, sir? It's not for me to mind. But as you say, I thought we'd just got up and running . . . and now we've no troops on the Continent and Jerry's overrun it . . . we'll have our work cut out. Everyone who can nick a rowing boat in Belgium or Holland will do it . . . and Jerry'll put spies in among 'em sure as eggs are eggs.'

'Quite,' said Thesiger at this brief summary of what they all knew.

'But it won't be for long. They want you to help with the internment of enemy aliens. You do know London, you speak German and you've probably more experience of working with foreigners than nine out of ten coppers. They're putting together a three-man team to take charge. You'll answer to Chief Inspector Steerforth . . .'

Stilton realised he had winced slightly at the name, and hoped Thesiger hadn't noticed. Steerforth was a good copper, but was also Stilton's idea of a 'bit of a stickler' and a 'pain in the arse'.

'. . . And you'll have under you a sergeant, name of Troy, Frederick Troy . . . who is some sort of wunderkind at the Yard.'

'I've met Troy, sir.'

If he'd let his feelings about Steerforth show, Stilton wouldn't give a flicker over Troy – of whom his personal opinion was 'a bit wet behind the ears'.

'Me too,' Leigh-Hunt chipped in. 'We were at school together. Matter o'fact, he's my oldest friend. Do give him my best, won't you, Walter?'

It was at moments like this that Stilton always failed to summon up the 'one nation' feeling that he knew was the only patriotic position in wartime. It was bollocks and he knew it, and the old school tie always yanked the old class issues out of whatever box he had dutifully crammed them into. There might be pleasure in this assignment, but he doubted it, and given a choice between catching enemy spies in the company of these two toffs, whose talents he respected, and rounding up the poor, beleaguered immigrants of Stepney with a toff whose talents he didn't much respect . . . then Burnham-on-Crouch won hands down. On the plus side, being back in Stepney meant well-rounded platefuls of his wife's cooking and a well-rounded bedful of his well-rounded wife.

'Fine, sir,' he said simply.

'Okey-dokey,' said Thesiger with a flippancy that Stilton could never quite get used to. 'Six o'clock, Leman Street Police Station. And, Walter, don't worry, old man . . . we'll still be here when you get back.'

§78

They stood in Troy's old office at Leman Street, cooling their heels. Troy hadn't set eyes on Inspector Stilton in a while. He hadn't known him well in his Stepney days, although he was always a 'figure-on-the-Green', big, fat even, moustachioed, friendly. But Stilton was Branch and it was Branch policy not to mix. But for George Bonham, he doubted he'd be on more than nodding terms with the man. Bonham and Walter went back at least as far as 1910, and he rather thought George had known Mrs Stilton a hell of a lot longer. Walter was a northerner – another 'immigrant' just like Stanley Onions . . . big and bluff and Derbyshire . . . but lacking in the machiavellian streak that made Troy and his boss so alike and so wary of one another. Walter was, by common consent of those that knew him, 'a good bloke'. You'd prop up a bar with Walter Stilton. You'd never do that with Stanley Onions. And if you did, Stan would always have a hidden motive.

Stilton took out a cased silver pocket watch from his waistcoat, popped the lid and looked at the time.

'What do you make it, Mr Troy?'

Troy pushed up the sleeve on his right arm.

'Six thirty. I think we can call this the privilege of rank, sir.'

'Indeed we can, lad. And we're going to be on the same team, call me Walter. It's Walter unless there's brass around.'

Brass appeared. Steerforth burst in – a diminutive figure in a tasteless, ill-fitting brown suit – slapped a full briefcase on the desk, set his hat next to it – all the pretence and palaver of man-in-a-hurry. Troy knew at once he was not going to like Chief Inspector Steerforth nor he Troy. Onions would never do this, it was his habit to pass off the important almost lackadaisically – to seize the attention of his subordinates by a slow deliberation – the odd bout of temper notwithstanding. He'd never bother with this 'I'm a very busy man' routine.

'Right. I don't have a lot of time to waste.'

A sheaf of papers was pulled from the briefcase and all but thrown down in front of Stilton.

'We're stuck with this. Rounding up a bunch of Yids and Krauts. Ought to be kids' stuff. Waste of Branch time. God knows, we've done it before. But ... there are a few do-gooders in parliament whingeing about the hows and whys. So there's two ends to play off against the middle. There's a quota and there's a time limit. I don't care about the pace, suit yourselves. Just get everyone on that list collared by the end of the month. And the other end is ... some of these buggers have been here a while. Let's just avoid any letters written to MPs, shall we? I don't want to hear a peep from the Commissioner. So if you have to get heavy, just make sure it's with someone who doesn't know enough English to do anything about it. You have to thump some bugger, make sure nobody sees you.

'Now you two are in charge – ask for all the paddy wagons you need. Just get this lot carted off. Collar the lot. Some names have a destination against them. Most don't. There'll be a bus to Lingfield race course every morning from outside the nick, and another to St Pancras for the ones going north. After that they're not our problem And I wish to God they weren't now.

'Now if you've no questions ...'

He stared at Troy and Stilton, daring them to speak.

'... I've got bigger fish to fry.'

'No sir,' Stilton said calmly and politely. 'No questions.'

'Right.'

Steerforth grabbed his case and hat. He'd not been in the room five minutes. He turned in the door, looked at Troy with the first hint of acknowledgement in his eyes.

'You're Troy, right?'

'Yes, sir.'

'From Stanley Onions' team?'

'Yes, sir.'

'One o'them Troys?'

'That too, sir.'

'Fine. Just remember. This is the Branch. It's rank that counts on this team, not privilege.'

Troy made no answer. None was expected. It had been an audience with the headmaster. Steerforth banged down the corridor, a small man trying for a large presence. A weasel wanting to be a fox.

Stilton picked up the sheaf of papers off the desk, a dozen or so pages, double-spaced.

'Do you think, sir, that we just got shafted?'

'I do, lad. And like I said, it's Walter.'

'Do you think we'll never see the Chief Inspector again?'

'We won't be that lucky.'

Stilton turned a few pages, sucked air like a plumber offering an estimate and said, 'Y'know, lad, I don't feel much like disturbing the evening meals of "Yids and Krauts" tonight. What say we go down the Brickie's Arms and go over the list with a pint or two in our hands?'

§79

The Bricklayer's Arms stood at the corner of Hannibal Road and Redman's Road. A stonesthrow from Stepney Green, and roughly halfway between Stilton's house in Jubilee Street and George Bonham's flat in Union Place. Troy had almost grown used to the idea of having a 'local' during his time as a beat bobby, but could never quite get used to the idea of a public house in the first place. To him they were grim and joyless, and the explanation for this no doubt lay in matters of class. He'd known his presence as a copper take the fun out of any pub. Given that the Brickie's was frequented by two local coppers anyway, the job alone would not stun *this* pub to silence. But he'd known his accent do that. A few sentences in received pronunciation and voices would hush and heads would turn. Or maybe it was the landlord – Eric the Grim. A northerner, too stingy ever to redecorate, hence the pub had long ago assumed a permanent nicotine hue. The only splash of colour came from the two union jacks, either side of a portrait of Winston Churchill over the bar. Troy was prepared to bet that the portrait had only been up since Dunkirk. He tried to remember who Eric had had in the place of honour before Churchill. He rather thought it had been the exiled King Edward VIII. Or was it Gracie Fields? Eric was as likely to put a musical comedy star in the place of honour as he was a king or a prime minister. And if a nag on which he'd bet five bob each way came in before the British Army next won anything, then Troy had no doubt that Winston would be replaced by the winner of the 2.30 ... the 3.30 ... at New-market ... Redcar ... Sandown Park.

Stilton brought drinks from the bar. Troy went over the papers Steerforth had left them. An alphabetical list of the flotsam and jetsam of Europe, wave upon wave of refugees going back, he guessed, to the turn of the century, now beached in the East End of London – a list that some dull mind in Whitehall had assembled into a potential Fifth Column. Bum fodder.

'Oh hell,' said Troy.

'What is it?'

'I've just got to the Js. Jakobson. 11a White Horse Lane.'

Stilton supped and thought for a moment.

'Funny. I don't think I know a Jakobson in White Horse Lane. I know a couple of Jakobsons, but none in White Horse Lane. There's a family in the Commercial Road, and another in Ben Jonson road. But I don't know of any in White Horse Lane.'

'Well, Abel Jakobson, which is what we've got here, is the name over Billy Jacks' shop in the Mile End Road, and 11a White Horse Lane is where he lives.'

'Odd. I thought Billy was as English as me. What nationality does it give?'

'German. Born Danzig, 1898. Admitted 1902.'

'What? Billy?'

'It's here in black and white.'

Stilton mused.

'I think I get your drift.'

'Quite. Which of us wants to go round and tell Billy Jacks he's nicked.'

'Worse, lad. Which of us wants to go round and tell him he's German. I've known Billy thirty years. Since he was a lad, and he's always had "Light Blue Touch Paper and Stand Well Back" tattooed onto his forehead. As they say in these parts . . . he'll do his nut.'

'Worse . . . he'll write to his MP. If anyone can make Mr Steerforth's nightmare come true, it's Billy.'

Stilton thought again.

'Let's bump him down the list a bit. Leave him till later, and try and give him a bit of notice.'

'We give him notice, who's to say he won't put pen to paper?'

'Do you really care about that?'

'Not a damn.'

'Me neither. Billy may be the most irascible bugger on the Green, but he's also what's called a pillar of the community. Chamber of Commerce, Parochial Committees, that sort of malarkey. I bet he's in the Rotary Club or summat like that. Let's show him a modicum of respect.'

'Does the Rotary Club admit Jews?'

'Haven't the foggiest. But . . . let's cut him some slack. Let's put off that encounter as long as we can. God knows we'll catch enough abuse doing this without him going off like a Roman candle.'

Troy pretended to drink his half of bitter. He couldn't abide beer – he accepted or bought it in the cause of sociability and usually managed to leave most of it unnoticed.

However – they weren't going unnoticed. Over at the bar Bonham was in conversation with a young woman whose head turned every few seconds to look at Stilton. Titian-red hair bouncing off the collar of a greenish military style macintosh, all epaulettes and buttons. It seemed to Troy there were too many shades of green – the green of her eyes, like wine bottles, the combat green of her mac . . . the lurid tint of green cordial in her gin and lime.

'That young woman's been looking at you ever since we got in,' he said.

'Doubt it,' Stilton said.

'She's looking away now.'

'First off, you're thirty years younger'n me – I'll bet it's you she's looking at. Second off, she's my eldest daughter, our Katherine.'

It was odd that Troy had never set eyes on her before. If he had, he would surely have remembered? Kitty Stilton had gone through Hendon a year ahead of him and left a fierce reputation for outspokenness and tenacity in her wake. After Hendon she had asked for a posting 'up West' and got it. Stilton read his mind.

'Must say, I'm surprised you don't recognise her. Mind, last few years she's had her own place in Covent Garden. Doesn't treat Stepney like home any more. I can see why . . . her mother can't.'

Now both George and Kitty Stilton were looking their way. Bonham had a hand in the air, pointing towards a side table where two other men were setting out dominoes.

'Do you fancy a game, Sergeant Troy?' Stilton said.

'I'll be fine where I am,' Troy replied.

Troy didn't fancy a game. Troy fancied Kitty Stilton. Kitty Stilton was a stunner. Fat chance.

Stilton joined Bonham. For a minute or so Troy and Kitty simply looked at one another. Troy wondered at what point in the scale of decency looking became staring, then she picked up her gin and lime, walked over, put a hand on the back of Stilton's chair and said, 'My dad not coming back?'

Troy said nothing.

'Then you won't mind if I sit here, will you?'

She slipped off the macintosh – Troy had thought it unnecessary, given the weather – and he realised its purpose. Kitty was still in uniform, the blue-black of the Metropolitan Police Force – three bold stripes on each arm. He'd have worn a mac too rather than go for a quiet drink dressed like that.

His first words to Kitty were, 'Congratulations. I hadn't heard.'

'I got me own station. Bow Street. First and only woman station sergeant in the Met. It'll be in the gazette next month.'

She downed her gin and slid the empty glass across the table to him. 'Just one more. I'm driving.'

Troy obliged, still managed to leave his half of bitter untouched.

'You working with Dad now?'

'Yes.'

'I can't figure out why we haven't met before. I mean, we haven't have we?'

'I'd remember,' he said.

'I mean. I know you by sight. I seen you about when you was a beat bobby.'

'Then you had the advantage of me.'

Kitty thought about this upper-class euphemism, and decided it meant nothing.

'And o'course everybody sort of knew you.'

'They did?'

'O'course . . . toff on the beat. You could hardly expect that not to be good gossip now, could you?'

'I suppose not,' Troy said, and then blundered on with, 'What other gossip was there?'

'Gossip?' she said, as though she herself had not uttered the word. 'Gossip?'

She leaned in closer. Troy had little choice but to follow and join her in this spurious confidentiality, already regretting he'd asked.

'Well, there are those that think a posh voice goes with bein' a bit of a poof. But you're not are you?'

Troy said nothing.

'I know you're not.'

The pause was a killer. Troy was sure he could hear his heart beat.

'Me and Judy Jacks is good friends. So I know.'

Troy's heart sank. 'Big', 'mouth' and 'shut' struggled for space in his thoughts. This was not the conversation to be having with someone he'd met a matter of minutes ago.

'Would you say that was common knowledge?'

'Wot? You an' . . . ?'

'Yes'

'No. I wouldn't. Like I said – me and Judy's good friends.'

'So Billy doesn't know.'

'If Billy knew he'd have clobbered the livin' daylights out of you.'

So he would.

Walter Stilton was right – Billy Jacks was best left as long as they could.

§ 80

Afterwards Troy could remember very little of what they'd said to one another. He'd aimed for small talk, anything small enough to prevent a return to the matter on which she'd kicked off. At the point when she was ready to leave, Troy was only too happy to leave too.

The domino players were still hard at it. Kitty said goodnight to her father, and Stilton looked up at Troy and said, 'An early start, wouldn't you agree, lad? Six thirty, my house?'

'Of course,' Troy said. He hated mornings. He'd catch the Underground home now and get his head down. With any luck he could be asleep by ten o'clock.

Outside Kitty said:

'You got your car, Sergeant?'

'No . . . no . . . I haven't. I came on the Underground. I'll go back the same way. District to Charing Cross, and then it's just a short walk.'

'Where do you live then?'

'Goodwin's Court, just off St Martin's Lane.'

'That's right by me. I got a place in Henrietta Street. I could give you a lift if you like?'

The lift surprised him. An Ariel Square 4, four-cylinder 1000cc motorbike and sidecar, in fire engine red.

'I just got it. I'm thinkin' of unboltin the sidecar, but that can wait till me brothers are home on leave. Meantime, you got a choice, chair or pillion?'

Troy knew he'd feel a fool doing either and muttered something about being quite alright on the Underground. But, as arguments with his Uncle Nikolai had proved in the past, bikers were a species of lunatic not known to take no for an answer. Pressed again, he chose pillion, marginally less silly than sitting in a dolly tub with plastic curtains and being whizzed along at gutter level.

'You just hang on tight and I'll have you home in a jiff.'

He hung on tight. Hands on her waist. A not altogether unpleasant experience.

Kitty stuck just within the speed limits all the way to Trafalgar Square – and Troy could only assume his nervousness had seeped through to her. She pulled up the bike by the rear entrance to Goodwin's Court in Bedforbury.

'O' course . . . without the sidecar I'll be able to let 'er rip.'

'The speed limit in the blackout is twenty miles per hour.'

'Yeah – but we're coppers.'

'Silly me.'

'O' course . . . I could walk home from here,' she said.

'We both could.'

'Yeah, but ain't you gonna stick the kettle on? It isn't even half past nine. It's still light. You can't be thinkin' of callin' it a night when it isn't dark yet. That's what night is. Dark.'

It was irrefutable logic.

Troy left her in the sitting room while he made tea.

'Look through the records,' he said. 'Find something you like.'

Just before the kettle blew he heard the steel twang and wooden creak of the gramophone being wound, and Art Tatum's 'Sweet Lorraine' crackled out of the brass horn. When he got in she was seated on the floor by the unlit fire, shoes off, legs tucked under her. He rather thought she was pulling a face.

'What's up?'

'I put this on 'cos I liked the name of the song . . . you know, girl's name, "sweet" . . . but . . . don't you have any dance bands?'

'Yes. I think you'll find Duke Ellington fits that description, officer.'

She smiled at this, said, 'No ... I mean ... *dance* dance bands. British dance bands. This is ... well you couldn't dance to this could you? I mean it's all twiddles.'

'Actually, they're called *arpeggios* ... it's what Tatum does when he improvises.'

'Eh?'

'Makes it up as he goes along.'

'Makes it up? Then why does he bother with a tune in the first place?'

'It's somewhere to start, I suppose.'

'Still can't dance to it. He doesn't leave you enough of the tune.'

Tatum rippled out. The only sound was the needle orbiting in the final groove. If neither of them stopped it it would do that until the spring wound down.

Troy compromised. Riffled through the records he kept in the cupboard under the stairs – not much listened to any more, but more probably to his guest's taste.

He called out the names of bands from the cupboard door.

'Billy Cotton?'

Someone must have given him that – he would never have gone out and bought it.

'Wot? "Maybe it's Because I'm a Londoner"?'

''Fraid so.'

'Strictly for the mums and dads. It's the sort of stuff my mum plays when she's feelin' sentimental.'

'The Waldorfians?'

'Who's singin' with 'em?'

'Doesn't say. Carrol Gibbons? "Night and Day".'

'The one with Al Bowlly?'

'Yep.'

'Great. Anything with Al would be fine.'

Troy flipped through the pile, and picked out records by Roy Fox and Lew Stone – Al Bowlly had fronted both bands for a while. He found a good half dozen – 'Isn't It Heavenly', 'Just Let Me Look at You', 'My Woman', 'Love is the Sweetest Thing' and 'Fancy Our Meeting'. They weren't to his taste any longer – indeed he wasn't at all sure they ever had been, but when he was eighteen they had been 'all the rage'. Bowlly's voice was not pleasing. He 'crooned', which meant he was one of the new singers whose vocal technique had been developed for the electric microphone. So had Bing Crosby's – the difference was Crosby's voice pleased.

But even Al Bowlly couldn't quite ruin 'Night and Day'. After Kitty had gabbled through her career since Hendon, and they'd played the lesser Bowlly side for side, he put 'Night and Day' on one more time meaning it to cue the evening's end.

It was, he thought, Cole Porter at his best. A song he thought of as starkly romantic – a song delivered without jollity or flippancy – obsessively seductive. Designed to draw you in.

She kissed him. Leaned over and kissed him, halfway through the song. He thought he might be blushing. His response was not half-hearted, but it was inadequate.

She pulled back to look at him. It was getting dark now – time to black out the windows – and whilst he couldn't see for certain, he knew she was staring, big green eyes locked onto his.

'You think I'm a bit previous, don't you?'

Troy had been baffled by her attentiveness. He'd been ready to write the evening off as copper talk – the wish to talk shop with someone who knew the job, but wasn't on the same team. Coppers got that way. It was one reason they spent too much time with one another, and one reason they became such ready bores. Now, he couldn't believe his luck, and lacked the courage of his desire.

'Forward might be the word,' he said.

'But it's not forward if a bloke does it.'

'You're not a bloke.'

'So you noticed?'

She kissed him again. He got the better of his nerves and kissed back.

'That's better. You're not so shy now, are you?'

'Yes I am,' he said truthfully.

'Get used to it, Sergeant Troy. London's full of forward women. Who's gonna wait on a bloke plucking up the nerve or polishing his chat-up lines when we might be blown to kingdom come tomorrow?'

'"The grave's a fine and private place, but none I think do there embrace."'

She'd been poised and pouting, ready to kiss him again. The word 'grave' pulled her up sharply.

'Did you just make that up?'

'No, I wasn't improvising. It's an old English poet called Marvell.'

'How old? Like Shakespeare?'

'Give or take fifty years.'

'We ain't got fifty years. There's a war on.'

She kissed him again. The record spun into its final groove, the needle clicking back and forth – click, schtuck, click, schtuck.

Kitty took it up.

'Don't you know there's a war on – click, schtuck. Don't you know there's a war on – click, schtuck.'

'I noticed that too.'

'Don't you know there's a war on – click, schtuck. Come on, Sergeant Troy. We ain't gonna live forever.'

She stood up, stretched out a hand to him and pulled him to his feet.

'This place does have an upstairs, doesn't it? A bedroom, I mean. That other "fine and private place".'

It was blatant. He'd never heard a woman talk like this before. Women didn't talk like this.

'I'm on early tomorrow,' he bleated, running away from what he wanted one more time. He was being pathetic and he knew it. 'You heard your father. Six thirty, Jubilee Street.'

'I'm not on till noon.'

'Meaning?'

'Tiptoe past the end of the bed and I'll let meself out around ten.'

Blatant.

'Do you always get what you want?'

'Not always, no.'

'But you find it pays to ask.'

'I don't bother with askin'. There's a war on. Haven't you heard? Click, schtuck.'

Blatant.

§ 81

At six thirty in the morning, Troy, never a morning man, felt elated. It was as though he'd been reborn into a better body. He hoped her father did not notice. He hoped the afterglow of sex did not show in his flesh like stigmata. He hoped never to have to own up to last night.

Troy left his Bulinose Morris outside the Stiltons' house in Jubilee Street. Stilton said they'd use his Riley Kestrel.

'You're looking bright and cocky this morning?' he said as they got into the car.

Troy's heart sank. Did he have to say 'cocky'? Surely 'breezy' went better with 'bright'?

'Nothing like a good night's sleep,' he lied.

'Aye, well, I reckon today'll ruin a few nights' sleep for the poor buggers on that list. There are days when I hate this job – far outnumbered by the days when I love it but I wish there were none at all. Now ... who first?'

'Franz Hermann Neuberg. From Dresden. Lodges with a family called Wax in Aylward Street.'

Stilton slipped the Riley into reverse, turned the car around and headed south.

'Do you know Mrs Wax?' he asked.

'No. Do you?'

'Oh yes. If she's taken to Herr Neuberg she'll give us an earful.'

'And if she hasn't?'

'Then she'll like as not pack his bags for him.'

Mrs Wax, stout and fifty-ish, hair tucked under a mesh net, pinny on, slippers bulging bunions, nose bulging veins, folded her arms and stood squarely on the threshold when she saw who had knocked at her door at a quarter to seven in the morning.

'Spit it out, Walter. I'll not make this easy for you.'

'Mornin' Dora. You took a shine to Mr Neuberg then?'

'It's Professor Neuberg to you. He's an educated man. Deserving of a bit of respect.'

'He'll get it, Dora. Now, I need to talk to him. How good's his English?'

'Talk to him? You mean nick 'im, don't you, Walter Stilton?'

'Just ask him to come to the door.'

She turned around and bellowed, 'Professor!'

Troy wondered if it were possible to be quite so loud and show respect at the same time.

'He's havin' his breakfast. Getting ready to go to work. He's at a college up west. You'll have to wait.'

'Could we wait inside?'

'You just want to scrounge a cup o' tea, that's what you want.'

'Well, Dora . . . it's not as if it's rationed is it?'

Troy was amazed at the warmth and charm Stilton put into a simple statement. Like daughter like father. He would never have thought of charm as a Special Branch secret weapon. There was nothing special about the Branch, they were the most ordinary of coppers – but he was beginning to think there was nothing ordinary about Walter.

'It will be, Walter Stilton, you mark my words!'

Her belligerence vanished. She wasn't smiling, she might even be a long way from smiling, but she led them into the back room of the house and told them to sit down.

Troy found himself facing a little man with wisps of white hair spiralling up off his head – standing at the oilclothed table in shirt and braces, a collar half attached to his shirt sticking out like starched wings, paused in a breakfast of poached eggs and toast by Dora Wax's warning roar. He was getting their measure, doing nothing until he knew them for what they were – standing almost to attention, straining, Troy thought, to appear obedient, respectful and compliant. No direct eye contact. A man who'd been arrested before. Troy saw this and clearly Stilton did too.

'It's OK, Professor,' Stilton said, smiling. 'We're not wearing jackboots.'

'Do I have time to pack?'

'Of course.'

'Time to finish my meal?'

'That too.'

The professor sat down again. The norms of the transaction so established, he seemed to Troy to be no further perturbed and in no hurry – which suited Stilton. Dora Wax set out tea for the two of them. Stilton eyed the full rack of toast, standing on edge by the professor's plate.

'Any chance of a bit of toast, Dora?'

'Wot, ain't your missis fed you today?'

'Of course . . . but that was over an hour ago.'

She took a slice of toast off the rack, slapped it on a plate and pushed it towards Stilton.

'Help yourself. Go easy on the butter. That is rationed – or hadn't you heard? Now, Professor, knock back yer tea and let me have the cup.'

She spun the dregs of tea around, upended the cup over the saucer and then peered into the pattern she had made around the inside.

'Ooooh . . . I see a journey,' she said.

Troy and Stilton looked at each other. Stilton grinned over a mouthful of buttered toast.

'A car journey. Not a long one. Then a dark place.'

'Where, Dora?' Neuberg said simply without looking at her. 'And will there be light enough to read?'

'Dunno. Hard to say. Just dark. Then another journey. A long one this time. Far, far away. Then . . . 'Ang on . . . Yeah . . . I see water . . . a sea crossing . . . . Professor, you're going overseas!'

Neuberg finished his eggs, stood up, said, 'Right now, Dora, I am going upstairs. You will excuse me, gentlemen. I will not keep you long.'

Troy found Dora Wax towering over him.

'Drink up, young copper, and I'll do you next.'

His heart sank. Stilton was close to giggling into his tea. Troy obeyed and handed her the cup. Swirl, tip, peer.

'I did you, young copper, 'cos I know wot a septic Walter Stilton is. And you know what I see? I see a woman in your life.'

Stilton was holding in the laughter now by force of will. Oh God, Troy thought, let not this woman have red hair. He couldn't bear the end of Stilton's 'septicism'. He couldn't bear to have to explain.

'Oooh . . . A dark woman – lots of thick black hair and coal-black eyes . . . wicked woman! A wicked woman is going to enter your life!'

Good, thought Troy. He was a policeman . . . from his point of view the world was full of wicked women. Dark or otherwise.

Neuberg appeared in the doorway. A briefcase under his arm, a small overnight case in one hand, a homburg on his head.

'Gentlemen, I am ready.'

Troy drove. Stilton sat in the back of the Riley with Neuberg.

'Do you know where this dark place is?' Neuberg asked.

'Probably just the cell at Leman Street. After that you will be going on a journey. Dora was right about that. I just don't know where.'

'Away from Dora.'

''Fraid so.'

'Ach! The woman could drive a man mad, you know. She no longer believes in the God of her forefathers and seeks faith in the random arrangement of tea leaves in a cup. She looks in, states what is obvious and is falsely reassured by the illusion of her own wisdom. Of course I'm going on a journey. I'm a refugee. When are we not in transit? The woman could drive me mad. What she does not realise is that everything is numbers. If she wants the secret of the universe, it lies in numbers.'

'Does it?' Stilton said, sounding incredulous.

'Trust me. I am – was – Professor of Mathematics at University College. Numbers are everything.'

He tapped Troy on the shoulder. Relaxed enough now to treat him as though he were no more than a chauffeur.

'Would you pull up at the corner? I would like to buy a newspaper. Who knows how long I shall be in your dark place.'

§ 82

If there was a pattern to the day's work, thought Troy, it lay only in that initial sense of caution the men displayed. No one jumped to conclusions, no one assumed anything about the nature of them as coppers until it became self-evident, as though each and every one of them suspected that somewhere in the hidden heart of England Churchill had been saving his storm troopers for a day such as this. Once they were certain they were dealing with nothing more than a couple of unarmed London bobbies, the full gamut of reaction was possible. Herr Schwartz in Jamaica Street had wept buckets, as had Herr Franzen in Commercial Road and Herr Bernstein in the East India Dock Road. Herr Tauber of Ropemaker's Fields had made a run for it – Stilton had left it to Troy to mess up his suit and rugby tackle him, and Herr Musil of Wapping Lane had adopted Gandhiesque tactics and lay rigid on the floor of his landlady's sitting room in an act of civil disobedience. The landlady had helped carry Herr Musil out saying, 'If you wasn't behind with your rent it'd be a different matter. I can let yer room to some bugger wot pays proper.'

By the end of the day Troy had seen little opportunity for his supposed local knowledge or Stilton's grasp of German to be much use, and said so to Stilton.

'It's a shabby job.'

'It's a job like any other, lad,' Stilton said. 'And who knows what the Chief Inspector has in store for us?'

Troy called in at the Yard on his way home to check his in-tray. There was one note:

'Station Sergeant at Bow Street called. 6.12 p.m. Asked if you would return call.'

For a moment he had no idea who the Station Sergeant at Bow Street was or why he might be calling. Then he remembered.

'Kitty Stilton, please.'

She came on the line.

'I get off at eight,' she said. 'We could . . .'

'What? We could what?'

'We could go out for a bite to eat. Make the most of the light nights.' Her voice dropped to a whisper. 'Before we make the most of the dark.'

Troy thought. He could not be taken aback at any of this. He had called her. It had been perfectly possible not to call her, but he had. And her initial suggestion was a good one – proper though it was. Dining out might take away the shabby taste of the day.

'Fine,' he said. 'But I'm not going anywhere on the back of your bike. I'll pick you up in my car in five minutes. We'll drive to my house, and then we'll walk.'

He found her under the white lamps of Bow Street nick – white because Queen Victoria would not have those ugly, garish blue lamps opposite the Royal Opera House if it were to be truly royal; the queen had been dead thirty-nine years, but the lamps remained white. Kitty slid in beside him, leaned over to kiss him, found her gas mask case jammed painfully between them and slung it on the back seat, as symbolic as a discarded item of clothing.

'Glad you're free. I'd no idea how long Dad would keep you.'

Troy slipped the car into gear and set off up Bow Street and into Long Acre.

'Do you and your father not talk?'

'Not shop we don't. I'm just uniform I am. A plonk. He'd no more tell me Special Branch business than he'd tell me how to nick the crown jewels in the Tower o'London. It was just like that when I was a nipper – "Where you goin' Dad?". "See a man about a dog." I got fed up hearin' that.'

'I'm not Branch. So I can tell you . . . we spent all day rounding up Germans and Austrians, mostly middle-aged and middle class, Herr Doktor This and Herr Professor That, banging them up in Leman Street and then watching them get shuffled off to St Pancras or Lingfield.'

'Wot they done?'

'Nothing.'

'So?'

'So it's distasteful. I'd sooner be chasing murderers. That's what I do. And as for the crown jewels . . .'

'Yeah?'

'The ones in the tower are fake, so I wouldn't bother. The real ones haven't been on display since the days of Captain Blood.'

He parked in Bedfordbury. She slipped an arm in his and they walked along New Row and up as far as Seven Dials.

'I know a nice little Italian place. Gepetto's. Not much of a regular menu, but an astonishing array of specials on the blackboard every day, and a decent wine list. It's usually jammed, but I've known Gepetto for years, he'll fit us in.'

'I never drunk wine.'

Troy supposed there was a first time for everything. Perhaps most English women had never tasted wine? He had grown up with wine. His parents had settled in England after a few years in France. Almost the first thing the old man had done was stock his wine cellar.

Outside Gepetto's the blackboard was bare. Inside Gepetto's Gepetto was seated alone with a bottle of wine and a glass, his head in his hand.

Troy tapped on the window. Gepetto looked up, a sad-eyed seventy-year-old, brimming with tears. He beckoned to them to come in. Turned over two more glasses and poured.

'What's happened?'

'Ah . . . Freddie . . . Where I begin?'

'At the beginning?'

'After lunch today . . . two coppers come . . . they ask for Gepetto Zocchi . . . when I say that's me they say "no, it must be your son", and my son my Joe, my cockney Joe, he come out and he talk to them, and he say you buggers got to be kidding and next thing I know he got his hat and coat and they take him down nick and put him in chokey and say he not be back . . . he is . . . how you say . . . impermed.'

'Interned,' Troy said.

'Impermed. Interned. Still chokey, yes? An' I say what he done, and they say he a wop and that enough . . . they say they are coppers on the wop, Kraut and kike run. And they laugh and they take my Joe away. So I got no cook, no customers . . . so I go walk and I go over to Soho . . . and I ask around and they nick also Gobbi from Mario's and Spinetti from Quaglino's, and the bloke from the Café Royal, and those two blokes at the ice cream parlour in Old Compton Street . . . I tell you,

Freddie, this night you cannot get a good Italian meal this side of Milan!'

Troy took out his notebook, said, 'Jot down Joe's full name for me, date and place of birth, and let me look into this. I can't make any promises. But I can at least find out where he's gone.'

Gepetto scribbled.

Troy felt a hypocrite.

Troy felt unclean.

Troy felt a liar.

Troy took up his glass of wine, hoping he could hide behind it or anything. The sooner he got out of here the better.

He sipped. It was superb. It sapped at his sense of hypocrisy. He felt it begin to wane almost at once. He turned the bottle to see the label. Gepetto had chosen to drown his sorrows in a Bruno di Monticello 1926.

'You good copper, Freddie. Not like these bums who come today. You never lock up bloke just cos he a kike or a wop. I tell you what. Let me feed you and your young lady.'

Hypocrisy, good wine and the prospect of food fought for space in Troy's conscience.

'It not be much. Just a little pasta and *putanesca*.'

He vanished into the kitchen.

Kitty was staring at him, her glass untouched.

'Try it,' Troy whispered. 'You'll like it.'

'How can you *not* tell him?'

'No . . . that's the wrong question. How *can* I tell him?'

'It stinks, doesn't it?'

'Yes, I told your father as much earlier on . . . but the wine doesn't and nor will the meal. And when did you last dine in an empty restaurant with the proprietor?'

Kitty tasted the wine, pulled a face just like the one she'd pulled at Art Tatum.

'I could get used to it . . . anyway . . . pasta . . . that's spaghetti . . . pasta and what?'

'Putanesca.'

'Wossat mean.'

Troy wished she hadn't asked.

'Lady of the night.'

'Oh, nice.'

'Less literally, Whore's Sauce.'

'Thanks a million, Troy.'

'It just means olives and tomatoes and . . .'

'Troy . . . just shut yer gob.'

§ 83

Afterwards. A warm night. The window open. Kitty lying with her red mane spread across his chest, he said, 'I had my fortune told today.'

'Wot? Who by?'

'Dora Wax.'

'Dora Wax reads tea leaves She couldn't tell you the Titanic had sunk or Mafeking been relieved.'

'She said a wicked woman was about to enter my life.'

Kitty's head rose up, a glint in her green eyes.

'Wot . . . your *putanesca*? Your Lady of the Night?'

'Yes . . . but it's not you.'

'I should think not. And one more crack about whores and I'll thump you.'

§ 84

Every day Troy worked on the wop, Kraut and kike run with Walter Stilton. Every day tasted worse. Every night he met up with Kitty Stilton, and whether they went to a restaurant, a pub or a cinema they always ended up in his bed. Every day tasted better.

Came Friday.

Steerforth appeared at Leman Street at lunchtime. Neither Troy nor Stilton had set eyes on him since Monday evening.

'I need you two in Hampstead this afternoon. Finish what you're doing . . .'

They were drinking tea and eating sandwiches in Troy's old office.

Stilton never lost an opportunity for food or tea, and Troy had grown used to the fact that each morning Stilton would cajole a second breakfast out of whichever household they invaded first.

'... And be outside Hampstead Library at two thirty.'

Steerforth left without another word to them.

Stilton bit into his bacon sandwich, spat crumbs and said, 'Do you want to guess or shall I?'

'Book burning,' Troy said. 'He'll have us tipping books off the shelves and burning them in the street.'

Later, Troy wished he had put more imagination into his answer.

They arrived at Arkwright Road to find three Black Marias and a couple of dozen uniformed coppers lined up outside. Steerforth was bristling. It seemed to Troy that what passed for his moustache was twitching with anticipation. He picked two uniforms from the ranks and told Troy and Stilton to follow him inside.

Inside, the library was full of people, almost entirely men, some snoozing, most bent over books and newspapers, some even taking notes. It was a typical Hampstead Library Friday afternoon. Troy had come here as a boy to change his library books after school. The watchword had been silence. One disturbed nothing in Hampstead Library. Fingers pressed to lips and whispered 'hush'. The librarians even wore rubber heels. One librarian sensing impending trouble came up and asked if she could help. Steerforth ignored her, went over to the counter, raised the access flap and slammed it down three times, until every head in the room had turned to look at him.

'Everybody up! Everybody stand!'

Confused, people obeyed slowly and sporadically. Suddenly, Troy had worked out exactly what Steerforth was up to. The more obedient they were, the more they gave themselves away. Troy could spot the Europeans just by looking at them. No Englishman would leap to his feet just because a policeman said so.

'Mr Stilton, take the left-hand side of the room, Mr Troy the right. I shall be centre.'

So saying he walked up to a tall, elderly, bespectacled man who had risen slowly to his feet by the first table and said, 'Repeat after me – "Heil Hitler".'

'Certainly not,' came the reply. 'Bugger off.'

Steerforth didn't bat an eyelid, moved on to the next man.

'Repeat after me – "Heil Hitler".'

The only right answer to this preposterous request was indeed 'Bugger off', but this time the 'Heil Hitler' was all but whispered back to him in accented English.

Steerforth put his face only inches from his cringing captive's and said, 'Now say "God Save the King"!'

'Gott Save de King.'

'You're nicked! Mr Stilton, Mr Troy! Nick anyone who can't say it right.'

Stilton looked at Troy in disbelief. He hadn't twigged. Then he said as gently as he could to the first man in his aisle, 'Would you mind just saying "Heil Hitler" and "God Save the King" for me?'

Steerforth roared, 'Don't ask them! Tell 'em!'

Troy walked out.

Five or six minutes passed, then the remaining bobbies lined up to form a corridor and thirty-odd men were hustled out of the library straight into Black Marias. As the first van moved off Steerforth caught sight of Troy standing by the Riley and strode purposefully over.

'What the hell do you think you're playing at?'

Troy said, 'Mr Steerforth, what you did in there was disgusting –'

Steerforth punched him in the mouth. Troy tasted blood. Steerforth pulled back for a second blow and found his arm held by Stilton.

'Remember what you told us, sir – nobody gets thumped while there's witnesses.'

Stilton pointed back at the crowd they'd drawn. Steerforth shrugged him off, glanced quickly round at the staring faces on the pavement. But for them Troy was sure he'd hit him again. Then the finger wagged in his face.

'You ever . . . You ever disobey an order of mine again and I'll see you busted back to pounding the beat.'

He turned his back on Troy and strode off.

Troy wiped the blood from his lip.

'It was also illegal,' he said to Steerforth's back. Steerforth turned and ran at Troy. Stilton, almost twice his girth, got both arms around him and said, 'For Christ's sake, sir. Not in public!'

Steerforth freed one arm and a finger to wag with.

'Cross me again, son, and you're through. Gettit? Through! You won't be worth dogshit on the pavement!'

Stilton said nothing until the street had begun to chatter. Then, blending authority and civility, said, 'Do you want to be a copper when you grow up?'

Troy looked down, spat blood onto the tarmac.

'I'm right, Walter. This . . . this farrago is illegal.'

'I've no doubt you're right. You're the educated one. But you work for Stanley Onions. I thought you'd have learnt by now that if there's one thing brass hates it's a barrack-room lawyer and that's just what you came across as to Steerforth. You waved a red rag at a bull. Worse, you just made a powerful enemy.'

An old woman stepped out of the crowd. Took a fancy, blue-edged hanky from her sleeve and pressed it to Troy's split lip.

'*Diese englische Polizei, ist nicht besser als die deutsche. Nur die braunen Hemden fehlen noch.*'

Troy understood little of what she'd said. 'Police' and 'brown', and not much else. He took the hanky from her, looked to Stilton for a translation.

'You won't like it. She thinks you're the one we've nicked and told you coppers're no better than the Brownshirts.'

'Just thank her, would you, Walter? Don't tell her I'm a copper. I think I'm ashamed to be one for once.'

Stilton obliged, and as she walked away said, 'Well, at least we're not locking up the women.'

'Not yet,' Troy said. 'But Steerforth'll have us doing that if we don't get off this assignment.'

§ 85

That night Kitty touched the scab on his lip, slipped a finger in his mouth to see if his teeth wiggled.

'I can't believe he did that.'

Troy said nothing but 'mmm' and sucked gently on the finger.

She pulled it out and said, 'What did my dad say?'

Troy told her.

'But you'll report him – the bastard – won't you?'

'No,' said Troy. 'No I won't.'

'Why ever not?'

'And have to call your father as a witness? Against Steerforth? He'd hate that.'

'Yeah – he would. He'd absolutely hate it. Steerforth – I could just murder him!'

'My experience with crimes of vengeance and murder – which is not inconsiderable – has led me to think that it's far better to let someone else do the deed for you. Murder Steerforth and who knows . . . It might land in my in-tray.'

'What? You? Investigatin' me?'

She kissed the injured lip, ruffled the injured pride.

'I can twirl you round my little finger any time I want.'

So she did.

§ 86

What does one do after the revolution? So long in coming, those who planned and achieved it have their roles mapped out from the first. The Second Under-Assistant Deputy Chief Commissar for Internal State Security (East) has known what his role will be from the night when he and the comrades met in an attic over a butcher's shop in an alley off a back street in some nameless provincial town far from Moscow ten and more years ago. But what of those who did not plan the revolution, opposed it or simply had no idea it was coming? After the failed revolution of 1905, Alex Troy, who had part-planned part-participated and part-exploited the event, scarpered. After 1917 – revolution or putsch? in either case Troy was not party – all he had to do was stay put in London, run his newspapers, expand his publishing empire and wonder (not that he did) how to spend all the money. Admiral Wolkoff, the Tsar's naval attaché in London in 1917, had also chosen to stay put . . . but not owning any newspaper, let alone a string of them, what was he to do? His choice was an odd one. He opened a café-restaurant – he called it a tea room, in fact quite specifically the Russian Tea Rooms, but café-restaurant it was – on the corner of Harrington Road and

Thurloe Place in South Kensington, directly opposite the Underground station (Circle, District and Piccadilly).

The Russian Tea Rooms appealed primarily to right-wing exiles known as Whites, of which there were plenty, several of whom had been all but blackmailed into pro-Bolshevik activity – but for exiles of the Left it presented an irresistible, if often resisted, opportunity merely to drink tea from a samovar and to listen to the seductive susurrus of their native tongue. Troy couldn't give a toss. He liked to hear Russian spoken, but few things bored him more than a bunch of old Russians sitting around banging on about the old country (one to which he had never been and to which he had no expectations of ever going). His Uncle Nikolai, youngest of his father's brothers, twenty years younger than Alex himself, the only one to make the journey westward, who had escorted Troy's grandfather, Rodyon Rodyonovich, to safety after the death of his mentor Lev Nikolayevich Tolstoy in 1910, felt differently. He liked the place, politics notwithstanding, and every so often badgered the young Troy into accompanying him.

Hence, the next day, the Saturday lunchtime, Troy found himself with a day off and emerging from the Underground station to see his uncle, short and stout and very Russian, waving at him from the other side of the street.

'Ah . . . dear boy . . . I smell the scents of Old Russia!' Nikolai said.

'Really?' Troy replied. 'I smell petrol fumes and the blocked drains of old Kensington.'

'For that you pick up the bill.'

'Fine,' said Troy. 'Lead me to it.'

Inside it was Saturday-packed, a sea of nodding, babbling heads. A liquid hubbub of Russian speech. At a corner table near the door, the stately figure of old Admiral Wolkoff himself, bushy white beard, head turning slowly to look briefly at every newcomer. At the counter his daughter, Anna, a frumpish woman in her late thirties whom Troy thought charmless but whose familiar broad slav features somehow put a twinkle in his uncle's eye.

On a quiet day, and he hardly ever seemed to be there when it was quiet, Troy thought the Tea Rooms might even be a relaxing place to take tea – dark-panelled, highly polished, elegant in its way and in winter often with a welcoming, roaring open fire. But they were too popular. People came in droves. It was said that the Tea Rooms served the best caviar in London. There were plenty who probably came here just to try it, but, to Troy's dismay, his uncle always opted for peasant fare, for food associated with his childhood. His favourite stank. Troy could not abide the smell, but knew as he saw his uncle scanning the menu that he would settle on a disgusting soup made from kidneys and sour cream, called *roscolnick*. No matter what they did to it it always reeked of offal.

Predictably, he lowered the menu, his eyes smiling at Troy across the top.

'*Roscolnick* today!'

'Really?' Troy lied. 'I hadn't noticed. And to follow?'

Troy picked out the next most unpalatable item, and mentally placed a fiver on Nikolai opting for jellied halibut.

'Oh . . . I think the jellied . . . sturgeon . . . no, no . . . the halibut. Yes, the jellied halibut.'

Troy would sooner eat snails.

'You may pick the pudding.'

Anna Wolkoff set Russian tea in silver-cased glasses in front of them, and prepared to take their order.

'We have not seen you in a while, Professor,' she said.

'War work, you know how it is,' Nikolai said, coyly, and rattled off his order. 'My nephew will choose the pudding.'

Anna paid attention to Troy for the first time.

'Ah, your nephew the journalist?'

'No, my nephew the Scotland Yard detective.'

Her head jerked up, she blinked. If there'd been a smile this remark would have wiped it from her face.

'I'll send a girl over when you've made your mind up,' she said, and left without a second glance at Troy.

'I do wish you wouldn't just blurt out things like that,' Troy said.

'Why?' Nikolai stirred honey into his tea. 'You're not ashamed to be the famous Scotland Yard detective, are you?'

'No. I'm not ashamed. And I'm not famous either. It's just . . .'

'Just what?'

'It's a bit of a show-stopper.'

'I didn't see any heads turn. I saw no one pick up a bag marked "swag" and sneak out the back door.'

'Well it got rid of her pretty sharpish.'

Nikolai shrugged this off – a gesture Troy himself had inherited.

'Perhaps she has something to hide?'

Another waitress came and took Troy's order for *gurevskaya kasha*, better known to former English public schoolboys as semolina pudding, but enlivened by the addition of nuts and cream.

Troy did what a good nephew should throughout the first course, and answered all his uncle's questions about the family.

What was Rod up to?

Writing a book about his time in Germany.

His father's disposition?

He and Churchill were still not speaking.

The mood of his mother?

Still taking everything too seriously.

The antics of his wayward sisters?

While the cat's away . . .

'And you, my boy? What of you? Always we talk of the others. But they are all of them married now. Only you left alone. Is there no one? A fine-looking boy like you, surely there is a girl?'

Troy looked at his fish rather than straight at his uncle. He would not answer this question if the old man shoved lighted matches under his fingernails.

'I'm rather busy at work,' he fenced.

'Ah, so. Murder.'

'If only. No . . . at the moment I'm rounding up German and Austrian nationals.'

Nikolai nodded, paused a little and asked, 'Kornfeld. Arthur Kornfeld. Did you round up Kornfeld?'

'No.'

'Franz Neuberg?'

'Yes. He was the first. Friend of yours?'

'No, but doubtless we shall meet. I have been asked to review the internment of anyone who might be useful to the war effort.'

'By our Military Intelligence?'

'Naturally.'

'You know it would make more sense if they'd asked you before they asked me to lock the poor buggers up.'

'Well, my boy, you know what they say. Military Intelligence – the perfect oxymoron.'

'Then we're all doomed,' said Troy.

As the prospect of jellied halibut sat before him, looking like something that had recently emerged from Moby Dick's groin, he caught sight of Nikolai looking past him towards the staircase that wound up just to the left of the door into what he presumed was an over-the-shop flat. He looked in the mirror behind Nikolai and saw in reflection what his uncle saw directly, the frequency with which men were ushered up with a nod and a gesture from old Wolkoff, without any seeming contact with the rest of the restaurant. He had assumed on entry, as he always had, that the old Admiral guarded the door, and did so with a mixture of proprietorial majesty and plain nosiness. Now he realised that it was this second, inner door he guarded. Not this room but the room above. And his uncle's remark began to seem more than casual, more than thrown out as banter. Perhaps Anna Wolkoff did have something to hide? He shifted his chair a little to show more of the rest of the room in the mirror, let his uncle's chatter wash over him, and spotted two men by the fireplace, sipping Russian tea with obvious distaste and clutching English newspapers they only pretended to read. Like Nikolai they seemed more concerned with the comings and goings from the upstairs room.

Nikolai had finished the fish.

'You haff hardly touched yours, my boy.'

Troy beckoned to the waitress for their bill.

'Are you not staying for the *kasha*?'

'No,' said Troy softly. 'And neither are you. You see those two blokes over by the fireplace. Coppers.'

'You don't say.'

'I do. Not just coppers, but I'd bet a penny to a pound they're Special Branch. You have only to look at the size of their feet. I don't know what you've heard, but something's going on here and you with your insatiable kitten's curiosity could not resist taking a peek. Fine. I don't know what you've heard, what tip-off you've received, but you've had your peek. We're leaving before whatever it is is going to happen happens.'

'Nonsense.'

Troy caught sight of a small boy in wire-rimmed glasses, ten or eleven years old, standing by the counter as he always seemed to be whenever Troy was in the café. He caught his eye and the boy came over. Troy cupped a silver sixpence in his hand, and let the boy catch a glimpse of it, before bunching his fingers around it, and saying softly, 'Len – those two by the fireplace. Are they regulars?'

'Nah. They was in yesterday as well, though. But I never seen 'em before yesterday.'

'Do they order anything?'

'Just tea, and they don't seem to like that much. They keep looking at their watches like they was afraid of missing something. And they don't seem to understand a word of Russian. Goes right over their 'eads. Even I understand "please" and "thank you".'

Troy opened his fist and let the boy trouser the sixpence. Turned to Nikolai and said, 'Now do you believe me?'

Nikolai knocked back the last of his tea, and muttered, 'Spoilsport'.

They parted at the Cromwell Road where a set of steps descend from a traffic island into a tunnel, and thence to the Underground. It had been a delight since childhood for Troy to vanish in this way. Even at twenty-four it was a touch surreal to pop down a hole in the road like Alice after the white rabbit.

As the stairs emerged into the tunnel, hands grabbed Troy and banged him back against the wall with enough force to knock the air from his lungs. The hands that pinned him belonged to a man far bigger than he, but the face that loomed up was Steerforth's.

'What do you think you're playing at?'

'I'm sorry, sir . . .?' Troy feigned.

'Tea Rooms, laddie! What were you doing in the Tea Rooms?'

'Having tea. Eating lunch.'

A blow to the solar plexus told him this was not the right answer.

'Who's the old man?'

As Troy had no breath to answer Steerforth yelled the question again – into his face.

'My uncle.'

'Why there? Why that caff? Why not any other caff?'

'He's Russian. He came over with my father. He's a regular at the Tea Rooms.'

'A regular?'

'He goes there to drink Russian tea and speak Russian. That accounts for about ninety-nine per cent of their trade, I should think.'

Another body-bending blow to the gut.

'You are too fuckin' clever by half. Did anybody ever tell you that?'

'Frequently.'

Another hammer blow that took Troy to his knees.

People coming down the tunnel from the Museum end stopped. The Branch copper let Troy fall. Steerforth turned on his onlookers, blazing.

'Police business. Move along! Now!'

And they did.

Troy was on the ground now – one more blow and he felt he'd puke. One kick to the belly and he did.

Steerforth knelt down next to him, a faux-avuncular tone in his voice.

'Son, I've tried to tell you. You just don't bloody listen. There's copper business, and there's Branch business. And you seem to get 'em mixed up. So you and your uncle fancied tea in a Russian caff. You just picked a caff I had under surveillance. You blundered onto my patch like a bull in a china shop. Do it again, and I'll make you wish you'd never been born. D'ye understand laddie?'

'Under surveillance?'

'Yes.'

'Then you need to learn discretion, Mr Steerforth. Your men stick out like redwoods in the desert. Those two blokes by the fireplace might just as well wear signs saying "Copper". If I spotted them, I'll bet your target did too.'

Steerforth hauled off and hit Troy in the mouth with his fist.

'You cocky little gobshite! This is your last warning! Stay off my patch!'

They left him there. On the floor of the tunnel. Puddled in his own vomit, a familiar reek of offal, a trickle of blood oozing from the corner of his mouth. A woman stopped, bent down to Troy and asked if he was alright. If it weren't that she spoke in English Troy would have been prepared to swear it was the same woman who had approached him after his last punch-up with Steerforth.

'I'll be fine,' he lied. 'As soon as I get to my feet.'

And he'd no idea how long that would take.

She gave him her hanky. Women did that. He'd no idea why, but he'd soon have a collection of women's handkerchiefs.

§ 87

'You've got to report him this time.'

'No.'

'You can't let him get away with this.'

Troy spat blood into the basin, felt Kitty's fingertips run down his back, healing, soothing, provoking.

'He won't. You're going to kill him for me. Remember?'

'Ha, bloody, ha.'

§ 88

On the Sunday they had lumbered themselves. Lunch with the Stiltons. Dinner with the Troys.

Earlier in the week, the conversation had gone . . .

'My mum wants to meet you. God knows why.'

'What have you told her?'

'I ain't told her a thing. Not a sausage. It's Dad.'

'What does he say?'

'How should I know? But it's obvious, innit . . . we're y'know . . . bound to be curious.'

They were in bed. Kitty slumped against him. His hand cupped around her left breast arousing a nipple.

'We're what?'

'Don't make me spell it out, Troy.'

'We're . . .'

'Don't you dare use that word! Don't you dare!'

She squirmed to look him in the face. 'All the others is nicer.'

'Of course. My mother is interested too. She asked if I'd care to bring my young lady to dinner on Sunday.'

'Wot? Next Sunday? But I said we'd have dinner in Stepney.'

'That's fine . . . dinner in Stepney is surely in the middle of the day, whereas in Hampstead it's never before eight in the evening.'

'You don't say?'

'Are you sneering?'

'Are you being snotty?'

§ 89

It seemed to Troy that he had been in countless East End rooms just like this over the last few weeks. At the same time nothing had been quite like Edna Stilton's vast kitchen basement, with its constantly running coal-fired Aga, its table for a dozen or more and its constant stream of children and in-laws.

Mrs Stilton stared at the bruise on his face and seemed too embarrassed to ask. Walter said simply, 'You do seem to cop it, don't you, lad?'

They were thirteen at table. He wasn't superstitious, but he'd have difficulty keeping track.

Brothers Kevin and Trevor, two young naval ratings home on leave, who shook his hand heartily but thereafter seemed to communicate only with one another. Miss Greenlees, the lodger – bottle-thick spectacles and a job at Finsbury Town Hall. Sister Rose and her husband, Tom, from the Ministry of Works. Sister Vera, not yet twenty and already her mother's rival for control of the kitchen – brother Terence, 'Call me Tel', the baby of the family, picked on by all who came before. And sister Reen and her husband, Maurice.

Troy had known Maurice Micklewhite before the war. He had thought him a wide boy. So many from Watney Market were, but Mo was clean as a whistle. Whatever it was he'd been up to he'd not been nicked. And he'd married a copper's daughter. Hence, this no longer being Troy's manor, he earned the benefit of what doubt there had been.

'I've volunteered, Freddie. Only way to beat the call-up. I'll be in the RAF in less than a fortnight.'

'Flying?'

'I hope so. What's the RAF if you're stuck on the ground twiddling a spanner or mashing tea? Not for me – I've asked to train as a pilot. I've twenty-twenty vision. They're screaming for pilots. Can't see 'em turning me down.'

Troy thought that class alone might be a reason the RAF would want Mo mashing tea rather than flying Spitfires, but he said nothing. Instead Maurice said it for him.

'I know what you're thinking. A cockney pilot. Accent like a pile o' broken brick, and no 'andle-bar moustache. But them days is over. Just you wait and see, them days is over.'

Crude, but touching. Troy hoped he was right. Troy sincerely hoped he was right. His sister-in-law clearly didn't think them days were over at all, and from the look on Edna Stilton's face nor did she. Walter, Troy had concluded weeks ago, was a brick, a prince among coppers – neither impressed nor dismayed by the upper-crust accent that Troy did nothing to leaven. Others there were who reacted as though the vowels of received pronunciation spelt snob – or as Kitty had put it a day or two back, 'snotty'.

Over rabbit pie . . .

'Your dad borrowed a shotgun and bagged four out in Essex.'

. . . Mrs Stilton quizzed Troy . . . about his job . . . his prospects . . . his family . . . and while Troy answered honestly and thought that there was no other way but honestly, Mrs Stilton seemed to him to be flinching at every response, and all but reeling from his accent. No aspect of his world touched any part of hers.

'So you ain't really a Londoner, then?'

'I don't think so. In fact, I'm not sure what I am. It's the kind of conversation I often find myself having with my brother.'

Uncertainty was not Mrs Stilton's *modus operandi*, and it was what had geared his entire life from the day his father fled Russia.

'I mean . . . I'm London born and bred. I was born in this house. My mum and dad bought this house straight off the builder in 1887. I lived here all me life. Till I married Walter there weren't even anyone from another borough in the family that I knew of. We was all Stepney.'

Stepney to Troy was more cosmopolitan than it was to Mrs Stilton. He'd spent weeks rounding up Stepney-ites whose origins amounted to a sampling of most of Europe, and if his dad's anecdotes were true, Joe Stalin himself had been one of Edna Stilton's neighbours a few doors down in Jubilee Street before the last war.

He was being warned off. He knew it, she knew it . . . Troy wondered if Walter did.

Stilton had no questions. But then he knew the answers. At the end of the meal he lit up his pipe, popped the top button on his trousers and seemed content to play a benign *paterfamilias*. Troy could not help feeling that he had been found wanting. Wrong part of London, wrong school, wrong accent, wrong origins, wrong man. And he could not help feeling that Kitty had not even noticed when her mother had slipped from questions into a busy, let's-clear-away silence. No, them days were not over.

§90

Kitty said she could not eat another meal.

Troy said that was OK. He'd call his parents and postpone.

Kitty said, 'Nah – let's get it over with.'

'It isn't meant to be an ordeal, you know.'

'You sayin' dinner with my lot wasn't?'

Troy said nothing.

''Cos I know what it's like. I know what they're like. Me mum's always got a thousand questions, me dad's watching his plate for the chance of seconds or watching my plate in the hope I'll leave something – Tom and Rose can only talk about Tom's job and Tom's next promotion and Kev and Trev are wrapped up in a world made up of just the two of them.'

So – she had noticed after all. Troy deemed discretion to be the better part of valour.

'I have twin sisters, you know.'

'Fine. They can't be as bad as my pair can they?'

But they could.

§91

It was not one of his father's good days. And if his father was not having a good day, the family wasn't having a good day. It was one of those days when he never got past the dressing-gown stage. A bee entered his bonnet at breakfast, usually over something he'd read in that morning's paper, and shaving and dressing he went to the wall until he'd worked through it.

His mother looked at the bruise on Troy's face and said nothing. His father did not notice. His uncle said, 'Ach, I leave you alone for a day and look what happens.'

Dinner was a poor showing. The twins' husbands were away in the armed forces, leaving them bored and restless. The only other guest was his Uncle Nikolai, seated next to his mother, and monopolised by her in French. Troy was seated next to his father as the one most likely to cope with his obsession if it ever found utterance, which left Kitty where he would not have put her, stranded between the sisters, Sasha and Masha. It left him craving Rod's company, the decencies and certainties of Rod's social code, but Rod was holed up writing his book on Berlin and Vienna and could not be tempted from it.

Troy heard Kitty telling his sisters that she was a policewoman, and he thought that perhaps they were all in a household where that remark might not be a show-stopper, when his father suddenly surfaced.

'Latvia.'

'Sorry, Dad. What was that?'

'Lithuania.'

Ah, that was the bee – Stalin's reoccupation of the Baltic States.

'Estonia.'

'Yes, Dad.'

'Churchill was right. It is a war of conquest. A land grab from both sides. The puzzling thing is why now? Why did Stalin not roll over these pygmy nations when he rolled over Poland?'

The plate was pushed away. Troy knew the gesture. He'd eat no more as it got in the way of talking. He wasn't the only one not eating. Troy could see Kitty picking at her food, and wasn't sure whether it was the company that put her off or the alien nature of the dish itself – a casserole of cock pheasant, out of season. A bit odd, a bit high. As desperate a dish as rabbit pie had been.

'It is to give with one hand and to take with the other – Lenin granted independence to Georgia. Stalin, took it back . . .'

Suddenly Kitty was on her feet.

''Scuse me. I need the er . . . toilet.'

She dashed out.

As Troy got up Sasha said, 'You might teach her the word "lavatory" while you're up Freddie.'

And he knew the meal was over.

'Sasha, you're a bitch.'

He found Kitty on the doorstep.

'I'm not gonna cry. I'm not.'

He pulled the front door shut behind them.

'You can if you want to.'

He put his arms around her. Her head touched his shoulder moment-arily and then rose up again, tears restrained in the corners of her eyes.

'They was talking about shopping. About clothes and that.'

'That's what they do. They shop.'

There was one other thing they did, but Kitty had banned his use of the word.

'And they asked me where I shopped. An' I said I made this dress meself on me mum's sewing machine and then it all went . . . went like they was taking the mickey out of me.'

'They were. They're bitches. I told them so.'

'Did yer?'

'Yes.'

'And then they started trying to give me make-up tips like I was some snot-nosed kid from the gutter who couldn't put her lipstick on straight. Just 'cos I said I made me own clothes. Everybody I know makes their own frocks. Me mum and Aunt Dolly, they was always sewing when I was a kid. They made all my clothes, all Rose's and Reen's and Vera's. I should think the only bespoke item in the whole house is me dad's best suit what Billy Jacks made for him. What's so bleedin' odd about makin' your own clothes?'

'It's still light. British Double Summertime. The day goes on forever . . .'

'Not this one. Not this one don't. This one's over. I'm not going back in there. Not with them two. You know what they are? They're just snobs, just bleedin' snobs!'

'I was about to say . . . let's go on somewhere.'

'But . . . your folks . . .'

'My dad is in a world of his own. He won't even notice we've gone. Let's go on somewhere.'

'Maybe . . . Archie Rice's got a new show at the Holborn Empire.'

'I was thinking more of a club. Let's go to a club. Let's see a band.'

'You never want to go to clubs.'

'That's usually because there's no one I want to see. Right now there is.'

'Like who?'

'Like Snakehips Johnson.'

'Who?'

'Ken "Snakehips" Johnson. He's on at the Café de Paris.'

'Snakehips? He's not black, is he?'

'You ever met a white man called snakehips?'

She had the makings of a smile playing across her lips now.

'I'm from Stepney. Everybody there's called Snakehips. Snakehips Cohen, Snakehips Kantor . . .'

§92

On Monday morning, Stan appeared in the doorway of Troy's office. Closed the door behind him. Looked at the bruise on Troy's face. Made no comment. Took his usual seat by the gas fire, which had been off since April. Stood up again, patted down his pockets. Said, 'Bugger. Can't seem to find me fags.'

Troy opened a desk drawer and handed Stan an unopened packet of Woodbines.

'I didn't know you smoked.'

'I keep them for you.'

'You never offered before.'

'You've never run out of fags before.'

Stan lit up, coughed up a bit of sputum and sat down again.

'Always meant to stop, y'know. My old dad were a pipe man. Always fancied meself with a pipe. Just never got round to it. Now there's a war on, seems like too much of a luxury to want to give it up.'

He coughed again.

'They're stale. Have you had 'em in that drawer long?'

'Since September. You don't have to smoke them.'

'Beggars . . . choosers. Now . . .'

He coughed again, this time a prolonged fit Troy thought might be put on to show how bad a stale cigarette tasted.

'When are you off to Stepney?'

'Any minute. A late start today just to let me and Walter catch up on our own offices.'

'Good, good. Now ... Chief Inspector Steerforth has asked MI5 to have you vetted. He's got on to B5b. Whatever that is.'

'Maxwell Knight's operation. Political Subversion,' Troy said. 'Nazi watchers ... and if the tide turns back, Commie watchers. They're not fussy.'

'I never know how you know these things. Spookery baffles me. But ...'

'But?'

'They've been asked to see if you're a security risk.'

Short and shocking. It required an equally stark answer.

'I'm not,' Troy said simply.

'I know.'

'Then get it stopped.'

'I can't. Wheels have been set in motion. It'll get bounced back to the Branch and someone other than Ernie Steerforth'll be checking you out. They'll be checking out your Uncle Nikolai too.'

'This is just bollocks.'

'I know. And I've no doubts you'll pass, but I'm powerless to stop it.'

'All because I bumped into Steerforth at the Russian Tea Rooms when I was off duty?'

'He says you nearly kyboshed an arrest.'

'I didn't.'

'Shut up and listen. I'm telling you more than I should, but I want you to watch your step from now on. Steerforth rounded up a lot of people at the Russian Tea Rooms and some bloke at the American Embassy too. There's even a whisper an MP will go down for this. All very hush-hush. And big, believe you me, big. Probably the biggest case Steerforth'll ever crack. And a peacock feather in his cap. He'll not take kindly to anyone trying to pull that feather out. So, I can't say I blame him having you checked out.'

'Vetted is a bit more serious than checked out,' Troy said.

'Whatever ... but this is orders not advice. Stay away from the Tea Rooms. Find some other caff that serves stewed tea without milk and calls it Russian – or you and your uncle could both end up in the shit.'

The blue eyes met his now in a steady gaze, searching out assent from Troy. Troy shrugged his assent, allowed a long enough pause to know Stan had taken it in and said, 'Stan, it may be indiscreet to say this ... but what do you think my uncle does at Imperial College?'

Stan said nothing.

'He's a scientific advisor to the intelligence services. And Steerforth knows it, because one of Nikolai's roles is to reassess all the boffins Walter and I bang up to see if they're of use to the war effort.'

Stan got to his feet now. Pinched out the Woodbine and dropped the stub in his top pocket for later. Headed for the door. Said with his back to Troy, 'Wheels within bloody wheels.'

'So Steerforth is asking MI5 to check out one of their own.'

'I don't care – walk a mile round it. All of it.'

Door open. Gone. Argument over.

§93

It was fuck-up time in the Jacks household. Given the disposition of the head of the house, a not uncommon occurrence.

Lena Jacks wanted a new coat. A new winter coat – in early summer – and she had expressed no wish that her father make the garment for her. She wanted her mother to lend her the money.

'I thought if you could lend it to me, I could get the coat now and not wait for winter. There's talk that there'll be rationing on clothes soon. So if I could get it now . . .'

Judy cut her short. They were in the kitchen – they might be out of earshot, but Billy had big ears.

'Don't say that in front of your father. He goes purple if you mention clothes rationing.'

And his voice boomed out from the living room, 'I ain't deaf yet, y'know!'

Judy put a finger to her lips to silence her daughter, hefted a plate of upturned spotted dick and pointed to the jug of custard. Lena followed. They set the pudding down in front of Billy, seated at the dining table, far from purple, far from peaceful.

'I just thought you'd like to finish your supper in peace,' Judy said.

Billy pointed to the vacant chair opposite, between Hummel and Schuster. Hummel bent over his copy of *Lord Jim,* Schuster staring calmy and idly into space, silently counting suet duff among his British blessings.

'Peace? With that great booby acting like something out of Old

Bedlam? I thought he might at least be in on his last night. Eat with his own family. Is that too much to ask?'

Judy served Hummel and Schuster.

Billy protested, 'You might at least wait. Is that too much to ask?'

'You sound like a record, Bill. What's the point in holding up a single course if Danny's out? You and me haven't eaten the same course at the same time for fifteen years, 'cos you always bolt yer grub. Nothin' new in that. And Manny loves his duff, don't you Manny?'

Schuster set his spoon upright, a tin soldier waiting for the duff.

Billy pushed his empty bowl away.

'I'm not hungry any more.'

Lena said gently, one hand resting on her father's forearm, 'Danny'll be back soon, Dad. He can't stay out too late. His train's at half past eight in the morning.'

'Is that it? Is that all I get? "Goodnight Dad"?'

'Won't be for long,' Judy said. 'There'll be leave, as soon as he's done his basic training.'

Billy sneered.

'Basic training? You got all the jargon off pat ain't yer? All bloody blanco and gaiters. Basic training for what?'

'For the war, of course.'

'Right. People don't come back from war, do they?'

'This one won't be like that.'

'Your dad didn't come back from the last.'

'And yours did. That don't prove nothing. They say we'll cop the worst of it this time.'

'Wot?'

'Papers have been full of. That Blitzkrieg thing. Like they done on Holland and Belgium. We could all get bombed silly. Wake up one mornin' and find your bed in a pile of rubble.'

Lena said, 'Mrs Wisby says we can go down her cellar.'

Judy said, 'We got our own cellar. I don't need to go down her cellar. And if I'm going to die I'd rather be hit by a German bomb than catch typhus.'

And Billy said, 'Shuuuttuuup!!!'

Schuster paused in his duff, Hummel looked up from his book.

'Dad!'

'Shut up! Just answer me one question, will yer? One straight answer. Where's Danny? And don't say out!'

'With his mates,' Judy said.

'In the Brickie's Arms,' Lena added.

'Fine. Right. Gottit. He's gone out to get legless. And I'll be up till bleedin' closing time!'

Billy rummaged in the pocket of his waistcoat for the end of a cigarette, got up, found matches by the fireplace, lit up and left his family to finish their meal in strained silence.

On the high mantelshelf, at eye level, was a sepia photograph in a shiny, chipped, shellaced green frame with an ivy motif. It had stood on the same spot for twenty-five years, ignored mostly, and occasionally, as now, observed. A middle-aged man in the uniform of a British infantry private, peaked cap and puttees, with one arm around a boy – recognisably Billy – of fourteen or fifteen. It was dated Christmas 1915 in his father's handwriting. One day in late 1914 Abel Sr. had stood at an open-air meeting on 'The Waste' – a patch of scrubby green at the point where Jubilee Street met the Mile End Road – and volunteered for what was soon nicknamed Schneider's regiment from the preponderance of Jews and tailors in it. The old man had, as Judy had pointed out, been one of the lucky ones. Survived to the end. Most who'd gone in as early had been annihilated. But the war had got to Abel Jacks. He'd never been the same man again. Home on leave the following year he had declined to describe anything of what had happened 'out there'. Billy had heard this unreligious man pray out loud that the war would end before his son was conscripted. His prayer had been answered. And it didn't make Billy one jot less the atheist.

He looked at his younger self, looked at the 'old man', knowing it had not been the greatest father/son relationship in the world but wishing the one with his own son were half as good. Danny had not waited on conscription, he had volunteered. With Billy yelling the lesson of 'Yer zayde' in his face, he had still volunteered.

§94

Way past closing time, way past midnight, Billy sat by the fireplace in his dressing gown and slippers, not even remotely dozing. The thump on the front door brought him to his feet.

'Who is it?'

'It's me. Ted.'

'What do you want? It's gone midnight.'

'It's what you want, Billy. I got Danny here. You can open up or I can just park him on the doorstep.'

Billy opened up to see his son propped up by an ARP warden in blue blouse and tin hat. The warden said no more, lugged Danny in and slung him down in the chair Billy had been in.

'I saw him. I'd just come off me break. I saw him reeling along Stepney Green. Swimming in it. Look, I can't stop. It was only me break. By rights I shouldn't really leave the street.'

'S'awright, Ted. You get off. I'll be fine with him.'

'Right – see yer Billy.'

Before the door closed, Billy said, 'Ted? Was there no one with him? None of his mates or nothing?'

'Nah, Billy. Not a soul.'

'Bastards. I owe you, Ted. I'm grateful, really I am.'

Billy drew up a chair opposite his slumped son and stared. The stare seemed to penetrate the boy's consciousness. His eyes flickered open.

'Dad?'

'Yes, my blue-eyed boy?'

'Where am I?'

'Aldershot.'

'Eh?'

'I thought I'd join up with you. We've got reveille in ten minutes.'

Danny looked around the room. Grinned.

''Ere. You're havin me oooooooon!'

And on the last syllable leaned over the arm of the chair and puked into the coal scuttle.

When his head rose again, sleeve wiping his mouth, Billy said, 'I waited up for yer.'

'I can see that.'

'What's it all for, son?'

'For King and Couuuuuntryyyyyyy!'

Puked again.

Billy said, 'I can see that. But I was talkin about the state you're in.'

'I thought you meant the war. Me joinin' up an' that. You been fixin' me with your beady for weeks.'

'However . . . now that you bring it up.'

So cued, Danny leaned over and vomited again.

'Not now, Dad . . . not now, for Christ's sake.'

'Oh . . . you don't think a father and his only son should have a bit of a chat the night before the son goes off to get hisself killed.'

'Thanks, Dad. That really makes me feel good.'

Billy had sat all evening on his temper, but no more. The rage surged to the surface in an explosion that would have scared anyone less drunk than Danny.

'You stupid little bugger! I thought I brought you up to have brains. Not to get 'em blown out. I never thought you were dumb enough to go for a squaddie! What've I told you? What've I told you? What've I always told you? Look after number one . . . Look after . . .'

'I heard you the first time. You been telling me that as long as can remember. I'll never forget seeing that 'orrible red phizzog of yours pushed up against the bars of me playpen saying "who's a pretty boy – look after number one".'

'Very funny. You're not too old for a back-hander you know.'

Danny staggered to his feet.

'Fine, Dad. I'm up now. Knock me down if you like. I don't bleedin' care. I'd rather make it up the stairs and sleep in me own bed, but you do what you're gonna do. Either way, get me up in the mornin'. Seven at the latest. Just don't give me another of your lectures. I know 'em all by heart.'

Billy stared at the space vacated by Danny as though the boy had not moved, listened to his son banging about in the hallway, at the foot of the stairs. Then, 'Dad? Dad?? I can't get up the stairs. Dad??? I can't get up the stairs. You'll have to help me.'

Billy did not move.

Billy said nothing.

'Dad??? Just now . . . I don't think I can look after number one.'

Billy sighed and got up.

§95

Danny peered in the mirror over the fireplace, picked at the bog roll on his chin, hoping it had staunched the trickle of blood from his shaving cut. His father sat at the dining table drinking his tea from the saucer, the way he had done, much to his wife's irritation, for twenty years and more. The irritated wife was out of sight in the kitchen. The clock read 7.15 a.m.

Billy said, 'How you manage to look so good at this time of day after a night like the last I just do not know.'

'Youth and clean living, Dad.'

Danny turned to his father and smiled.

'You see you do keep it clean.'

'Dad! Me mum's only in the kitchen, in't she?'

'Your mother is a woman of the world. She knows the facts of life a damn sight better'n you do. All I'm saying is if you go with a woman, go with a clean one. I know you – as soon as you get in with a bunch of lads, you'll want to prove yourself . . . just don't come back poxy. Ask the M.O. for some you-know-whats before you do anything daft.'

Judy came in with a steaming kettle to top up the teapot – she whistled louder than the kettle. Both men turned to look at her.

'Well, Bill. You always told me to whistle when men talk dirty and pretend I can't hear them. All the same, Danny, your dad's right. You'll like as not do what everybody else does just to be like 'em. Don't catch nothing you don't have to.'

'Leave it out, Mum. I know what I'm doing.'

Billy said, 'Just a bit of advice, son. Not often yer Ma agrees with me.'

Danny slipped his jacket of the back of a chair, and stuck his arms in the sleeves.

'Anything else the two of you think I should know?'

Judy ducked back into the kitchen, Billy thought about his answer, slurped at his tea.

'Not really . . . But . . .'

'Yeah?'

'If you conquerin' heroes get as far as Warsaw you could look for a pawnbrokers in St Francis Street. Your zayde pawned his pocket watch there in 1895. I'd quite like it back.'

Only Judy's laughter from the kitchen told Danny it was a joke. She stuck her head round the door, saw her son looking baffled, said, 'Danny, you're such a dummy – you never know when he's pullin' yer leg.'

'Are you, Dad?'

'Well, son. Your zayde did pawn his watch. But no . . . I don't expect you to get it back. I lost the ticket years ago.'

I don't follow you, Dad. Some blokes' dads would be encouraging and things. You . . . you play pop for three weeks and now suddenly it's a joke. I don't get it, Dad. I don't get you.'

'What do you want? A send-off?'

'I dunno.'

'Ignore your dad, Danny,' said Judy. 'You'll get your send-off. Lena's getting up . . . Joe and Manny'll be back from their walk round the green any minute.'

Five minutes later they were all stood in the street in the bright morning light. Danny with his brand new cardboard suitcase, his brand new trilby, and his hand-me-down macintosh rolled over one arm. His sister in her dressing gown, his mother holding in tears. Hugs and kisses.

Of the men only Schuster embarrassed him with an embrace. Hummel shook hands and smiled at him silently. His father stood with his hands in his pockets, expression flickering between his scowl and his smile.

Judy said, 'Remember to write, lazybones.'

'O'course.'

'Yeah. Just like you did at scout camp.'

'Dad?'

Danny looked at his father. Heard his mother's tears burst forth, saw his father whip out a handkerchief and pass it to her without even looking at her.

'You do what your mother says, son. You write to her.'

'And you?'

'I'll miss you, son. I really will.'

Danny hugged Judy one last time, straightened the brim of his hat, the way he'd seen film stars do, picked up his suitcase and walked off to war – up White Horse Lane towards the Mile End Road, just as a Riley Kestrel came down the lane in the opposite direction.

The car pulled up by the Jacks' house and two men got out. A tall walrus of a man of fifty-odd, and a short, dark, vaguely foreign-looking man half his age.

Billy flipped out his pocket watch, checked the time, swung it by the silver chain and flipped it back. A flash little display just for their benefit.

'Well, well, well, coppers at this time in the morning. What have I done to deserve a visit from you two?'

Stilton said, 'I'm glad to find you all here. Perhaps we could all have a word inside?'

Judy Jacks' tears dried at once, like the turning of a tap. She thrust the handkerchief back at Billy and disappeared into the house.

'All you say? All of who?'

'An assumption, Billy, that these two gentlemen are Mr Schuster and Mr Hummel?'

'Yeah, they are. They work for me. And they got jobs to go to. We all got jobs to go to.'

'It won't take long.'

Billy led off into the house.

In the dining room, he stuck his hands back in his pockets, stood mid-carpet with enough proprietorial swagger to let them know that coppers or no coppers they were on his turf. Schuster and Hummel sat at the dining table, fading paler as Billy waxed redder, anticipating what he couldn't.

'Right, Walter, woss all this about?'

'If you could just confirm your identities to me . . .'

'Identities? Bleedin' 'ell. I known you most of my life. And you might not have known their names but Joe and Manny here made that suit you're wearing last winter . . . on which I gave you a sweet little discount . . . or have you forgotten that . . .?'

Troy wished the floor would open up and swallow him. He wouldn't even mind if the floor chewed first, it would be preferable to what he faced now.

While Jacks ranted at Walter, Judy leaned against the door jamb, half in, half out of her kitchen, lit up a fag, exhaled a deep cloud and stared at Troy through the haze of smoke.

It had the desired effect. He was squirming inside if not out.

In 1936, a young copper on his first beat, he had been patrolling Whitechapel Market, right outside the Underground station, and had apprehended a petty thief named Moses Kettleman – better known by his street moniker of Mott Kettle. Mott had a thing – Troy could come up with no more accurate word – about women's underwear. He had been pilfering it from the open stalls on the market for some time. It had been a joke that had worn thin almost at once, and the stallholders wanted something done. None of them would name Mott and, even though Troy knew damn well who it was, the chances of catching him at it were slim. The uniform was as loud as a siren.

Troy got lucky, or Mott grew bold and thought it might be fun to try and outrun a copper. One Saturday morning, knowing Troy was only yards away, he had snatched a pair of knickers off a stall and walked off. It all but screamed 'catch me if you can'. Troy followed, and by the time they reached the Blind Beggar Mott was running, and Troy had chased him all the way past the Odeon in the Mile End Road to bring him down with a rugby tackle opposite Stepney Green. He had landed badly, all but knocked himself senseless, lost his helmet and had blood running into one eye from a cut on his head. Mott had shrugged him off, got up again and ran straight into the fist of George Bonham, who laid him out cold. Troy had staggered to his feet to find he had an audience of cackling Stepney housewives, laughing fit to bust their corsets.

'Freddie Troy, Freddie Troy . . . Bigfoot Bonham's little boy!'

Troy might have blushed. Under the film of blood who would have known? And a voice in his head said, 'All this for a knicker thief?'

Suddenly an arm was thrust under his.

A voice telling the crowd, 'You should be ashamed of yourselves! Supposin' they was your knickers.'

Which only produced more laughter.

Bonham hoisted Mott to his feet, slapped him into consciousness and said simply, 'Nicked!'

Judy Jacks took out her handkerchief, spat on it and mopped at the cut on Troy's head.

'It needs more than that. I only live round the corner, you come home with me.'

Troy looked silently at Bonham.

'You go ahead, young Fred. I'll get Mott booked and chalked down to you.'

Judy had picked up his helmet with one hand and steered Troy into White Horse Lane with the other. He found himself standing in front of her kitchen sink, his tunic being unbuttoned, his braces dangling like a toddler's reins, his shirt peeled from him.

'You're still groggy, ain't you?'

'Yes.'

'Do you know who I am?'

'Mrs . . . Jacks.'

'S'right . . . Judy. Call me Judy.'

She washed the wound, told him it didn't need stitches and was far enough into his hair not to leave a visible scar. She wiped the blood from his face, ran the flannel down his chest.

'Lot o'blood for such a bit of a cut. But it's stopped now. You'll be fine.'

Troy blinked, vision cleared . . . found himself eye to eye with a small, blonde woman about ten years older than he was himself. Her fingertips pressing a wet flannel to his right nipple. Not an organ he had ever thought of as erogenous. Until now.

'Be a shame to get scarred, wunnit?' Cos you're pretty, you are.'

'Pretty?'

'Yeah. You might be handsome one day. Right now you're pretty. How old are you? Eighteen?'

'Twenty-one.'

'Key of the door. All grown up.'

'And chasing knicker thieves for a living.'

'Yeah, well . . . that's why you got laughed at . . . sort of.'

'Because I chased a knicker thief?'

'Not exactly . . . you got 'em all puzzled. Ever since you got here. It's more why a toff like you would be walking the beat in Stepney . . . knickers or no knickers.'

Troy said nothing.

Her fingers let the flannel fall and moved to his left nipple.

'But . . . you ain't half pretty.'

'I'll have to get used to that word,' he said lamely.

'Yeah,' Judy said. 'You do that.'

Then she flipped the buttons on his flies, let his trousers slip to the floor, pressed her lips to his and cupped his balls with her free hand.

They fucked on the kitchen table. Over in an instant as Troy came.

He paused in a kind of mental limbo, mostly naked on top of a woman mostly clothed, not knowing the protocol for prising himself off a woman drenched with his own semen, whilst still on duty. But Judy said, 'Am I your first? You should've said.'

Troy woke from reverie to find Stilton and the three men all seated at the table.

'Is that what this adds up to? You and young Troy here have come to tell us we're nicked?'

'Not nicked, Billy. That's not the word. It's interned. It's a temporary measure. Safety of the realm, that sort of thing.'

'And you think we're threats to the safety of the realm? Me who's lived here all me life ... about as cockney as they come, me an' an old man in his seventies and a bloke so skinny you could play a tune on his ribs? What do you think we are ... the Tailors' Own Fifth Column?'

'Billy ...'

'I been Chairman of the Chamber Commerce twice! I was General Secretary of the East London branch of the Tailors' Guild from 1934 to 1936! Who do you think I am?'

Troy had gone back to the house in White Horse Lane on two further occasions. The first had begun with a 'nice cup of tea', but they had tumbled. The second they hadn't even bothered with the tea.

After the last time, Judy had said, 'You're still comin' too quick.'

And Troy had said, 'I can't do this any more.'

She never spoke to him again. He'd passed her many times in the street in the days before he transferred to the Yard, but she never spoke. One day in the autumn of 1938 he thought she might have smiled at him and the hatchet might be buried, but afterwards concluded he was mistaken, or worse, self-deluding ... for the blade of that hatchet now gleamed in her ice-blue eyes.

First he had come to cuckold Billy Jacks, now he had come to lock him up. He had no idea what Judy might be thinking – for all he knew she might be on the brink of dancing for joy and celebrating her freedom from grumpy old Billy with another pretty young boy.

'Suit you, does it, young Fred?'

'I'm sorry, Mrs Jacks ... I don't ...'

'The Yard. Everybody on the manor knows the Yard spotted you for a bit of a whiz-kid.'

'It suits me well, thank you.'

'Liked Stepncy while you was 'ere, did you?'

'Very much. Stepney was good to me,' Troy said truthfully.

'And this is how you pay us back?'

Troy said nothing.

Billy was ranting.

'I am not bleedin' German. My old man was a Polack. From Danzig ... in Poland!'

'Billy, it's here in black and white . . . born April 4th, 1898, Danzig.'

'S'right! Poland!'

'Danzig was in East Prussia then. Germany.'

'So . . . don't make me a Kraut, does it?'

Stilton paused, drew breath, said as gently as he could, 'Yes, Billy . . . It does.'

Judy took her eyes off Troy.

'What? What are you sayin', Walter Stilton? That Billy's not British?'

'He's not, Judy.'

'But he's married to me. Whitechapel Registry Office, 1920.'

'Doesn't make him British. Billy stated at his hearing last year . . .'

'Hearing? What bloody hearing?'

Nobody spoke.

'Billy!'

'I got sent for. A tribunal, they called it. I didn't think it much mattered so I didn't tell you. They said I was an alien, but not much of one. So I didn't think it mattered. I told 'em I'd got a War Office contract to make uniforms and they said I was just the sort of bloke Britain needed. Patted me on the back and told me to stay away from the seaside. That's why we didn't go to Canvey Island for Whit Week.'

'But you're British, you're English. You told me that when we got married.'

'No, love. I didn't. You just assumed it. And that's because I just assumed it. It turns out I never did the paperwork to get British.'

'But your old man fought in the last war. Dammit, Walter, he fought alongside o'you. Don't that make him British?'

'I'm afraid it doesn't.'

'My son, my Danny, just gone off to enlist in the REME . . . don't that make us British? My little girl, Sallie . . . she's been evacuated to Wales along with the rest of the kids in the street . . . don't that make us British?'

Judy snatched the portrait of Billy and his father off the mantelpiece.

'Look at this . . . just look!'

Only Troy did.

Hummel and Schuster looked at the tablecloth, Jacks and Stilton looked at each other. A few moments passed. Judy seemed suddenly weary and tearful, put the photograph back, went into her kitchen and closed the door.

'What now?' Billy said softly.

'We're trying not to muck people about. We're trying to be decent about summat that's frankly indecent. But we've orders to follow. Some days we've just had to knock on the door and tell some poor bugger to grab his things and come with us. There's plenty round here not had so much as an excuse me. It's because we know you – it's because I've known you since you were a nipper – that this is different.'

'How different?'

'Pack a case and be ready. It won't be long. We can leave you to the end of the list. But chances are I can only let you know the night before, maybe not even that.'

'And these two?'

'Joe'd better be as prepared as you. He'll go at the same time. Manny's over seventy. We won't be coming for him.'

Stilton turned to Schuster, 'All you have to do is avoid restricted areas. And all that means is no trips to the seaside.'

Schuster nodded.

'Pity,' he said. 'I always wanted to see Canvey Island.'

'You better not,' Billy said. 'Sounds like you'll be running the business. So, Joe . . . it'll be you and me for the skylark, eh?'

'*Ja*,' Hummel replied, not understanding anything but the bare fact of his impending internment. 'De skylark.'

As they walked back to the car, Troy heard Judy call his name.

He turned, she walked up to him, reddened in the face, but dry-eyed now. He'd always loved Judy's eyes – even when they had glared at him with contempt, he had loved Judy's eyes.

'Do you know where they'll take him?'

'Not for certain. There are camps all over the country. Race courses, mills, anything that could be commandeered. But the odds are he'll end up on the Isle of Man. Most do.'

'How long?'

'I don't know.'

'The duration?'

'I don't know.'

Judy turned away from him, walked back to the house.

Troy said, 'Judy, I didn't ask for this assignment.'

But he was not even sure she'd heard him.

He got back into the car, sat next to Stilton, feeling faithless.

'Do I detect a hint of history between you and Mrs Jacks, young Fred?'

Troy said nothing.

§96

Not knowing how long he might be gone, Billy thought it a good idea that certain of his company papers be burnt. If his wife was right about this Blitz thing, nobody would ever know and the next time the taxman came knocking he could just blame Hitler.

He and his daughter Lena sat by the hearth at midnight and fed papers into the fire.

'Nice,' Lena said. 'Some of these summer evenings you can start to feel a bit of a chill.'

'Sure,' Billy said, non-commital.

'Mum's takin' it better than I thought she would.'

'Yeah, well. She's got Danny to think about, ain't she.'

'He'll be OK. You can call him stupid if you like, but he volunteered for the REME, didn't he? If he'd waited for the call-up, what choice would he have had? Electrical Engineers won't be sloggin' it out in France will they? More likely some cushy little billet in the West Country guarding army surplus radios.'

A pause.

They slurped tea. Billy favouring cup over saucer for once.

'Dad? Why din't you tell Mum about the tribunal?'

'Why? 'Cos I felt a total pratt, that's why.'

'Eh?'

'Havin' to say how British I was.'

'There's people in this street'd've paid good money to see that.'

'There's worse . . . I had to point out I was Jewish . . .'

Lena giggled. Even Billy began to smile.

'I mean, how thick can these toffs get? Not knowin' a Jew when they see one. They might have known from the name, 'cos they kept referrin' to me as "Mr Jakobson". Like you get Jakobsons in Surrey or Hampshire. Jakobson, my arse. I even sign cheques as Billy Jacks. But . . . it was a farce . . . me sittin' there remindin' them of things I ain't give a toss about in donkey's years . . . bein' British . . . bein' Jewish . . .'

'I never seen you so much as open a bible.'

'Ain't one in the house. Not since your zayde came back from the Somme with one of his balls shot off. Wasn't exactly godfearin' in the

first place, but that made him a screamin' atheist, that did. He's lost one
... therefore there ain't no God ...'

A pause.

They slurped.

'Still,' Lena said. 'It gets yer.'

'Eh?'

'You can play the sarcastic old sheeny for all it's worth, Dad. But I've
seen twenty years of your act ... grumpy, stingy, whiney ... you've
played most of the seven dwarfs ... but this has really got to you.'

'I never thought about bein' Polish much. And not once did I ever
think about bein' German. I was two when we left Danzig. Don't
remember it at all. For the next couple of years we lived wherever your
zayde laid his hat. A few months in Cracow, almost a year in Rotterdam.
Pogromed here, pogromed there, old Macdonald had a pogrom ... and
that ain't strictly true neither ... we just moved ... moved before it
happened. "One step ahead of the Cossacks," he always used to say. Not
that he ever saw a Cossack. I got vague memories of Rotterdam, and I
remember landing at Tilbury, just like Manny and Joe did, but the old
man ... he filled me up with his memories. Told so many tales. It's like
I could remember Cracow and Rotterdam and all the other places ...
but I can't really. And the strange thing is, he took to England. As far as
your zayde was concerned, he was English. OK, so we never had a bible
in the house ... but we had a Union Jack.'

'Till he died. Then you binned it.'

'Like I was sayin'. He took to England. Became English. Didn't give
a toss about bein' Jewish no more. I never had a *bar mitzvah*. The Rabbis
come round he'd just tell 'em to bugger off. Only thing he kept out of
bein' born a Jew was speakin Yiddish. And I've always liked that. Yiddish
says things English can't.'

'You never passed it on to me and Danny and Sallie.'

'What would be the point? Your Mum's a cockney *shikse* through and
through. She'd never learn Yiddish. Knows enough to call me a *putz*
when she's narked and that's about it. Anyway ... the other thing the
old man passed on to me was something he didn't feel ... but like I
caught it from his memories ... I don't care about nationalities, he did
... I don't care about bein' British, he did. I can't explain it. I just grew
up that way. Like I was more shaped by his tales of being the Wanderin'
Jew than I was by the streets of London. If London took me in, that was
fine. But I took it for granted. I didn't much think about it. Now that

217

may sound ungrateful to you, you bein' English an' all, but that's the way it was. That's the way it was for a lot of Jews ... anywhere that didn't boot you out was where you stayed. And I always felt it could have been anywhere. Just so happens it was England, it was London, it was Stepney. Of the three the only one that matters the price of a bag o'fish an' chips is Stepney.

'I suppose I should say thank you to England. Took me in, gave me a home. But if it does this to me I won't forgive it. Me and your zayde spent thirty years building up a business. How long will it last now?'

'I can manage. With Manny to do the tailoring.'

'Manny's a tailor. He don't know nothin' about buyin'. Leastways not in London. And no disrespect to the old boy ... but the real talent's Joe. Joe can cut and sew fit for Savile Row.'

'Dad, I've fiddled your books for you since I was sixteen. I'll manage.'

'Kept − not fiddled!'

'That's why we're sitting here filleting the paperwork and sending half of it up in flames, is it? 'Cos we keep straight books? Leave it out, Dad.'

'As soon as I'm somewhere I'll write to you. Send you an address.'

'If they let you.'

'Maybe we can keep it all together long distance.'

'Trust me, Dad. You brought me up to have brains, didn't you?'

'I brought you up to look after number one.'

'Yeah ... well now I'm lookin' after you.'

Another pause.

They slurped.

Three floors up Hummel lay on his narrow bed. He had taken down his portrait. His suitcase stood packed at the foot of it. *Juif Errant* once more. He lay like an English knight depicted in brass upon a tombstone, legs crossed at the ankles, hands clasped across his chest. His eyes looked up to the ceiling, slanting down to meet the wall. His eyes looked up to the heaven he had never perceived, to the God he had never believed in, and his lips mouthed the silent word Job had never uttered, '*Wieder?*'

§97

Sunday morning came.

Troy was awoken by a hammering at his door.

Kitty's head rose up from deep in the sheets.

'Wossat? Wot time is it?'

'It's gone ten. And I've no idea who it is, but at this time on a Sunday they can just bugger off.'

Troy tiptoed naked to the window, parted the curtain half an inch and found himself looking down at the top of some bloke's trilby. The man drew back a couple of paces from the door, looked down the alley, pulled up his sleeve and looked at his watch. Troy stepped back.

'Good bloody grief, it's Steerforth.'

'Wot?'

'Steerforth. Outside. On the doorstep.'

'Wot's he want?'

'I've no idea. I haven't set eyes on him since the day he thumped me in the tunnel by the Russian Tea Rooms.'

'Then don't answer.'

'I'm not going to. I've two days off. I don't care what wop or Kraut he wants nicked. He can get somebody else.'

After sex, a bath, more sex (unplanned) and another (colder) bath, Troy caught the Northern line up to Hampstead, and saved on petrol. Lunch with his parents and whatever ad hoc family could be arranged. Some combination of sisters, brothers-in-law, the odd uncle. But the man sitting clutching a trilby hat in the hallway as Troy let himself in just after noon wasn't a brother, a brother-in-law or an uncle. He was a copper.

'Have you been looking for me? I was at home all morning,' Troy half-lied. 'There really was no need . . .'

Steerforth stood up. Knowing the man would not stand in the presence of a junior officer just for the sake of it, Troy turned to the door of the morning room to see who had appeared.

His father said, 'Come in now, if you would, Chief Inspector.'

And noticing Troy added, 'You too, Freddie. Your timing seems little short of magic.'

Alex held the door wide, Troy looked at Steerforth, Steerforth looked at Troy.

'I know what you're thinking, son. But I didn't ask for this.'

'Ask for what?'

'You mean they didn't send for you?'

'Send for me?'

'O'course not . . . you could hardly have got here from the West End in . . .'

'Gentlemen, if you would,' Troy's father cut Steerforth short.

Steerforth was out of his depth. Rank was no match for class. Troy extended an arm and waved him into the sitting room, past his father to face the assembled Troys. His mother looking ashen, his father looking solemn, Uncle Nikolai looking tousled as though they had dragged him from his bed for this . . . and Rod looking unreadable – not calm, not anxious, a neutrality that Troy found baffling. Steerforth pulled out his warrant card.

Troy's father said, 'Not necessary, Chief Inspector. No one doubts your identity.'

Steerforth put the card back into his inside pocket, but when the hand emerged it was clutching instead a small brown envelope.

'Mr Rodyon . . . Aly . . . Aly . . .' he looked down at the name and was grinding to a halt over the pronunciation of the patronymic when Rod baled him out.

'Rodyon Alexeyevitch Troy,' Rod said. 'That's me.'

'It's a letter of instruction, Mr Troy, telling you to report for internment the day after tomorrow, under the Registration of Aliens Act 1939. I won't read it out. I'm quite sure your brother will explain it all to you. It isn't a warrant. It could be, of course it could be, it's just that under the circumstances . . . well . . . we didn't think it was necessary. I won't be sending an escort either . . . I didn't think that was necessary.'

Troy noted the change from plural to singular in the course of Steerforth's decision-making. Rod took the envelope from Steerforth, slipped out the single sheet of folded foolscap, read it at a glance and said, '10.30 it is. St Pancras Station. I'll be ready.'

'Thank you, Mr Troy. Thank you for not making this difficult.'

'Not making it difficult!' Troy exploded. 'What the bloody hell is going on?'

Rank took over from class. Steerforth said quietly, 'A word outside if you please, Sergeant.'

Troy followed him to the front door, out into the street.

Steerforth turned on him, all but purple with rage, a vein throbbing prominently in his forehead, but his voice controlled – the anger simmering not boiling. The moustache twitching – again.

'I tried to tell you, but you don't bloody listen, do you? I tried to tell you. I didn't ask for this collar. I'm stuck with it 'cos I follow orders. Now, I accept that you don't understand the word "orders", which is why, in my opinion, you're a gobshite of a copper, a whippersnapper who'd be filing paperclips if you were on my team. But you're not, and I'm stuck with you all the same. But mark my words, son, I did you a big favour today. I could have come along here with a pair of uniform bobbies and dragged your brother off in a Black Maria. I didn't. Why? Because I've some respect for your father, and I've some consideration for your mother, and like it or not, you're a copper, and coppers stick together. I hate to say it, but you are one of us. I wish to God you weren't, but you are. If I were Stanley Onions I'd have you back in civvy street tomorrow morning. But I'm not Stanley Onions. I'm the poor sod who he stuck with you. Now I suggest you get back in there and explain to them all.'

'You could have told me yesterday.'

'I didn't bloody know yesterday. I knew this bloody morning. I called by your bloody house on my way into the bloody Yard two hours ago, I hammered on your bloody door and you were either in your bloody pit or you weren't home all morning 'cos no bugger answered. Now, bugger off back inside, *Sergeant* Troy, and see to your family.'

Steerforth stomped off to the end of the street, doing what Troy always thought of as copper's plod. A way of walking that summed up not so much a job as a generation. Inside hell had cracked open and spewed forth.

The row was going on in three languages. His mother was yelling at his father in French, his Uncle Nikolai was attempting mediation in Russian and Rod was saying in English, 'Will you all just calm down, please.'

Troy cut through it.

'For the last time will somebody tell me what's going on?'

It was loud enough to turn all three heads, but it was Rod who spoke first.

'There's nothing to worry about, Freddie. And it isn't a mistake. I am being interned as an enemy alien. The paperwork is all in order.'

221

'Enemy? What enemy? Alien? What alien? You're English. As English as I am.'

'No, I'm not.'

His mother exploded again – something about idiots and missed chances. His father put an arm around her and was shrugged off as she fished up her sleeve for a handkerchief to stem the tide of her tears.

'Well?'

Rod embraced his mother. Much taller than any other man in the room, the embrace seemed all-enveloping and she did not resist.

'Dad,' Rod said simply. 'Tell him.'

'Let us all sit down,' Alex said.

Nobody moved.

'Let us sit. Please let us sit.'

Rod steered Maria Mikhailovna to the sofa, Alex and Nikolai took armchairs, Troy perched on a footstool – the youngest once more, the baby of the family lost at foot level, feeling, as in childhood, that he was the only one who hadn't a clue.

'Many years ago . . .'

It was the sort of opening that had made Troy yawn as a child.

'Many years ago, I suppose it would have been around 1919 or 1920 . . . when I accepted the baronetcy . . . I changed the family name . . . and I accepted British Citizenship . . . for myself, for your mother and for the twins. For you it was not necessary. You were born in this house, the little Englander, as your mother was wont to call you. Nikolai and my father I left to their own devices. Neither of them much wanted to give up being Russian. My father died a Russian and a Troitsky. Nikolai still is Russian, and a Troitsky. The choice was his. But . . . we're not at war with Russia.'

'We're not at war with France either,' Troy said.

'Quite. But France is not the issue.'

'Yes it is . . . Rod and the twins were born in France . . . they were French . . . now they're English. I mean, dammit, you *are* English, aren't you?'

Troy looked across at his brother. Their mother had straightened up and was now merely sniffling. Rod was braced as though for impact, one large hand on each large knee.

'No,' he said. 'No, I'm not. And I'm not French either.'

'Rubbish. You lot have always told me that you lived in Paris before

222

you came to London. All of you. The twins and Rod were born there. Ergo ...'

Alex cut in, 'Before that we lived for some time in Vienna.'

'Eh?'

'I was born there,' Rod said. 'I'm not English or French, I'm Austrian ... and in the present climate that means German.'

'I don't believe this. I don't bloody believe this! Why are you German? Why didn't you naturalize when everybody else did?'

Alex said, 'It was my fault.'

Rod said, 'No it wasn't. Dad gave me a choice.'

'And?'

'I chose to stay as I was.'

'Rod, I swear I'm going to fucking throttle you!'

'I was thirteen ... an adolescent ... it was just a way of asserting my independence from family ... a way of being different at school. You said the same thing yourself at about the same age ... nothing like an English public school for making you wish you weren't English.'

Alex said, 'I should have made you do it.'

'No,' Rod said. 'You were right. You gave me the choice. God knows there've been plenty of opportunities to naturalize since and I haven't taken them.'

'Just a minute,' Troy said. 'Are you telling me you've been travelling all these years on an Austrian passport ... all those trips into Germany? You were even in Vienna in '38. On an Austrian passport?'

'Freddie, I haven't got any kind of state passport. I never have had a passport as such.'

'Then how do you get around?'

'When I was younger, travelling with the family ... no one asked ... more often than not we arrived in foreign parts on a ship Dad owned or chartered ... do you think anyone comes up to Alex Troy and says "who are you"? After that, more often than not all I ever had to show in Germany was a press card. Even when they kicked me out there was no paperwork. In fact, the only time I've ever had to show papers was Vienna.'

'So what did you show them?'

'My Nansen.'

Troy felt he might be in shock. He felt his jaw must have dropped and would not have been surprised to be told he was drooling. Nansen passports were the invention of the Norwegian diplomat, and quondam explorer, Fridtjof Nansen, who, under the auspices of the League of Nations, attempted to give papers to the stateless, to people who might otherwise – in an otherwise world than the one that existed after the Great War – have been citizens of countries whose borders had shifted or whose independent status had been simply obliterated. Specifically, the Nansen had been introduced to help Russian refugees. It was easy to see how Rod had been inspired to ask for one. Harder to see quite why they had given him one. He'd have worn it like a badge on the back of his lapel, as though he were a member of some secret school society. It reinforced his foreignness just when adolescence made it all the harder to be English. Nansen's had been a noble effort, almost half a million stateless people helped. Within the member countries of the League of Nations the passport had some validity. Notably neither the USA nor the USSR were members, and since Germany had stormed out of the league in 1933, Troy thought a Nansen in the greater Germany was probably not worth the paper it took to print. About as much use as wearing the school monitor's badge. Half a million stateless now seemed like a redundant statistic, mathematics for another age ... the zeroes as meaningless as those on a Weimar stamp – the homeless, the stateless, the nameless were already teeming in the millions, and we'd been arguing about what to do with them for years – a world of bureaucracy, of quotas, of visas, of 'send the Jews anywhere but here', Madagascar, Uganda, the Dominican Republic ... Pillar ... Post ... Palestine ... anywhere but here. For Rod to be posing – was that the word? posing – as one of them, to be playing the game of statelessness, to be travelling around Hitler's Europe on a fifteen-year-old scrap of paper was little short of ridiculous.

'A Nansen? You travelled around the Third fucking Reich on a fucking Nansen. Are you completely mad?'

'That's what Hugh Greene used to say. It's what the bloke from SS said when he saw me off at Tempelhof. And I was careless not mad, and I did get away with it.'

'Rod ... the Germans didn't bang you up. That's amazing ... absolutely bloody amazing ... now the British are going to do it!'

'And I'm going to let them.'

Their mother seemed to snap to life.

'What did he say?'

'He said,' Alex said, 'that he will not resist this internment.'

'But he must.'

224

The next thing Troy knew they were all talking at once, once more. Only Rod and Troy said nothing. Rod looked at him, sad in the eyes, biting on his bottom lip as though on the verge of explanation and apology that Troy dreaded hearing. He tuned out to the family, stared at the ceiling. Then one word in emphatic English cut through the Babel racket, his mother at the top of her voice, 'Enough!'

And she was gone, banging out – nought but verbal rubble in her wake.

'Jesus Christ,' Alex said softly. Then more audibly, 'Freddie, go to her. None of us can. Go to your mother.'

Troy stood in the hallway waiting for any sign that his mother's feet had touched earth once more.

A matter of minutes later he heard the sound of a piano coming from the red room – his mother playing a note perfect but far too robust *Cathédrale engloutie*. The piece lent itself to that – the left hand from hell or deep water, Poseidon plays. It was her way, one of her ways, of administering morphine to the soul. Anger had often driven her to the piano during his childhood. She was an angry woman. His father was not an angry man, indeed Troy had scarcely heard him raise his voice, but the twins drove him to distraction ('Is it my fault? Have I taught them to so ignore the court of public opinion that they think they can get away with anything?') and he and Rod drove his mother to rage. One summer, Troy was almost certain, she had got through both books of Debussy preludes, one day, one prelude, at a time, as piano therapy for life with small children underfoot.

She stopped, hands poised, twitching above the keyboard.

'Can't remember what comes next.'

Neither could Troy.

'Is it the ninth or the tenth?'

'Tenth – I'm pretty certain of that.'

The lid slammed down.

'Then I'm stuffed.'

She sat, fingertips on the lid as though still touching the keys. A silent chord played for no one.

Suddenly she was up, facing him and into a tirade in French so rapid he could not keep up.

'*Lentement*.... *lentement* ... and preferably in some other language.'

She switched to Russian – ignored the hint – and spoke to him slowly in her French-tinged nineteenth-century Muscovite Russian, the sort of accent that got you put up against a wall and shot these days.

'Why are they doing this to me?'

'To you?'

'To me. You do not remember the old country.'

Of course Troy didn't remember the old country – he'd never even been there.

'You should know. I was born here, and unless you've shocking news for me, it was you gave birth to me.'

'The old fortress,' she went on, ignoring him. 'Peter and Paul. Throughout my childhood people vanished into it. After we left, in 1912, my brother Pierre was arrested by the Tsar's secret police. He too went into Peter and Paul. And in 1921, after the putsch that Bolsheviks insist was a revolution, my brother André was snatched by the Cheka or the OGPU or whatever set of initials they had for it in those days. He too went into Peter and Paul. I never saw either of them again.'

Good God, thought Troy, the things this woman had not told him.

'Now the English Cheka want to put my son in a camp. They do not tell us what camp. They merely say present yourself at such and such a railway station at such and such a time. And I know nothing. For all the English tell us it could be Peter and Paul . . . it could be Dachau.'

Troy said, 'The station Rod has to turn up at is St Pancras. That's the line that goes into Manchester Central. I'd say they were shipping him to the Isle of Man.'

'The Isle of Man?'

'It's all on its own in the Irish Sea between England and Ireland and Scotland.'

'And what is this island like?'

'I don't know. It's British, but sort of independent. Its own parliament and that sort of thing.'

'Independent?'

'Sort of.'

The sigh was massive, continental in its breadth and exasperation.

'Oh God . . . not another small, faraway country of which we know nothing?'

'Sort of . . . I really don't know – but I should hardly think it's Dachau.'

§98

Just before lunch the next day, Troy felt the specific gravity of the house change. It was close to mystical, the sense that something in the house had changed. He looked into his father's study. The old man was standing in the open window, holding his pince-nez in place with a forefinger and staring down at an open volume in the other hand. Yet again searching for the verse that caught his mood or the mood. No change at all.

His mother passed him in the hallway, vanished into the red room before he could even turn to look at her, and he knew the source of the feeling. She was trailing her mood in a rough wake that only his father would not feel.

He followed. She stood by the piano, dropped her handbag, pulled off her hat. The hat spun across the room to land neatly on a chair.

'I have been into town.'

'Liberty's,' he said, lying hopefully. 'Harrods? Army and Navy?'

'Downing Street. I have been to see that man Churchill.'

Oh fuck, thought Troy.

'And how was that man?'

'I do not know. I had assumed that in view of the number of times I have sat at the dining table with that man that whatever differences might now exist between him and your father I would be received. They, that is the *Cheka Anglais*, would not let me in. I gave them my card and a flunky came out, a private or a personal or a parliamentary secretary – I could grasp neither his name nor his title – returned the card and told me the Prime Minister was not available. I was left standing on the steps with a London bobby, feeling like a knife-grinder being shown the tradesman's entrance. Do you know what he said to me? This London bobby? He said "Don't you know there's a war on madam?" '

She lifted the piano lid – began, appropriately, at the beginning – got halfway through 'Danseuses de Delphe' and stopped.

'You play so much better than I. Play for me Freddie.'

Time was Troy would have agreed with her. The Troys had thrust music at all their children. The twins had sung like angels, Rod still wasn't half bad on the violin, but in the eyes (ears) of his mother it was her son Frederick who shone. Now, he felt rusty, suddenly out of practice – too long living in a house without a piano. He picked up 'Danseuses' pretty much where his mother had left off.

'I looked at the sheet music in that shop on the high street today. The one we could neither of us remember yesterday was "Puck".'

'Of course,' she said. 'Play "Puck" . . . play anything.'

§ 99

Rod had a small house on Holly Mount – about a quarter of a mile from his father's house. From the top floor he could see across London all the way to Crystal Palace and beyond that to the North Downs. Troy found him pretty much where he expected to find him – sitting at the top of Holly Bush Steps, settling for the lesser view down what he called his *petit Montmartre*, to Heath Street, his two-year-old daughter, Nattie, sitting at his side displaying remarkable patience as Rod ad-libbed a story about fieldmice and hedgehogs. Troy sat down next to him. Rod paused the narrative.

'She's furious,' Troy said simply.

'She doesn't get it,' Rod said as simply.

'I'm not sure I do either.'

Rod sighed.

'Perhaps you'd better tell me,' Troy prompted.

Still Rod said nothing, and for a minute or more all three of them stared down at the slate roofs of Hampstead.

'It'll make us English at last,' Rod said.

'At last?'

'Yes. At last, finally . . . in the end . . . dammit Freddie, you surely don't think we're English yet?'

'Of course we're not. I don't feel English.'

'And you were the only one of us born here.'

Troy nodded his head towards Nattie.

'Different generation,' Rod said. 'That matters. I'm sure my son and daughter will grow up to be English. But I'm not and you're not.'

'You're more the Englishman than I am.'

228

'That, *brer*, is because I have not resisted it the way you have.'

'And it's why you're not resisting now?'

'Quite.'

'So letting my flat-footed friends lock you up and bung you in a camp will somehow make you English?'

'Yes.'

'A camp in all likelihood devoid of the English, but full of Italians, Germans, Austrians . . .'

'And Nazis . . . and Jews. Yes, Freddie, a thousand times yes.'

'Then I still don't get it.'

'Daddy,' said Nattie. 'What happened to the mousie?'

Rod whispered in her ear. She stood up and ran for the house – through the front door and clattering down the hallway.

'What happened to the mousie?' said Troy.

'I told her he was living under the squeaky floorboard in the dining room.'

'Do you know what kind of a camp you'll be going to.'

'No – but I'm sure you'll be able to tell me. Besides, it can hardly be Dachau, can it?'

'That's what I told Mother. That's what she doesn't get. She equates any camp with Peter and Paul, which is pretty well Dachau in her vocabulary. People disappear into them and vanish without trace.'

'I won't, and we both know I won't. And with a modicum of effort we can get that through to her. You can describe the camps to her surely?'

'Some . . . I've never seen the inside of any of them. I know there's an old mill in Lancashire somewhere. That sounds grim. Most likely it'll be the Isle of Man . . . "come to sunny Douglas" . . . they've cordoned off whole streets of B&Bs with barbed wire.'

'So . . . if the worst comes to the worst, I'll be getting a cheap pre-war holiday just like thousands of Manchester mill workers. I won't be in Peter and Paul or anything like it.'

Troy weighed up his next sentence – uttered it just the same.

'She lost two brothers in Peter and Paul.'

Rod leaned back – sprawled full length across the flagstones – big feet in odd socks dangling off the steps.

'Good God. The things that bloody woman doesn't tell you.'

Troy walked back via Hampstead High Street, bought a second-hand piano at Parker & Trewin – an upright Bösendorfer made, they told him,

229

in 1907, the year of his brother's birth, in Vienna, the city of his brother's birth. It seemed somehow appropriate whilst packing his brother off to an unknown fate on a remote island in the Irish Sea to install a wooden substitute at home. It symbolised the nature of the problem in walnut and ebony. He wrote a fat cheque and asked for the piano to be delivered to Goodwin's Court.

§ 100

They were prompt. 10 a.m. Sharp. Troy had wangled a morning off by convincing Stilton that a visit to St Pancras Railway station to ensure the departure of a detainee was work. He had omitted to mention that the detainee was his own brother and, if Steerforth had told Stilton, Stilton wasn't giving so much as a hint. 10 a.m. Sharp. Two men from Parker & Trewin turned up with his chunk of old Vienna rattling like a badly improvised boogie.

'Are you sure you want it in 'ere guv'ner. Room ain't much bigger than the joanna.'

That was the problem, the price he'd paid for beauty. Houses in Goodwin's Court were tiny. They looked as though they had started their life as shops sometime in the eighteenth century – bow-fronted, narrow, beautiful. The first time he had seen it he'd been able to imagine the Tailor of Gloucester sitting cross-legged in the window. After East End digs the house had felt big enough when he'd moved in, and he'd moved in early 1937 after a blow to the head had left him senseless at the battle of Cable Street the year before and the impossibility of recuperation without privacy had come home to him. He had had all the privacy he could have asked for in any of his father's homes. He'd none at school, and the former forever failed to compensate the latter. Living 'on the manor' had been considered a necessity to learning the shoe-leather, corn and blister craft of coppering as a beat bobby, and he'd given it more than a year before he succumbed to the lure of a place of his own. The price was living accommodation only marginally better than boarding school – although the food was much the better. Goodwin's Court, cramped and cosy, was the first home he had chosen for himself. His mother referred to it scathingly as his 'bachelor quarters'.

'There's nowhere else,' he said simply. 'It's got to fit in here.'

They tugged and strained and manipulated the beast in burr walnut until it sat spanning most of the right-hand wall of the living room.

'We's'll tune up in a mo, guv'ner,' the first man said, while the second leaned on the piano and muttered something about being 'parched', a phrase Troy had come to accept was only ever used by tradesmen. He took the hint, stuck the kettle on and looked at his watch. He'd have to be out of the house in ten minutes. He sat at the piano, lifted the lid and struck a minor chord. It was off.

'Like I said, guv'ner, we's'll tune 'er up when we've had a cuppa. I'm just a shifter me, but Ted 'ere ... he'll 'ave the old girl singin' for you in half an hour.'

Troy ignored the bum notes and began to play.

''Ere ... know this one ... it's ... don't tell me ... it's ...'

Troy stopped, took his jacket of the peg, fished around for his house keys and tossed them to the shifter.

'It's called 'Tea for Two'. And you two'll be making your own. The caddy's on the draining board. It'll be rationed any day now, so try and leave me some, will you?'

Troy followed a cab all the way into the station, hoping to flash his warrant card and be able to just leave the car among the cabs between platforms 5 and 6, but the concourse was awash with people. He'd not seen a scene like this since the mass-evacuation of children last September in the final forty-eight hours before the declaration of war.

He stopped the car and got out. Dozens if not hundreds of people milled around him. In and out of uniform. Soldiers, sailors ... children. Half a dozen children numbered and labelled like luggage. All met by joyous parents. All but one. This one grabbed Troy by the hem of his jacket.

'Have you seen me mum?'

A little girl, aged ten or thereabouts, in a summer frock, a cheap plastic slide in her dirty blonde hair – a worn man's tweed jacket for a topcoat, frayed at the collar and cuffs – a brown paper parcel tied up with string and bursting, a yellow, balding teddy bear under one arm.

'Me mum said she'd be here.'

Troy looked down at her. He was useless with kids and he knew it.

'What are you doing here? Are you going to the country?'

'Nah. Been there. We comin' back now. Had enough of the bloomin' country, I 'ave. You can stuff yer bloomin' country.'

'All of you?' Troy asked. 'All of you coming back to London?'

''Spose so. I don't know none o' them others. I was vaccywated wiv me cousin. Only 'e done a bunk in March. We was in Llandudno. We 'ated Llandudno. We was wiv Mrs Sproat. Mrs Sproat 'ated us. 'Ated all cockneys. Me, I'm a Stepney girl, I am.'

This was madness. A winter away from bombs that never fell, and now they returned in droves just as Hitler seemed to have London and the Southern Counties in his sights.

'Stepney, you say? I may be able to help you there.'

The child reached up and took his hand, and as she did so he caught sight of his brother, mired among the mites, trying to stride over them like a giant in seven-league boots.

'I thought you'd never make it!'

It pleased Troy that some anxiety had etched itself into his brother's expression.

'Is Cid here?'

'No, no. She's not. It's not the place for a farewell, is it? Not the place for the wife and kids.'

'Really?' said Troy, holding up the child's arm, her hand still locked into his.

'Who's she?' Rod said, as though it was only now he'd noticed that his brother was welded to a child.

'No idea,' Troy replied. 'I'll find out when you're on the train.'

A uniformed copper examined Troy's warrant card at the barrier.

'I'm to see him onto the train,' Troy lied.

'Must be someone special – a right villain if the Yard send a personal escort. Most of 'em we herd in two dozen to a bobby.'

'Oh, he's special alright,' said Troy moving on.

'That might not exactly be helpful, you know, Freddie,' Rod said. 'I don't want them thinking I'm any sort of a fascist.'

'I think this is where I mutter something about bed, made, lie in it.'

'That doesn't help either, you know.'

Rod looked at him, sadly, Troy thought. They rarely understood one another.

'When you get on that train, nothing will help. You have no idea with whom you'll be banged up. For all you do know it'll be every half-arsed

Hitler impersonator in Britain. It'll make Saturday night at the music hall look like high realism.'

Rod looked at him, angrily, Troy thought. They rarely understood one another.

'But you do know, don't you, Freddie. 'Cos you're the one banging them up. So, *brer*, don't take your guilt out on me, just tell me the truth. How many little Hitlers have you found in the last few weeks?'

Troy thought of Billy Jacks and smiled.

'Well ... mostly you'll be sharing digs with Italian chefs and Jewish tailors. But take it from me ... one or two of those really will be little Hitlers.'

As the train moved off, Rod yanked on the leather strap, sent the window clattering down, stuck his head out and yelled, 'Tell Cid ...'

But the train chose that moment to let rip with a head of steam, and whatever it was Troy had to tell Mrs Rodyon Troy was lost in the great black cavern of St Pancras's engine shed. Over Rod's shoulder Troy could almost swear he'd seen a pair of eyes glaring out at him from the darkness of the carriage.

The train chugged out of the engine shed. Troy watched until the lamp on the last carriage became a dot and disappeared. His brother had waved until the curve in the track leading to Kentish Town had obscured his view, and Troy had thought of a lifetime of arrivals and departures, of a common childhood spent at docks and railway stations and aerodromes, of a big brother with whom he was usually at loggerheads and often felt he hardly knew. It seemed possible now that he might never know him. It seemed odd in the extreme that Rod had waved like a schoolboy packed off for the new term.

Something small and warm appeared to be attached to him, and as the noise dipped he could hear a small, high voice saying, 'Bye ... Bye bye.'

The child was still waving at the back of the train.

Troy said, 'Your mum promised to meet you, did she?'

'Not 'zackly. I wrote and said she was to meet me please.'

Troy led her back down the platform, towards his car.

'When did you post the letter?'

'Las' night just before I got on the train. There was a pillar box on the platform.'

'Stepney, you said.'

'S'right. I'm a Stepney Stunner, I am. Me mum says if we lived in

233

Bow I'd be a Bow Belle, but we lives in Stepney so I'm a Stepney Stunner.'

The space around his car had cleared. Kids had been met and collected. Instead a group of soldiers in khaki were sat in front of his Bullnose Morris, perched on kitbags, smoking and dealing cards. He reversed neatly away from them, under the arch, spun the car around on the ramp and set off again in the direction of Stepney.

'We goin' 'ome now, are we?'

'Yes. Just tell me where you live.'

The girl looked at the numbered tag on her tweed jacket as though needing to be reminded not of where she lived but of the official record of living somewhere.

'Child number 1155, female, White Horse Lane, Stepney Green, London E1. Sept. 2nd 39. dob. 3.8.30.'

Troy dodged an errant cyclist as they crawled up the Pentonville Road, then said, 'September 2nd? Is that how long you've been gone?'

'Yeah. Ages. Wonder I don't sound bloomin' Welsh, init?'

She launched into what Troy took to be a mickey take of her recent foster mother.

'Eat it up now, 'cos if you don't there's plenty of little gurrls'll be glad of it. What do you mean "gristle"! 'Ow durr you call my best streaky bacon gristle!'

Pulling into White Horse Lane Troy asked what number, and when she said 11a stepped so hard on the brake they both shot forward.

'What did you say your name was?'

'Child 1155, but really I'm Sallie Jacks.'

Oh shit, thought Troy, oh shit, oh shit.

Judy Jacks yanked open the door, and before she could take in the whole scene had said, 'Oh no, not you again.'

Then she had spotted her daughter, peeking coyly behind Troy's back, snatched her from him, smothered her in kisses, and finally said, 'Where did you find her?'

'At St Pancras. She was wandering around looking for you.'

'What, at the station just now?'

'Half an hour ago,' said Troy.

'Then it's a wonder she didn't bump into her dad. Walter Stilton came round at breakfast, told him he was taking him an' Joe this morning for a ten thirty train. Bangin' 'em up in chokey they are. You know, Troy, you should be ashamed of yourself! You should be bloody well ashamed of yourself!'

The door slammed in his face. He had always loved Judy's eyes. And then he recalled with nagging clarity the two eyes that had bored into him from the darkness as Rod stood soft and sentimental in the carriage window.

§ 101

There is a short tunnel just north of St Pancras that plunges a train into momentary darkness and the smell of soot and steam. A sensation little different in the spring of 1940 from what it was in the spring of 1868 when the station opened. Only the novelty has worn off. Passengers, or, in this case, prisoners, still emerge from it blinking and slightly startled. The parting is over, the adventure has not yet begun – far too early to look at one another. One would not do that much before West Hampstead, and one would certainly be un-English to speak much before St Albans – and these men, foreigners all, are all keen to be English.

Packed in four-a-side, the outsiders watched London crawl from boroughs to suburbs to countryside. Kentish Town and Cricklewood, Mill Hill and Hendon, Elstree and Radlett. Insiders read posters advertising the attractions of Matlock Bath and Monsal Dale. Rod read that morning's copy of the *Post*. He was the only one with the foresight to pack a newspaper, although the chap next to him had gone one better and brought a book – two books to be precise: J.B. Priestley's *The Good Companions* and an English-German German-English dictionary. He bent to his book as soon as the light returned, and seemed to Rod to be curiously content, humming, as he was, softly to himself. Priestley had begun broadcasting to the nation only a week or so ago, on the Home Service after the nine o'clock news on a Sunday night. It seemed obvious, reasonable, that a foreigner seeking a handle on the English language might begin with the momentarily most famous novelist we had – although what he might make of life in Bruddersford was another matter.

Round about Market Harborough Rod was onto the letters page and became oddly conscious of being watched. Opposite him was a short, dark, angry – oh so angry – man glaring at him with big brown eyes. A homburg crammed onto his head, his belongings in a battered gladstone bag, clutched between his knees. The worst case of five o'clock shadow at eleven-thirty in the morning that Rod had ever seen. Only the suit gave him away. It was too good. Surely this man had to be one of the Jewish tailors that his brother had flung in his face at parting? And what was it he'd said about little Hitlers?

Pulling out of Loughborough, across the dull plain of the English midlands, at about ten past one, Rod had exhausted every inch of print in his paper and would have paid ten pounds for a copy of *Reveille* or the *Beano*. He folded the *Post* and offered it silently to the man opposite.

The man looked at the folded paper as though it were some kind of weapon, then he looked straight at Rod and said, 'That copper.'

Rod realised he was expected to deduce something from this and said, 'Yes?'

'That copper what saw you off.'

'Yeeess,' Rod said slowly, wondering where this was leading.

'Friend o' yours?'

'Well . . . no . . . actually he's my brother.'

Now Rod was aware that they were both looking at him – the man opposite and the man next to him.

'It was him nicked us. Him what banged up me an' Hummer here. Ain't that so Hummer?'

Hummer hummed and nodded.

Oh shit, thought Rod, oh shit, oh shit.

The little man leaned forward, one stubby finger stabbing at the space about halfway between them.

'So, if you're a copper's brother, what the hell are you doin' here? Spyin' on us?'

Rod babbled something about being a prisoner just like them, but the humming man cut him short and said something in Yiddish, very quickly. So quickly that he had to repeat it when the angry man looked uncomprehending.

'You're kidding,' he said in English. Then he turned to Rod and said, 'Then we'd better introduce ourselves. Billy Jacks, tailor of Stepney Green.'

Rod had no idea what had defused the situation, and was simply grateful that something had. He stretched out his hand, 'Rod Troy, journalist of Hampstead.'

Billy shook the hand and nodded his head in the direction of the man next to Rod.

'And this is 'Ummer. Leastways I call him 'Ummer. Real name's Hummel. He don't say much but he hums a lot.'

Rod shook hands with Hummer, still wondering what the man had said, regretting that a sound knowledge of German still left him baffled by Yiddish idiom, never guessing that it had been, 'Leave him alone, Billy. He's one of the good guys. I knew him the moment he got on board. He's the big Englishman who saved me from the SA on Kristallnacht.'

And neither Hummer nor Billy translated for him.

§ 102

At Derby they were allowed to stretch their legs. Soldiers lined the platform – locals, civilian and free, peeked through to look at the motley threat, this fearsome horde of pastry chefs and tailors, the detritus swept in from Europe. The prisoners strolled around under the dirty, blacked-out glass canopy, high equinoctial sunlight slanting in through the gaps where the paint had peeled. A summer's afternoon in the railway heart of England, huge whooshes of steam from all directions, the earth-shaking rattle of steel on steel, the roar of heat and smoke. The thunder of manufacture beating ploughshares into railway engines. Derby. A place Rod had never bothered to imagine, a place he felt sure many of his fellow passengers had never even heard of.

They had begun to know one another. Mr Jacks the tailor, once released from his animosity, had been most forthcoming – he had told Rod about the unfortunate accident of his birth, how unfortunate to find that he was German (Rod had been able to tell him all about the history of Danzig that had made his birth so unfortunate) and mercifully he had asked Rod no more questions about his brother – he surely would later, but for now it was a small mercy gratefully received. The man he called Hummer had retreated back into his novel and his dictionary –

'Din't speak a word when he got here,' Billy Jacks had told him. 'Now he soaks it up like hot jelly poured on sponge cake. Says bugger all for days, then he comes out with a string of long words the half of which he can't pronounce proper, on account he's only ever seen 'em written down, the other half of which I don't understand in the first place.' Rod had learnt that Hummer was a refugee from Vienna. He'd like to talk to him about Vienna if he ever surfaced from Bruddersford. Perhaps they knew the same parts? Perhaps they'd been there at the same time? The chap in the far corner, diagonally opposite Rod, had introduced himself. A Berlin Jew named Rosen who'd had the foresight to get out in 1933. The two blokes next to Hummer spoke no English, did not respond to Jacks' cockney Yiddish, and spoke in polysyllabics that Rod could not place anywhere on the map of Europe. If he'd been sitting next to them Rod thought he might run the gamut of his European tongues and have a go at them in his decent French and his far from decent Polish. As a last resort he might even talk to them in his native Russian. Next to Jacks was an Italian chef from Soho, a Mr Spinetti, who baked pastries at Quaglino's (Rod had eaten plenty of them in his time), who spoke English as well as Rod or Billy Jacks. Next to him, between him and Rosen, was a man in his sixties who looked at them all, responded with his eyes, blinking blue behind gold-rimmed spectacles, and the occasional nod, but would not or could not speak despite the obvious understanding he had of what they were saying.

Misunderstanding the nature of the occasion, the nature of his charges, a uniformed sergeant had yelled out, 'You may smoke!' Most of them were anyway, lighting up one cigarette from another and flicking the butts onto the track. The silent man was at the platform's edge, staring down at the tracks. The rails began to rattle and hum with the approach of an express. He turned and looked at Rod as though he had somehow felt Rod's eyes upon him. Then he straightened up, tugged his jacket neatly and strode over, hand outstretched.

'Hugo Klemper. How pleasant to know you.'

Rod took the hand, wondered at the inflection of what the man had said. It sounded like parrot-work poorly learnt, too much emphasis on the first syllable, rising too high at the end of the sentence, as though the 'how' were the question it wasn't.

'Professor of Electrical Engineering, Dresden.'

'Rod Troy, I'm a journalist,' Rod began, but before he could recip-

238

rocate full chapter and verse, Herr Klemper had moved on to shake hands with Jacks.

'Hugo Klemper. How pleasant to know you.'

It was breath for breath the same sentence. As though they had dialled up the speaking clock and got that infuriatingly precise woman with her infuriatingly unvarying vowels.

'Professor of Electrical Engineering, Dresden.'

Again, as soon as Jacks could rattle off the potted version of life as a single occupation, Klemper had moved on, to waste his words on the men who spoke no known language, and, seeking out everyone he shared the compartment with, Herr Rosen and Hummer, both of whom he addressed in English despite the common bond of German.

'Hugo Klemper. How pleasant to know you.'

The tracks hummed louder.

'Professor of Electrical Engineering, Dresden.'

The tannoy crackled to life and a woman's voice told passengers on Platform 1 to stand well back as the 2.25 to Sheffield passed.

Then Rod knew. This had not been a formal introduction, it had been a summary farewell. He lunged for Klemper, only to find Jacks and Hummer had him by his jacket. He watched, submerged in the rush and roar, silent inside the bubble of noise, as Klemper stepped off the platform and vanished under the train.

§ 103

It was, Rod thought, a form of madness. Each side going mad in its own way. The panic among the prisoners more than matched by the reaction of the troops, advancing on the helpless, hysterical captives as though they had themselves been attacked, rifles at waist height, barrels aiming into the crowd, boots banging down, sergeant and corporal barking orders. They herded them back across the platform to their own train, shoving them back inside and slamming the doors.

Somehow they flowed around Rod. At six feet two it seemed odd they should miss him, and suddenly he found himself behind enemy lines, looking down the track for a sign of Klemper. Twenty yards down the platform, Spinetti emerged from the gents, ''Ere, what's all the commotion?' and 'Bloody Hell' as he caught sight of the remains of Klemper. He leaned into the wall of the gents to throw up. Rod ran towards him, but by now the soldiers had spotted him, and two of them stepped in front of him and slapped their rifle barrels across his chest.

'Let me through,' Rod said softly.

'Back on the train, mate, back on the train.'

Rod pointed down the track to Klemper's mangled corpse.

'Good God, man, do you have no decency?'

The received pronunciation, the clipped speech of the officer class seemed to hit an automatic deference in them. They followed him down the platform. Spinetti was pale and groping around desperately in his pockets for a cigarette. Klemper was in three pieces, one arm, his head and then the rest.

'See,' said one of the Tommies. 'Ain't nuffink you could do.'

'Then perhaps it should be one of you. Get down onto the track, find his papers and see that someone informs his family.'

They were staring at the blood – a crimson slick a yard across, seeping into the limestone chips between the sleepers. Rod jumped down, put a hand inside Klemper's jacket and pulled out his wallet. Willing hands helped him back to the platform, but none would take the blood-stained wallet from him. Rod opened it, two ten-shilling notes, a letter from the Ministry classifying him as a Category C Alien, a blue-grey National Identity Card bearing an address in Willesden, a buff-yellow ration book ... and nothing else. Not a single personal item.

'What was you expecting?' said a Tommy.

'I don't know,' said Rod. 'Letters, a photograph, some memento of a wife or child. Some sense of family.'

'Maybe he got no family?'

Then Rod realised. They had been his family. Seven total strangers on a train. Seven men whose names and jobs he had to know before he died or die alone. Rod let himself be shepherded back and, with Spinetti all but thrown in behind him, the train started up once more, northward. Out of Derby, criss-crossing the Derwent every few miles, bridges and tunnels all but beyond number, for Manchester and points north.

§ 104

'Why?' said Billy, for the umpteenth time. 'Why would he just . . . bleedin' jump?'

For the umpteenth time Rod declined to answer. It seemed hubristic in the presence of so many refugees for this debate to be taking place between the compartment's resident Englishmen. But Rosen, after twenty minutes or more, had recovered his composure and seemed combative enough to want to answer.

'Mr Jacks, I heard you say you have lived your whole life here. Am I right?'

'Yeah. My old man brought me over when I was a nipper. Before I'd even learnt to speak. He was a Pole. I thought I was a Pole, when I didn't think I was English that is. Suddenly . . . I'm German . . .'

'*Ja, ja.* It is so. But you have never been back to Germany?'

'Course not.'

'Then you cannot possibly know. I was a prisoner of the Nazis for only a few weeks in 1933. The Oranienburg camp near Berlin. It is closed now, but worse have arisen in its place. The experience was enough to make me leave for good. I was lucky that I could leave. Many who go into the camps are never seen again.'

Billy was thinking about this, but Rod could tell from the puzzled expression – he wasn't getting it.

'So?'

'Perhaps Professor Klemper had been in a camp too. Perhaps his experience, like mine, was enough to drive him from his homeland. Perhaps the prospect of another camp, for that is surely where we are headed, was enough to make death seem preferable.'

'That's . . . that's just bleedin' ridiculous . . . these aren't yer Nazis these are English Tommies . . .'

'And they are?'

'Whaddya mean by that . . . they are . . . what they are.'

'They are men with guns taking us to a camp . . . of which we know neither the name nor the location.'

'Does that matter?'

Rod found Stahl's words to him on the matter of camps rising

241

unbidden to his lips. It had been a startling phrase at the time, a glimpse into Stahl's vision of it all, and, more than ever, it seemed appropriate.

'*Nacht und Nebel*,' he said softly but loud enough for all to hear.

There was a pause. Rosen looked at Rod expectantly. The two non-speakers stared straight ahead, Spinetti and Billy looked at one another.

'What's that mean?' they said together.

Rod was about to tell them, when Hummel spoke.

'Night and Fog, Billy. Not a phrase I have heard before but so resonant. So very resonant. I wish I'd thought of the phrase. But I have no gift for poetry. I almost vanished into night and fog myself.'

'See,' said Billy, much to Rod's despair. 'I told you 'e'd come out with a mouthful sooner or later.'

§ 105

They sat an age in a railway siding just outside Manchester. It was late afternoon now, but approaching the longest day of the year, and far from twilight. About half past five, the train shunted slowly into Manchester Central – a building conceived in its black misery to make even St Pancras look cheerful. Rod stuck his head out of the window. A soldier was patrolling right outside, ten paces up the platform, ten paces down, rifle slung over his left shoulder.

'Is this it?' Rod asked.

'No, mate. It ain't.'

'In that case, is there any chance we could stretch our legs? It's awfully hot in here and we've been cooped up since Derby.'

'If it was up to me you could. But it ain't, so you can't. You just pop yer 'ead back inside. You'll be on the move before you know it.'

Truer word was never. Before Rod could step back into the compartment, the carriage lurched and the train reversed slowly back out of the station. He staggered to his seat.

Billy Jacks said, 'What's 'appening?'

'Not much. I rather think we just changed engines, that's all.'

'Looks to me as though we're headed back to London.'

Fat chance, thought Rod, but he said nothing.

The train took a westward curve over points at the south end of the station and crawled in a lazy half circle around the centre of the city, across the Irwell and into Salford, into a landscape of tall chimneys and soot-blackened mills.

By nine o'clock they were in a siding, pulled up at freight platforms next to one of the mills. At last the cry went up, 'Everybody out.' And, for the benefit of non-English speakers, someone was running the length of the platform yelling in crude German, '*Raus! Raus!*' Several hundred tired, cramped and dishevelled men stepped down from the train – all with one question, 'Where are we?'

Rod was the last to leave the compartment. He reached up for his bag, took it down and realised his was not the last. There was still an attaché case up there on the netting. Brown leather, reinforced at the corners, with the labels of a hotel in Stuttgart and another in Paris stuck to it. It had to be Klemper's. Who else's could it be? And rather than leave it he took it with him, half wondering if there might yet be someone to whom it could be returned. 'Everybody has somebody' was a truism of which he was beginning to doubt the truth. It now seemed perfectly possible that Professor Klemper had nobody. That they, in their present captivity, were nobodies. That they could jump to their deaths alone and uncounted. It struck him as a form of oblivion – death as a statistic, to have existed only never to have existed, *Nacht und Nebel* again – the saddest fact of death, that there was no one even to tell. He shook the moment off – told himself he had a wife and two kids, both parents living, two sisters ... to say nothing of an irritating little brother.

Attempts to square the internees military-style into ranks of three amounted to nothing. Those that understood wouldn't or couldn't and those that didn't understand outnumbered those that did. So they slouched across cobblestones, through the makeshift barbed wire gates of the mill, more mob than squad, with a disbelieving infantry sergeant bellowing at them to 'Shape up!'

As they passed under the main archway into the mill itself, Rod looked up and caught sight of the company name chipped into the stone lintel in big, cusped letters, all the boldness of the nineteenth century caught in a font. He glanced off to his left and caught Hummel doing the same. Hummel could not resist a smile. The sign read 'Friedrich Engels and Co.' Perhaps Hummel had the same thoughts Rod was having – did Engels write *The Condition of the English Working Class* here? Did he put his two penn'orth into the *Manifesto of the Communist Party* here? And was his ghost watching as men were led beneath his name if not into chains then certainly into captivity? Hummel, he decided from the smile, had a sense of irony. He wouldn't bother trying to explain this to Billy Jacks.

It was poorly lit inside – naked bulbs dangling almost periloulsy to shed circles of light and shadow without creating enough of either to give anyone a clear sense of where they were. In front of them was a row of trestle tables, manned by uniformed soldiers, who in turn were guarded by armed soldiers under the command of a corporal of the Lancashire Regiment.

'Right you Krauts an' Eyeties and what have you. Kit on the table and turn out yer pockets!'

This produced a prolonged hiatus as those that spoke English translated for those that didn't.

'Get a bleedin' move on!'

A man four places ahead of Rod in the queue obediently put down a green oilskin case and began to rummage through his pockets. The case was flipped open, its contents roughly tipped out onto the table. Rod watched this happen to one package after another, the length of the room. Saw the flash of movement as wallets and watches disappeared like a bad conjuring trick.

'My God,' he said, thinking aloud. 'They're fleecing us!'

'Fleecing, *ja*.' He heard Hummel say, another colloquialism logged.

'I thought it was an inspection . . . but they're just confiscating anything they want.'

A tap on the arm with the barrel of a rifle urged Rod up to the table.

'Your stuff, on the table, now, Fritz!'

Rod had a firm grip on his own bag but saw Klemper's snatched from him and plonked down, saw the soldier's fingers fiddling at the latch. Calmly Rod placed a hand over his.

'The case is not mine. And it certainly isn't yours. Its owner died today. Would you steal from the dead?'

'What? Who the fuck are you?'

'I'm the man in charge, and what you're doing is theft.'

'In charge? In charge o' what?'

'In charge of this case. Now who's in charge of you?'

Rod followed the man's gaze, craned his neck to see the corporal approach.

'What's the hold-up 'Iggins? Keep the buggers moving!'

'It's this bloke, Corp. He say he's in charge.'

The corporal was a little bulldog of a man, pigeon-chested and a good eight inches shorter than Rod. Rod stood up, stretched to his full height and drew on memories of being in the OTC at school.

'You, man. Who's your commanding officer?'

'You what?'

'Stand to attention when you address me. I said, where's your commanding officer?'

'I . . . er . . . I er . . .'

'Don't fluster man, just go and get him!'

Slightly, but only slightly, to Rod's amazement it worked. The corporal turned on his heel and vanished into an inner room of the mill. The soldiers at the table froze, every one of them looking at Rod. The internees set up a susurrus of whispers in half a dozen languages, and they too stared at the big man who'd bellowed orders in the received pronunciation of the King's English. English and foreigner had but one thought between them – friend or foe?

The corporal returned, led by a captain of the Lancashires. The captain pointedly flipped the press stud on his holster, Rod just as pointedly flipped his Old Harrovian tie.

'What's going on here?'

Then his eyes flickered down to the tie, then up to Rod's face, down to the tie and back again. The press stud was clicked back into place with his right hand and the left took Rod gently by the elbow and steered him towards the edge of the room, where moonlight streaked in through a broken window.

'I know you,' the captain said simply. 'You're one of the Troy brothers, aren't you?'

'Yes,' said Rod. 'I'm Rod.'

'Johnnie Eynsford-Hill. I was two years below you at school. Your brother fagged for me.'

'Well, if I ever get out of this den of thieves I'll be sure to remind him.'

'Look, old chap, would you mind keeping your voice down?'

'Thief is thief even if I whisper it,' Rod mock-whispered. 'These men are robbing their charges. If you know about it and condone it, you're as guilty as they are. If you don't know then you're a poor excuse for an officer. But now your face comes back to me, "old chap", you were a pretty poor excuse for a cadet, as I recall.'

The man blushed. Guilt seeped like a beetroot stain on a tablecloth.

'I've come a long way since then. Sandhurst. Passed out well. Commissioned. And believe you me, I'd rather be in a combat regiment than in charge of this bunch of skiving layabouts.'

'Fine ... prove it.'

Eynsford-Hill blushed again.

'I find it pays to let them do things their way.'

'One of us has to give an order. If not you, me. And if I do it and any of these "skiving layabouts" jumps to it, you'll never have the respect of a British Tommy again. Do it. Do it for your own self-respect.'

Eynsford-Hill turned to face the room. Rod took a step back to let him.

'Right, listen here. All packages are to be examined. But you are only to confiscate anything that might be used as a weapon. Does everyone understand?'

The corporal saluted, a dozen begrudging voices said 'Sir.'

Rod went back to the table. Picked up his bag and Klemper's and stepped out of the queue. If they still wanted to search him he'd be amazed. Eynsford-Hill beckoned him back to the window.

'I do have a question,' he said.

'OK. I owe you that. Ask away.'

'What are you doing here?'

§ 106

They were led to the top floor, up five flights of winding stairs to a long weaving shed lit only by the moon through the rooflights. Even so, Rod could see what they were in for. For eighty-odd men there seemed to be no more than twenty beds, none of which had mattresses. Most of the old machinery had not been removed and the accommodation was fitted in around looms and cranks and over head cam-belts. If it weren't for the filth, the litter and the neglect − puddles under the broken rooflights where it had rained the night before, broken wooden bobbins everywhere − it was possible to believe the factory had shut yesterday merely to reopen as a prison today.

Rod turned to see the reaction in the others only to find they were all looking at him. He couldn't quite decide whether the look was respect or desperation, then Billy Jacks half-whispered to him, 'Flashing the ole school tie to scare a bunch of Tommies shitless is one thing – worked a treat, if you ask me – but this lot need a leader, and they're lookin' at you and you can't say you didn't ask for it. Toffs is as toffs does.'

'Oh bugger.'

'Just tell 'em what to do, 'Ampstead. They'll listen to you.'

'Er . . . er . . . right. Mr Jacks, go back to the British and tell them that we've none of us eaten for almost twelve hours and we'd appreciate rations issue.'

Jacks called him a bastard but set off for the staircase.

'Now . . . beds. Is there anyone sick or lame?'

The translations moved swiftly and half a dozen hands went up.

'Right – you get the beds. The rest go to anyone over sixty. Now . . . blankets. Mr Spinetti . . . back to the British, tell them we need more blankets.'

Slowly the men spread themselves out. A natural democracy ensued. No squabbles over who was sicker than whom. Or who was older than whom. It was a mess turning into an organisation. For a brief hubristic moment, Rod felt a deluding flush of pride – then Eynsford-Hill was standing in front of him again, red-faced and trying vainly to hold in his anger. Spinetti and Jacks behind him, pleased at the trouble they were causing.

'You're asking an awful lot, you know. It's practically dark, it's close to ten o'clock . . .'

Rod said, 'Are you saying you have no rations?'

'No, but . . .'

'Then break them out and feed the men. Are you saying you've no blankets?'

'No we haven't any more blankets. What you see is what there is. It's all we've got. Troy, what you don't seem to understand is that no one was expecting you. You've been shuffled around in railway sidings half the evening while we found somewhere that would take you. We already have seven hundred and fifty men here! I'll feed you, of course I'll feed you, but there's not much more I can do.'

'Blankets for the sick, and a visit from the MO?'

'The MO will be here in the morning. I can probably drum up

enough blankets for the sick . . . my men will surrender theirs . . . depends how many are claiming sick.'

'Seven. And a dozen I'd just call elderly.'

'OK. Leave it with me.'

Eynsford-Hill pushed his way between Jacks and Spinetti. They were, Rod thought, grinning like idiots, revelling in the minor skirmishes of the class war, delighted, smugly pleased to see toff versus toff work in their favour. What bothered him was that they neither of them seemed to grasp how serious it was. What bothered him was that their perception of him as their champion could be at best temporary.

Half an hour later half a dozen soldiers brought up trays of bread and cheese. Rod felt a slap on the back from Jacks that he could well have done without. The bread was stale, the cheese faintly green with the onset of mould.

'Oh, bloody hell,' said Jacks. 'This is disgustin'. Get those buggers back up here and give 'em a piece of your mind, 'Ampstead!'

Rod chewed on his iron rations, thinking this must be how the escaped convict had felt in *Great Expectations*. Awful it was, and way better than nothing at all.

'Tell you what, Mr Jacks, try flashing *your* old school tie for a change. I think you'll find they don't do room service. Or did you think I could work miracles?'

'Alright, alright . . . keep yer wig on. I only asked.'

Jacks bit into the bread and cheese, pulled a face at Rod, chewed almost stoically and looked around him. Bad as it was the meal was being wolfed by almost everyone else.

Herr Rosen said softly to Billy, 'You see, Herr Jacks, we have many of us been here before. Eat first, complain later, if at all, for you may end up with nothing. Believe me, I have eaten worse. And you, Herr Troy – miracle, shmiracle . . . don't be so modest.'

Rod lay on the floor, used his bag for a pillow. This must, he thought, be what a coffin feels like. Or, as his metaphor enlarged, what it feels like to be a lead soldier in a toybox . . . lying as he was ramrod straight between a ramrod straight Rosen and a ramrod straight Hummel. Some-where over to his right Jacks was squirming, 'I can't get comfy.'

'Sssh, Billy,' Rod heard Hummel say, then Jacks was up and yelling, ''Ere, wot the bleedin'? . . . It's a rat . . . a fuckin' rat just ran over me!'

A shaft of moonlight from the roof showed Jacks leaping from one foot to the other, armed with a shoe.

'It's a rat, a fuckin' rat!'

In seconds he had the room in turmoil, old men wrapped in blankets shuffling around and shouting at one another in German.

'*Ja! Ja! Hier!*'

Jacks pounced with his shoe, walloped and missed. Spinetti came at it from the other side, walloped and scored. He picked up the rat by its tail, but before he could say a word, the cry went up from the other side of the room, '*Noch eine, noch eine.*'

Soon half the men in the room had taken off one shoe and were pounding away at the floorboards, at rats real or imagined in a mad cacophony of drumming.

Another Lancashire corporal appeared suddenly at the top of the stairs, a man either side of him with rifles levelled.

'What the bleedin' 'ell is going on 'ere?'

Silence. Then a lone voice said, '*Ratten.*'

Then dozens of voices took it up, '*Ratten! Ratten!*'

'What!?'

'Rats.'

Hands went up among the prisoners, three dead rats held by their tails.

The corporal muttered, 'Jesus H. Christ', motioned to his men to lower their rifles, and as he did so there was a cry that seemed to come from a thousand miles away. Faint and clear at the same time. Rod looked behind him. A window had been forced open. He looked out and down, the corporal rushed to his side. Five floors down they could see the outline of a man, splayed across the cobblestones.

Rod had no idea who it was. The sight, the idea of another suicide took his breath away. Billy Jacks came up beside him.

'Not another?' he said gently.

'Yeah,' said the corporal. 'Another bloody jumper. My third this fuckin' week! Now I've got to fill out fuckin' forms an' fuckin' chits and make a report to the fuckin' captain. And then the fuckin' captain's got to make a report to the fuckin' colonel. Why do they always pick my fuckin' shift? Why can't you fuckers do it on the day watch? Why can't you do it before you fuckin' get here?'

He barged his way out, took his men with him. Rod looked down at the body, looked at Jacks, looked down at the body, at the posse of uniforms gathering around it.

Hummel was standing behind them. Poked his head between them and he too looked down.

'Always they yump,' he said and turned away.

Rod turned back to the room, a sea of frightened faces, and found his voice.

'Who?' he said. 'Does anyone know who?'

And no one did.

Later, cold and miserable, craving a blanket, ramrod straight again between Hummel and Herr Rosen, Rod heard Billy say over him, 'Ummer?'

'*Ja*, Billy.'

'You said "always they yump".'

'That's because they do.'

'Sure. All I meant to say was it's "jump" with a J.'

'Thank you, Billy.'

Later, Rod heard Billy start to snore and knew then what the music of the night would be, the bass rumble of his snoring underscoring the arpeggios of urine landing in firebuckets as the elderly got up to pee, one after another, all night – but then why should he sleep? When had he ever known two deaths in a day before, let alone two suicides? It was a recipe for eternal insomnia. The stuff of which dreams are not made.

§ 107

Roused at six. No breakfast. No Medical Officer. Shuffled back onto a train, unwashed, unshaven, bleary. Eynsford-Hill sticking his head in through the carriage window to say, 'What you've got to understand is –', only to be cut short by Rod's curt 'Fuck off' and the train juddering into motion.

At Liverpool Pier Head Rod finally realised his brother had been right. They were headed for the Isle of Man. They lined up for the noon crossing to Douglas aboard the RMS *Ben My Chree*.

For a while, for the few hours it took to cross the Irish Sea on a calm, beautiful summer's day, it was almost possible to ignore war, captivity and the rumbling of his stomach. It was bliss to watch land fall away, it was bliss to watch nothing but sea, it was bliss to watch new land come into sight. Even half a dozen Spitfires circling briefly on a training exercise did not dent the illusion.

Late afternoon brought them to disembarkation in Douglas harbour, another stupid sergeant bellowing at them. A miserable, downtrodden private to march them off again. A haphazard path across the town, up the hill to another ring of barbed wire.

It seemed to Rod that 'camp' was hardly a good description. The Army had cordoned off whole streets of seaside boarding houses. Simply rolled out barbed wire and declared what was within a camp. The landladies of these establishments had been told to pack and go, the houses stuffed to the eaves with refugees of all (enemy) nations and, in the absence of proper screens, the windows painted black. It looked bizarre. The bright, garish colours of the seaside punctuated by the lightless panes of black.

They stood at the gates and waited. Voices from behind the wire called out names to men in line ... Manny, Asa, Yonny? ... it's me ... Hans, Josef, Willi!

The miserable private on guard duty came out to talk to the miserable private who'd marched them up from the quay.

'Wot? More? We can't take this lot. We're stuffed. Where do they all come from?'

'They just marched up the hill.'

'Well march 'em back down again, they can't come in here.'

'Maybe Port Erin will take 'em?'

'Maybe. So long as they don't come here.'

Rod could hardly miss this.

'I say ... do I understand that you're moving us on somewhere else?'

'S'right mate. They reckon this place is full.'

'So ... more walking?'

'Bound to be some walking.'

'No,' Rod said firmly. 'I'll walk, and so will the younger men. But the sick and the elderly get off now. They've been travelling for two days. You push some of these chaps an inch further and they'll collapse.'

The two soldiers exchanged glances.

'But ... that's most of 'em. Most of 'em look sick or old.'

'Then they'd better stay here, hadn't they?'

The guard looked behind him as though seeking support, as though an officer might helpfully appear on the scene at any moment, but none did. Only a bobbing sea of heads still waving and calling out to those they recognised.

'Alright, nobody wants any bother. But just the sick uns and the old uns. OK?'

'OK,' Rod said.

The gates opened. Rod called out in German that anyone who felt unwell or was over sixty should go inside. Men shuffled past him. Men who looked sick, men who looked old, men who looked neither and the two who spoke no known language. This whittled their numbers down to a handful. Nobody stood still long enough to be counted.

They marched back down the hill to the railway station, to a quaint narrow gauge railway, where pot-domed little tank engines pulled brightly coloured carriages along a three-foot track.

Their guard handed them over to another with a tired, 'All yours, mate' and 'Watch out for the big bugger with the posh voice, he's a trouble-maker.'

Their latest escort didn't seem a bad sort. Grinning rather than smiling, but that was at least an expression and far better than the way the soldiers had behaved last night or this evening. He ignored the warning, turned his grin on Rod and said, 'You're one of the lucky ones, mate.'

'Lucky. We don't even know where we're going. We just get bounced from pillar to post.'

'Trust me, mate, in less than an hour you'll be in heaven.'

The grin had become a smile, Rod could not but trust to the honesty of the man. 'In heaven', clearly, was no euphemism for meeting one's maker – they weren't about to be put up against the wall and shot. After all, the British didn't do that sort of thing, did they? And as soon as the thought had achieved language in his mind he realised how difficult it would be explaining that to the Jews, the Germans and the Austrians on this train, who had fled persecution, who had fled camps, and probably did think they had leapt from frying pan to firing squad. They had seen two countries that they may well have thought above that sort of thing descend into casual murder and political thuggery. Who, prior to 1914, would not have considered Germany amongst the most civilised of countries? Why should it not happen here?

§ 108

It was like the descent into a dream. The descent from a dream. He would never be sure which. Steam from the locomotive wreathed around his ankles, the smell of a childhood summer drifting to his nostrils, smoke and soot mingling with the steam, the racing clouds across the sky, the heavy hint of rain in a summer evening, rounding off a day of glorious summer sunshine, the awed, gentle hush of Mitteleurope hissing behind him, soft as smoke and steam. And as the last puff from the engine dies away, the platform clears, and in front of his eyes the station name board, *Heaven's Gate*. And a poem of Edward Thomas's surfacing in his mind, *Adelstrop*, remembering the slow train stopping in obscurest Oxfordshire or Gloucestershire, the singing of a blackbird and of all the birds for miles around – and then a blackbird did sing, and it seemed to him he was wrapped inside the dream, wrapped in birdsong, wrapped in steam, wrapped in a soft, shlooshy murmur of enquiring Yiddish. How improbable was Heaven's Gate? How much the stuff of dreams?

'Told yer.'

It was the soldier who'd chatted to him on the platform in Douglas.

'Not quite,' said Rod. 'You dropped a hint.'

'Nah, if I'd told you there was a place called Heaven's Gate, it'd ruin the surprise and you'd never have believed me.'

'I'm not sure I believe you even now.'

'Suit yerself, but don't hang about. If you ask me it's going to piss it down.'

Out of the dream. Rain and night. Out of the dream. Piss it down.

§ 109

It was a matter of less than a quarter of a mile to their destination. Rod did a head count to please the soldier and realised for the first time that they were down now to less than twenty. Mostly middle-aged. Indeed the youngest seemed to be made up entirely of those with whom he had shared a compartment on the journey from London. They'd lost the two Incomprehensibles at Douglas, and they'd lost Klemper. The five remained – Rod, Jacks, Hummel, Spinetti and the still rather enigmatic Herr Rosen. He shrugged off the word survivors – unbidden in his mind and not yet appropriate, and said to the soldier, 'I make it nineteen.'

'Me too.'

'How many of us should there be?'

'Search me. I'll just tell 'em nineteen delivered and leave it at that.'

Rod and he walked side by side, down a dusty lane, thick with dog roses and honeysuckle, away from the station, the raggle-taggle band of old Jews trailing along behind, all a-mutter. They dribbled to a halt at two large stone gateposts. The gateposts had lost their gates, no doubt being melted down to make spitfires or dreadnoughts, the iron hinges stuck out like severed limbs, but two inscriptions remained. The newer read 'St Margaret's School for Girls. Est. 1921', and the one above, its lettering black with age, the contrast between stone and carving almost dead flat, read 'Heaven's Gate, Convent of the Sacred Heart. 1866.'

As at Engels' mill, makeshift gates had been knocked up from three-by-two and barbed wire. One half lay propped open, and in the space another infantry man stood puffing on a cigarette in lazy expectation.

'Another lot?' he said simply.

'Nineteen, Ted,' said the first soldier, adding a truthless, 'All accounted for.'

'Anything to sign?'

'Leave it out.'

Then the soldier smiled at Rod, said a gentle, 'Good luck, mate' and walked back the way he had come. The reluctant gypsies stood at the gates of heaven.

'Well, you gonna stand there all night or are you comin' in?'

Their new guardian pulled the second gate wide and beckoned to them.

'Straight down the drive, up to the porch, can't miss it. Kettle'll be on. I bet you blokes are parched.'

Rod said, 'Are you not meant to escort us or something?'

'No mate, it's going to piss it down. I wanna be back in me box. You lot toddle off to Little Vienna.'

'Little Vienna?' Rod said, but the soldier had gone back in his box.

They shuffled through the gates, down the driveway lined with peeling plane trees, under a sky now heavy with the threat of rain.

Jacks drew level with Rod. 'You know that thing you get in detective stories, when the bad geezer "lulls his victim into a" ... a wotsit ... "a false sense of security"?'

'Quite,' said Rod.

'I got that now. It's like a tightness in yer bollocks.'

'Indeed it is,' said Rod.

Rod found himself thinking of the novels he'd read set in grand houses, *Jane Eyre, Mansfield Park* – more recently *Rebecca* – but soon settled on the image of his father's house in Hertfordshire, of the way the driveway had been shaped to create and withhold revelation – little twists and little turns that presented the house in fragments, a window here, a glimpse of roof there, until the trees fell away and you arrived at a full view of the southern side of the crumbling Georgian pile in all its ramshackle glory.

Heaven's Gate appeared to them as huge slate roofs, occasional turrets, high, narrow leaded windows, until the last bend in the drive, the last overgrown plane tree and the clear sight of a Victorian mansion, clad in ivy – gloom and neglect registered so well in a single plant.

As Rod set foot on the porch, the first drops of rain pattered onto the roof above him, the door flew open and a disembodied, accented voice said, 'My word, just in time. Such a capricious summer. Come, come. Inside all of you. We were expecting you hours ago. You must all be starving!'

And they were.

'*Mehr licht, mehr licht!*'

A chandelier high over their heads, missing half its bulbs, flickered on. Rod found himself facing a small, bright-eyed little man in his sixties, white hair and a goatee beard – every inch the cartoon professor. If David Low had ever caricatured Trotsky and Einstein – and Rod could not remember one way or the other – this man would be the hybrid.

'*Würden sie Deutschen oder Englisch bevorzugen?*'

Offering him a choice of languages in the same tone in which one said 'Indian or China?'

'I'm fine with English,' Rod said, 'although there may be one or two who ...'

'Quite, quite. Let us proceed in English until we learn of another necessity. Let me introduce myself. I am Maximilian Drax, of Berlin. Welcome to the Isle of Forgotten Men.'

'And I'm Rod Troy ... of Hampstead.'

'It helps,' said Drax, 'and it will not detain us long, if we state for the record our city of origin.'

He gestured towards a chunky mahogany dining table that had been trundled in to serve as a desk. Behind it sat a young man in his late twenties, pen in hand, a notebook splayed on the table before him, smiling benignly at them all. Smiling seemed to be the order of the day. On the far edge of the table sat a steaming, hissing urn of hot water and another man, back to Rod, bent over it filling tea pot after tea pot, thoroughly preoccupied.

'Arthur Kornfeld, of Vienna, keeps records for us. We all feel it helps to know where we all come from. To have something written down by us rather than by the British. Helps us not to ... not to lose touch. A matter of identity. No small matter you will agree.'

Rod did agree. It was a matter of identity that had brought him here in the first place.

'In that case,' he said, perfectly willing to play the game, 'I'm Rodyon Troy, also of Vienna. Indeed, I think you'll find more than a few of us are.'

Drax stuck out both hands to shake one of Rod's, beaming at him as though he'd found a long-lost son. Behind him Rod heard Jacks plonk his gladstone bag on the table and say, 'Billy Jacks, Stepney Green.'

Kornfeld said, 'It won't hurt, you know. And we're all in the same boat.'

Billy shot a surly glance in Rod's direction, looked back at Kornfeld.

'OK, OK, whatever 'Ampstead says. Abel Jakobson, Danzig. Now, where's me bleedin' tea?'

The man at the urn turned with the deftness of a canteen lady in a cotton mill, splashed tea into half a dozen mugs at once, and said, 'Right here, Danzig. Hot and wet, as they say in your part of London.'

He handed a cup to Billy, picked up another for Rod and stared. Rod stared back. It was Oskar Siebert – Detective Sergeant of the Vienna Police HQ.

Before Rod could speak, Kornfeld did, 'Forgive me, Herr Jakobson, but I ask this of everyone, do you play the violin?'

Jacks said, to Kornfeld's bafflement, 'Worked a few fiddles in me time, never actually played one.'

Kornfeld sought explanation in Rod's eyes. Rod took his eyes off Siebert and said, 'As a matter of fact *I* do.'

256

'Oh marvellous,' said Kornfeld. 'We have been so lucky here these last few months – we have a good library, we have been able to set up a small printing press and an active university and a patisserie, but our string quartet has always lacked a second violin. Herr Troy, would you care to be our second violin?'

Rod introduced a pause, looked at Siebert and said, 'A patisserie? Are they kidding?'

'No, Mr Troy, they are not. And you'll find the coffee's not bad either.'

A new face slipped in beside Kornfeld. Rod heard Hummel say, 'Josef Hummel. Vienna. I play nothing.'

Then Kornfeld was waving at him.

'Of course,' Rod said. 'Second violin. Why not?'

Herr Rosen stepped up to the table.

'Viktor Rosen. Berlin. Piano. Sugar in my tea, if at all possible.'

Rod beckoned to Siebert. Other willing hands had appeared to man the tea, a new burble of voices and questions – 'Anyone here from Hamburg . . . Berlin . . . Düsseldorf?' They would find a corner to talk in. Away from the refugees' tea party. Then he heard Kornfeld say, 'Max, Max, do you see who we have hear. Viktor Rosen. Viktor Rosen! *Mein Gott!*'

Then Kornfeld too was on his feet, both hands extended to grip Rosen's as Drax had gripped Rod's.

'I heard you play the Tchaikovsky First in 1932 with the Berlin Philharmonic. I have . . . I mean had . . . all your records.'

§ 110

Siebert showed Rod to his billet on the second floor. A small room with four narrow cots, neatly folded blankets and clean sheets. It looked to Rod to be a pleasant, light room, a panelled rectangle in pale oak and cream paintwork – high windows darkened only by the rain battering against them. It was all familiar.

'It's crowded, but better than dormitories. This place began as a nunnery, hence there tend to be small rooms, some absurdly small – I think you might even say cells – rather than dormitories. I share with Kornfeld. Drax has his own room. This room is entirely empty. Pick who you wish, although I would advise against anyone over sixty-five. They tend to piss all night and you get no sleep.'

Rod looked at the pegs on the wall next to the door, leftovers from the recent days when the house had been a girl's boarding school – fading white labels in tiny metal windows – 'Rosalind Twist', 'Eleanor Twist', 'Margaret Mayes'. To which list he added his own name, seeing once again the row of pegs at his old school bearing the names 'Troy, R.A.', and 'Bentinck, J.P.Q.' and half a dozen others. Bentinck J.P.Q. had the requisite three initials of an upper-class English public schoolboy, and had been Rod's best friend in a small world where best friends lasted forever. Rod had lost touch with him years ago.

It was all familiar enough to be reassuring.

'Tell me,' he began.

'What am I doing here?' Siebert said.

'I'm sure the question applies to us both . . . but . . .'

'Me first, eh?'

Siebert sat on the nearest cot, then stretched out with his hands clasped behind his head on the pile of blankets and pillows. Rod perched, less relaxed, on the edge of the next cot.

'Well . . . you kept your word. Nothing you wrote about Kristallnacht mentioned me by name. All the same, the account you gave had in it a glaring gap that could only be filled by me. I was not the favourite son of the Vienna police to begin with – a non-Nazi in what you rightly observed was pretty much a Nazi organisation to begin with. After Kristallnacht I was suspect. They made no move against me, but I knew it all the same. In the January of '39 we obtained an extradition order on a jewel thief who had fled to Zürich. It had been my case, naturally I was the one to go and collect him. It was probably the easy solution for everyone. They knew I'd not come back. I abandoned my apartment . . . it was only rented . . . I abandoned all my possessions . . . I crossed into Switzerland, with my extradition order, my warrant and my passport . . . and with the contents of my bank account wrapped around my waist in a money belt. Who knows, perhaps you have heard a dozen stories like this in the last few days? The money belt has replaced clean underpants as the sine qua non of travel. I let a jewel thief go. I let myself go. I was in England by March, and not without difficulties. Being a former police-man helped and did not help. It showed I might be honest, and implied

I might be a Nazi . . . hence when the round-up came I was one of the first. I've been here since October. Indeed, I count myself lucky not to have been shipped to the colonies, to Canada or Australia.'

'Good Lord, are we . . . I mean they . . . doing that?'

'Yes. That's why Heaven's Gate has room for you. They shipped out a couple of dozen only days ago.'

'Poor buggers.'

'Some were innocents, some were Jews, but mostly they were Nazis. An unpleasant crowd. They taunted the Jews, and only the fact that they were outnumbered stopped anything worse. Good riddance was the general feeling. In fact, I rather wish they'd taken them all. We have one left, just the one, and with a bit of luck you'll never need to have anything to do with him.'

Siebert stretched and sat up again.

'And you?'

Back at school, soaking up the imagery of his very English childhood – if only there were a cricket bat parked in the corner, a muddy football boot under the bed, or a dog-eared *Kennedy's Latin Primer* on the windowsill – Rod found the phrase that had eluded him for ages now about to burst on his lips.

'I am the . . . I am the ambiguous Englishman. The Home Counties, Harrow and Cambridge . . . a plum in my voice, a striped tie at my neck, the label of a Mayfair bespoke tailor on the inside pocket of my suit . . . but born in Vienna as my parents passed through from Russia, to Paris . . . to London.'

'Ah . . . I had not guessed. Stupid of me. But why were you not naturalised?'

'That's a long story,' the ambiguous Englishman said.

§ I I I

Downstairs the lobby was full. The whole house had turned out at the news of new arrivals. He found Hummel listening intently as two men talked at him in rapid German, oblivious to the fact that Hummel was saying not a word. Found Billy, standing on the sidelines, mug of tea in hand, munching on a flaky pastry.

'They really weren't kidding about the patisserie, then?' Rod said.

'Nope. I got me cake. In fact I'm on me third slice.'

Rod heard the silent 'but' and uttered it for him.

'But it's weird. Not just that I don't speak German ... I mean they seem to switch between German and Yiddish all the time ... and my old dad brought me up to speak Yiddish so ... it's just ... I dunno.'

'It's just that all this ... otherness, this Mitteleuropeanness, this ... this Viennese picnic makes you feel English?'

Billy pulled a face at this as though it were a phrase too far in his thinking.

'No. I don't feel English. Maybe I'll never feel English again. Maybe your brother kyboshed bein' English for me when he and old Stilton come round to tell me I was nicked for a wog. Maybe I never was English. Me with an accent like a gobful of whelks. Maybe the only thing you can be is you. Maybe the only thing to do is look after number one.'

Rod changed the subject.

'I've been allocated a room for four. Are you and Hummel coming in with me?'

'Sure, why not?'

'We'll need a fourth.'

'Not one of them old buggers. They piss all bleedin' night!'

And Rod thought he'd snored through it all.

'I meant ... Spinetti or Rosen?'

'Rosen. Spinetti talks too much. Bleedin' wops never shut up.'

§ 112

Stilton and Troy were dealing with stragglers now. Men so far down the list they were literally last, even if the list itself possessed no logic. Or men who had not been home when they called or not reported when asked.

Ivor Kempinski fulfilled both categories and added a third by making a run for it when Stilton and Troy turned up at his home during his late evening meal. He had upended his boiled beef and carrots over Stilton, ran for the back door with his napkin still tucked into his collar, clambered nimbly onto the roof of the outside khazi, leapt into the alley and vanished.

Troy yanked at the yard door, heard Mrs Kempinski say, 'I wouldn't bother, if I were you. Ain't opened in twenty years.'

Stilton bumbled into the yard, brushing mashed potato from his jacket.

'Legged it? Over the wall?'

'Yep.'

'How old do the notes say he is?'

'Fifty-four.'

'Fit for his age,' Stilton said. 'Well, he runs to fight another day. I'm not chasing him tonight. It'll be dark in ten minutes.'

Mrs Kempinski folded her arms under her bosom and looked as though this sort of thing happened to her every day.

'You won't be wanting yer cup of tea then?'

'Some other time, Hilda. Some other time.'

They drove back towards Jubilee Street, where Troy had left his car outside Stilton's house.

Halfway down Parnell Street, a brewer's dray had shed half its load and blocked the road. Broken barrels and a sea of ale. Troy stepped out of the car, looked at the dead horse between the shafts, at the patient survivor, ears up, head down, standing bunkered next to the body, and made no argument with the driver. Breweries had worked overtime since the war increased demand. He'd read somewhere that Hitler had raised the level of alcohol in German beer, to boost morale. *Blitzkrieg, Pisstkrieg.*

He told Stilton, 'Let's cut through Buxton Street, the alley that runs behind the synagogue.'

'Just so long as we don't meet anything coming the other way. It can't be six foot wide.'

Stilton reversed the Riley, then swung right into a long, curving alley. No traffic, no blockages and they'd emerge close to the Mile End Road. It was only just dark now, but with no moon, high walls on either side and the merest glimmer of light from the shielded headlamps, they might as well have driven into hell.

Stilton said, 'Ye Gods, it's black as Satan's armpit down here. You could –'

The bump thrust up the passenger side of the car and brought it down with a crash.

'What the —? Must have hit the kerb.'

The engine died.

Troy said, 'There is no kerb.'

He got out, wished he'd had the foresight to bring a torch, and groped around under the car

'Walter, drive on a bit. There's something under the back wheel.'

Troy flattened himself against the wall, Stilton rolled the car on a couple of feet. Troy had a partial sight of the obstacle now, fractionally lit up by the glow of the rear lamps and revised his phrasing. There had been some*one* under the wheel. Someone big and black and hairy.

Stilton came round the other side and handed him a bullseye torch.

'Oh Christ. Is he dead?'

Troy held one wrist between finger and thumb.

'Yes.'

Shone the torch on the face.

'It's Isaiah Borg.'

'What?'

'Rabbi Borg, from the synagogue.'

'What?'

Stilton turned, seeking something in the blank appearance of the synagogue's back wall.

'You mean he just stepped out . . .'

'No. I don't. He didn't step out from anywhere. I'd have seen him. You'd have seen him. He was on the ground when we hit him. We went over him, and then he got stuck under the back wheel.'

'What do we do?'

It sounded more innocent than it was. It seemed an odd question for one copper to be asking of another, but murder was Troy's business. It wasn't Stilton's.

'You'd better drive on. Call in at the London Hospital. Phone the nick from there. I'll stay here until the ambulance arrives.'

'It's leaving the scene of a crime, surely?'

'We didn't kill him, Walter. He was dead when we got here.'

'You're sure?'

'I'm sure.'

Troy heard a *sotto voce* 'Poor bugger', watched Stilton get back in the Riley and drive off.

He retraced their route to the head of the alley, walked slowly back towards the body, swinging the bullseye torch methodically from side to side. Fifty yards on a fat, black book lay splayed upon the cobbles.

It was in Hebrew and, from what he had learnt of Jewish life in his time in Stepney, he rather thought it was a teaching bible, annotated for the purposes of instruction. There were a couple of sheets of white paper, scribbled in English, tucked into the end papers. The sort of thing a Rabbi used when preparing boys for rites of passage. Apart from *bar mitzvahs*, Troy wasn't at all sure what these were.

Another hundred yards and he reached the body.

He waited a quarter of an hour for the ambulance. Stilton arrived with it. But by then he had worked most of it out in his mind.

'George Bonham's getting in touch with the family.'

'What family? I thought Rabbi Borg was a widower.'

Troy had met Isaiah Borg a few times during his days on the beat. Although none of those few had been in the last two years. He was affable enough and lacking in the pomposity Troy thought characterised all priests – he even went by the nickname Izzy. But he could recall no mention of any family.

'There's a daughter somewhere. I knew her when she was a girl. But she's not had much to do with her father or the East End since she grew up. Got a bit snotty, I heard. Scholarship girl. Educated. Lots of letters after her name. You know. Oxford, Cambridge. That sort of thing.'

Troy knew. He'd narrowly avoided going there himself.

As the body was manhandled into the ambulance, Stilton said, 'I've arranged for us to make statements first thing in the morning. Then we can get on with the round-up. Should be our last day at it . . . This thing ought to be open and shut. Accidental death, after all. And being Jewish an' all, they'll want him underground as soon as possible.'

From the moment the car bumped the body and banged to earth it was obvious to Troy that Stilton had been shaken. It made sense – however guiltless, he had been driving the car when it ran over another human being. And no policeman who had never served on the Murder Squad would ever be so matter-of-fact about death as one who had. All the same, it was time to tell him.

'I think I'll make my statement tonight. I won't be in till ten in the morning. I have to drive out to Hendon.'

'Hendon?'

'Forensics. I've asked for the body to be taken to Forensics. I want a complete examination of everything he's wearing and a full post-mortem.'

'Eh?'

'It wasn't an accident, Walter. Izzy Borg was murdered.'

§

Under moonlight,
infectious moonlight,
a madman dances,
chanting numbers,
two, three, five, seven, eleven.
Smeared in excrement,
naked as nativity,
Lord Carsington dances.

§ I I 3

Rod had slept. Much to his surprise he had slept. A nudging hand from Billy woke him.

'Roll call.'

Rod looked up, for a second or two not recognising either the room or the man.

'Roll call?'

'Yeah. They probably want to count us again.'

Now he knew. Prison. The island. Heaven's Gate. He looked around. Rosen had dressed and left, Hummel was buttoning his shirt and seemed to be staring at a sketch of a wide-eyed, skinny man he had pinned to the wall opposite his bed. It was the sole decoration in the room. Rod wondered idly if it had been there the night before and he had not noticed or whether one of them had pinned it up. He swung his feet off the bed, looked down at his feet, peeping out from under the white and blue stripes of his pyjamas, which, but for his wife having packed for him, he would entirely have forgotten to bring.

'Don't 'ang about,' Jacks said. 'They say there'll be breakfast straight after. I could eat a horse. Worse, I could eat Hummer.'

Alone now, Rod dressed slowly, and as he looked around automatically searching for a mirror — always tied his tie in front of a mirror — he caught sight of the sketch again and went closer. It was Hummel. A Hummel even skinnier than the Hummel he had known for two days. A Hummel looking out at the world as though seeing it for the first time. Big eyes, big ears and something like numb astonishment in his expression. Rod thought it odd Hummel should pin this up, but who else would have? And then a distorted cliché came to mind, *memento vivi* or would it be *vivens* ... whatever, a reminder not of death but of life, another life, another place. And for a moment he could see Hummel as Hummel saw himself. Astonished by the fact of his own life. Looking at this sketch as though it were another version of himself rather than simply himself when younger, thinner ... and older, oh so much older ... looking at the world for the first time through old, old eyes. Rod turned away. Did up his shoelaces. He hoped Hummel might take it down soon, for it seemed to him like a form of punishment.

Out in the yard, standing among the puddles from last night's storm, they were counted, counted about as efficiently as they had been on arrival.

A lackadaisical lieutenant in an ill-fitting uniform told them to stand to attention as though he were asking them politely to move along in a bus queue. His voice was scarcely audible above the prattle of German, Yiddish and English and, when no one did, he didn't even bother to repeat the order. A major appeared. Tall, handsome, but for a brutal moustache, and looking thoroughly bored by the whole business.

'All present and correct, sir,' the lieutenant said.

'You've counted them?'

'As best we can, sir. They're not used to taking orders.'

'Why do I even bother? Right, Jenkins, on your own head be it. Dismiss them. If they feel like being dismissed that is.'

With that he was gone.

Rod was baffled — not by the inefficiency of it all — the last forty-eight hours had taught him to expect that at every turn, muddling through had become bumbling through — but by a hint of recognition.

He turned to Drax. Drax was coughing into his handkerchief.

'Do you know the major's name?'

Drax drew a deep breath and passed the query on to Siebert.

'It is Trench, is it not, Oskar?'

'*Ja*. Trench.'

'Surely not Geoffrey Trench?'

'No,' Siebert replied. 'I too made that mistake on first seeing him. The resemblance to the madman in parliament is amazing. So, I conclude they are twins. This one is Reginald. Geoffrey has not yet seen fit to serve king and country by enlisting. And given his fascist politics, we might wonder which country he would choose to serve.'

They drifted back into the house, following the older inmates to the refectory.

'Does this Trench share the other's politics?'

Drax answered, 'I do not know. He says so little. This morning's performance was verbose by his standards. I have known him inspect us without a word or a glance. His utter indifference to us has the benefit of laissez-faire and the hazard of neglect. I could escape. Would he notice? I could be dying. Would he notice?'

'He would rather be elsewhere,' Siebert added. 'Like so many stuck in this role he sees himself as a hero, lacking any opportunity to prove himself. The result? A cold bastard, a lazy bastard who leaves the running of his camp and our welfare to his NCOs. Decent enough men, by and large.'

Breakfast was toast, tea and porridge. Fine by Rod, and plenty of it. But he wondered as he watched Hummel pick at his porridge how Scotland's national dish went down with Mitteleurope.

Hummel hesitated too long. A man appeared before them like a jack-in-the-box, popping up from nowhere.

'You haff finished?'

Hummel stared at the apparition. The newcomer looked like a shabby parody of a banker, the city gent in the striped suit and the carefully knotted tie. But the suit had seen better days. Its owner had seen better days. Fifty-ish, slightly balding, dark hair slicked back from a high forehead escaped in wisps, adding to the overall impression of a stock-broker who might suddenly have thrown his bowler and brolly and caution to the winds and run off to the seaside with the pretty, blonde waitress from the tea rooms. All in all, it was Pooterish.

'You haff finished?' he said again.

'The burnt bread and the stewed leaves I want,' said Hummel, teasingly literal. 'The salted oatmeal paste, you are welcome to.'

It was snatched away before he could change his mind, and the question repeated at every table in the refectory where a hesitant diner might be seen to linger over his porridge.

'Oatmeal paste,' Billy said. 'That's a good one. Just about sums it up. I always 'ated porridge. He must be starvin' to want more.'

Spinetti said, 'He don't actually eat the stuff, y'know.'

'Come again?'

'I share a room with him. He won't eat it. He won't eat any of it.'

'What does he do with it then?'

Before Spinetti could answer, the eager face of Arthur Kornfeld appeared. He sat next to Spinetti, opposite Rod, Hummel and Billy, a notebook and pencil in hand.

'I was hoping to catch you,' he said. 'All of you. But you in particular, Herr Troy. We will be rehearsing later today, I wondered if you might join us.'

'I didn't actually pack a violin, you know. My mind was on more mundane things – like socks.'

'This used to be a girls' school. We have a room full of hockey sticks and lacrosse racquets and another full of instruments. If any of you play the tuba, we have six going begging. To say nothing of a sousaphone, a harpsichord and what appears to be a bass saxophone, if Herr Sax ever invented such a thing. Would any of you . . .?'

Nobody would. They munched burnt bread and swilled stewed leaves and left Rod and Kornfeld to it.

'No matter. We rehearse in the music room on the ground floor at two.'

'Fine,' said Rod. 'I'd be happy to. Do you have a piece in mind? Come to think of it, do you have a performance in mind?'

'Yes,' said Kornfeid. 'Yes in both cases. We are aiming for a . . . how would you say? . . . concert party? . . . in a week or two, and we have chosen the Elgar "Quartet in E minor".'

Rod's heart sank a little. He was partial to Elgar. It had been the music of his childhood when new. It had nursed in the Edwardian era. Those few short years of long summers. The peace that could not last. He was about the same age as Elgar's two symphonies. He'd heard them all his life. Elgar had died only a couple of years back, but in Rod's mind his music would always be associated with the years just before the Great War. However, the string quartet was a dreary piece. Elgar firing on two

cylinders with carburettor trouble. Playing it would be a bore. Listening
to it had been a bore when his dad had taken him to the work's premiere
at the Wigmore Hall just after the War.

'Anything else in mind?' he said, meaning 'any other music'.

Kornfeld misunderstood and said, 'Oh, *Ja*. Most evenings we have
Heaven's Gate University. Lectures and discussions. On Monday Professor Drax will speak. His field is politics and history. Next Thursday I
make my own modest contribution. I was a theoretical physicist in the
old country. Perhaps one of you would care to speak? We always have
room for more.'

To no one's amazement this was greeted with silence.

Then to everyone's amazement, Hummel spoke.

'*Ja*. I will speak. Put me down for . . . for Man and God.'

Kornfeld scribbled, muttering to himself, 'Man and God. Man and
God. Ah . . . you were a theologian, Herr Hummel?'

'No, a tailor.'

Then, 'Thank you, gentlemen, thank you. At two, Herr Troy?'

And he left.

Billy had turned to stare at Hummel.

'Are you quite sure about this, Joe?'

'Sure I'm sure.'

§ 114

Early the same day Troy drove out to Hendon. To the Metropolitan
Police Laboratory. The brainchild of the eminent forensic scientist Sir
Bernard Spilsbury. On occasion Troy had dealt directly with the great
man; more often than not, and certainly out of choice, he dealt with
one Ladislaw Kolankiewicz, a Polish exile of undoubted qualification
and talent – one of those talents being an ability to swing between the
tender and the obstreperous in a matter of seconds. He had been, at
necessary moments in Troy's life, the best listener in the world, avuncular
in the positive sense of the word. On other occasions Troy would arrive
to find him mid-dissection, hunched over a corpse, swearing with all
the power of the many languages available to him. His oaths were the

stuff of legend at Scotland Yard – there were those who saw only the funny side, the man who called Chief Inspectors of the Yard 'Dog-wankers' to their face – and there were those who could not abide him – Onions was one – and there was Troy, for whom Kolankiewicz seemed to hold an abiding, if abusive, affection.

'What you want at this time of day, smartyarse?'

'Rabbi Borg.'

'Oh, he was one of yours, was he?'

'Found him myself. I was in the car that ran over him.'

'You drive?'

'No. Stilton drove. But, to be accurate, I was in the second car. It was the first killed him, right?'

'Right.'

'When?'

'8.58.'

'So precise?'

'The impact broke his pocket watch . . . so unless he carried a stopped watch in his waistcoat pocket . . . and it fits in fairly well with the onset of rigor . . . but tell me . . . *you* think he was murdered. Or you wouldn't be here at a time when you are usually in bed. Why?'

'Two things. I found his bible a hundred yards or so from the body. From thereon I think he was running. I think he ran until the car following hit him . . . caught him round about the backside or thighs, I should think . . .'

'Correct. Broke the right hip, then ran over the torso crushing the ribcage. Both lungs pierced. Poor bastard drowned in his own blood in less than a minute. Still warm when you got there, when . . .?'

'About an hour later. Still warm . . . and . . . the other thing – still sweaty. I could feel it on his wrist as I tried for a pulse. Dead men don't sweat.'

Kolankiewicz could argue for a continent and two countries, but he didn't.

'So far, smartyarse, ten out of ten. Yes, he was soaked in sweat. I'd say he'd run more than a hundred yards. Even allowing for his age, and he was sixty-ish, his weight, and he was stout, and the preponderant weight of traditional Jewish clothing on an August night, he had sweated . . . shall we say . . . unnaturally. He had, as you deduce, been running. Not a habit among rabbis, I think. Can't remember when I saw a rabbi so much as dash for a bus. As for the annual rabbis egg and spoon race . . .'

'Anything else?'

'I could probably come up with a tyre print off the back of the suit. But they're not fingerprints. One car has the pattern, so do a thousand. And you and Stilton somewhat queered the pitch when you ran over him a second time.'

'Any marks on the body not consistent with hit and run?'

'He was trussed for a hernia. Not a device ever used as a murder weapon, as I recall. He was immaculate in his habits. Clean fingernails, clean underwear, clean hanky, trimmed beard. He'd eaten around five in the afternoon, and he'd pissed in his pants before he died. I conclude ... a dignified man whose death had anything but dignity.'

It seemed to Troy that that simple statement said something timely about the condition of Europe at that moment, to sum up things that had happened in Berlin or Vienna or Warsaw. But to say so was to risk a discussion that might last all morning.

'You're right ... that was Izzy Borg as I remember him. Dignity. A dignity he didn't stand on. A nice guy.'

'A *mensch*.'

'Quite. So who would want to ...?'

Kolankiewicz handed Troy a paper bag containing the contents of Rabbi Borg's pockets – two pencils, a fountain pen, a pocket diary, two mint humbugs in wrappers, the stub of a railway ticket from Liverpool Street to Cambridge and three shillings and sixpence halfpenny in change.

'There's almost nothing of any use to you. What you need is an eyewitness.'

Fat chance, thought Troy. That was the thing about life in the blackout. Witnesses, if they saw anything at all, saw only shadows. He had no high hope of solving this one, but that was no reason not to try.

§ 115

They stood in Troy's old office once again that lunchtime. Drinking tea. Stilton's stomach rumbling.

'What do you want me to do?' he said.

Troy said, 'How many names on our list? Half a dozen?'

''Bout that.'

'Would you mind handling them on your own? I could look into Borg's death today.'

Stilton paused, thought, set his teacup back on the saucer.

'You're still saying it was murder?'

'Yes, and so is Kolankiewicz.'

'And Mr Onions?'

'I haven't told him yet. But I will.'

'And I'll have to tell Steerforth.'

'Do you really have to?

'You're being naïve, Mr Troy. O'course I have to tell him. And there'll be consequences. Ructions.'

'Such as?'

'He'll be mad as hell with both of us. Spittin' feathers. I can hear him now. "It's none of your business . . . make your statements and get on with the job in hand." And then his spook mode'll cut in. I can hear that too . . . "Murdered rabbi? . . . just as we're rounding up Jews? Keep it to yourself." He'll tell us it's Branch business and want it kept a secret. Politically sensitive that's what he'll say. And if you don't think the spooks in MI5'll back him up then you really are naïve. They'll sit on this. Penny to a quid they'll not want this getting out now.'

'Then would you mind waiting until I've talked to Onions?'

'I think I can manage that, but why?'

'If I make this Scotland Yard business, Murder Squad business, it won't be Branch business and the only man who can tell me *not* to investigate is Onions. Steerforth can rant and rave, but short of MI5 going to the Home Secretary and the Home Secretary leaning on the Met Commissioner, the buck will stop with Onions.'

'Onions lets you investigate anything you deem to be murder?'

'Has so far.'

'You know, for a young un you've got an awful lot of power. Most of us just do what we're told.'

Troy had never been much good at that.

§ 116

It had been an agonisingly scratchy, scrapey couple of hours in the music room. He was the least practised of the quartet and the least accomplished, but that was nothing compared to the dullness inherent in the piece Kornfeld had chosen. There was nothing of *Nimrod* about it. There was nothing hummable about it. You didn't listen to, let alone attempt to play, Elgar's only string quartet and come away humming anything. It was, to use the parlance of the *palais-de-dance,* anything but 'catchy', Rod thought. Lady Elgar had supposedly referred to some aspect of the piece as 'captured sunshine'. But it was bottled boredom.

Rod asked 'why the Elgar?'

Kornfeld said, to the eager smiles of Herr Lippmann, his viola player, and Herr Schnitzler, his cellist, 'It is England, the epitome of England. We were keen to do something that showed England, that showed our willingness to be of England, to be English. We intend, of course, to invite all the British in the camp and some of the villagers on the island. This piece has . . . a quality of light . . .'

'Captured sunshine?' Rod said, only to find the quotation and the sarcasm wasted and returned with more smiles.

'Exactly!'

'Y'know,' Rod said slowly and carefully. 'I'm pretty keen on Elgar myself. Saw the young Menuhin boy play the violin concerto a few years back, listened to the symphonies all my life . . . or so it seems . . . but I can't help feeling that we should be . . .'

Oh God, he couldn't say it.

'Yes?' Kornfeld urged him on.

'Well. We're all from Vienna, aren't we?'

'Herr Lippmann is from Salzburg.'

'Fine . . . I think my point will withstand the geography . . .'

'Yes?'

'Why not something by Haydn or Schubert?'

Kornfeld looked at Lippmann and Schnitzler, Lippmann and Schnitzler looked at one another.

'What does that prove?' Kornfeld said eventually.

'Nothing you can prove by playing a piece of second-rate Elgar. None of it makes us English, it's merely playing politics. We should be playing music, music that means something to us – we can at least give the English something of ourselves and as Vienna has so much to give that is first rate ...?'

Rod let the sentence trail off.

Shrugs all round.

'You think our guards will like Haydn or Schubert more?'

Time to lie. Rod didn't think they'd give a damn about music at all.

'I haven't a clue. But we will. Let us be true to the name they've landed us with.'

More shrugs. They hadn't heard.

'You didn't know they call this place Little Vienna?'

'No.'

Kornfeld led Rod across to a huge cupboard built into the alcove formed by the chimney breast. He swung back the door to reveal a dozen shelves of alphabetised sheet music from floor to high, high ceiling. Thomas Arne to Richard Wagner. You'd need a ladder to reach Arne and anyone ahead of Chopin. There were dozens of them, hundreds of them. Rod began to regret ever having spoken.

'Perhaps you could find the right piece for us?'

Rod stared. There might even be thousands here.

'That's very good, you know – "playing music not politics". *Ja*, very good.'

Behind him Rod could hear Schnitzler muttering 'something of ourselves' over and over again – the sound of him getting nearer. Then he shuffled between the two of them and reached into the heart of the cupboard, to the section labelled M.

'Mozart,' Schnitzler said pulling out a dozen folders of bound sheets and dropping as many more on the floor. What was left in his hand he seemed to regard as the product of serendipity. He stared down at the top sheet and read out the title to them all.

'The 23rd in F. Hmmm. I played it first as a boy. It is as you say ... something of myself.'

He handed the music to Kornfeld.

'You will find it livelier than the Elgar. I would even venture to say it is spritely. Not quite jazz, but spritely.'

§ 117

He'd talked to the caretaker at Borg's synagogue. He'd gone to Borg's home and he'd talked to two surviving sisters – grief-stricken women not bothering to restrain their tears, easily deceived by Troy's reassurance that his questions were the stuff of routine. There had been a crime committed – it was illegal to drive away after being involved in an accident. But it was no more than that. He fended off questions about the autopsy, about the release of the body, assuming that the truth could only worsen their grief.

Rabbi Borg's diary showed a 7.30 appointment in a community hall, less than a mile from where his body was found. Borg had spent an hour with six thirteen-year-old boys, and a further half hour chatting with the father of one of them. He'd set off home in daylight, he'd been run down in daylight. And no one had seen a thing. As ever ... he was 'a man with no enemies' and 'who would ever want to do a thing like that to nice man like ...' – their voices echoed those of Borg's caretaker and sisters.

Troy arrived back at the Yard, not much wiser.

The phone rang.

'Stilton,' the voice on the other end said.

'Are we done?'

'We're done with refugees, fifth columnists, pastry chefs, professors of physics and little Hitlers. Are you done with dead rabbis?'

''Fraid not.'

'Then we'd best meet.'

Troy looked at his watch. 6.05 p.m.

'I could come over to you by seven.'

'No. This is off the record and off the manor. I don't want flapping lug'oles. Do you know the Hand & Shears in Cloth Fair, between Smithfield and Barts Hospital?'

'No, but I can find it.'

'Seven it is then.'

Troy liked the streets behind Barts. It was as though they'd been deliberately hidden from the rest of the city, tucked into the shadow of Smithfield and forgotten about. Streets as narrow as Goodwin's Court, built for a very different London. Public houses no bigger than the front room of a terraced house. The etching on the street door read 'Snug' – it was. The Hand & Shears was tiny – a spit-and-sawdust pub that probably catered to porters from the meat-market at nearby Smithfield. It was empty but for a fat-faced, walrus-moustached copper seated at a corner table, just about big enough for four pints and an ash tray. This was why Stilton had chosen it – a pub that was full to bursting or empty because it relied for its trade on men working shifts – all in or all out. He was on his first pint, a fringe of white froth on the end of his moustache.

'I didn't order for you. I get the feeling you don't much like ale anyway.'

Troy ordered a ginger beer. *Sotto voce.* It seemed unmanly not to like beer.

Stilton said, 'I thought there were a couple of things we should get straight before I set off back to Burnham.'

'Say hello to Charlie.'

'I will. Now . . . this Izzy Borg business . . . I'll say it one more time . . . it couldn't just be an accident?'

'No.'

'It's pitch dark in that alley. I could see bugger all. Maybe the bloke who ran him down couldn't see either.'

'I have a precise time of death. It was light when Borg died there. We're on British Double Summertime, remember?'

'OK . . . OK . . . cut me some slack for being sceptical. I've never been on a murder in all my years on the force. And I'll never get used to double summertime. But I wanted to be sure, to be sure you're sure.'

'I am.'

''Cos if you go on with this, you'll go up against Steerforth sooner or later. And he is a vindictive little sod.'

'Thanks for the warning,' Troy said, remembering two vicious encounters with the man.

'And that incident at the Russian Tea Rooms didn't help.'

'Ah . . . I didn't know you knew. Kitty?'

'No, our Kit's got some discretion. Steerforth told me himself. And that's another thing. He's not well liked in the Branch . . . always looking for the main chance . . . can't resist a bit of bragging . . . not good in a Branch copper . . . out to make a name for himself.'

'In which case, he's in the wrong outfit.'

'Do I detect a hint of smugness, Sergeant Troy?'

'You do. He'll never get to be "Steerforth of the Yard" working for Special Branch. Murder is what matters. Murder's what sells papers. Whatever went down at the Tea Rooms hasn't even made the small print in the late extra. I don't suppose it ever will. He may brag a bit to fellow officers, he brags to the papers he's done for.'

'Well, he works with what he's got. That's why I thought he might declare Rabbi Borg's death to be Branch business. Given the way things are, he'd not have much difficulty justifying it. He might see it as an opportunity. Summat to be kept under wraps, hidden from the likes of you and investigated with an eye to impressing his masters. You make a meal out of it, you go around saying it's murder . . . he might just do that.'

'But he hasn't?'

'Not yet. But if he wants the case . . . and if he wants an opportunity to shaft you . . .?'

Stilton shrugged the sentence into inconclusion.

'OK. I take your meaning. I've made an enemy.'

'You've a knack for that. The missis isn't too keen on you either.'

This sounded to Troy like a complete non-sequitur. He wasn't sure whether Walter had changed the subject or not.

'Was it something I said?' knowing full well it was everything he said.

'No. I don't think there's a thing you could have said to please her, less you said it in a cockney accent. No . . . forget I spoke . . . think nothing of it . . . she never has a good word to say about anyone who courts our Kitty.'

'Courts?'

'The missis's word, not mine, but while we're about it, there is one other thing.'

'There is?'

'What *are* your intentions towards my daughter?'

Troy felt socked, blind-sided, sucker-punched.

'I . . . er . . .'

'Only jokin' lad.'

A big walrus-faced grin, a sip of ale, the glass set down again. Another fringe of white foam.

'But if you do go up against Steerforth. Keep her out of it. Her career matters to her. As I'd hope you've noticed.'

And now he wasn't joking, and it dawned on Troy that they had at last reached the real reason for this off-the-manor bit-of-a-chat.

§118

Spinetti showed Rod and Billy the room he was sharing. Among his room-mates was the man who pinched bowls of porridge at breakfast. The first thing they noticed was the smell. Faintly mouldy, wafting around the door and out into the corridor. The second thing they noticed was the source. The window sills were crowded with what appeared to be abstract sculptures, blobby, loopy and, to the undiscerning eye, formless.

'Bloody hell,' said Billy. 'It's never ...'

He poked a finger into the nearest 'statue'.

'It is. It's ... porridge!'

'Told you so,' Spinetti said. 'A nutter, a bona fide nutter.'

Rod leaned in a little and sniffed.

'You know in Scotland they're rumoured to keep the stuff for days. Make it in advance and store it ... rather like making bread.'

'This ain't been here days,' Spinetti said. 'I reckon Schwitters made some of these weeks ago.'

'Is that his name?' Rod asked.

From the doorway Kornfeld answered.

'Kurt Schwitters. Surely you have heard of him? The Dadaist?'

'Rings a bell,' Rod replied. 'Wasn't he one who turned his house into a work of art?'

'Yes. The Merzbau.'

'Art, shmart! Merz shmerz!' Billy said. 'You toffs can dress it up in all the fancy words you like. It's still just mouldy porridge.'

'Then come with me and I will show you all something more appetising.'

Kornfeld led them down the staircase, out into the grounds and across the lawns to the perimeter fence.

'Patisserie day,' he said to no one's understanding.

A stout old woman in a headscarf and a long, billowing skirt was approaching from the other side of the fence, carrying a large wicker basket on one arm. From their side a guard was approaching, rifle slung across his shoulder, his pace leisurely to the careless. He waved at the old woman as he passed, called out 'Hello, Aunt Doris' and got back 'Hello, young Tony' in return.

When she drew level with Kornfeld she smiled hugely, whipped the teacloth off her basket and said, 'I got everything you asked for. Two dozen eggs, three pounds of white flour, a pound of raisins and a bag of mixed nuts. I've put the word out for marzipan, but it'll take a while. Wasn't much call for marzipan even before rationing. But I'll do me best.'

With each phrase an item was passed through the wire.

'Thank you, Mrs Kelly. If you would add it to my bill I'll settle up at the end of the month.'

'Whatever you say, Arthur. Your credit's good with me.'

She eased her weight into one hip momentarily and looked at the newcomers, each one clutching an item of contraband and feeling slightly baffled.

'New boys are you? You like your grub, you lot, I must say. Talk about a sweet tooth. Well, can't stand 'ere gabbin all day. Same time on Thursday Arthur.'

She ambled off. In the distance the guard had reached the corner of the house and had turned around to slouch back their way.

'I don't believe this,' Rod said. 'Smuggling right under the guard's nose?'

'As you will have gathered, the boy is her nephew. But that is scarcely crucial. They none of them . . . what is that evocative English phrase . . . give a "toss". Why should they? We trade honestly with the villagers.'

'How? I mean how do you pay for it?'

By cheque. Drawn on my account in Cambridge. King's College still pays my salary. I haven't been fired or suspended. Merely interned. Did you not bring your chequebook?'

'As a matter of fact, I did, but . . .'

'But what?'

'Nothing. I just find it all a little odd.'

'Oh it's odd alright. But it keeps our patisserie in fresh ingredients. And since you have brought your chequebook, I'm sure that, if there was anything extra you wanted sent in, Mrs Kelly and her husband would be only too happy to oblige. Indeed, if there's anything you want sent out, anything you don't want Trench's censors to read, I mean, that can be arranged too.'

'Does Trench know about this?'

Kornfeld shrugged.

'I've no idea. But who would ever want to tell him?'

The guard passed them again, nodded, said a soft 'Afternoon Mr Kornfeld' and walked on.

§ 119

Another day of routine police work, the simplicity of questions, brought Troy nothing. He might as well let Steerforth have the case of the Hit-and-Run Rabbi.

One thing remained. He'd go to the funeral. He'd no idea why, but he would. Then he rationalised the impulse. He'd make it known he was a policeman. There was just a chance someone among the mourners would come up to him with a snippet of information. Murder, as Dorothy L. Sayers had put it, must advertise, however much Stilton wanted discretion.

He rang George Bonham. Kolankiewicz had released the body, the coroner had read his report and delayed the inquest pending a report from Troy. The funeral must surely be imminent?

'It's tomorrow morning,' George said. 'I was planning on going meself. I knew Izzy all me life.'

'Would you let the family know we'll both be there? It might yield something.'

'Family? He was a widower, y'know. There'll be his sisters and his daughter. I see Miriam and Martha from time to time. Doubt I've set eyes on the daughter since . . .'

'Yes. I heard. A bit of a cow.'

'Freddie? Have you ever been to a Jewish funeral?'

He'd been to Freud's, but he didn't think that counted.

'No. I've been to a couple of *brisses* though. But . . . they can't be that different can they?'

§ 120

Somehow he'd got it into his head that it would be a small affair. Something to do with there being a war on, and something to do with Borg having next to no family. It wasn't.

They stood outside the House of Prayer in Mile End Sephardic Cemetery – the house itself was packed.

Bonham whispered, 'I been to do's like this afore. You stand when they stand, sit when they sit and keep yer trap shut. Piece o'cake.'

'George, I don't think we're going to get the chance to sit.'

'Whatever . . . when the blokes come out with the coffin, just fall in line.'

'What about the women?'

'They'll do their own thing. A lot of it'll be blokes only.'

'I thought you said Borg only had a daughter.'

'There'll be some bloke doin' the doins at the graveside, bound to be.'

Troy found no opportunity to talk to anyone. He'd anticipated too much, that it might be just a little like a Church of England funeral – and he'd managed to avoid those since childhood – guests and mourners, greetings and handshakes, and what Bonham probably called 'a-bit-of-a-do' afterwards. It wasn't. It was austere – not a wreath or bunch of flowers in sight – it was heart-rending, it was spare, and it was moving, and it was, to the uninitiated, often as not confusing. Troy lost track. There was so much to-ing and fro-ing. More ritual than he could keep up with. The immediate mourners emerged following the coffin. At the grave side a nephew read *Kaddish*.

'To the departed whom we now remember, may peace and bliss be granted in the world of eternal life. There may they find grace and mercy before the Lord of heaven and earth. May their souls rejoice in that ineffable good which God has laid up for those that fear Him, and may their memory be a blessing unto those that cherish it.

'May the Father of peace send peace to all troubled souls, and comfort all the bereaved among us. Amen.'

A cousin gave a personal eulogy – testament to the character and scholarship of the deceased, and where the C of E would have a priest at the graveside there was not a rabbi in sight. Then the men were invited forward to shovel earth onto the coffin, Bonham and Troy included.

'What?' Troy whispered.

'Just do as I do,' Bonham whispered back, and Troy did as he was told, followed Bonham and tipped earth into Izzy Borg's grave. Then back to the House of Prayer. Men and women behaving like separate tribes. He'd hardly set eyes on the women – the most immediate of Borg's family – distant figures wrapped in black scarves, heads down. He'd sort of expected this, and he sort of hadn't.

When they emerged a second time, it was obvious even to Troy that they were into a new phase – now he could see the women clearly.

Borg's sisters were dumpy, grey-haired, identical, little women – obligations to grief and surrender to ritual competed with native capability as they now organised those around them. Who would drive back with whom, who would visit when. Just as well. His only descendant, a daughter of thirty or so, seemed aloof from it all. Only too happy to let others organise. Also, unlike her aunts, she was tall, dark and beautiful. When those who had seen her grow up chose to emphasise her brains, her defiance and her much-vaunted indifference to faith and tribe, they almost always forgot to tell him she was tall, dark and beautiful. George Bonham had called her 'a difficult little girl', 'too clever by half' and Stilton had said she was 'the sort of girl who grows up to be the sort of woman bound to break her dad's heart, if not every man's heart.'

Only slightly to Troy's surprise she came right up to him.

'*Police at the Funeral*. Isn't that the title of a Marje Allingham novel? You didn't tell me you were a policeman.'

'You didn't tell me you were Jewish.'

She laughed out loud. Heads turned. She wiped the laugh back to a smile and restored just enough of the decorum of a funeral.

'My real name's Borg – but I suppose you know that, don't you?'

'Poor excuse for a copper if I didn't.'

'And Isabella – Izzy – was a joke. I suppose it was at my father's expense. Hardly seems in good taste now. I'm called Zette. And what do I call you? Troy?'

Troy said, 'Call me Sergeant Troy.'

§ 121

Now she whispered.

'This isn't a courtesy call, is it?'

'No. But it's meant to look like one.'

'You don't think my father died in an accident at all, do you?'

'I'm a detective with Scotland Yard Murder Squad. I don't bother much with road accidents.'

'Of course. But the East End thinks it was an accident. If you want them to go on thinking that . . . well, you're at a Jewish funeral . . . gossip will spread from here faster than a bush telegraph . . . they'll know in Bialystock by midnight, and Brooklyn by breakfast.'

'Then perhaps we should stop whispering and go somewhere where we can talk.'

'I'll be at home this evening.'

'I can't come to Cambridge.'

'Don't worry. I may not be a cockney sparrow any longer, but I'm still a London girl. I have a top-floor flat overlooking the park. 112 Stanhope Place, just past Marble Arch. Shall we say eight o'clock?'

'Shouldn't you be here? Shouldn't you be sitting *shiv'ah* at your father's house. I thought *shiv'ah* lasted quite a while?'

'*Shiv'ah*? What did you do? Look up "Jew" in an encyclopedia?'

'Yes.'

Troy thought she might laugh again, instead she said, 'Do you think I give a damn? I want to be out of here before they start praying again. Be there at eight. I'll provide the bacon and eggs, you bring the champagne.'

§ 122

The lift was like a gilded cage. Two fat ladies could not have stood side by side. It whisked Troy to the top floor, jerked to a halt and disgorged him, Taittinger in hand, opposite the open door of Zette Borg's 'penthouse' flat. He pushed gently at the door, a waft of scent across the room, a hint of steam and talcum from the bathroom, a wireless softly airing a Benny Goodman Concert – Helen Forrest crooning 'Smoke Gets in Your Eyes' a little too jauntily.

The sitting room faced south-west, and from this height Troy had a clear view above the treetops across Hyde Park. It was light, it would be light for a couple of hours. It was, he thought, a flat chosen for sunsets. Perhaps sunset was what Zette had in mind.

An arm snaked around his waist. The waft of scent grew stronger with the lips pressed to the back of his neck, the chin resting on his shoulder. He knew the fragrance – his sisters had used it for years now – *Indiscret* by Lucien Lelong. It summed up their joint character, or at least would do so until the advent of a scent called *Who Gives A Damn?*

'I know what you're thinking.'

'You do?'

'You're thinking Lindfors has set me up in a love-nest.'

Which was exactly what Troy was thinking.

'I'm not his only one, you know. He likes clever women. He's had affairs with most of his female staff.'

'Do you mind?'

'Nope. Sauce for the goose. Just so long as I'm *numero uno*, as long as I don't find some other woman's knickers in the laundry basket ... I couldn't give a damn.'

Her head left his shoulder, she turned her back and said, 'Zip me up, Troy.'

She was wearing a Schiaparelli trouser-dress, the sort of thing Marlene Dietrich always seemed to be wearing when there was a photographer around. The trousers billowed from waist to ankle, the top clung to her like a second, simple black skin. The end of the zip was all but in the cleft of her buttocks – a line of white flesh peeping through black silk, from neck to arse – no knickers, no bra.

'Don't be shy, Troy.'

He yanked it up, was about to take a pace backward when one hand came over her shoulder and pointed at her spine.

'Oh no, you don't get off that lightly. Kiss.'

He kissed.

'You know,' he said into the scent and the flesh of her backbone. 'I rather thought you told me not to make plans.'

'Who's planning anything? I've nothing planned beyond midnight. Now – you did remember the champagne?'

'Next to your gramophone, well chilled.'

'How do you manage to chill champagne at this time of year?'

'You plan ahead. You lower a bucket of water into the coalhole outside your house and dunk the champagne in it for as long as you can. Then you wrap it in last night's newspaper, jump in a cab and get here as fast as you can.'

'Supposing the coalman calls?'

§ 123

She had pinched his shirt. Troy wandered around in trousers, sockless. Zette stood at the stove scrambling eggs and crisping bacon. All he'd had to do was pop the cork on the champagne while it was still cold.

It was a sparse flat, close to bare. Unengaging shades of cream. Chunky leather furniture. Immaculate lines and surfaces. Bland watercolours that looked as though they'd been acquired as a job lot after Huntley & Palmer had used them on biscuit tins. Everything in it cost, but also everything in it told you no one lived there. It was like being in a hotel. Troy pulled open a drawer in the sideboard half-expecting a Gideon bible – it was empty – opened a cupboard next to the fireplace – that was empty too. How long did you have to spend somewhere before you wanted to put your mark on it, to introduce some personal object, some well-read book, some framed photograph of some loved one? It struck Troy that this was the opposite of all those Jewish homes he and Walter Stilton had invaded this summer – they were crammed with memories, stuffed with the signifying junk of life – this flat was stripped of them. How long did you have to spend somewhere ... how long would you spend dressing up, all that Lelong and Schiaparelli, knowing you would all but rip it off in minutes?

They had tumbled into bed so quickly he wondered that she had bothered to ask him to zip her up.

Afterwards she had made no comment on his amateurishness. It was understood. He was better at it than the last time they'd met. He'd give

Kitty Stilton credit for that, were it not that he was pushing Kitty Stilton as far from consciousness as possible.

'Now, Troy!'

Zette rushed in, shirttails flapping, a gust of bacon and brown sauce trailing behind her. Slapped their after-lights-out dorm feast on the table by the picture window on the park. It would soon be dark, the sun was a reddling blush on the horizon. And with darkness came the blackout.

'Not that I'm saying bolt your grub or anything, Troy, but I can't abide the blackout. I usually put out all the lights instead. Often as not I just sit here. Before the war, of course, one watched London light up, now it never does, as though a giant had leaned over London in '39, huffed just once and out they all went.'

After bacon and eggs, after most of a bottle of Taittinger, she said, 'Just so you don't think I'm utterly heartless ... tell me how my father died.'

The question took Troy by surprise. But what didn't? That their wake for Izzy Borg had been to fuck each other senseless had taken him by surprise.

He told her as briefly and as clinically as he had told Onions.

'And,' she said at last, 'you have no doubts?'

'No.'

She said nothing while they drained the bottle, then, with a suddeness that was startling, she stood up, peeled the shirt over her head, threw it at Troy, stood naked before him and said, 'Get dressed. Time we went out.'

'What – a club or something?'

Troy did not do clubs – he'd somehow missed out that phase of his education.

'Yes,' she said. 'Or something.'

She disappeared into her bedroom and reappeared in a macintosh and soft shoes.

They crossed the road into the park, she slipped an arm through his. A couple of hundred yards and she steered him across the grass, towards trees, but they stopped just short of them.

It was a dark night, but not so dark he could not discern the vague shapes of bodies on the grass around him. Not so dark that he could not see that Zette was face to face with him. And no depth of dark could mask the sounds of coitus coming at him from every direction. If there was one couple coupling, there were a dozen or more.

'I discovered this in the spring. People come here every day just to do it. Even before dusk.'

'They do?'

'It's almost a tradition. Indeed, a new London cry is to be heard nightly, the cry of ye olde rubber johnnie seller. We might even see one. Condoms on sticks like candy floss, and the cry of "Five bob new, half a crown used".'

'Used! You're kidding?'

'Nope. A good rinse and a light dusting with chalk and a rubber johnny ought to last a month. All depends how hard you go at it. But ... we don't need him, because we have ...'

There was just enough light to see the french letter in its tiny paper envelope, like a thank you card from an elf, that she held up to him.

'Er ...'

'Yeees?'

'We don't need him, but we don't need the park either, we have ... your flat. These people probably have nowhere else to go.'

'No Troy, they do it here because they can. They do it here because they want to do it here. It's the "aphrodisia of war". It's pure Freud. It's pure sex. We need to do it here, Troy.'

'No we don't.'

'Oh, but we do. We do. We most certainly do.'

She let the macintosh slip. She'd a simple cotton frock on. She hoisted the frock to her waist, bunched the skirt in one hand – knickerless still – and thrust the condom at him with the other.

'Let's do it.'

'I ... I ... I ... er.'

And a voice from the dark said, 'Fer Gawd's sake, fuck 'er, mate. If you don't, I bleedin' well will. Maybe then she'll shut 'er great clangin' gob!'

Later, heaped with embarrassment, glistening with sweat, trousers round his knees, groin locked to hers, pale moon of arse in the air, wondering what he'd do if a policeman stopped by, Troy found everything an inhibition.

'Come, Troy. Come. *Viens! Viens! Viens!*'

Like it or not he did as he was told, and at the wettest moment of the great wet rush, she whispered in his ear, 'Catch this bastard for me, Troy. Catch him. Promise me you'll catch him!'

For no reason he could think of Troy was suddenly reminded of Dora

Wax reading tea leaves for him. Something about a dark woman entering his life. A dark woman, a wicked woman.

§

Under moonlight,
infectious moonlight,
a madman dances,
chanting numbers,
two, three, five, seven, eleven.
Smeared in excrement,
naked as nativity,
smeared in his own blood,
throat bared to heaven,
Lord Carsington dances.

§ 124

As Izzy, henceforth known as Zette, and Troy repeated their night-time feast on scrambled eggs, crispy bacon and Taittinger, Rod Troy and his new-found friends mulled over the pleasure of their cuisine in their dormitory three hundred miles away.

Hummel said, 'Have you considered that this might indeed be heaven? We have beds with sheets, we have indoor plumbing, sufficient entertainment and diversion, we have three square meals a day . . .'

'Squar*ish*,' said Billy. 'The grub ain't that great and there's hardly ever seconds of anything. There's no booze. And you can get fed up with kippers every day.'

Hummel conceded, 'Squarish then. If heaven lies in the security of the basic necessities of life . . .'

'Food that falls from the trees?' said Rod.

'Kippers don't fall from trees.'

Hummel ignored Billy and picked up from Rod, 'Exactly, then

Heaven's Gate might not be heaven, but as you more aptly suggest Eden?'

'Wot are you on about?'

'He means, Billy, that one could get used to this.'

'Do you 'Ummer?'

'Indeed I do. I begin to wonder if I might not spend the rest of my life here in fruitful idleness.'

'You don't 'arf talk some bollocks.'

Rod and Hummel said nothing. Billy could always be relied on to fill a silence, and clearly, he was thinking.

'Where do kippers come from?' he said at last.

And from the farthest bunk Herr Rosen said, '*Mein Gott*, do you cockneys know nothing?'

§ 125

A couple of days later, Troy found a postcard on the doormat as he and Kitty let themselves in early in the evening.

He glanced at it. A view of the backs and the river at Cambridge.

```
Tied up for a while. If you succeed you can
always reach me here, at the Cavendish. Z.
and ps. You can make a plan now. Just the one.
Don't go Mad XXX
```

'Wossat?'

Kitty's head on his shoulder, peering at the card.

'Nothing,' he lied, folding the card. 'My old pal, Charlie. Works with your father out at Burnham.'

'You live in a world of old pals, you lot, don't yer?'

§ 126

Rod found himself looking forward to the idea of Heaven's Gate Makeshift University. It would pass the time, much as playing second violin in the string quartet would pass the time, and it might kick his brain into gear the way things did when he was at Cambridge. He was not at all surprised to find that Rosen and Hummel joined him – after Hummel's offer to speak on the matter of God, it was to be expected. What surprised him was to find himself seated between Jacks and Lt Jenkins.

Jacks said, 'It's gotta be better than twiddlin' yer thumbs, ain't it?'

Rod said, 'Are you under orders, Mr Jenkins?'

''Fraid so, old man. Besides, you can't keep it a secret, and I'd've come anyway.'

'Mr Trench will not be joining us?'

'Nope. He'll get whatever potted version I choose to give him. He's expecting subversion and dissidence. Anything less and he'll probably dismiss me before I get to the end of my first sentence.'

Drax's first sentence was incredibly long. As was his second and his third. He coughed into a hanky every so often, otherwise he launched into a convoluted account of 'Our Times.'

It was disappointing. Drax, the most interesting conversationalist Rod had met in his imprisonment, was all too predictable as a lecturer. Rod felt he could have written all this himself. It was too familiar. It was the rubber-stamp, left-wing interpretation of the inter-war years, a potted account of the rise of Nazism, and potshots at every other wing of politics for not resisting it. It sent Rod into daydreams. Jacks nodded off. Jenkins and Hummel looked alert enough, but Jacks was definitely asleep, his snore punctuating the boredom as regularly as Drax's cough. Rosen looked engaged, engaged and angry.

'In conclusion . . . the development of National Socialism in Germany in all its horror is not an aberration from the human values extolled by the capitalist system but a direct consequence of them. I would even say their apotheosis, and propaganda is now being used to convince the British of their fundamental difference from the Third Reich, whereas in fact the difference is at best one of superstructures . . . not of fundamentals. When we hear of "the Enemy Within" – ourselves, gentlemen, ourselves! – and are urged to vigilance, it is only intelligent to recognise that the enemy has been "within" for one hundred and fifty years, and if war is now being fought in terms of nationalities, it conceals rather than cancels the war between capital and labour.'

Rod all but sighed with relief when Kornfeld got up to offer a vote of thanks.

'You know, Max, if you talk like this you'll be locked up.'

And under the cover of laughter Rod slipped out of the room.

§ 127

His next postcard from Zette was in an envelope. The same picture of the Cambridge backs and the river, but it was clear why she'd put it in an envelope.

```
I said `catch this bastard' - of course I meant
`kill this bastard'. You can do that, can't you,
Troy?
```

§ 128

Kornfeld stood before the class, looking far too young to be a professor of anything, but exuding self-confidence.

'I must apologise for the use of a blackboard. It is not designed to make you feel you are back in kindergarten.'

Kornfeld paused for laughter, but there was none.

'Those of you who have been here a while will know that until my internment I was a fellow in theoretical physics at Cambridge University. Theoretical Physics is mostly numbers – indeed I trained as a mathematician – and I think we will all find it a little easier if I write down some of the formulae so we all may see them.

Again for the sake of newcomers, I will begin by recapping a little of my winter lectures on Unified Field Theory . . .'

'What theory?' Jacks whispered to Rod.

'Haven't a clue,' Rod replied.

'. . . before I embark on my theme, which is, of course, as it were, the complimentary notion of the Steady State . . .'

'Are you keepin' up with this, 'Ampstead?'

'I think he said it was all about numbers.'

'I think I'll nip out for a fag.'

§ 129

It was Thursday. Kitty worked the nightshift on Thursday. It saved Troy from any sense of dilemma.

Shortly after ten in the morning the telephone had rung in his office and he had heard Zette Borg say, 'What plan did you make?'

'I . . . er . . .'

'You didn't? No matter. I'll be in town for the night. Be at my flat by nine.'

Troy said nothing.

'You can do that, can't you, Troy?'

The echo of her last postcard was inescapable. But the wisp of a dilemma turned to mist before his eyes and blew away.

'Yes,' he said. 'I can do *that*.'

They got in from the park at midnight. Lay on the bed as though they had lain there all evening rather than in the fresh-cut grass of Hyde Park. He could still smell mown grass, stronger than her *Indiscret*.

Small talk would have been nice – would have been appropriate – but she was saying nothing. Her face was in the pillow.

'You know,' he began. 'I don't know much about you.'

'I rather think that's why we're here.'

'I know nothing about your job.'

'I know nothing about yours.'

'I'm a copper. I think it might be easy to imagine my job. I used to wear a pointy hat and boots and carry a truncheon. Now I wear a suit and ask a lot of questions.'

She turned her face sideways, out of the pillow, not looking at him but at least he could hear her clearly now.

'Oh God ... do you really want to know? Fine ... it's all about numbers.'

Troy knew he'd heard this phrase before – then it came back to him. The first alien he and Stilton had rounded up, the chap who lodged with Dora Wax, had dismissed Dora's tea-leaf prophecy with 'everything is numbers. If she wants the secret of the universe, it lies in numbers.'

'You've heard that old adage that a Ph.D. is more and more about less and less? Well it applies to low temperature physics in spades ... we're talking, we're asking, more and more about the infinitessimally small.'

'Atoms?'

'Beyond atoms ... sub-atomic particles ... the activity of the building blocks of the universe ... and it all comes down to numbers, to numbers, ratios and equations. Do you know who Heisenberg is?'

'No.'

'Schrödinger? Won the Nobel for physics in '33?'

'No.'

'Dirac? Shared the Nobel in '33? Talks of the poetry of mathematics?'

All Troy knew was that, with names like that, he and Walter Stilton would probably have locked them up by now if they lived in England.

'No.'

'OK. OK. If I were to sum up what they've achieved in my field in the last fifteen years, I'd say they put the maths in place for the understanding of anything bigger than the nucleus of the atom. Now ... we're going below that ... down to the point where you don't know whether you're dealing with matter or energy ...'

He found the words of old Dora's lodger on his lips ... 'the secret of the universe'.

He'd half expected her to sneer at this, but instead he seemed to have caught her attention. She propped herself up on one elbow to look at him.

'Yes. If you want. That's exactly what it is, and if we can keep the would-be-mystics out of it, we'll find it.'

'Would-be-mystics?'

She flopped down again, face in the pillow, her tone of voice the same exasperated one she had used when she'd told him not to make plans.

'People like my father.'

While she slept Troy thought of the difference between his relationship with Kitty and his relationship with Zette. She was right, they did not know one another, they were as elemental as matter and energy, and he and Kitty surely did know one another? But in not knowing, so many of the obstacles vanished. Between Troy and Zette, class, race, tribe, faith mattered not a damn.

§ 130

They each lay full length on their cots. Only Herr Rosen had chosen not to return. As though each of them felt the same sudden exhaustion – but nothing had taxed them physically. Rod knew what he felt after a Drax talk. It was the force of Old Drax's anger. The years of knowing that it was all preventable, and nothing had been done. After Kornfeld's he was baffled and mind-numb. He wondered what might be tiring Billy and Hummel, as he lay between them. Like the largest tin soldier in the box. It could not be the same, surely? But it was.

Billy spoke, 'What was that about then?'

'Search me,' Rod replied.

'Y'know 'Ampstead. There are times when I think you and me are the only ones who don't know.'

'Really? I used to think I had certain intellectual strengths. History, y'know, Metternich's Europe and all that ... Modern Languages ... a smattering of Economics ...'

Billy saved him from a list of his own inadequacies, 'Whereas me – not bein' college – I know two things ... how to run a tailor's and how to –'

'Look after number one,' Rod concluded for him.

Billy propped himself up on one elbow, surprised but not in his habitually angry way of confronting the new.

'How d'yer know I was gonna say that?'

'Billy,' Hummel said softly from the other side of Rod's bulk, all but invisible to Billy, 'it is your battle cry – you ride with it wrapped around your crest like a crusader legend. You drum it into your wife, you shout it at your son and you use it as a sophist's bludgeon in any negotiations with Schuster and myself.'

Billy spoke to Rod, 'Did you understand that?'

'More than you did.'

Hummel had not finished.

'But, my friends ... let us consider the question you asked first. "What's it all about?"'

'I'm all ears, cock.'

'There is a certain common ground in what Professor Kornfeld is saying in his talks and what I shall say in mine. We are both dealing with the greatest human failing of all – the necessity of meaning.'

'Eh?'

'Kornfeld is asking you to consider where science has been headed since Darwin.'

'Who?'

'Later, Billy,' Rod said. 'That's an easy one. I can answer that one for you. Let Josef speak.'

'Darwin,' Hummel said on cue, 'removed the hand of God from creation – a momentous decision for a devout Christian, one has no difficulty in understanding the great delay in making his conclusions public – yet in so doing, in taking God's heavenly hand from the earthly tiller, he ironically left order ... genus, species, category ... call it what you will, it's order ... even though the very principle appears to be that everything is random, accidental and hence meaningless. That much-abused phrase 'The Survival of the Fittest' might be better rendered as 'The Survival of the Freaks'. We are freaks with overly large frontal lobes and opposing thumbs as surely as the long-necked Galapagos tortoise is a freak. Now, with what remained of order – and absence of God might be lightly termed the absence of whimsy ... the duckbilled platypus might make more sense viewed as the product of divine whimsy, never-theless it evolved ... practically, in interaction with the rest of nature ... and nature is the greatest freak, the consummate all-pervading freak ... with the order remaining science has sought, however unconsciously, to reinvent God. Not the God of the laws of our fathers, nor the Christian God of love, no God with human form ... but the God of First Principles, first causes ... of teleology.'

The last word, if not all the others put together, had clearly thrown Billy, yet surprisingly he managed to hit the nail on the head.

'I get it. God is dead. Long live God?'

'Exactly,' said Hummel. And with this in mind Herr Kornfeld, while not quite subscribing himself, is telling us that some of his fellow physicists seek God in unity. In the idea that everything at some sub-molecular level is one – that energy is matter, matter is energy and so on . . . I do not have the science to put it better. In their very different fields both Gregor Mendel and Albert Einstein sought to show us the God of First Things – a Catholic monk and a German Jew . . . the order of inheritance in a garden pea on the one hand, the singularity, the oneness of time and space on the other . . . the great unified theory of everything. One big jam pot to hold us all.'

The pause was natural. Perfect timing on Hummel's part. Rod could hear Billy breathing, Billy bursting.

Hummel resumed, concluded, 'Whilst I, on the other hand, am arguing the opposite.'

'Which is what?'

Rod answered for Hummel, 'That there is no God, Billy. That there is no unity and hence no meaning. I think you'll find Josef says this, or parts of this, on a fairly regular basis.'

'Thank you, Herr Troy. A simple message. But mine own.'

'Alright . . . so everybody's lookin' for God?'

'Ja,' said Hummel, 'because everyone wants meaning.'

'OK. What about Old Drax, then?'

'Ach, Billy. You should have no difficulty understanding Herr Drax. Herr Drax is talking to you about a necessity so close to your own heart.'

'Eh?'

Rod spoke for both of them, 'He means "looking after number one", Billy.'

§ 1 3 1

It was with some reluctance that Rod attended Drax's next lecture. Herr Rosen had talked both him and Billy Jacks into going.

'He might yet surprise you, Herr Troy. And you, Herr Jacks, does it matter where you take your siesta?'

'I wasn't asleep!'

'Oh – do you snore when you're awake?'

'No. But I might grunt a bit.'

Jenkins sat next to Rod again, passed out pencils and scraps of paper, saying, 'I managed to get hold of a few things. You wouldn't believe the shortage of pencils or the number of chits a chap has to fill out to get one.'

Drax coughed. He coughed a lot. He seemed to feel the cold too, and from somewhere had produced a fur coat which he had taken to wearing even indoors. Rod could not help but think it made him look like a Jewish Bud Flanagan about to sing 'Underneath the Arches' with Chesney Allen, until he remembered that Bud Flanagan was Jewish in the first place. Drax coughed, and opened the session.

'The theme I wish to pursue today is one of information and response, of access and concealment, of clear vision and self-deceit. The role of the British Press is central in this. Not only as they responded to the events of 1933, but in the way they shaped public response to those and subsequent events – to the SA's reign of violence, to the setting up of the concentration camps, the dissolution of the trade unions and political parties, the persecution of the communists – the persecution of the Jews to the descent into night and fog –'

Rod's head, all but noddding off in the cupped palm of one hand, jerked up at the sound of these words. It was like a poke with a sharp stick. He kept hearing that phrase, as though it were something in the ether, half-formed, intellectually embryonic, struggling to break into common parlance. Night and Fog. *Nacht und Nebel*. It struck him now as sharply as it had the night Wolfgang Stahl had first used it to him last May.

'– the descent into night and fog of one of the most civilised cultures in the world.

'Certain British newspapers saw fit to make a national crusade of Mosley's Blackshirts. The *Daily Mail*'s 'Hurrah for the Blackshirts', the *Dispatch*'s competition 'Why I Like the Blackshirts'. And I do not hold up these headlines as peripheral – I hold them to be central to British thinking in the last decade. It bespeaks a failure to read Nazism alright. A misperception of the enemy on a tragic scale.

Why does the British ruling class fail to see Nazism for what it is? Could it be that they have common values? That the same anti-Semitism that infects Germany infects Britain, that the people in power are not repulsed by the moral implosion that is Germany, that they themselves would support fascism as a bulwark against communism if only Hitler's nationalist demands were more "reasonable"? That the same deep-rooted anti-Semitism which flourished in the Chamberlain government now blossoms in Churchill's?

'Gentlemen – think about it. Most of you were locked up long before Sir Oswald Mosley. The man was not considered a threat. He was part of the British establishment. The threat is you – the little Jewish professor from Berlin, the little Jewish tailor from Vienna – you who have never donned a black shirt, a brown shirt or a jackboot. You whom Churchill has rounded up. And meanwhile the British fascists remain at large.

'Why is Lord Carsington allowed his freedom? Why is Professor Charles Lockett allowed to teach his racist theories in universities ... why is Geoffrey Trench, brother of our commandant, allowed to retain his seat in parliament?'

'Oh bugger,' Jenkins whispered to Rod. 'I do wish the old boy hadn't said that.'

Before Rod could say anything there was an interruption from the floor. Herr Rosen was on his feet, asking that Drax permit him a moment. He alone, it seemed, had used Jenkins' pencil and paper to take notes. He stood for a second looking down at them, then he looked straight at Drax.

'It is undoubtedly true that the English could and should have been less naïve about the true nature of the Nazis. You and I, Professor, have both lived in Berlin, have both been in a concentration camp. Let us call it the privilege of living the nightmare. We know. We do not doubt. We know. But ... let us give the English perhaps the benefit of the doubt.

'When I arrived here I spoke some English, but I was by no means fluent. Of the culture I was entirely ignorant. I knew so little of their history, their art or their literature. Worse still, I had no clue as to the strange taboos and customs which make the English such a strange and exasperating people. I had no suspicion that such class divisions as the English still maintain existed anywhere in Europe. I had never heard of "understatement", and could not for the life of me see why when asked "How did your concert go?" it was wrong to answer "Splendid, the house was packed" instead of saying "Not too badly." I could not understand why I should not ask a man about his profession, income, how much he paid for his suit, and whether he voted Liberal, Tory or Labour. All of them, one might have thought, perfectly justifiable questions in the eyes of any sane human being; and why it seemed to be "not done" to get excited or indeed passionate about a subject, and why it would be wrong to try and shine in conversation ... these were mysterious questions to me. I could not, indeed still cannot, understand their preference for ball games over reading a good book.

'I came from a country torn by civil strife, wrecked by inflation, where your liberty and indeed your life was often in danger, where you could be arrested and sent to prison or a concentration camp without trial, and where your race, creed, political opinions could put not only you but your entire family in jeopardy. England – or so it seemed to me – was a paradise, a country without suffering, changeless, excluded from the common lot of mankind, a happy isle of lotus eaters.

'Most amazing of all, there were policemen who carried no guns, called you "Sir" and asked you to sit down when you went to report a change of address.

'Certainly my first impressions were superficial, but I cannot see how they could have been very different. It seemed to me a stranger country than any I had known before, and her people still seemed to be living in the Edwardian era. It is, as Herr Schwitters reminds us every day, a surreal country – in which a Minister of Defence can proudly announce that there have been 436 and a half volunteers for the army while Hitler has millions of men ready for war; a country where people, who seem to be sane in every other way, were until recently willing to believe the word of a madman but refused to believe in concentration camps, and suspected that my motive for imploring my new-found friends to re-arm was due to nothing more than a refugee's craving for revenge.

'At first I was very little impressed by London, which I compared – to its disadvantage – with Paris. Trafalgar Square was nothing beside the Place de la Concorde, Whitehall a poor substitute for the Champs-Elysees, and the Thames was not a match for the Seine. But I fell in love immediately with rural England. Everything was new – everything unexpected. I discovered the Cotswolds: Burford, Chipping Campden, Winchcombe; I discovered Cambridge and Bath. But above all I fell in love with the English people. What a change from the open rudeness of the Germans and the thin varnish of politeness of the French. These people are tolerant, kind, helpful, good-mannered, disciplined, friendly, and less selfish than people anywhere else. Rudeness is exceptional, violence rare.

'This seems strange, because I cannot imagine any other country where one could live with so little interference from others. Yet all the time the influence is there. It is in the quiet voices of people in buses and the Underground, making the excitedly talking foreigner drop his voice, unconsciously trying to adapt his ways to his surroundings. It is in the polite way in which you are treated when you have dealings with the authorities at the police station, or the food office. Abroad, officials make you feel that you are a nuisance, a necessary evil. At first I was staggered by British officials. I am sure they themselves do not realise how much the newly arrived foreigner is impressed by their quietness and courtesy.

England is an amazing country. To anyone coming from the Continent it is a haven and a heaven. Gentlemen, it deserves our thanks. And its people our understanding.'

With that Rosen sat down again, stuffed the sheet of paper into his pocket. Rod could scarcely believe his ears. Rosen had glanced occasionally at his notes, but he'd spoken unaided for more than five minutes. And as he sat he'd brought the room to its feet. Jenkins stood and led, hands clapping furiously, like the winning captain at cricket leading a round of applause for the gallant losers. And man for man they rose with him. Hummel, Spinetti, Schwitters . . . all clapping. Rod was almost the last to join. It was a stunning statement of 'Englishness' with which he was not wholly certain he could agree. But Billy Jacks abstained. As the ripple died away, he turned to Rod and said, 'No copper ever called me "sir". Chipping Campden? Chipping bloody Campden? Rosen may know Chipping bloody Campden. Bet he's never been to Stepney Green. Two cheers for England, eh, 'Ampstead?'

It had been a muddled speech, a disjointed speech – insightful, objective – a resounding, an optimistic, generous response to the bitterness of Drax – but also shot through with sentimentality. Whilst he would never agree with Drax, it pained Rod to feel he agreed more with Jacks than with Rosen. But it was a hymn to Englishness, and he felt no impulse to make one himself – just yet.

Drax took it all in his stride. He knew that he had lost his audience for the day. They'd be back.

'Until next week,' he said, stacked his notes and left.

§ 132

One day in the first week of August at nine o'clock in the morning Troy was putting off the paperwork, wishing Scotland Yard made a decent cup of coffee, leaning in the window of his office, glancing out at the Thames, and reading a censored letter from his brother on the Isle of Man.

> I'm in a camp called — —. It's a nice old
> building just outside Port —. Not bad. Might
> even say comfortable, and actually nowhere near
> as rough as you might think. There were
> 'incidents' on the way here, but if I try to
> tell you what happened it'll just get —, but
> the bunch of squaddies we have guarding us are
> decent blokes. Let's test the — —, they're all
> from the — Regiment. Did that get through?
> Thought not. Some interesting company too. The
> Cambridge physicist Arthur Kornfeld - the more
> I talk to him the more I'm sure I'd come across
> his name in the newspapers before the war, but
> also the German pianist Viktor Rosen. Knew
> Mahler when he was a boy! I find that amazing.
> And we have a complete nutcase called Kurt
> Schwitters who calls himself a Dadaist. I have
> the vaguest memories of them. Anarchic bunch.
> Nikolai seemed to admire them for turning
> everything into utter nonsense, but then he
> would, wouldn't he? A grumpy, but really rather
> dear old socialist, Max Drax, goes around in a
> fur coat looking like Bud Flanagan . . . and an
> equally grumpy Tory from the East End called
> Billy Jacks. I'd be amazed if you hadn't come
> across him. From Stepney. That was your old
> beat, wasn't it? I've learnt a new word -
> *zwangsgemeinschaft.* Sounds like a mouthful of

marbles but it means a compulsory community.
Blokes bunged together who didn't choose one
another but nevertheless form a community. All
puts me in mind of that Conrad line - forget
which novel - to be free you must first belong.
  I'm keeping busy. We have a university going -
not kidding - and we have a concert party in
the offing. Believe it or not I'm on second
violin. Resin on me fingers for the first time in
God-knows-how-long. Come to think of it,
Schwitters has volunteered to do a turn. I dread
to think what he's got up his sleeve. Do tell
Nikolai I've met him, he'll be so impressed.
And . . .'

The telephone rang.
    'You busy, young Fred?'
    'Save me from it.'
    'Eh?'
    'Paperwork, George.'
    'Oh . . . if it's a trip out you want, I'm your man. You'd best get back
to Whitechapel as quick as you can.'
    'No problem . . . where do you want me?'
    'Market Street Synagogue.'
    'Not another dead rabbi?'
    'Yep.'
    'George, I was joking!'
    'I wasn't. Old Rabbi Adelson. Found dead in his own synagogue this
morning. Get yer skates on.'

§ 133

Elohim Synagogue, the formal name of Market Street Synagogue, E. 1.,
faced Market Street with a vast frontage. It was surprising Troy had never
looked closely before. He could hardly miss it. A huge circular window,

a stained glass star of David twenty feet wide, and dozens of little columns, all contributing to a rather Moorish effect, a hint of southern Spain and Granada. In short, it was grandiose. Brick testament to the first generation of Jewish immigrants to make money in Brick Lane – 'we're here, we're staying, we're Jews'. They'd spent their money on this – a dignified statement about God or a fist in the face, depending on your viewpoint. The next generation had spent their money on detached houses and pretentious porches in Golders Green.

All public buildings seemed to Troy like fakes, like pretentious porches. Promises and preambles that could not deliver. The synagogue reminded him of the casino at Monte Carlo – reminded him of the Palace of Westminster and St Pancras railway station. What they all had in common was that they could never be what they pretended to be. This was as true of Elohim Synagogue as it was of St Pancras. Public space lacked intimacy. Without intimacy space was hollow space. Gild it every which way, it was still the gilt of gold-leaf on gypsum. As fake as a film set, as real as a casino. That God and Mammon should have tastes quite so similar was neither here nor there.

Bonham was waiting inside the door.

'You wasn't quick enough.'

'What do you mean?'

'His doctor's here already. Mrs Adelson sent for him. Dr Guildenstern. A real stickler for the doins – wants the body carted off and cleansed. The works. You'll have to be sharpish or they'll have the old boy under ground before you can say truncheon.'

'Sounds like a pain in the arse.'

'He is.'

The electricity to the synagogue was down. Oil lamps had been lit. Troy picked his way through the pews to find Dr Guildenstern kneeling over the body of Rabbi Adelson, medical bag open at his side. A second man stood holding a torch, aiming it at the body.

'Rosencrantz,' he said. 'I mind the place.'

'Troy,' said Troy. 'Scotland Yard.'

At this the doctor stood up, dropped his stethoscope into his bag, turned to Troy. A small man of sixty or so, short white beard, wire-rimmed glases, a homburg pushed to the back of his head. An I've-seen-it-all look about him that Troy so hated in the middle-aged. A voice that all but rippled with practised sarcasm.

'So, someone sent for the big boys, did they? Well, there's nothing here for you or Scotland Yard, Mr Troy. Aaron died of natural causes. Quite simply, his heart stopped. Can't say I'm surprised. He was seventy-two and he'd been complaining of angina to me for six or seven years. And last night? Well, I reckon there's a fair few dropped dead of fright last night.'

Troy said nothing. He peered past Guildenstern to look at the body in the dim light. It was hunched. Almost foetal, as though Rabbi Adelson had curled up into a corner. He turned to the caretaker.

'You found him?'

'S'right.'

'Exactly where he is now?'

'More or less.'

Troy looked at Guildenstern.

'I turned him. Had to. Had to get at his chest. When I found him he was face down, against the floorboards.'

'I see,' Troy said. 'Then he didn't drop dead?'

'Mr Troy, I've been a physician forty-odd years ...'

'He didn't *drop* at all. He must have crawled in there.'

Guildenstern looked a little flustered at this, but stood his ground, made a fussy display of repacking and closing his bag.

'People do odd things when they're frightened ...'

This was Troy's point, but he saw no merit in spelling it out.

'... And if there's one thing you learn in my job, Mr Troy, it's people.'

'Frightened of what?'

'Air raid. There was a false alarm last night. I know. I was awake half the night myself. I should think most of the East End was. We've been expecting it for weeks, months even. It can be terrifying. Until you hear the all-clear. You haven't a clue whether they're up there or not. If I'd been here maybe I'd've crawled into a corner too.'

'But you were in a shelter?'

'As it happens, I was. I've an Anderson in the garden ...'

Those that had gardens had Anderson shelters. Most houses in this neck of the woods didn't have either.

'And the rabbi?'

The caretaker answered, 'Rabbi has an Anderson too.'

'Then I need to ask, why wasn't he in it? If he felt the need to shelter, why here?'

'I don't think you do need to ask. A man's found dead of heart failure

303

after the sirens go off? I've no doubts. I've no suspicions. I'm happy to give the family what they want.'

'And what's that?'

'A funeral today. I'm signing . . . natural causes.'

Troy knelt down, looked at the hands and the face, at the chest where the doctor had exposed it. Took one wrist and felt for the extent of rigour.

'Would you mind shining your torch again?'

The caretaker flicked it on. Troy could see no signs of violence, no cuts or bruises, no tears in the clothing. Just dust and dirt from lying on the floor. He stood up again.

'I'm afraid I can't let you do that just yet,' he said, trying to make 'no' sound more than monosyllabic and more conciliatory than it was.

Guildenstern shifted from flustered to angry, a broad band of colour spreading across his cheeks.

'You're not Jewish, I take it, Mr Troy?'

Troy said nothing.

'And you clearly know nothing about our traditions . . .'

'I know enough to know the importance of the ritual cleansing, the watch over the body, the immediacy of a funeral, but you're only going to get that if the law is satisfied it's natural causes. Right now I am the law, and I want a forensic scientist down here to examine the body. If he agrees with you, you can sign off on the case. I'm not trying to create obstacles.'

'And if he doesn't agree?'

'I'll ask for a post-mortem.'

'You'll ask for a post-mortem! You'll have him cut up? I suppose it's too much to ask for a little respect?'

§ 134

It would take Kolankiewicz more than an hour to get to Whitechapel from Hendon. Out of respect, Troy talked not to the widow, but to the sister-in-law.

'Aaron always said he'd never use a shelter. He could be like that, stubborn as a mule. Said he hadn't lived seventy-two years to run and hide from tinpot dictators like Hitler. After that first false alarm the day war broke out, that Sunday morning, he always said he'd take his chances. And, if God decided to take him, that was that − in the street, in his house, in the synagogue ... but he wouldn't be caught by his maker cowering from Nazis in a tin hut in the back garden. Said if God wanted him for a pilchard, he'd have been born a pilchard. There've been a few since, he ignored them all. I heard the siren about nine o'clock last night. No idea whether it was another waste of time, or whether this was really it. I mean, you never do know, until it is *it*. I went down the shelter with Sarah. The all-clear must have sounded about an hour and a half later − but by then we were settled, so we neither of us thought of coming out till gone seven. We got a few hours sleep. I expect a lot of people did. When we went into the kitchen to make a cup of tea, Aaron wasn't home. Only when we'd had a cup of tea did we think to wonder what had become of him.'

'Did he disappear often?'

'No ... I wouldn't say he ever disappeared. He walked a lot. He knew every street for miles around by the soles of his feet. But when he couldn't sleep he'd often be in the synagogue. And I reckon that's where he was when the alarm went up. So he stayed put. He read a lot at night, you see.'

'And if he'd heard the alarm?'

'If? He'd have had to be dead not to have heard it.'

That, too, was a possibility, but Troy said nothing.

'Would he have ... panicked ... hidden from it?'

'I doubt he'd have so much as looked up. I've seen him read the paper right through the whole rigmarole − siren wailing, lots of running about, kids screaming, not knowing a thing, then that awful silence, then the all-clear ... and Aaron hadn't budged.'

§ I 3 5

The electricity was back on by the time Kolankiewicz arrived. Troy had the lights turned up full.

'Troy, do you not think we could let him have this one?'

'The man's a fool.'

'Respect . . . not for the doctor but for the patient perhaps?'

'I know what you're saying, and if we can avoid a p-m we will. But I'm not releasing the body for burial until we're sure we've nothing else to learn.'

'It looks like heart failure to me. Given his medical history . . .'

'Given that he's the second dead rabbi in a matter of weeks . . .'

'Ah . . . so we're still chasing the ghost of Izzy Borg?'

'Did you think I'd give up?'

'No, my boy, I suppose not.'

'This looks like heart failure. Borg's death looked like a traffic accident. We both know it wasn't.'

'OK . . . so talk me through it.'

'Look at the toecaps of his shoes, the knees, the palms of his hands. Then look at the scuff marks on the floorboards. Guildenstern thinks he dropped dead. I say he crawled twenty-five feet from the nearest aisle to get here. Guildenstern reckons he died of fright when the sirens went off at nine last night. I say he died nearer midnight. He wasn't in full rigor when I got here, and he's only just in it now. What do you say?'

Kolankiewicz said nothing for more than a minute, working over the stiffening body with his hands and eyes.

'Crawled? Yes. I agree. Dirt and dust consistent with having crawled on his hands and knees. The man's clothes and shoes are otherwise immaculate. There are even splinters of wood in the hands to support your theory. Time of death. Between midnight and 2 a.m. If it were nine last night when he died he'd be set like concrete.'

'Dead men do not crawl.'

'The attack might not have killed him outright.'

'Do men crawl after heart attacks?'

'Troy . . . it's perfectly possible this one did.'

'But is it likely?'

'No. I would tend to see it as immobilising. Literally a near-death experience – your instinct would be to lie still, wait for help.'

'Not crawl into a corner where any help would be more than likely to miss you?'

'Probably not.'

'So, what do you say?'

'I say I think we caused offence to the Borg family when we delayed old Izzy's funeral, and I think we will now be doing the same to this lot . . . name as yet unknown to me . . .'

'Adelson.'

'. . . Particularly if you then do not say outright to the family that you do consider the death to be murder – you did not tell the Borgs, if I understand you aright?'

'I asked the questions I had to ask and tried not to suggest one thing or the other.'

'But you didn't tell them as clearly as you would me or Onions that you were investigating a murder.'

Thinking of all he'd said to Zette Borg, Troy chose his words with care.

'Not all of them, no.'

How neatly half-truths become half-lies.

§ 136

As if to think of her was to summon her up by word magic, Aladdin's genie sprung from the stage-trap. He knew the knock on his door could not be Kitty. He had given her a key, and it was Thursday – Kitty's day on the all-night shift. On his doorstep in the fading light of day stood Zette Borg, wearing the chic black outfit she'd been wearing the first time he'd set eyes on her on the Monte Carlo train. She'd not done this before. Her summonses had been imperious. She'd never just turned up on him.

'I called your office,' she said. 'You've been out all day.'

'I . . . er . . .'

'Hesitant again, Troy? Why not just ask me in?'

Troy pulled the door wide.

She walked in, turned full circle to take in the room in a single glance and finish facing him.

'I heard. I heard there's been another killing.'

'News travels.'

'It does.'

'Is that what brought you all this way? After so long?'

'Some,' she said. 'Some.'

§ I 37

'So it might have been an accident?'

'No – not an accident.'

'Troy, you know what I mean . . . natural causes.'

'It might. But I don't believe that's all there is to it and Kolankiewicz is holding his breath.'

'And your boss . . . that Onions bloke?'

'I gave him the gist over the phone. He's sceptical.'

'Sceptical?'

'I can't paraphrase for you . . . sceptical.'

'Good God . . . how many dead rabbis does it take? Some bugger kills my father and now kills Aaron Adelson too. How much does it take?'

Troy didn't want to answer. In so short a time, in so few meetings, he'd seen Zette in moods that rendered her completely unpredictable. He didn't know if this was one of them. It was. Rage gave way to tears. Almost the last thing he'd expected. And tears gave way to lust. First hers. Then his.

Afterwards she said, 'Tell me.'

'The post-mortem revealed nothing out of the ordinary. He died of a heart attack.'

'Died instantly?'

'Kolankiewicz thinks so, but as I said he's . . .'

'. . . Holding his breath. So you released the body?'

'I released the body, and I took an irate phone call from Adelson's physician telling me I was young, ignorant, a disgrace to the force and that I had no respect. Well, I knew that. And then I told the family.'

'Told the family what?'

'That it seems to be natural causes.'

'Seems? Seems . . . seems . . . seems! . . . I know not seems! How long are you going to go on telling lies of omission, Troy?'

§

Under moonlight,
infectious moonlight,
a madman dances,
chanting numbers,
two, three, five, seven, eleven.
Smeared in excrement,
naked as nativity,
smeared in his own blood,
wailing like a dog in pain,
throat bared to heaven,
mouth the perfect O,
Lord Carsington dances.

§ 138

It had been their first night in his bed, rather than hers, rather than the damp grass of the park. In the middle of the night he was wide awake. He was pretty damn certain she was too.

'What did you mean about your father being a "would-be mystic"?'

'He would not have said that himself. He'd have said he was a scholar.'

Troy remembered the tributes at Izzy Borg's graveside – gentleman and scholar.

'Well ... that rather went with the job, didn't it?'

'He didn't just study the word of God – he studied Kabbalah.'

'What's that?'

'It's more numbers. There are actually idiots who believe that the Torah is a numerical code ... sort of full of hidden clues from God ... it's called Gammantria, and when you work out what the numbers are you recite lists of numbers ... the word of God reduced to a game of lotto and the first to yell 'house' gets ...'

'Gets what?'

'That's the bit I could never quite get. I suppose they think they will receive divine revelation or some such bollocks. Because, believe me Troy, it is bollocks. There were even rabbis who thought you could conjure up a golem with the right recitation. All I can say is, we've been in need of a few regiments of golem since 1933 and they're not exactly thick on the ground, are they? The only thing Kabbalah has in common with anything meaningful like science or logic is the use of numbers. Although, I suppose, like quantum physics, it seeks meaning in the tiniest of things.'

'God by numbers? God in numbers? I suppose the entire *modus operandi* of religion is to be able to extrapolate the big picture from the small ... you know ... the world in a grain of sand.'

'Or ... "we're all in the gutter but some of us are looking at the stars"? It's bollocks, Troy, it's all bollocks. I gave up trying to talk sense to him long before he died. I know there are people in Stepney, people who knew me when I was a child, who think I've grown up snotty and aloof. Well, let any one of them try living with an assault on intelligence like my father's hocus pocus. It shrinks the mind. I almost said shrivels the soul, but that would be playing right into the old man's hands.'

'You know . . . we met in a house of numbers.'

'You mean the casino? Troy, there is as much meaning in the random dealing of cards at chemin-de-fer as there is in all the gobbledegook I ever heard in a synagogue or in my father's study. I play because I like to see numbers unfold in front of me. I don't pretend there's a pattern. And the only meaning is in the exercise of my judgement, of my brain. Meaning means winning. I usually win. I no more believe in luck than I believe in God. If my father believed there is a God – and I don't and nor do you – then surely that God gave him his brain to use?'

Troy said nothing.

Then.

'I knew him, you know.'

'You knew the affable old East End rabbi. A smile for everyone. Goyim and all. I knew the crank who rotted his own brain and tried to rot mine too.'

Troy's father was a crank too – Troy rather thought crankiness began in the adult male when its sperm finally met an ovum – he'd built an empire on the combination of his crankiness and his intelligence. But Troy would hate it if all that the world remembered about his father was the man eating Sunday dinner in his dressing gown while his daughters ran roughshod over his guests.

'Tell me something good about him.'

Zette was silent for a while. All he could hear was the depth of her breathing.

'He . . . he believed in belonging. I'd like to say that even if he lost his faith, which is unimaginable, that the notion of belonging, of being a Jew would still have meant everything to him. I respected that. I can de-louse myself of faith – easy-peasy – I can't de-louse myself of being Jewish, nor would I want to, and nor would society let me. I'd wear the yellow star with pride. My father was right, in his own daft way, to be free you must belong.'

'You know, my brother said something very similar in his last letter to me.'

'Your brother "belongs"?'

'It's beginning to look that way.'

'But you don't, do you?'

§ 139

Hummel was approaching the end of his lecture. Several amongst his audience had fallen asleep, one or two were sighing with exasperation.

'I have always thought it fascinating that neither Descartes nor Darwin could ever relinquish the notion of God – indeed the struggle for Darwin must have been agonising. But neither of them were in a position to address the centrality of the matter – although it becomes central with Descartes' *cogito, ergo sum* – the centrality of consciousness, for even now we have no science of consciousness. Consciousness alone is in the end what distinguishes us from the beasts, we are all of us self-aware and the crux of self-awareness is the awareness of our own mortality. We alone know we must die. The domesticated cat who deals in death every day has no notion of death, and no notion of its own death. It knows aggression and it knows fear. That is the cat condition. Our condition is this – to live until we die and to know the inevitability of that.'

It wasn't that Hummel wasn't making sense, indeed Rod found his argument far easier to grasp than anything Kornfeld had to say, and at least fresher than anything Drax had said so far ... but his mind had begun to wander ... from Hummel to the leaded windows, from the windows to the lawn ... and from the lawn to memories of cricket at school. He'd adored cricket. The perfect ritual in the perfect togs. White upon white with an optional cap in a silly colour. He even loved the sound of cricket, the soft thwack of willow on leather, the distant ripple of applause, like doves taking flight. He remembered the long holiday after his first year at Harrow – he'd tried teaching cricket to his brother on the south lawn at their father's country pile, Mimram House in Hertfordshire. He didn't think Freddie could have been much more than six ... but it wasn't so much his not getting it as his utter refusal to want to get it. Perhaps it was all to do with the boy being left-handed. At the end of a very frustrating afternoon the boy had asked of cricket, 'But will it get me into heaven?' It remained to this day the only question of faith he'd heard his brother ask ... and remembering this brought him back off a lawn a world away, back through the leaded windows and back to Hummel.

'. . . After much thought I have reached a conclusion I cannot reconcile with any of my arguments ... consciousness is the central problem of modern philosophy ... yet, and I hesitate to say this, I fear that consciousness itself seems to be an illusion.'

A ripple of applause. The dozy awoke. Hummel looked at them all waiting for questions. There always were questions, even though, as now, there was prolonged and cogitative silence.

Rod thought a bit. He'd missed something vital daydreaming. There'd been a seven-league leap in Hummel's argument. Rod spoke, 'An illusion of what? Without consciousness there can be neither certainty nor illusion. You say "seems", seems to whom or what? What or who is the entity so deluded or deceived?'

Hummel smiled, and said, 'I wish you hadn't asked me that.'

§ 140

It had come together in an unexpected if intended way. The British had turned out for the Viennese, the Berliners ... the odd Italian ... in their re-creation of Red Vienna. The enlisted men sat at the back, ordered to a concert and as uneasy as if they'd been invited to a nudist camp, Lieutenant Jenkins sat up front, as though representing the absent commandant, Major Trench.

It had come together. Rod was pleased. He knew he wasn't a great or even a good second violin, but he was capable and felt he had shown it. Kornfeld was ecstatic, Herr Schnitzler wept tears of joy, and the audience belted out the applause and demanded an encore. Kornfeld apologised that they had none of them had enough vanity ever to think they would require an encore and hence had not prepared one – and they left the stage to a second round of clapping.

They were to be followed by Schwitters. Rod took his seat next to Billy Jacks.

'It's nothin' to do with porridge, I 'ope.'

'The programme says a sonata. That's a piece for solo instrument.'

'How do you know he hasn't found a way of playin' a tune on porridge?'

Schwitters strode onto the stage. He'd wetted his hair to stick down

313

his errant wisps, and Rod could have sworn he'd concealed the holes in his increasingly tatty black jacket by dabbing ink onto the shirt underneath. Dignity, it seemed, was the vital setting for the absurd.

'I shall now perform for you ze presto, foursz movement of my Ursonate, originally composed in ze late 1920s, but wiz furzer additions in later years.'

Rod couldn't see what instrument Schwitters had in mind. Was he going to walk over to the piano? Was he suddenly going to whip out a Jew's harp from his trouser pocket and start twanging away?

Schwitters did not move. He stood stock still, almost as though at attention, opened his mouth and began to babble.

It sounded to Rod like . . .

   'grim

       blim

           bim'

and

   'bnim

       bim

          bum'.

Or was it? No, it was 'bum' it was definitely 'bum'. And it went on for several minutes, perhaps the best part of quarter of an hour, via . . .

   'oo

       bee

           oo

              bee',

   'lula

       lula

          lula'

and . . .

     'rinza

        kette

           bee'

to end up pretty well where he'd started at . . .

'grim

    blim

        bim.'

Rod wondered, in view of Schwitters' statement about the piece being 'composed', whether he had memorised all this gibberish or simply made it up as he went along. It had a certain rhythm to it, a generous mind might even say a certain music. Jacks did not have a generous mind. As the too-polite applause died down he whispered, 'What the bleeding 'ell was that?'

Rod said, 'I'm sorry, I haven't a clue. But remember he's an artist.'

'Artist, my arse! It was a load of Chipping Campden, that's what it was.'

Chipping Campden had proved such an emotive phrase for Billy, it had all but replaced both 'fuck' and 'bollocks' in his vocabulary since he had first heard Herr Rosen utter it. It was the compression of all his contempt for England into four syllables – deploying the name of a quaint Cotswold village as an obscenity had a poetry to it that Schwitters might appreciate.

'I've heard more sense out of any o' my kids while they was still in the pram. He should stick to carvin' porridge.'

'Well ... he's down for another number in the second half. I suggest you put your fingers in your ears, or nip out for a fag.'

'Nah ... I'll stick with it. If I catch him actually making sense or using real words I could maybe ask for me money back.'

'You know, I think you might just have invented a new parlour game. First person in a bollocks-talking contest to accidentally make sense loses.'

After the interval, Rod sat between Drax and Jacks, the big man book-ended by two little men ... half a dozen blokes recited poetry in German – chunks of Schiller, snippets of Goethe – another bloke did indeed get on stage, pull out a Jew's Harp and twang away tunelessly pretty much like a cockney dad bashing away on a pair of spoons under the fond delusion that it was music, a counter-tenor sang something obscure and excruciating ... and that left only Schwitters' second number, whatever that might turn out to be, and the finale, Viktor Rosen playing Beethoven's 'Pathétique' sonata on a Bechstein abandoned by the girls' school upon their departure, and personally retuned by Rosen himself.

Schwitters took the stage again to an apprehensive silence. All Rod could hear was Drax wheezing, but then Drax seemed to be wheezing a lot lately. Either Schwitters was clutching what appeared to be a rifle carved out of wood or he'd found a way to set porridge rigid.

'I sing for you now ze smash hit of 1912, lyrics by George Norton, music by Ernie Burnett.'

Rod hadn't a clue what to expect. Jacks whispered, 'I know this one. My old dad used to sing this. Da de da de da da da de dada.'

Schwitters sloped arms and began to sing, his left hand upheld in a 'Heil Hitler' salute:

'Komm to me mein melancholy babeeeee ...'

And as he sang he turned his head slowly, mechanically, almost as though on a ratchet and gazed a gorgon gaze upon his audience, unflinching, unsmiling, bone-chilling. Rod found the sentimentality of the words evaporating like Manx will-o'-the-wisp under Schwitters' withering gaze. For the second verse he held his torso rigid and goose-stepped up and down the stage. For the third, he unslung his rifle, and aimed it at individuals in the audience, stamping his foot after each phrase to simulate a gunshot.

'Cuddle up!'

Bang!

'Und don't be!'

Bang!

'Shy!'

Bang!

On 'shy', Rod rather thought the wooden rifle was pointing at him or Drax. It was a chillingly effective little stunt. He doubted there'd be two hands put together to clap at the end of it. On 'bang' Drax slumped forward, chin on chest. Rod was amazed. He'd never have thought Drax willing to play along with a piece of Chipping Campden like this – but as Schwitters left the stage to a gobsmacked silence Drax did not move, and when Rod gently grasped a shoulder and asked, 'Are you OK, old man?' he slumped to the floor.

§ 141

Rosen was approaching the end of the second movement when Drax came to. Rod had laid him out on a sofa in a small room next to the concert hall. He'd been light as a feather. Rod realised he so rarely saw the man without his Bud Flanagan fur coat that he'd an utterly false idea of his size. He doubted he weighed more than eight and a half stone.

'How long?' Drax asked.

'About ten minutes,' Rod said.

Drax swung his feet off the sofa.

'Ach, for twenty years I wanted to hear Viktor Rosen play . . .'

He lost his balance. Rod caught his head and laid him gently down again.

'Not so fast.'

'Ach . . . It is only a cold. It has been coming on for days.'

Hummel peered down, spoke up.

'No, Max. It is longer than that, you have coughed and wheezed almost since we met.'

'Can you be surprised? We have had some terrible rain this summer. I have caught a cold. No more than that.'

Rod said, 'Colds don't cause you to pass out.'

Drax said nothing to this, looked back as though silently imploring Rod to change the subject.

'I think you should see the MO.'

Kornfeld said, 'Medical Officer? What Medical Officer? We don't have a Medical Officer.'

Rod got Jenkins out of the concert.

''Fraid he's right, old man. We've no resident MO.'

'What? For a hundred men?'

'Are there a hundred? I've never really been able to count. But no, it sort of never got organised.'

'It'll have to be organised,' Rod whispered. 'It looks more like pneumonia than a common cold to me.'

Jenkins knelt down next to Drax.

'Max, old chap, how are you feeling?'

Drax responded with a fit of wet-coughing, drenching his handkercief in sputum.

'I shall be fine,' he lied.

Jenkins took Rod into a corner.

'I think you're right. I'll find the major. Something will have to be done.'

'Tonight?'

'I do hope so. But you know as well as I how elusive the good major can be. Hasn't been to roll call for a week. Hasn't set foot in the mess for longer. And written on the wall in the enlisted men's latrine is "What's the difference between God and Trench?"'

Rod looked blank.

'Sorry, it's an old gag – I thought you might have heard it. It goes . . . 'God is everywhere, Trench is everywhere but here". But, I'll find him.'

§ 142

Trench was blunt.

'I know your sort. You're a rabble-rouser, Mr Troy. You're the thing the Army hates most. A barrack-room lawyer.'

'I'm not in the Army and neither is Professor Drax.'

'I'm so glad we agree on that because I have no provision for medical treatment of civilians.'

Even now Rod had only half of Trench's attention. He was standing behind his desk, rifling through piles of paperwork.

'There's surely an MO for your men?'

'In Douglas, yes. If one of my chaps gets ill I'd have to send to Douglas.'

'Then send for him for Drax. He's ill. Quite seriously ill. I think it might be pneumonia.'

'No can do.'

'Then send for a GP from one of the villages.'

Trench banged a fist down on the pile of paper.

'You see this lot? Army regulations. Army bumf. Comes in by the barrowload every day.'

His other hand lay flat on a second smaller pile.

'You see this lot? Home Office bumf. Right now jurisdiction over your raggle-taggle bunch of Germans and Jews is with the War Office. Any day now it shifts to the Home Office. Don't ask me why. All I know is the transition means twice the bloody bumf, and it gets bigger every day. If I have power to summon a civilian GP ... *if* ... who knows, the regulation might be in this lot somewhere. But right now I don't have that power.'

§ 143

Rod said, 'Isn't there a doctor in camp? All these degrees and diplomas, surely one of us knows something about medicine?'

Siebert said, 'You may recall I mentioned that there is one remaining Nazi?'

'Vaguely,' Rod said.

'Massmann.'

'Eh?'

'Massmann, he's the Nazi. He's also a doctor.'

'Oh bugger. Have I met him? I don't think I've met him.'

'Takes his meals in his room since they shipped out all the others. You and Billy might pay him a call. The rest of us are known to him, most of us have clashed with him at some time. He has a room to himself on the top floor.'

'A room to himself?'

'Did you think any of us would share with him?'

Massmann's room was in the attic, high in the gable. Enough room for a palliasse, a constantly hissing cold water tank, a washbasin and little else. Rod and Billy peered in through the open door. The room was higher than it was wide or long. Just as well – Massmann appeared to Rod to be close to six foot six and as skinny as Hummel. He was stretched out on the palliasse, one hand behind his head, the other clutching a book. Rod tapped politely on the door. The eyes flickered up to look at him, but Rod could swear not another muscle in his body moved – the eyes were the enviable Aryan blue, the skin taut across his forehead, the cheekbones high and his skin pale.

'What is this? A delegation?'

'After a fashion. Doctor Massmann . . .'

'When a Jew comes to me, things must be in a sorry state on the lower floors.'

'Actually, I'm not Jewish.'

'But your little friend is, and while you are hell-bent on sticking to your English manners and your Queensberry rules, your friend would like to strangle me. I can see it in his eyes.'

Rod was utterly thrown by this. Almost speechless.

'Come, little Jew. Say what you are thinking – spit it out. Tell me to my face. You would like to strangle me, would you not?'

'Yeah,' Billy blurted out. 'Right on all counts, Jerry. I'm a Jew, I would like to strangle you but I've come to ask a favour.'

Massmann laid the book face down on his chest.

'So, the air is cleared. And now such honesty must surely be rewarded. Ask away, little Jew. Your Englishman is clearly still tongue-tied.'

'We got this mate – been taken sick he has. We reckon it's pneumonia. He says he's always been prone to a touch of bronchitis – but now it looks worse. You're the only doctor in camp. We'd like you to take a look.'

'Another Jew?'

Billy looked at Rod, Rod looked back.

'Well? Yes or no? Another stinking Jew?'

'Yes,' Rod said at last. 'Another stinking Jew.'

Massmann stood up, stood at the end of his bed, turned on the tap above the basin, not speaking until the groaning in the pipes had shivered to a stop.

To Rod's surprise he switched to German.

'"*Da aber Pilatus sah, daß er nichts schaffte, sondern daß ein viel größer Getümmel ward, nahm er Wasser und wusch die Hände vor dem Volk und sprach: Ich bin unschuldig an dem Blut dieses Gerechten, sehet ihr zu!' Die, die in Ubereinstimmung mit Juden stehen, sterben als Juden. Laß ihn kreuzigen! Laß ihn kreuzigen!*'

All the way back down the stairs Rod could hear '*Laß ihn kreuzigen!*' ringing in his ears. He had almost to drag Billy with him, kicking and screaming, 'Bastard, you complete fuckin' bastard.'

Only at the bottom of the stairs, shrugging off Rod's hand did he ask, 'What was that about? What did he say?'

'He was quoting the bible. New Testament. Matthew, I think.'

'I ain't never read it. Come to think of it, I ain't read much of the old one neither.'

'Pontius Pilate was the Roman Governor of Judaea who condemned Christ to death – literally washed his hands of him.'

'Yeah well – I don't need that bit spelled out. I could see that for meself. You don't need to be no scholar to work out he was washing his hands of old Drax. What was he sayin' about Jews? I know he said something – I definitely heard "Juden".'

'If you – and I think he meant me – line up with Jews you can expect to die as one.'

Billy thought for a moment but the best he could come up with was 'Fuckim'.

Then Rod said, 'Stinking Jews' as much to himself as to Billy.

'Yeah. Why did you say that? Have you gone stark starin' bonkers or what, 'Ampstead?'

'He's right. We're all stinking Jews now. *Wir sind die stinkenden Juden.*'

'Oh . . . Chippin fuckin Campden!'

Billy stomped off, uncomprehending, unforgiving.

Half an hour later Jenkins found Billy and Siebert in the gardens, cutting nettles.

'I heard you were asking for me,' he said. 'What are you doing?'

'Cuttin' nettles for nettle soup.'

'Do you really think the rations are that bad?'

'It ain't for us. It's for old Drax. Best thing for lung trouble, nettle soup. My old man used to swear by it. When I was not much more than a kid, during the last war, I used to raid disused gardens for nettles. My mum must have poured nettle soup down dozens of people. You won't remember that flu epidemic, last year of the war, will you?'

'I'm not that young, Billy. I'd be four or five – I heard about it.'

Billy seemed to think they had cut enough, stopped swinging the bread knife and wrapped what he and Siebert had cut in a towel.

'You heard that Nazi won't treat Drax?'

'No – but I can't say I'm surprised.'

'Ever occur to you to wonder why he's here?'

'He makes that obvious, he wears his politics next to his heartlessness, on his sleeve.'

'I mean – why he's *still* here?'

'I don't follow.'

'Oskar here reckons all the Nazis was shipped out just before I got here. Every last one, 'cept for Massmann. So ... why not him, why is he here and not on his way to Canada or Australia or at the bottom of the ocean like some poor buggers?'

'I don't know.'

Siebert spoke, 'You know, Billy, there was a lot of shuffling about, people changing places with one another. It wasn't a list so much as a quota. Mostly it was younger men trading places with the elderly. Drax himself was down to be shipped – a younger man took his place. As long as the numbers were right Trench seemed content.'

'Do you think anyone would have swapped places with Massmann?'

'No, probably not.'

'So we look for another reason why he's still here, and I'll give you one. He had to be down for deportation – paid up fuckin' Nazi after all – and what I say is this, he bought his way out. Greased somebody's palm.'

Jenkins looked surprised and innocent. 'But whose?'

Billy said, 'Well there's only two people in camp with power to bump his name off a list – even if you do call it a quota – there's you ... and there's Trench.'

The light dawned on Jenkins.

'Oh bugger,' he said. 'Oh bugger, what do you want?'

'We want,' Siebert said. 'A key to Trench's office.'

§ 144

Thus far Hugh Greene's war had proved no less eventful than Rod Troy's. He had escaped the fall of Poland by fleeing to Rumania, had escaped the fall of Belgium by fleeing into France, and had escaped the fall of France by boarding the SS *Madura* at Bordeaux, out of East Africa bound for England. Late in June he landed at Falmouth, and made his way back to London. He had been in London a couple of days when it occurred to him to call Rod, and he rang the house in Hampstead. Alex

Troy invited him round at once, and brought him up to date on his son's plight.

'It's outrageous. *It's bonkers!*'

'I know,' said Alex.

'All that . . . dammit . . . all that talent going to waste . . . the kind of talents we need to win this war. Surely you talked to Churchill?'

'No, no. I didn't.'

'But surely . . .?'

'And Rod expressly asked me not to. There have been questions in the House. Cazalet has taken up the cause of the unfairness of it all, the uselessness of it all – but neither he nor I have spoken directly to Churchill.'

The old man was getting . . . well . . . old, Hugh thought, but to leave his son wallowing in some godforsaken hole in . . . well . . . where exactly?

'Isle of Man. Heaven's Gate, near Port Erin. I gather it is some sort of lapsed stately home, run as a girls' school since the last war and now commandeered for the purpose. We write. Letters can can take two days or two weeks, and they are censored.'

'I shall write at once,' said Hugh.

And he did.

It was three weeks before Rod Troy received the letter. Nothing had been cut. Hugh stated that he was undoubtedly going to end up in the forces pretty damn quick. Most probably the RAF. Rod's reply took a further fortnight, and after the censorship, which blanked out anything of interest about life at Heaven's Gate, ended, 'The RAF? Wish I was joining you.'

By now Pilot Officer Greene was a translator/interrogator with RAF Intelligence at Cockfosters, on the northernmost edge of London. His superiors were impressed with his command of languages and one of them, one day towards the middle of August, lazily remarked that they could do with half a dozen like him.

'Half a dozen? I could get you one, but an absolute corker.'

'What languages?'

'German, French and Russian, smattering of Polish too.'

'Good German?'

'Three years in Berlin. Reported on the Kristallnacht from Vienna. Got booted out of Germany same time as me.'

'And where is he now? In the RAF?'

'Not quite.'

'How not quite?'

'He's in one of the camps – interned.'

'Oh – you mean he *is* a German?'

'Absolutely not. Harrow and Pembroke, Cambridge. Just had the rotten luck to be born in Vienna.'

For reasons that would never be wholly clear to him, Hugh seemed to have struck a chord in Wing-Commander Perkins.

'Locked up! Half the buggers in the country seemed to be locked up. Krauts, naturally … but Jews, and Iteyes and … and bloody Austrians. What the bloody hell's going on? It's easier to ask who haven't we locked up! Well – if he's in War Office custody, I'm sure the War Office will have to let him go if we say we need him. Half the blokes in those camps would be more use on the outside. Do you know they locked up my tailor? What's the bloody point of that? I curse the bloody War Office every time I lose a button on my flies! I have to go around with my flies flapping like some old pervert on the Brighton Line, just because they can't tell a Nazi from a … and they locked up the chef from Quaglino's too – can't get a decent meal anywhere in Soho these days! Do you know what I had to eat the last time I was up West? Fish and bloody chips! That's what! And they were cold! I ask you, is this what we're fighting this war for, for the freedom to go around with our wedding tackle flapping in the breeze, and to eat cold fish and chips? And they nobbled that bloke who used to do hand-made ice-cream every summer at the corner of Old Compton Street! And my brother-in-law's accountant, who turned out to be Viennese – and all the time we thought he was Welsh! I'll get on the blower to the War Office right away. What's your chap's name?'

This was where his surge of belligerent enthusiasm might just hit the buffers, but when Hugh said, 'Troy, Rod Troy' Perkins simply reached for the telephone half-muttering 'Any relation to that old fool who writes all those cranky editorials?' And the next minute he was bellowing at some poor underling in Whitehall.

§ 145

Rod found Hummel and Jacks in their room. Billy was stretched full length on his bed looking bored, blowing smoke rings from a roll-up ciggie so thin it was scarcely fatter than a matchstick. Hummel was sitting on the window seat, mending trousers for Herr Rosen, needle and scissors flying, and feeling plagued by wasps attracted by the tall pear tree just outside his window. A quick wave of his arm and he had snipped three of the insects in half as they flew.

'Amazing,' Rod said. 'How do you do that?'

Hummel merely smiled.

'Would you do something for me, the two of you.'

'I'm so bored, 'Ampstead, I'd do a tap dance for you with feathers up me jacksie if you asked.'

'Thank you, Billy – but what I had in mind was a spot of tailoring.'

'Wot exactly?'

'I need lots of yellow stars of David on white armbands.'

'Why?'

'Can you do it?'

Hummel said, '*Ja*, we sacrifice a sheet for the white armbands. Perhaps we use yours?'

'Of course,' said Rod. 'By all means take both the sheets off my bed. We need to make an armband for everyone in camp. Now, what about the yellow stars? Any ideas?'

Billy said, 'Ain't there an art room from the days when this joint was a school? Find us some yellow poster paint.'

'And,' said Hummel, 'Bob's your uncle.'

'I don't know where he picks it all up, I really don't.'

'And,' Rod said, 'I need them tomorrow.'

§ 146

At roll call Rod spread the word – the entire camp stayed out in the yard. It was a fortuitously sunny morning, but it had not been one of the mornings when Trench had graced them with his presence. Jenkins had done one of his hopeless head counts, told them to dismiss in his inimitably lazy fashion and had not seemed at all bothered when they hadn't.

Rod looked around – he could see Hummel, he couldn't see Billy or Siebert. It looked as though they had legged it.

Watching Kornfeld slip on the armband, he felt a twinge. What was he asking them to do?

'I'm sorry, Arthur. I suppose this is all too familiar.'

'No,' Kornfeld replied. 'It is . . . new to me.'

'I thought all Jews had to wear the yellow star?'

'In Poland perhaps, but it is only a matter of time . . . and . . . I'm not Jewish. As a matter of fact, I'm a Lutheran. A rather obviously lapsed Lutheran.'

'With a name like Kornfeld?'

'What's in a name, Mr Troitsky? What's in a label?'

Kornfeld seemed to have set himself to musing. The two of them stood at the edge of the courtyard watching Rosen, Spinetti and half a dozen volunteers hand out the armbands.

'It's nothing new, you know. So little the Nazis come up with is. A badge of some sort to tell the Jews at a glance has been around for centuries. Every other tyrant seems to have entertained the idea. Popes and kings and emperors – your own King Henry III, to name but one – and for centuries there was such a thing as a Jewish hat. A quirk of fashion made compulsory. Yellow stars are merely the latest manifestation.'

'They all seem to be going along with it.'

'Oh, they will, they will. There was a slogan a few years back, "*Tragt ihn mit Stolz, den gelben Fleck*." I often think you are the most reluctant leader I have ever met, Troy. Yet you handle a man as plainly disagreeable as Billy Jacks with skill, a man as deeply odd as Josef Hummel with understanding and a man as prickly as Viktor Rosen with tact. So, in this you lead and they will follow – they will wear the yellow star with pride.'

'There's a bit more to it than that.'

'Oh really – what do you have in mind?'

Rod briefed them all. They murmured almost with one voice it seemed, a baritone hum rippling across ninety-odd faces. They turned to look at one another, to mutter, to nod, to agree.

'Of course if anyone feels that they can't . . .' Rod began.

But Herr Rosen finished for him, 'No, Herr Troy, there will be no dissenters. Not this morning.'

Rod almost blushed with pride.

Kornfeld, standing at Rod's side, hands behind his back, the way they'd seen Jenkins stand when playing the subordinate, whispered, 'And those who stand in line with Jews.'

Rod suggested they wait for Billy and Siebert.

Kornfeld said, '*Carpe diem.*'

So they did.

Jenkins was first on the scene.

'Oh bugger! What are you chaps up to?'

And the chant drowned out every last syllable.

'*Jude! Jude! Jude! Jude! Jude! Jude! Jude! Jude!*'

Ninety-odd voices – a single word.

'*Jude! Jude!*'

Jenkins dashed back inside.

They took a breather.

Schwitters appeared, carrying a large roll of paper nailed to two sticks. He gave one end to Spinetti and then walked away from him unrolling the paper until it was about ten feet long and its text clearly visible:

'We Are the Stinking Jews !'. . . in letters a foot high.

'Such a telling phrase. I had originally intended to do it in German,' Schwitters said, 'but then I thought of your intended audience.'

'Fine,' said Rod, 'Fine,' thinking all the while 'bloody hell!'

They took up the chant once more.

'*Jude, Jude, Jude!*'

Trench appeared in the doorway, hatless and red-faced. He turned and shouted at Jenkins. Rod wished they'd paused in the chant long enough for him to hear what Trench was saying.

Jenkins came over, shy and almost embarrassed to be cast as the errand-boy. He and Rod found themselves conducting their conversation at shouting pitch.

'The Major says whatever it is you think you'll achieve by this, you won't!'

'We want a doctor for Drax! That's all!'

'I'd sort of worked that out for myself. Not entirely a thicko, y'know! Is that what you want me to tell Major Trench?'

'Yes.'

'And if . . .'

'If he says no we'll stay here till he does.'

'Really. Till dark? Past dinner time?'

Rod had not thought that far ahead, but 'yes' was the only answer.

Jenkins went back inside. Five minutes later he was back.

'Message from the Major. You can stay here till you freeze or starve. He isn't even going to turn out the guard.'

Rod's heart sank, silently. He waved an arm in the air, the chant of '*Jude!*' slowly fizzled out.

'Bugger,' he said softly to Jenkins.

'Bugger indeed.'

'I'd sort of counted on a reaction. If not immediate acquiescence, at least something that tied up lots of soldiers all doing nothing when they should be doing something.'

'Can't help you there, old man. If I turn out the guard I could be on a fizzer.'

'Jenkins!'

They both turned, Trench was in the doorway bellowing.

Jenkins said, 'Start your chaps up again,' and dashed across.

Rod saw the confrontation as mime, drowned out once more by the chant, Trench all arms in the air, the comic face of British bluster, Jenkins doing what he did worst, trying to stand to attention.

Then Trench was gone, and Jenkins was running across the lawn to them waving madly. The chant stopped, this time almost as one.

'He said yes. He's sending for a physician, for a doctor from one of the villages!'

'Why?' Rod said.

'Does it matter? He's agreed! God knows why, but he has. You can call it off now!'

Rod looked at Kornfeld, Kornfeld looked at Rod. Shook his head. Looked at the ground.

Rod looked at Jenkins. 'When we see the doctor arrive, then we'll stop.'

He turned to the crowd to be certain they'd heard him, and saw the nods of assent.

'We'll stop chanting, but we stay here until the doctor arrives. If he doesn't arrive in an hour, we might find our voice again.'

'Fine by me,' said Jenkins. 'Absolutely fine.'

As Jenkins left, Jacks and Siebert ambled out. Late and shameless.

'Missed the show 'ave we?'

About three-quarters of an hour passed, then the main gate opened and Rod saw a Bullnose Morris, not unlike the one his brother drove, pull up to the house. A doctor – with a homburg and a gladstone bag he could be no other – stepped out, glanced momentarily at the crowd of protestors and vanished into the house.

Billy Jacks was standing facing Rod and Kornfeld. His yellow-star armband dangling at the elbow, hands in pockets flicking out the fabric of his trousers for all the world to see, like a schoolboy playing with his private parts. Like the cat that got at the cream.

'Can we have breakfast now?' he said. 'I'm starvin'. I'd never thought I'd see the day I yearned for porridge, but yearn is what I do. If I don't get some oats in me in the next five minutes, I'll eat one of Schwitters' obbjydarses.'

§ 147

Trench sent for Rod. Rod would have been surprised if Trench had not sent for him.

'That was quite a show you put on out there.'

Rod said nothing to this. If Trench was going to play the headmaster, fine. They stood in his office, barely adapted from the headmistress's study. Several generations of hockey First XIs still askew on the walls, a glass-fronted bookshelf stuffed with pocket-sized Loeb dual-language classics – Horace, Cicero, Polybius. It was at least a fitting venue.

'Don't think it swayed me.'

'Something did.'

'I gather Professor Drax does have pneumonia?'

'That's what the doctor's treating him for. It's not as if there's a pill one can take.'

'Quite.'

They'd reached an impasse. Whatever 'It' was Trench had to say he wasn't saying it.

'I know ... I realise ... when you first got here ...'

Rod declined to prompt him.

'You put me down as ... as a particular type ... a particular type of chap. I think you made the mistake of confusing my opinions ... my behaviour with that of my brother. It's obvious you know who he is. If one or two of the others read newspapers more often they'd all know who he is.'

'Of course I know who Geoffrey Trench is. My father was present when Mungo Carfax threw him out of the House with a boot up his arse. You're lucky that didn't make the newspapers.'

'Quite. However, it remains, yours was a rush to judgement. I'm no kind of fascist, and my politics are my own business. In denying your request for a civilian doctor I was merely following guidelines.'

'Then why did you change your mind?'

'I changed my mind because they are only guidelines and not regulations. It was a matter entirely for my discretion. And I did that to convince you that I am a man who acts independently. I am my brother's twin not his carbon copy.'

Rod had one thought.

'I don't believe you.'

He kept it to himself.

§ 148

Rod told Billy Jacks and Oskar Siebert what Trench had said to him.

'Of course he's kidding himself. I think the sound of us chanting was a huge embarrassment to him. Made him look as though he wasn't in control. In front of Jenkins and the men, I mean. No officer could stand that sort of thing.'

Jacks was doing that fiddling thing in his trouser pockets again – it struck Rod as faintly obscene. But one hand emerged, clutching a folded sheet of paper.

'There is one other thing,' he said. 'We let him get a gander at what you lot was up to out in the yard, and then we gave him this.'

Billy handed Rod a folded sheet of thin white paper. At first glance it seemed to Rod to be a child's scrawl, awful handwriting, perfect spelling – then it dawned on him Jacks had done a word for word, comma for comma copy of a letter that had originated on headed notepaper.

```
           Lascelles & Abercrombie Bank
                  Regent House
                 Hanover Square
                   London W1
                                   June 2nd 1940
Major R. A. C. Trench
Heaven's Gate
Port Erin
Isle of Man


Dear Sir,
   We hereby confirm clearance of a cheque for
£750, drawn on the account of Dr. Manfred
Massmann, The District Bank, Amersham. The money
has now been credited to your deposit account.
   Yrs Faithfully


J.B. Morton
Manager
```

'Where did you get this?'

'Oskar an' me turned over his office night before last. Idiot kept it in his desk drawer. Didn't know enough to burn the bleedin' evidence.'

'You burgled Trench's office!'

'No,' Siebert said. 'Not burgled. I had a key made. Young Jenkins gave me an impression of the original in a bar of soap.'

Rod waved the letter at them.

'And where's the original of this?'

'We sent it out by the patisserie run yesterday. My missis should get it in a day or two now. Trench don't play ball one copy goes to my MP, and another copy goes to Scotland Yard. My missis'll hang on to the original.'

'And that's what you told Trench?'

'Straight up.'

Rod did not know what he felt. Elated, deflated, victorious, defeated.

'You shouldn't be bothered,' Jacks said. 'You'd done wonders waving the old school tie. You got us fed back in Manchester, you got the sick and the old uns taken in at Douglas, you got this lot up an runnin'. You done good, you really have. But what you did today ... OK it was moving ... it was stirrin' ... an' we are all Stinkin Jews now ... you was dead right ... but it was never gonna work with a total tosser like Trench. All a sit-down was gonna get you was a row of cold arses.'

Rod folded the letter and passed it back to Jacks.

'Of course,' he said softly.

'He's right, Troy,' Siebert said. 'Gandhi-style civil disobedience was never going to work. As your English phrase has it, it was time to fight fire with fire.'

Rod looked at them. He could not see what they had in common. They were the same height and the same complexion – short, dark men – and that was about it. In peacetime, one would surely have been having his collar felt by the other?

He said, 'And to fight crime with crime? Do you know what an unholy team you two make? You should see yourselves, the East End wide boy and the career copper on the same side.'

'War,' Siebert said, 'makes strange bedfellows of us all.'

§ 149

Trench sent for Rod again the following day.

He too unfolded a letter and passed it across the desk to Rod.

'Came from the War Office this morning.'

Rod took it in at a glance and then re-read it slowly word for word.

Trench said, 'It's an order for your release.'

'I can see that.'

'You should be delighted.'

'And so should you.'

Trench declined the bait.

'You want me gone. Supposing I won't go?'

'Your charges will be safe with me. You've played Snow White among the Seven Dwarfs too long even for your own amusement. You'll go. Of course you'll bloody well go. It isn't a request ...'

Trench's finger tapped down on the paper.

'... It's an order. RAF Cockfosters. Seventy-two hours from now. You're in the forces now. Like it or lump it, Mr Troy, just bugger off!'

§ I 50

Rod arrived at Cockfosters wearing an ill-fitting off-the-peg uniform. There had been just enough time to get issued with the uniform, to drop in on his wife, children and parents and to ring his tailor and order a uniform tailored to his bulk. His father's obsession with, as he still insisted on calling it nearly forty years after the Wright Brothers, 'powered flight', had led Rod at an early age to indulge his father's hobby for him. The old man had bought an aeroplane in 1922 ... Rod had flown it for him and with him. He was a good amateur pilot, qualified longer than most professionals now in service and he had rarely lost a chance to fly. He'd kept up the hours in England, Ireland, France and, until the Nazis had grown suspicious of him, Germany too. Hence, it was with no small pride that he pinned his wings to the baggy RAF blue blouse before reporting to Wing Commander Perkins.

'I say, old man, you do realise wings are strictly for pilots?'

'I've been flying since I was sixteen. More than fifteen years.'

If Rod had wanted to stay in Intelligence it was the wrong remark to have made. Forty-eight hours later he found himself reporting to 56 Fighter Squadron, Fighter Group 10, in Boscombe Down, Wiltshire.

§151

It seemed to Rod that it had been a glorious summer. He'd seen it in London, he'd seen it on the Isle of Man, he'd glimpsed it one day at Cockfosters and now in rural Hampshire only twenty-five miles from the English Channel. He drove his HRG 1100 Sports two-seater down from London, his suitcase strapped to the back. Either side of the road out of Winchester the farmers were taking in the harvest. Heavy horses plodding in front of the whirling blades of reapers. Steam engines bellowing, fly wheels flying, leather belts spinning, threshing the corn. It was an odd combination of scents in the air. Steam and soot and the indescribable smell of mown wheat. He had no word to capture it in its ambiguity. It was the smell of summer – but it presaged autumn. The heat of the day always held that first cool breath of autumn, 'rotten before 'tis ripe' as some fool in Shakespeare said of the medlar – but for the life of him Rod couldn't remember who.

At the gate they told him to report to the Squadron Leader. The skies above were clear and empty. Somewhere across the airfield he could hear the sound of Forces Radio, the jaunty burble of the BBC Variety Orchestra. The Squadron Leader – Alec Bremner, a Scotsman as tall as Rod was himself, which went some way towards reassuring him that he might actually fit in a Hawker Hurricane – was sprawled in a lacquered Lloyd Loom chair, hands locked behind his head, staring into the blue yonder.

'That's a good sign.'

'What is?' Rod asked.

'I was watching you. When you'd parked the car the first thing you did was look up. You didn't look around or look for me, which was pretty much what you'd been told to do, you looked up. First sign of a pilot. You know who make the best pilots? Not rugby players, not football players or any other sporty type. It's musicians.'

Rod looked up again.

'Beautiful flying conditions. Not a plane in sight. And I play second violin.'

Bremner eased himself out of the chair. Returned Rod's belated salute with a handshake.

'And I bang away at the joanna when no one's around. Let's be grateful for small mercies, shall we? Now, how many hours?'

'Honestly couldn't say. More than a thousand, that I do know.'

'Good bloody grief, where have they been hiding you?'

Rod did not think this quite the moment to answer.

'OK, then, how many hours on Hurricanes?'

'None. Not a sausage.'

'OK . . . have you ever flown a monoplane?'

'Yes.'

'Anything with retractable wheels?'

'No . . . nor anything with machine guns. I've put in the hours, but I am an amateur.'

'Amateur? Bollocks. We've been taking anyone we can get since June. Ferry pilots. Green kids in their teens. Poles and Czechs who can't speak a bloody word of English. Canadians . . . even the odd Yank, and more Aussies and Kiwis than you could count. Amateur is no longer an applicable term. The only people we haven't taken are women . . . and I wonder how long it will be before we do.'

Bremner left no time to unpack, and got him up in a Harvard trainer right away. Less than forty-eight hours later, during a lull in the fighting, he was flying solo at the helm of a Hurricane, the squadron leader flying rings around him to teach him the tricks of aerial combat; the constant weaving to avoid enemy fire, sudden sweeps from behind, blinding attacks from out of the sun, the voice crackling through the headset 'Takka takka takka takka! You're dead, old son.'

Two days later it was real.

§ 152

High over Ventnor, Isle of Wight, a fleet of Heinkel 111s is in search of a target. The radar station, one of a chain dotted along the southern and eastern coasts, feeding into Fighter Command HQ at Stanmore, which gave the RAF advance notice of raiders from across the channel, had been taken out by Stukas less than a fortnight before. It was possible the Luftwaffe didn't grasp the extent of their success, but the Heinkel 111s ignored the remains of the radar station, lumbered on in the direction of Portsmouth. The 111s were slow planes – if a plane could ever be deemed slow by those on the ground below, harvesting by horse and reaper as they had done for two hundred years and more. Flying at no more than 225mph, a Heinkel 111 packed a bomb payload in the region of 3,000 lbs. Without the Messerschmitts they were vulnerable. Bremner had split the squadron into two wings – he would lead the more experienced pilots to tackle the escort, the 'new' boys, and there were two others as green as Rod, would try to take out the bombers, although the word 'try' had only been used once by Bremner, as in 'try not to get yourself killed'. A Heinkel was not only well-armoured, it was structurally all but impossible to break it up with bullets alone. Bremner had told him of bombers taking thousands of rounds with no significant damage to their capability in the air.

The tactic worked. It seemed to Rod almost too easy. To defend the bombers the fighters had to defend themselves – at cross-purpose when squadrons of Spitfires and Hurricanes closed in. The Messerschmitts peeled away from the Heinkels in swirling dogfights.

Flight Sergeant Milner led Rod and four other Hurricanes in a wide circle away from the action to come at the Heinkels side on, from the West, sun behind them. A Heinkel had no tail gunner – the firepower was all forward. Two gunners in the nose, two in the belly and one on top.

The top gunner in the nearest Heinkel opened up at once. Milner's voice came over the RT uttering the last words Rod had wanted to hear after staying within fifty feet of him since they left Boscombe, 'Break, break, you're on your own!'

A Messerschmitt 109 came down upon them. The German and Milner exchanged fire, and Rod took his Hurricane up into cloud out of harm's way. It was an instinctive move, and he knew, quite the wrong one. 'You're here to fight, laddie.' But he had not known how to engage the German without getting in the way of Milner. He put the plane into a tight circle, feeling the pull of G-force, and dropped sharply, too sharply, back down with no clear idea of where he was, out of cloud, and realised he had come down right in front of a Heinkel – facing its two forward gunners. A burst of fire from the Brownings in his wings, his first at a living target, a sound like ripping calico, fear fighting relief when he realised he had missed both gunners. Relief fighting fear as he realised they had both missed him. A second, almost unbidden burst of fire and then the shock as he saw the glass bubble in front of the two German pilots shatter and splatter with blood – and then the Heinkel dipped sharply, just as he rose. An unnerving bump as his tail wheel clipped the top gun turret and then flying free and fast, turning tightly once more to see the Heinkel spiralling out of control, down to earth.

Bremner had told him from the start that they all wanted 'a kill'. And he'd heard for himself the raucous claims in the mess afterwards, but Bremner had also said waiting for the proof was a dangerous vanity. 'The enemy is not the bloke you've just shot up, he's the bloke you can't yet see.'

Rod turned the plane northward just in time to see the 109 he had eluded minutes before send Milner's Hurricane plummeting – a trail of black smoke, then a billowing white cloud as Milner bailed out. But the Messerschmitt pilot hadn't heard Bremner's rule. He watched long enough for Rod to line up behind him, behind his armour, and open fire.

The blast as the Messerschmitt exploded sent Rod reeling westward. Down, down, down. When he levelled out of the dive, he was far below the battle. For a moment he seemed not even to be able to hear the sound of his own engine. As though he had slipped through a hole in time and space. Cocooned in a bubble of silence. Blasted into memory. He was in a bar in Berlin. Any bar would do. Nameless. He and Greene drinking German beer. And the voice in his head was asking if any of the young Luftwaffe officers he rubbed shoulders with night after night were amongst those he had just killed. Nameless.

Then Bremner's voice sounded, clear and present, loud and real and now, in his RT, 'Pancake! It's all over, you hooligans. Back to base. Repeat, pancake.'

§ 153

Bremner had unzipped his flying boots and came flapping up beside Rod.

'Milner?' he said simply.

'I saw him bail out. Saw the 'chute open.'

'Then we'll get him back soggy and sorry in an hour or two. And you?'

'Me?'

'You've made a spectacular start. Don't let it go to your head, but you have. I expected you to have a crack at a Heinkel. Fat lot of use if you can't. But to take the bugger down, and then the 109, that was something. How do you feel?'

Rod had been feeling rather a lot. If there was a gamut, it ran from elation, through surprise to a sad regret at the loss of life . . . to some rough-hewn sentiment he recognised might be patriotism.

'I feel . . . I feel . . .'

He stopped. Bremner and he face to face.

'What was it the PM said in May? . . . he quoted General Weygand's phrase about the Battle of France, said the Battle of France is over . . . blahdey-blah-de-blah . . . the battle about to begin will be the Battle of Britain. That's us, right? Battle of Britain?'

'Catchy, trips off the tongue,' said Bremner. 'But then I've always felt Winston had one eye on the history books.'

'So, if this is the Battle of Britain, I feel . . . well . . . British.'

It had taken a long time for Rod to arrive at this point. He had been aware for some time that it was a journey he had embarked upon long ago – quite possibly on the day almost twenty years ago when he had told his father that he would not be naturalised ('Well, Dad, not just yet anyway.'). He had never expected to reach this moment thousands of feet up in the skies over England, or in combat, but reach it he had. Would Bremner get it? He'd have had this conversation with whoever had asked him the question. He dearly wished he could have had it with his brother. But it had been Bremner, and only Bremner was listening . . . and he didn't know Bremner. He liked him – hard not to, he thought, but he didn't really know him. Would Bremner get it?

Bremner roared with laughter, slapped Rod so hard on the back he lurched forward.

'British? British, you Viennese Russki Sassenach bastard? Bugger British, I'm staying Scots!'

They scrambled again less than two hours later.

Bremner peeled them off by numbers to left and right. Rod heard Bremner on the headset to him, 'OK, Red Seven?' And then he heard him singing 'Wi' a hundred pipers, an'a an'a . . . we'll up and we'll gie 'em a blaw a blaw'. Then he heard him laughing like a maniac.

§ 154

Drax pulled a face, not for the first time, and set down his spoon.

'No disrespect to your mother – but I'll never get used to the taste of nettle soup.'

Billy said, 'Get it down yer. It pulled me through in 1921.'

Drax succumbed to a fit of coughing and asked for water. Billy went into the bathroom and came back with a tumbler. Drax drained it at one gulp, eased his head back on the pillows.

'Y'OK now?'

'I have been worse.'

'Bet you've eaten worse too.'

'True.'

'Like in that camp.'

Billy was pacing gently up and down the room, hands stuffed in the pockets of baggy trousers.

Drax said, 'Whatever it is you want to know – ask.'

Billy stopped in front of the window, stared at the cloudless September sky.

'When was you inside?'

'Nineteen thirty-three.'

'As soon as old Adolf got his knees under the table?'

'If I understand your idiom aright, yes.'

'And just 'cos yer Jewish?'

'There were many more than Jews in the camp.'

'Oranienburg, right?'

'How did you know?'

'Rosen was there too. Bleedin' miracle you didn't bump into one another.'

'I was there because I was . . . am . . . a Communist. I was a member of the Austrian party during my time in Vienna just after the last war. When I moved back to Berlin I did not join the German Party. All the same, after the burning of the Reichstag, when they needed scapegoats, the Nazis seemed to know who was a Communist and who was not. There was even talk that the membership lists had been supplied by

Moscow. They knew. They needed the merest excuse to arrest me. I gave it to them.'

'Things you said, like you do here?'

'Less ... much less. I asked students not to wear party uniforms in my lectures. The same day I was arrested. Two SA men came to my door at midnight. They gave no reason for my arrest, gave no time to pack or prepare. I was bundled into the back of a truck. They did not tell me the destination, although it was obvious. Everyone in Berlin knew about Oranienberg, although many pretended they didn't. Ironically, I remained on the payroll of the university for the next ten days until the Nazis passed an act forbidding Jews to join the civil service or teach in the universities. So I would have been fired anyway. The following month, having nothing else to do, they burnt books all across Germany, and no doubt some of mine were among them. Ironically – and this war is full of ironies – I would be offended if they weren't. I was released in the December. The camp closed soon after. But there are others now, bigger camps – Dachau, Sachsenhausen, Ravensbrück.'

'All a bit familiar, in't it?'

'Herr Jacks, are you really comparing this to a concentration camp?'

Billy shuffled his feet, moved away from the window, still not quite looking at Drax.

'Dunno – It's the nearest I've been to one. Lots o'blokes here got the midnight knock.'

'I suppose I do recognise it. In my own mind I've been comparing the two since the day I got here. I can tell you this. The food is better. It's not rancid and there are no maggots ... the shortage of marzipan I would term a minor hiccup – and boredom, any amount of boredom, is better than forced labour. But I know the real difference. This is a prison, and only a prison. I hate it – I know you do – and in my conscious mind I discriminate between a prison and a machine. If we are here five years, if the Germans do not come, it will still be just a prison. In five years, probably less, camps like Dachau will be part of the machine.'

'What machine?'

'The killing machine. There won't be enough bullets in the world to do the job.'

'Killing who?'

'Jews. Those who ... what were Herr Troy's words? ... those who stand in line with Jews.'

'Never pays to stick yer neck out.'

'Have you never "stuck your neck out", Billy?'

'Yeah. Just the once. I was at Cable Street. You know what that was?'

'Of course, I was in England by then.'

'I reckon that was my fight. Not just standin' in line with other buggers who thought it was their fight. My fight. Not because I'm Jewish or anything. The papers reported it as the East End takes on Mosley's Blackshirts. Maybe it was. And maybe that's part of why I was there. My East End, not bleedin' Mosley's. But there was also a chance of bungin' a brick at coppers. I may know nothing about Blackshirts, but I sure as hell know a blueshirt when I see one. I've always 'ated coppers. Wasn't Blackshirts dragged me into me old man's workshop by one lug'ole just 'cos I'd 'alf-inched a packet of fags. It was coppers. Wasn't Blackshirts tickled my ribs with a truncheon when I was fifteen, it was coppers. Wasn't Blackshirts or British Tommies that came knockin' on my door at midnight waving their internment orders – it was coppers. I got one mate who's a copper, known him since I was a nipper. He's alright. The rest? It's a battlefield.'

'Quite so. It's everybody's battle. You are so stubborn in seeing it as being yours alone. We are part of human kind, Billy. "Everyman's death diminishes me." Don't ask me which of your English poets I am quoting, I've no idea. But we are a whole, a collective, a community.'

'I'm not a Commie and you won't make me into one. It's just my attitude that's bolshie, not my politics. Like I said, I was bungin' bricks at coppers. I was lookin after number one.'

'And now you're looking after me. Feeding me your mother's dreadful concoction.'

'Can I get you some more?'

§ 155

7 September 1940

Of course they'd been expecting it all along. They'd been told to for years now. It was the received wisdom of the last decade. 'When the bombing starts whole cities will be levelled.' 'Seventy thousand dead expected in the first raid on London' – 'the ARP stockpiling papier-mâché coffins.' And it went back even further than that, in all probability to before the attainment of powered flight. H.G. Wells had been predicting 'the Blitz' in everything but name since he first put pen to paper. *The War in the Air* had been a novel of his middle age, published the best part of ten years before the Great War.

On 24 August, the Luftwaffe 'accidentally' bombed Central London. An 'accident' involving one hundred warplanes. The following night, on Churchill's orders, a modest RAF fleet of twenty-two planes made a reciprocal raid on Berlin.

A week or so later Hitler, as bonkers as Wells had said more recently, told the assembled Nazis in the Sportpalast that, 'We will wipe out their cities.'

And on 7 September the Luftwaffe tried to give him what he'd asked for.

Down in Dulwich, to the south-east of London, Harold Hapgood, a senior Fire Officer with the London Fire Brigade, was off-duty. It being a sunny, exceptionally sunny, Saturday afternoon, he was in civvies on his back lawn, collar-stud popped, braces dangling, top button of his flies open for comfort and digestion, relaxing with a cup of Earl Grey, four rich tea biscuits, a packet of Craven A cork-tipped cigarettes and a copy of that morning's *News Chronicle*. It was five o'clock or thereabouts, and had he not been so engrossed in his newspaper, he might have heard the distant wail of central London air-raid sirens letting rip at four minutes to five.

Instead, when concentration lagged, he glanced up into the sky, and saw to the north and east what looked like a swarm of insects, a black, moving mass, dotted with puffs of smoke. For fully ten seconds the lure of aesthetics and mystery took hold of him. They couldn't be insects, could they? And as reality returned, he realised ... more German bombers than he'd ever seen in the daytime sky ... hundreds of them, three hundred and seventy-five, as records later showed, and a fighter escort of twice that size. And the puffs of smoke were London's own ack-ack opening fire. He ran for his uniform. 'It' had begun.

Earlier that day, Ed Murrow, London correspondent of the American radio network CBS, had driven down to the mouth of the Thames through the East End of London. He had driven through the territory policed by George Bonham, and so recently purged of its Jews by Troy and Stilton, and remarked to his travelling companions, and later to the American nation, on how peaceful and pleasant it seemed in Commercial Road, the East India Dock Road ... by five o'clock Mr Murrow was at an RAF airfield out on the Thames estuary, watching the 'insect' swarm fly upriver to bomb London.

Outside Scotland Yard, Troy and Onions stood on the Thames Embankment, ignored the wailing siren and the rush of people around them and stared downriver. The image that came to Troy's mind was more precise than the one that had occurred to Fire Officer Hapgood – they were not just insects, they were moths, moths pursued by gnats.

'Bloody hell,' said Onions. 'Is this it?'

Troy had distinct feelings about 'it'. 'It' struck him as a ready willingness towards the irrational, a superstition ... like the 'historical imperative' or 'manifest destiny', both of which he thought to be complete bollocks, politics masquerading as faith – chance and circumstance elevated to the preordained. Telling Onions so would be a waste of time, so he said simply, 'There is no it.'

They went back to work. About an hour later Troy heard the all-clear sound – a two-minute wail of the siren – and looked up from his desk to see Onions in the doorway, macintosh on, cloth cap on, gas mask case across one shoulder. The cloth cap, Troy had learnt, meant Onions-in-disguise.

'They've stopped. I thought I'd heard nowt for a bit. D'ye fancy a drink? It's Saturday. Let's have a quick one and get home before the buggers come back again.'

Troy had an arrangement to meet Kitty out of work at eight o'clock. There was plenty of time to do both.

'St Stephens?'

'Too many toffs.'

Toffs meant politicians. Politicians to Onions meant flapping ears.

'Let's go the other way. Summat wi' a few dark corners. Villiers Street. Underneath the Arches.'

Onions always wanted a pub with dark corners. It didn't matter whether he was slagging off the bosses or merely telling you what he was growing on his allotment in Acton.

In the street, stepping eastward, Troy was suddenly disoriented to find himself walking into the sunset. Then it struck him. The glow on the horizon was London burning.

Onions bought a round. They stood at a window. Sipped ale.

Onions said, 'What was that you were saying earlier on? There is no "it"?'

It had not struck Troy as having a deal of philosophical depth, but clearly it troubled Onions. What in the realm of ideas might trouble Onions was never predictable.

'It seems to me,' Troy began tentatively, 'that we've worked up a sort of fatalism over the last year or so. Probably caused by that vacuum when nothing much seemed to happen, then exacerbated when what did happen happened so quickly.'

'Like Dunkirk, you mean?'

'Exactly. We had a long time to brood about it. And we've worked up an expectation of the worst. An old friend of my dad's rang up the last time I was with him, an old boy who's decided to see the war out from his retreat in Wiltshire. You know what he said? He's got hold of cyanide from the local chemist's – just in case.'

'Just in case o' what?'

'My point exactly.'

'You mean he'd top himself?'

'Most likely knock it back at the first sign of a German parachute floating down.'

'Bloody hell.'

'And of course ... it would be a paratrooper dressed as a nun or a Red Cross nurse.'

'What?'

'I heard that one in the canteen yesterday. That idiot Gutteridge regaling the Yard with rumours he'd heard that the Germans will land dressed as women.'

'Man's a twat.'

'If they do ... I have several friends in Fitzrovia who'd be delighted at the thought of big butch soldiers dressed as women.'

'God ... you know some queer folk.'

Onions sipped and thought.

'Fatalism? Like that saying from the last war ... "if it's got your name on it"?'

'Yep.'

'You don't buy that?'

'It's bollocks, Stan.'

Onions sipped and thought.

'But if "it" happened. If you knew it was all up for us ...?'

'I don't know,' Troy said.

'If I'm going to die,' Onions began, '... I'd like to be out on me allotment, get me parsnips lifted first. Leave things neat. And you?'

'Dunno,' Troy lied, wondering whether he would prefer to meet his maker between Kitty Stilton's arms or Zette Borg's thighs.

§ 156

Kitty emerged from Bow Street nick – tin hat boldly marked POLICE slung across one arm, gas mask in its cardboard case hanging from a shoulder – pale, worried, gabbling.

'Thank God you're 'ere. Stepney's taken a pasting. I got through to me mum. She's spent three hours in the coal cellar. I don't know what to do. I don't know whether I should be there or not.'

'Is she alright?'

'Oh yeah, nothing actually fell in the street. But she said she could hear it all around her. And the earth shook. And she had Aunt Dolly and Mrs Wisby with her. And Mrs Wisby's always been a bag o' nerves ... and ... I don't know ... I don't know what to do!'

'You got through to them?'

'No ... Mum called me. Seems like a miracle all ...'

A hand waved to the heavens.

'... This! And after all this the phones still work. No gas ... half the bleedin' windows gone and the phone still works. I should be there, Troy. I should be there.'

Looking at heaven again.

'I don't know what to do!'

Germany answered for Troy. The air-raid siren howled again. Kitty looked up into the sky, darkening in the west, still glowing red in the east.

'Oh bum. Oh arse!'

'You can't go now,' he said. 'Stick to plan A. Come home with me.'

'No ... I gotta go.'

'I can't drive you there while there's a raid on. We'd just be an obstacle.'

'Then I'll walk!'

Two steps and Troy had her by the arm.

'And when you get there, if you get there? Kitty, this war doesn't need spectators.'

She turned on him, red-faced and angry.

'See this blue outfit? I don't wear it 'cos it's me favourite colour. I'm a uniformed copper and I'm trained. Or has it been so long since you wore one you've been and gone and forgot?'

'Trained to find your family dead? Trained to see your own house blown to bollocks?'

'Don't say that!'

Then a tear, rolling from the corner of each eye.

'I ... I couldn't bear that.'

Her forehead slumped to his chest.

'Oh Jesus Christ.'

'Come home with me. We can go to Stepney the second the all-clear sounds.'

Her head lifted. A hand wiping at her eyes.

'No ... we ought to ... we ought to ... surely to God we ought to find a shelter?'

'I'm not going in a shelter. The world and his wife will be in the shelters. Cramped, crowded, stale, smelly, a hundred people all breathing the same pocket of air ... every chance of catching some disease ... I'd sooner take my chances in the open air. I'd sooner take my chances at home.'

Green eyes flashing – all anger again.

346

'What is it? The great unwashed? You know, you're such a bloody snob sometimes . . .'

'Of course. Now come home with this snob.'

He held the car door open for her. She hesitated, looked up at the eastern sky once more.

'Your mum will want you to be safe. You can't get to Stepney while there's a raid on.'

He served her a dinner of leftovers. Mashed potato, cabbage and a hint of bacon, half a sausage each, fried up in lard into a passable bubble'n'squeak. Her spirits had not recovered. They ate in silence – or rather in the absence of words. The world outside was alive with noise. She had just pushed her plate aside, with half the meal still on it, saying, 'Sorry, I'm just not that . . .' when a bomb landed so close the windows rattled and the door blew open. A crash, a boom, a gust of air. A ghost in the room.

'Oh God . . . that wasn't the East End, that felt more like Trafalgar Square.'

Troy closed the door.

'Would you really like to go to a shelter?'

'Nah. I want to be with you. I mean . . . here . . . with you.'

Close to midnight, he was certain she had nodded off. It had taken a couple of hours of her tossing and turning, wanting to be wrapped up in him, wanting to be fucked.

He slipped on his clothes, picked up his shoes and tiptoed to the bedroom door.

'Wot yer doin'?'

'I thought you were asleep.'

'With this racket going on? Can there be anybody asleep anywhere in London? I said – wot yer doin'?'

'I was just going outside for a while.'

'For a walk, you mean?'

'Yes. I thought I'd just take a look. See how far east I could get.'

'You mean you're going to walk to Stepney?'

'Sort of,' he lied.

'Troy – "this war don't need spectators". Or had you forgotten that?'

'It's the sound . . . it just . . .'

'Yeah?'

'Sucks you in.'

'Oh God . . . you are such a nutter. If you're that desperate to see, why don't you just peel back the blackout and look out the window?'

His bedroom window looked almost due south, across the flat roof of the bathroom. Leaning out and looking east, London burnt so brightly it was almost like daylight. He looked at the face of his wristwatch and found he could tell the time clearly. Five past twelve.

He opened the window wide and slid down to the flat roof, heard Kitty behind him say, 'Nutter.'

A drainpipe led up to the pitched roof, a quick scramble and he was at gutter height, a careful tiptoeing up the tiles and he was level with the chimney stack. He sat down just below the ridge, set his back against the stack and gazed eastward.

'Are you staying up there?'

'I won't be long.'

'You are bonkers, Troy, completely bonkers. Sitting on the roof in an air-raid!'

The risk seemed slight. Fire-watchers perched on rooftops every night. A hit from the Germans and he'd be just as dead in the room below. British shrapnel? He could see it streak across the sky like shooting stars – but there were no anti-aircraft guns this side of Hyde Park. He'd be very unlucky to be killed this night by his own side.

'Don't leave me alone.'

'I won't,' he lied.

He stared into the night sky. The night sky was not black it was pink. The barrage balloons, great silver cartoon whales tethered to a giant's fingertips in the sky, were not silver they were pink. And the giant's fingers were the searchlight beams, scouring the sky from Primrose Hill and Regent's Park. London's ack-ack defences puffed shells into the sky – the shooting stars. Silver on pink, pink on black. And the more Troy stared the more the colours ran like pastels in rain, spreading out in sponge-like shapes, like oil on puddles, colour leeching into colour, leeching into nothingness. Incendiaries falling from the sky, scattering in dozens and hundreds – a lethal war confetti – to explode in blinding blue-white pinpricks of magnesium light, turning yellow as the core caught, and taking on the hues of whatever they had ignited – black and red and orange, spreading ever outward in a burning tide, red into orange into pink – pink on silver, pink on black.

The bombers were concentrating on the docks that packed both sides of the Thames from Tower Bridge, around the bulge of the Isle of Dogs and out into the estuary past Woolwich Arsenal – St Katharine's Docks,

Surrey Commercial Docks, the plainly named London Docks ... the exotically named East and West India Docks, the royally named Albert and Victoria Docks ... and dozens of lesser harbours ... Canada, Quebec, Russia ... trade, empire, monarchy all written in brick and stone, and it seemed to Troy now that they were all burning, that Heinkels and Dorniers in wave after wave simply followed the twisted arrow that was the Thames into the heart of London. Some strayed. The bomb that had shaken the house looked to him to have fallen in the direction of the Strand and Charing Cross, the cloud of dust and smoke still hovering almost directly overhead – and with smoke and flames visible in the south-west it was clear that some had got as far as Victoria, and perhaps as far as Chelsea and Fulham.

It was the sound as much as the sight that kept him there. The sound that sucked him in. A dissonant London orchestra played a metropolitan cacophony and he had a seat in the gods – high explosive that fell with a crump and exploded with a boom – gunfire that yapped like a pack of fox terriers or cracked like thunderbolts. And the silver whoosh-whish of falling shrapnel, rattling across roof tiles and sparking like flint on paving stones. Bombers that growled dully like lazy lions or ground away monotonously like electric motors. Fighters that chattered endlessly. Surprisingly, in the midst of all the noise from above, noise from below punctuated the interludes – interruptions from the stalls, the drunken man in the third row – yelling at street level, the sound of running, boots banging down, breaking glass – so much breaking glass – and whistles – a never-ending unmelodious stream of whistles and bells.

§

Under moonlight,
infectious moonlight,
a madman dances,
chanting numbers,
two, three, five, seven, eleven.
Smeared in excrement,
naked as nativity,
smeared in his own blood,
wailing like a dog in pain,

throat bared to heaven,
mouth the perfect O,
face tilted to night,
eyes wide open,
eyes tight shut,
Lord Carsington dances.

§ 157

Troy had fallen asleep. The all-clear woke him sometime after four in the morning. He was cold and damp. He looked up into the sky. The stars he saw were real. Firmament and permanent. The man-made shooting stars had stopped. The night above had gone quiet. London seemed to hum below him now, and overhead was silence, and the glow of the East End burning. He slid down the roof, stumbled at the gutter and fell with a thud onto the leaded bathroom roof.

He expected to hear Kitty's voice, calling him an idiot or some such, but when he pushed aside the blackout curtain he found her tangled up in the sheets, foetally hunched, just her mop of hair peeping out, sound asleep. He crawled in beside her. He had promised to take her to Stepney as soon as the all-clear had sounded, but he crept in beside her and slept in his clothes.

As soon as she was up Kitty made Troy phone Stepney, but the line was dead.

'It'd be a minor miracle if it wasn't,' Troy said. 'We've got gas. That's something. The water's boiled. We have tea . . .'

If Kitty smoked she would have smoked now.

'I feel like . . .'

She sipped at her cup of tea, closed her eyes and let the sentence trail.

'I want to know. I want to talk to my mum.'

Troy had whipped up breakfast and set down scrambled eggs in front of her.

'I just want to talk to my mum. To be able to talk to my mum.'

Tears formed at the corners of her eyes.

'Eat up.'

The tears coursed towards her chin.

'Kitty. Eat up.'

She breathed in. Looked reluctantly at her plate.

'Smells great.'

Picked up a fork, hesitated with it poised, sunk it in and tasted.

''Ere . . . how many eggs you put in this?'

'Three each.'

'What? With eggs at two bob a dozen!'

Troy sat opposite her at the kitchen table, took a mouthful off his own plate.

'My mother keeps chickens.'

'Wot . . . out at your stately pile?'

Troy said nothing. Her tears had dried. He rather thought her counter-snobbery and her plain rattiness might be preferable to her tears.

'Pheasant . . . home-grown chicken . . . all them forks and knives at the dinner table . . . It's another world, innit?'

'So you keep saying.'

'Do I? Oh God, Troy. Will we ever be . . . wossaname . . . compatible?'

It was not a conversation Troy wished to have. He'd no idea she knew a polysyllabic as complicated as 'compatible'. The ringing of the phone spared him any need to reply.

'I thought you said it was dead.'

'It was.'

Troy picked up the receiver.

'It's me, George. I got something for you. How soon could you get over to Stepney?'

Troy looked at Kitty. Almost tearful again now. Apprehensive.

'A body?' he said wishing there were any other word as obvious, but what else would Bonham 'have' for him?

'Stepney's full o' bodies. But this one ain't down to Hitler.'

'I'm sorry . . . ?'

'Rabbi Friedland from Lindley Street.'

'What makes you think it wasn't the raid?'

'The knife stickin' in his chest.'

'I'll be as quick as I can. It'll all depend on the roads.'

'OK. I'll be waitin'.'

'George, Lindley Street's off Jubilee Street, isn't it?'

Kitty sat rigid. Troy could swear he saw the blood drain from her face.

'Yeah. That's where I am now. I'm in Edna Stilton's front room using her phone and drinkin' 'er char.'

'Is she there?'

'You want a word?'

'No, but there's someone here who will.'

Troy held out the telephone to Kitty.

'Who is it?'

'George Bonham. He'll put your mum on. I think she's fine.'

§ 158

Getting into Stepney was an obstacle course. It took an hour of diversions and doglegs, an hour of Kitty's mute anxiety and straining silence, before he finally pulled up the Bullnose Morris outside the Stiltons' house.

Kitty leapt from the car into her mother's arms. Into the house and never looked back. Troy was left standing by the car. A suddenly vacant moment after the intensity that was Kitty. He seemed to be surrounded by a haze of dust. It was like emerging into the aftermath of a sandstorm. Dust seemed to hang suspended in the air, to settle on his suit and hair like a coating of talcum powder or, worse, dandruff. Out of the dust a tall man with thick dark hair and a bad case of shaver's shadow was walking slowly down from the Mile End Road towards him, a spiral-bound notebook open in one hand. He scribbled a few notes and came closer.

He stopped by Troy's car, looking around him all the time. Up at the smoke billows suspended in the sky, across at the gutted building opposite them. Then he smiled at Troy, said 'Good Morning' and added 'How nice to be able to say those words,' in a strong, fag-soaked American accent.

'Press?' Troy said simply.

'CBS.'

'Will they believe this back home?'

'It'll be my job to make them.'

'Good luck,' said Troy.

The American smiled again and walked on towards Wapping. Troy had no idea who Ed Murrow was any more than Ed Murrow knew who Troy was. His brother would have known, his brother would have introduced them, but that is neither here nor there.

Troy looked down Lindley Street. It was impassable to traffic, littered with rubble, blocked by the burnt-out remains of a car. A big man in a police uniform was bending over a tarpaulin. It was Bonham.

Troy picked his way across a chequerboard of broken brick towards him. Only when he got close did he see that the tarpaulin was covering a row of bodies, laid out neatly in a row like lead soldiers in a toy box, each one a bump in the canvas, and only the telltale of a woman's foot sticking out at the far end to spell out the fact of death.

Bonham looked up. White in the face, a grey stubble on his chin, red rims to his eyes.

'They was in an Anderson,' he said. 'They're not a lot o' use when the house collapses on top of 'em. Bit like a sardine tin under a lorry.'

'Did you know them?'

'Who don't I know? I reckon everyone that died last night in a half mile radius was someone I knew. And that'll run into dozens. Across the manor it'll run into hundreds. Course I knew 'em. So did you.'

'Who?'

'Spendloves from number 14.'

Troy knew them. Old Tommy Spendlove had been a petty thief in his day. Only old age and incompetence had made him passably honest. His sons were tearaways, stealing anything that wasn't nailed down, from the age of ten. But his wife, Annie, cleaned in a West End hotel and his daughters, June and Pat, had worked on the counters in Woolworth's. A family torn apart by men, patched together by women and destroyed by Hitler.

'They really didn't deserve to die this way,' Bonham said.

'All of them?'

'Young June survived. Didn't like the shelters. Stayed in the house. When the back end caved in and fell on the shelter she was in the front parlour under the table. Saved her life. She ain't said a word since we give 'er the news. She's in with Edna Stilton and Aunt Dolly now. Sweet tea and sympathy.'

'And ...?'

'And the rabbi? Left him where I found him. C'mon I'll show yer.'

Half a dozen houses along on the southern side. A late-Victorian terraced house with its front windows shattered, a few tiles missing but otherwise intact. Bonham pushed open the door, led Troy down the corridor to the back kitchen.

Rabbi Friedland was sitting bolt upright and stone dead at the kitchen table. A carving knife had been rammed to the hilt into his heart. The pool of crisped, brown blood had settled on the oilskin tablecloth, spilled to the tiled floor, pooled in the worn groove that marked generations of feet crossing from the hall door to the yard door, soaked into his clothes and into the book he had been reading. When the bomb had hit the Spendloves' house most of the paint – Troy thought it must be whitewash or distemper – had flaked off the walls and ceiling, leaving a pattern of fine cracks like crazy glazing and a dusting of white powder over everything, as though someone had come in with a shaker of icing sugar and emptied it into the room. It had settled on the pool of blood, it had settled on Friedland. It was like walking into the set of an insane pantomime hammily dressed for winter in woodland.

'That times it pretty well, doesn't it?' said Troy. 'He died before the bomb hit.'

'ARP have that timed as 12.07.'

Pretty well the time Troy had settled on his rooftop. Perhaps the first explosion he saw had been this one?

Troy leaned down to look at the face. Friedland was in his sixties. Very lined about the eyes and very grey of beard. It seemed to Troy that he could not have died in this position, that his killer had simply pushed the body back into place, set him upright, propped back into a parody of life. Each hand flat upon the pages of the book. He looked at the book – the bible, open at the book of Isaiah, King James, 1611 version. Troy found this baffling. Perhaps he liked the poetry of English? But then this whole case was baffling.

Bonham took the words out of his mouth.

'Anybody could have done this. Anybody.'

'Darkness, chaos . . .'

'Deserted streets . . . bombs and guns and fire engines and that . . . then people rushing all over the place. Nobody would have seen a thing.'

'Did you close his eyes?'

'Yeah . . . sorry, I know I should a left him . . . but I couldn't bear to see him like that.'

'And the hands?'

'No. He was like that when I found him.'

'Has anyone else been in, seen the body?'

'No. I been careful about that. There's been all sorts o' rumours since Izzy Borg was killed. I sort of thought you wouldn't want any more just yet.'

'Family?'

'Widower. Like old Izzy. But no kids. They had just the one. He got took before the last war. Be 1910 or 1911. Poor little mite died of pneumonia.'

'So there's nobody to tell?'

'There's the whole of Stepney to tell. But you been so cagey about Izzy and Rabbi Adelson . . . might be murder might not . . . I thought you'd want to be the one to say when this gets out. 'Cos there's no two ways about this, is there? You got your evidence. Cut and dried. So no more pussyfooting. 'Cept there'll be a ruckus, o' course. Nobody panicked over Borg and Adelson. They will over this. When they find the time, that is.'

It was the longest and smartest thing Troy had ever heard George say. London would panic at the thought of a methodical murderer picking off rabbis – but only when they found the time. Only when they stopped counting their dead. And London was piled up with our English dead. What was one dead man among hundreds?

§ 159

Onions said, 'One dead man among hundreds. What's one dead man among hundreds?'

'It's the business we're in. The one-dead-man business.'

'Exactly. Exactly.'

'I had George send the body over to Kolankiewicz, but I hardly need wait for the report.'

'Have we got a single damn thing to go on?'

'No, George was right. Nobody saw anything. The streets were empty when the bomb fell and awash with people once the all-clear had sounded. No one to see, and then everyone too busy to see. Anyone could have nipped in and knifed Friedland, anyone at all.'

'Doesn't mean these deaths are linked though, does it?'

'Yes. It does.'

'We have one definite murder and two possibles.'

'And now that we do have the one that's definite . . .'

'You're going to open it up? Go public?'

'Yes.'

'You don't think . . . well . . . mebbe . . . dead rabbis . . . it's a political matter?'

'Yes. It's that too.

'A Fifth Column at work?'

'I think that's another of the phony war's myths, Stan. I don't think there's a Fifth Column, and if there was wouldn't they have better things to do than kill harmless, pensioned-off rabbis? Shouldn't they be taking potshots at Churchill instead? The Fifth Column is something dreamt up to keep Special Branch busy.'

'The Branch?'

'The Branch.'

'And Steerforth?'

A pause. The only sound the distant clicking of rotary dials somewhere on the phone line.

'Fuckim,' said Troy, and Onions did not argue.

§ 160

Kolankiewicz called Troy about three hours later.

'The fingerprints on the knife are blurred, but I suspect they all belong to the victim, and that the knife was simply picked up in the room. The only clear prints I have are on the tea cup and the bible.'

'George sent the bible over?'

'George even sent the tablecloth. You should be pleased someone takes your orders literally.'

'And the print is clear?'

'Too clear, and alas it belongs to the victim also.'

'How can a print be too clear?'

'Is as though I had taken it myself, rolled the finger across the ink pad and then rolled it across the book. Except that the ink is blood in this case.'

'You mean Friedland didn't touch the book?'

'Not while he was alive.'

'Are you sure?'

'No. But it seems highly likely. Besides what would an Orthodox rabbi be doing with an English translation of the bible? It would be like you reading Dostoevsky in English.'

'I've been asking myself that all morning. So it wasn't his? You think what? That the killer brought it with him?'

'Yes. I think he brought it with him. And as there's a Hatchards sticker in the end papers, I think he bought it at Hatchards.'

'At last,' Troy said. 'Something resembling a clue.'

He was about to ring off when the meaning of the 'clue' struck him.

'The print? Where was it?'

'Index finger, right hand.'

'I meant, where on the page?'

Kolankiewicz went to look. A few seconds later he picked up the telephone again and said, 'Isaiah 34:8. "For it is the day of the Lord's vengeance and the year of recompenses for the controversy of Zion." The print is on the second line, next to the word "Zion". Does this help in any way?'

'God knows. But it does seem like a message to us from the killer, doesn't it?'

'Such an arrogant message. Equating himself with God. That said, he could have plonked the finger down almost anywhere in this chapter and come up with something appropriate, meaningful even. We would be compelled to see significance in a random act. It is all of it apocalyptic in the extreme ... "the indignation of the Lord is upon all nations" ... "the sword of the Lord is filled with blood" ... streams turning into pitch, dust into brimstone ... smoke that rises forever ... I might be tempted to think it was a prophecy fulfilled all over London in the last twenty-four hours.'

§ 161

It was Sunday. Troy could not call Hatchards until the morning. At dusk Kitty called him.

'I won't be over tonight.'

'Where are you?'

'I'm still at me mum's. We got June Spendlove here. She ain't said a word all day. In fact, we got half the street here. The electric's still off and God knows when we'll get gas, but Mum cooks on coal so we're OK. She's been boiling kettles for everybody. It's like we've opened a caff. Churchill come down the street this afternoon. Mum and Aunt Dolly stood on the front step and chatted to him. They was thrilled to bits. More than if the King had come round. Mum asked him in for a cuppa but he told her he'd a lot of people to get to see. I wanted to be thrilled to bits, but I couldn't. I don't know why. I just couldn't. Aunt Dolly had a Union Jack to wave. God knows where she found it. I took meself out for a bit of air afterwards – I almost said fresh air, but it ain't fresh. It stinks. Like burning paint. Like ... like rotten eggs. And it's more than a smell ... it's like it sticks to the back of your throat or something. Like you could cough it up, but you can't cough it up. Anyway ... there's this big pile of rubble at the bottom of our street. And someone had stuck a Union Jack on it. Like we'd just climbed a mountain. And we was proud of it and we was like claiming it for England. Like Jerry could see it.'

'Perhaps the Prime Minister saw it.'

'You think he needs cheering up? If he needed cheering up he'd have had the cup of tea with Mum and Aunt Dolly, wouldn't he?'

Troy ignored the sarcasm.

'You're staying on, aren't you?'

'Yeah. Just for a bit. I feel better knowing me mum's OK, but I'll spend a few nights here. My dad won't be back for ages yet. He's not got a free weekend until the end of the month. She hates sleeping alone. And ... I mean ... you never know when *they'll* be back, do you?'

Troy would not have been the one to tell her, but he was certain they'd be back any minute.

And they were.

358

Around ten o'clock, with no Kitty to restrain him, he did what she would not let him. He turned up the collar on his overcoat, stuck his hands in his pockets and walked east into the glow of London's burning, walked into the shooting stars, the whines and the whistles of London's war – walked into 'it'. And as night became day and silence burst around him into noise that seemed to inhabit the skull, he was put in mind of Yeats' best-known line, 'A terrible beauty is born.'

He would have liked to be thrilled by a visit from Churchill, but the truth, the awful, the absolute truth, was that he was thrilled by this – by 'it'. It was like the descent into a dream. The descent from a dream. He would never be sure which.

§ 162

The bloke in Hatchards was blunt.

'That's a very tall order. A rare book, a rare book bought on account, we might be able to tell you quite quickly. The bible? Do you even know the edition? We must sell dozens, hundreds. Do you know when? Last week? Last year?'

Troy had one clue – and he'd just seen it run through his fingers like sand.

§ 163

Kitty did not return. He found he did not much mind. He found bodies to preoccupy him. Was the gunshot victim found almost headless in a mansion block off Gloucester Road a suicide or a murder?

Troy examined the body, sent for Kolankiewicz. They agreed on suicide.

The following day a man found pooled in blood in a shop doorway as wardens picked their way through Soho after the all-clear was found to have his throat cut. The wardens cried 'murder' and called Scotland Yard. Troy examined the body, took out his penknife, cut a sliver of shrapnel out of the wooden shopfront and sent it to Hendon with the body.

'Poor bugger,' Kolankiewicz said. 'Takes shelter from the Hun and a piece of British shrapnel slit his throat for him.'

'The blood groups match?'

'They do. You're not having a lot of luck, are you?'

'Never a good body when you want one.'

Still Kitty did not return.

When the local warden, Cyril Spender, knocked on his door and asked if he could firewatch on the roof of the Coliseum Theatre in St Martin's Lane Troy said that, duty permitting, he would. He did not have the engagement of a uniformed copper – Kitty had been right about that – he had received no extra training, all that had happened was that he'd been issued with a tin hat and a gas mask, neither of which he ever carried. Bonham had insisted on showing him how a stirrup pump worked, and he had paid no attention. Now, Spender taught him how to handle incendiaries. He had a duff one to demonstrate. It looked to Troy like a thermos flask.

'The trick is to smother it, stop it igniting in the first place. If it does, you're stuffed 'cos it burns at 648.8°C.'

'Hot, is it?' Troy asked, not being able to think in anything but Fahrenheit.'

'Hot enough to melt steel. Twice the temperature you'd need to burn yooman flesh!'

'Interesting statistic.'

'Yep. One o' them little buggers gets to you there'd be sweet f.a. left.'

Onions had been clear, 'We've a big enough job on our hands as it is. We're not auxiliaries to anything. Do you think crime stops just 'cos there's a war on? Don't go volunteering.' But to be so casually enlisted to firewatch on occasional nights was like being sanctioned – like being pardoned for the folly of his night walks, like having his seat in the Gods paid for. The conflict of fear and curiosity resolved with simplicity.

Midweek, he sat three nights on the roof of the Coliseum and watched heaven light up with the terrible beauty that he found almost irresistible. Suffering and death, terror into beauty. The suffering and death might next be his. Logic told him that; this was no more ordered than it was beautiful, it was random death and illusory beauty, but he was not a man wholly free from superstition – every cell in his body told him he would live through this, and a voice in his head said, 'who are you kidding?'

On the second night he had his only direct encounter with battle – an incendiary clattered down onto the roof and rolled towards his feet. He thrust it into a bucket of sand just as Spender had taught him and thought no more about it. But the sound of the night had changed. The guns were nearer now and seemed almost to surround him. Anti-aircraft guns had been mounted on trailers and dotted around the city, mounted on barges and towed into the Thames. He felt he could discern them as individual voices, as though each gun had its own unique sound. The battery near Hungerford Bridge barked, the battery somewhere in Bloomsbury twanged like a giant bow at Agincourt, firing arrows. But each night, when dawn broke, he heard the same noise from the street below. He had at first described it to himself as a hum, but now, from higher up, and closer to Trafalgar Square, it sounded more like a sigh – a gigantic sigh. And then he realised. It was London breathing. The inhalation and exhalation of a city breathing. The same rattle of broken glass, the shouts and the ringing of steeled boots on paving stones, but over it all and under it all, the inhalation, the exhalation, the great sigh of London drawing breath. A city licking its wounds and living.

§ 164

On Saturday evening the gas went off all over central London. He could flip the iron upside down and fry an egg – he'd done that more than once when electricity prevailed over gas. Or he could go on the scrounge. He phoned Hampstead. His father answered.

'Yes, I have gas, I even have a meal on the go. What I do not have is a family. Your mother has retreated to Mimram. So, I dine alone.'

'I'll be right over,' said Troy.

The old man served him rainbow trout and new potatoes – new-ish, they had been in store since the end of June. Raised by Troy's mother – her favourite Aura second earlies – and stored in sacks in darkness. She had rallied to the call of 'Dig for Victory' and rendered them almost self-sufficient in vegetables.

When they'd finished, and were settled in his father's study, Troy asked almost idly, 'Where did you get the fish? Almost seems like a novelty these days.'

'From your mother.'

'I thought she was at Mimram.'

'Indeed. She posted them to me. They arrived in the second post this morning.'

'She posted fish?'

'Why not? The food parcel is now as ubiquitous as the umbrella . . . or perhaps I should say the gas mask. All over England people are posting meals to their relations on the assumption someone somewhere is going short. But you did not drop in to talk about food, surely?'

'No. I didn't. I was wondering what you made of this.'

Troy took a sheet of paper from his coat pocket. He'd jotted down the verses of Isaiah 38.

Alex read it through, and said, 'Savage stuff. The God of the Old Testament in all his wrath. It seems rather apt. It could be describing the Europe of today. Hardly among the most quoted of verses, though. In fact downright obscure. Why do you have it?'

'It was left at the scene of a murder.'

'Then I'd say it was self-explanatory. Self-justification. The very arrogant assumption of divine vengeance. On whom?'

'A rabbi. An East End rabbi named Friedland. And he isn't the first victim. In fact, I think he's the third. Borg, Adelson, Friedland. But only the last had this as a sort of clue.'

Troy knew the look on his father's face. The concentration of memory, the pride, the relentless pride, of an old mind determined to forget nothing at the point when the body is willing to surrender everything.

'Run those names by me again, would you, my boy?'

'The first was Isaiah Borg, then . . . Aaron Adelson and the most recent was Moses Friedland.'

'In that order?'

'Yes.'

By now Alex was rummaging around in the centre drawer of his desk.

'Can I help?'

'No, it is here somewhere. I saved it, I'm sure I saved it. Though quite why . . .'

'Perhaps because you save everything?'

'I left so much behind in Russia. I will admit that to your mother's

362

dismay I have parted with almost nothing ever since. Every last scrap of paper came from Vienna, and every last scrap from Paris, so this should be ... Aah! I have it!'

He handed his son the letter.

'The signatures, and the name typed after each one.'

Troy looked.

'Daniel Shoval, Isaiah Borg, Aaron Adelson, Moses Friedland, Elishah Nader, David Cohen, Jacob Kossoff.'

Troy had met half these men in his time as a beat bobby – the old rabbis of East London. East European immigrants most of them and, in Kossoff's case, a man as Russian as his father – although his father spoke the better English. These were the parish priests of Judaism, serving the shifting, new, ever-renewing communities of the East End. Not one of them destined for the board of Deputies. And, Troy felt, not one so much as wanting it.

'Three of them,' said his father. 'Three of them on the list. Were it not for the oddity of the first not being among the dead, I'd have said someone might systematically be working down it.'

It was one of those moments Troy hated. Much as he loved having the pieces on the table, there was often a moment when the voice in the head told him he'd been stupid and forced him to backtrack.

Troy said, 'Daniel Shoval is dead. Last August. A matter of days before the war broke out. I investigated myself. It was my last case before I left Stepney, before you phoned up to whisk me off to Monte Carlo. Shoval was found dead in an Underground station. Fell on the escalator. No one saw him fall – middle of the afternoon, a Tuesday, hardly the rush hour – and, in the absence of anything to the contrary, I wrote it up as accidental death. If I'd known about this letter then, I'd have had grounds for suspicion. Now ... I'm beginning to think I was hasty. But I'm also beginning to think a systematic killer of rabbis just a bit too bizarre. It's like some Polish Gothic novel. *Der Golem Revisited.*'

'Then,' said his father, 'it is the other names on the list that should interest you the more. The people the rabbis wanted locked up. The word bizarre sums them up very well.'

Troy read the letter out loud, racing quickly through the demand for the internment of, together with reasons for ... until he came to the names.

'Sir Oswald Mosley, Archibald Ramsay MP, Oliver Gilbert, Victor Rowe, Roland Rollason, Lord Carsington, Major Harold Haward-Pyke,

Professor Charles Lockett, Sir Michael Redburn, Viscount Blackwall, Geoffrey Trench MP.'

'I received that letter last summer. The same day the Board of Deputies wrote to me calling for the suppression of Freud's last book. It caused some initial confusion. I published the letter about Freud. Freud would not have it otherwise. The letter from the East End rabbis I would willingly have published but for a request from the Home Office. I gather several other newspapers received the same letter and the same request. No one published. A request and, I might add, a reassurance.'

'What?'

'I was told that these men, or at least those of them who really are dangerous, would be locked up as the rabbis requested when the time was right. MPs and all. Aristocrats . . . and all.'

'Well . . . that takes care of Mosley,' Troy said with scarcely suppressed sarcasm.

'You think we have not locked up enough?'

'More that we have locked up the wrong people.'

Alex took the letter back.

'As your illustrious predecessor Sherlock Holmes used to say . . . "let us eliminate the impossible, what remains is fact however improbable".'

'Probably my suspect, you mean?'

'Quite. Now . . . Mosley, as you say, is interned for the duration. Rollason is dead, I wrote his obituary myself. Heart attack playing golf, as I recall. Blackwall volunteered as soon as war was declared. Went to France with the Royal West Kent Regiment, the one I think they call the "Buffs". He never returned from Dunkirk. I've had his obituary ready for weeks, but there is no confirmation that he is dead.'

'He might be a prisoner?'

'That's possible. Although I would have expected some news of him by now if he were. Haward-Pyke was interned in May on the same day as Mosley – Gilbert and Rowe about three weeks after the war broke out – and Ramsay only a matter of weeks ago. Not long before Rod, as I recall . . . and, unless I'm mistaken as a direct result of that fracas at the Tea Rooms that you and Nikolai blundered into. No one is quite sure why he was interned but . . .'

Troy merely shrugged and said, 'I blundered. I doubt that Nikolai did. I think he went for the show.'

'Whatever,' his father continued. 'That leaves only four . . . Redburn, Carsington, Trench and . . .'

'Lockett,' said Troy. 'A professor of something, I gather?'

'I had to ask myself. I'd scarcely heard of him. Indeed, I confused him with the reputable Lockett who runs the Psychoanalytic Society. Since it was necessary to talk to Freud that day, I asked him. The men are brothers. Charles Lockett is the elder, Nicholas the younger. Charles is quite possibly the last practitioner in England of a fake science that was known as "bumpology" when I was a boy, and even then so few people took it seriously. It's proper name was phrenology, and its vile offshoot has been racial stereotyping – of which the Nazis are so fond, of which we see so many crude examples in *Der Stürmer* . . . all those dreadful caricatures of Jews looking like a badly illustrated Merchant of Venice – it all leads to eugenics, and that has followers galore. Even seemingly rational men, men without apparent Nazi-sympathies, will expound the need for eugenics. I would say I have sat at half the dinner tables in London at one time or another – particularly in the years just before the last war – and listened to crackpot theories not necessarily on the superiority of one race over another but most definitely on the "inferior type" and selective breeding and the culling of the mentally or physically disabled. They seem to have a problem uttering the word murder.'

'Well, one of them doesn't seem to have any problem committing it.'

'But which? Do peers of the realm stoop to murder? Do university professors?'

'Yes'

'But which? Ah, well . . . I suppose that's why you became a policeman, isn't it? All those penny dreadful novels you read as a boy. It gave you a love of the chase . . . a passion to know "who-dunnit"?'

'No, Dad. Absolutely not. Who-dunnits are the lowest form of fiction. Somewhere between whelks and snails.'

'Does not a killer who kills in the order of signature on a letter strike you as a mite novelletish? I mean to say, that is the conclusion one would draw, is it not? . . . these rabbis have died in the order in which they signed.'

'They have. And more than anything it strikes me as a paucity of imagination – the ticking off of names on a list.'

'So, where will you start? Carsington, Redburn, Trench or Lockett?'

'None of them, I'll start with Elishah Nader. I have to tell him there's someone out there who's about to try and kill him.'

Sitting outside his father's house in his Bullnose Morris, he looked at the letter his father had given him. Nader's address was a show-stopper.

A name you clocked once and never forgot – Heaven's Gate Synagogue, London, E.1. As if there could be such a place.

§ 165

15 September 1940
Battle of Britain Day

Heaven's Gate was in utter contrast to Elohim. The road frontage was tiny. A solid pair of doors, a set of rusting railings, wedged between two shop fronts, at most eight or ten feet across. It looked more like the back entrance to a block of flats than the gates of heaven. Nothing screamed 'God' at the passer-by. You could look for this and still miss it.

Troy pushed at the door. It opened into a long, dark corridor. He walked about fifty or sixty feet, finding it so dark, he needed to trace his way with one hand along the wall. It grew lighter where a staircase branched off to either side and light filtered down from above. He found himself facing another set of doors. He pushed and daylight streamed through, bright as noon. He stepped in and looked up instinctively. There were gaps in the roof – an empyrean, rich, cerulean ceiling, a promise of heaven through which the blue of the real heaven now peeked in a dozen ragged holes – and a gap in the wall the size of a London double-decker bus. He could not swear this place had taken a direct hit, but if it hadn't the building next door had.

There'd been some effort made to clear up. There were still broken tiles, roofspars and bits of blue plasterwork littering the floor, but the way was passable and most of the fittings seemed to have survived. It was, he thought, a near-tragedy. Unlike Elohim, this really was beautiful, an intricate wooden maze in walnut, brass and glass, like being inside a chinese box – it was layered, it was simple and complex, sturdy and delicate all at the same time. It was everything Elohim was not – it was subtle, it was intimate. At the back of the synagogue the ark was flanked by two pastoral views, of what he took to be Israel. They were framed as though they were windows, a trompe l'œil that didn't quite work, but a quality of craftsmanship that compared well with anything he'd seen by Burne-Jones or Holman Hunt. He was contemplating this – maybe they were Holman Hunts? – did the pre-Raphaelites ever paint synagogues? – when a figure popped up from behind the *bimah*.

'Can I help you?'

A young rabbi. About his age. All in black. Not quite enough beard about him. As though he had yet to grow into the part he was playing. Troy assumed he was the 'curate'.

'I was looking for Rabbi Elishah Nader.'

'You found him.'

'I was expecting an older man.'

'Ah . . . you mean my father.'

The rabbi came round the *bimah* and extended a hand to greet Troy.

Troy shook the hand and said, 'Sergeant Troy, Scotland Yard.'

'My father and I are both called Elishah. But if it's him you want, it's me you get. My father has been in hospital since the beginning of August.'

Troy wondered for a second if there'd been an attack he'd missed, but Nader said, 'His heart. I doubt he will live long, but that's not why you're here, is it? Heart attacks are hardly police business. It's about the scrolls. You've found them?'

'Scrolls?'

'Scrolls of the Torah. Stolen the morning after the big raid. Come, I shall show you.'

He led the way over smashed tiles to the ark and slid open the doors. They glided past like silk running over glass – not a sound. The interior was huge, almost like a cabin on a sailing ship – lined throughout in crimson velvet, it reminded Troy of his mother's jewellery box. He knew it was the ark, Nader didn't need to tell him that – but he'd no real idea what an ark was for.

'My father had this done early last year. So many refugees. We'd been taking them in since I was a boy. After Kristallnacht the trickle became a flood. So many of them brought scrolls of the Torah from synagogues in Europe that had been closed, destroyed or simply abandoned. We had them stacked up all over – from Germany, Austria, Czechoslovakia. My father said the place was turning into a museum. Then he decided. It was a museum after all. The Torahs were priceless, some of them centuries old. And he had the ark re-built and enlarged to store them safely. Ventilated at the back with air bricks to prevent mould, and virtually fireproof at the front with three-inch thick oak doors and a solid concrete roof. Fireproof, but not burglar-proof. On 7 September we all caught it. Jew and Gentile, God and Mammon. The bombs did considerable damage, as you can see. And, on the morning of the eighth, I came in to check the extent of the damage and found the doors of the ark open and not a single scroll left. All thirty-one stolen. And you've come to tell me you haven't found them?'

'Rabbi Nader, I'm with the Murder Squad.'

Despite the nature of his tale, Nader had been smiling throughout. Troy's words wiped the smile away.

'Who's been murdered?'

'Izzy Borg, Aaron Adelson, and Moses Friedland.'

He'd get to Daniel 'Digger' Shoval later.

'Of course. I knew about Rabbi Friedland, but Rabbi Borg was run over in the blackout surely? And Rabbi . . .'

'Rabbi Nader, they were all murdered. Someone is killing East End rabbis.'

'And?'

'And?'

'And why are you telling me this?'

'Your father was next on the list.'

'Ah . . .'

Nader looked down, stirred a few chips of dust and rubble with his shoe. Then he looked Troy straight in the eye.

'Or do you mean, Mr Troy, that I am next on the list?'

§ 166

They crossed the road to Nader's house. He led Troy down the corridor to the back, past the open door of the front room, heavily Victorian, deep in its velvets and chenilles, its oak and mahogany, its booklined walls, to sit at the kitchen table. It was like being in Rabbi Friedland's kitchen. The same plain, square deal table. The same oilskin cloth draped across it.

'My father keeps the parlour strictly for the flock. But you're not flock, are you?'

'No, I'm not.'

'Think of it as a manse. Then think that we will both be more at ease at the kitchen table.'

Nader stuck the kettle on and shifted gear, saying simply, 'What list?'

Troy told him.

'When exactly?'

'The letter arrived at the office of the *Post* the day after Russia announced the Nazi pact. That would make it 24 August last year. It's dated the day before, the 23rd.'

'My father never mentioned it to me. But I was in Manchester most of that summer. In fact, most of this one too. You know, it would be like my father to sign something like this, but not to instigate it. I think the same was true of Rabbi Borg too. Yet you say his name was first in the signatures.'

'No – it wasn't. Rabbi Shoval was first.'

'But he died . . .'

'Last August – the 29th, five days after the letter arrived. I was a constable in Stepney at the time. I was called out to the scene. It looked like an accident.'

Nader poured tea and mused. Troy waiting to see where the muse led him.

'Daniel Shoval was the kind of man to have organised a petition. He was a campaigner. Or am I telling you something you know?'

'I heard of Rabbi Shoval. I'd never met him. Shall we say his reputation preceded him?'

'He was in the front line at the Battle of Cable Street, when Mosley led his Blackshirts into the East End in '36.'

Troy had been there too – in uniform, on duty, but he wasn't going to mention that.

'And now you think his death was not an accident?'

'It seems unlikely.'

'And Rabbi Borg . . . it is widely believed he died in a road accident in the blackout . . . . Rabbi Adelson . . . I was told had a heart attack . . .'

'And Rabbi Friedland?'

'Well . . . that was shocking. Is shocking. The whole East End is reeling at that.'

'But the whole East End didn't reel at the the idea of rabbis falling like flies and think something is wrong here?'

'"The Lord giveth, the Lord taketh away."'

'He's taken rather a lot just lately.'

It was a stupid remark. Troy could have bitten off his tongue.

Nader said, 'Are you talking dead rabbis now, Mr Troy, or the state of Europe? There are many among us who think God might have forgotten us altogether. But, yes . . . three dead rabbis in as many months has caused comment. It's one reason I came back to London. There's a shortage. I am covering for Rabbi Adelson as well as for my father. Getting bombed out merely creates an excuse to merge the services – Mile End synagogue has no rabbi, Heaven's Gate has no roof. We double up and we get by. And while none of us worked out that the death of quite so many rabbis might be a new plague, visited on us rather than Egypt . . . it would appear to have taken Scotland Yard a while to make their mind up too.'

Troy felt doubly crass. Sipped at his tea and bought a little time with honesty.

'Shoval was my mistake. But I didn't know he'd signed any petition at that point. After all, it was never published. But I've treated every single death since as suspicious.'

'Then why the fairy tales about heart attacks and road accidents?'

Why indeed? No one had specifically told him to fudge the truth – but it had kept the peace. He'd not had Steerforth on his back in ages. By the judicious use of a little fiction, he'd been able to investigate murder without Steerforth sticking his two penn'orth in.

'Special Branch's thinking, not mine. I was asked in a fairly subtle way not to say outright that I was treating these three recent deaths as murder. I think perhaps they feared a backlash of some sort.'

'I don't understand, but I suppose that doesn't matter. But what bothers me is this . . . if the letter was never published, how does anyone know what names appear on it?'

'I don't know. It went to several papers. All of which were told not to publish by the Home Office. I have no idea how many people read it before that decision was taken. But somebody knows. Somebody's working down that list and they've reached "Nader".'

§ 167

There were times when Troy thought *Who's Who* might be better titled
the Index of British Civil Servants and Colonial Officers. Chances were
if you needed the dope on someone urgently, he wouldn't be in *Who's
Who*. A minor baronet would be – indeed his father was, thereby gaining
Troy entry as one quarter of '2s, 2d'. A public figure from the wrong
class would not. You'd learn nothing about the well-known novelist Mr
J.B. Priestley or the music hall entertainer Monsewer Eddie Gray from
looking in *Who's Who*. Every Sir somebody would be there. Sir somebodies of such insignificance as to be immeasurable – the last interesting
fact in their entry being the word 'born'. All the same, he kept a copy
in his office, rather thought he was the only detective who did, and had
every expectation of finding an entry on each of the men his father had
named. He knew all there was to know about Lord Carsington, and
had a good handle on Redburn, but he began with the one he knew least
about. He'd never heard of Charles Lockett. He was not disappointed.

Lockett, Charles Jasper Wyatt, MC 1915; *b* 5 May 1886; *Elder s* of
the Ven. Herbert Lockett of St Albans, Herts, and Frances (*neé* Wyatt),
dau. of Bishop of Matabeleland; *Educ*: Radley; Kings, Cambridge; All
Souls, Oxford (BSc, MLitt, PhD). 9th London Reg. (Queen Victoria's
Rifles), 1915–18; Reader in Zoology 1919–23; Professor of Human
Biology 1924–present, University College, London. *Publications*: The
Criminal Skull, 1923; The Beast Within, 1929; Comparative Crani-
ology, 1931; A New Handbook of Phrenology, 1933; The Case for
Race, 1935. Recreations: fly-fishing, madrigals. *Address*: 44b South
Hills, NW3.

Military Cross in the Great War – can't knock his patriotism then,
thought Troy … but the list of publications was chilling, a course set
steady from the nineteenth century's half-baked obsession with assessing
the mind from the body's external features, to the paramountcy of racial
theory in the dirty Thirties. Troy did not doubt that professors of this,
that or the other got where they were through merit and effort and even
originality, but how easily they made fools of themselves with easy, lazy

populism. In this they were no different from politicians.

He looked up. Stan had appeared silently in his doorway, only the whiff of a Wills Woodbine had alerted Troy to his presence.

'Toffs again?' Onions said.

Troy wondered how much to tell him.

'I think I might be on a case in which every suspect is a toff.'

'Which one's this?'

'The rabbis.'

'So you still think they're linked.'

'Yes.'

'And you've someone in the frame?'

'Not exactly.'

'Fine, tell me how exactly.'

Onions took his usual chair by the unlit gas fire, hunched over in listening mode. Troy told him a clipped version of his conversation with his father.

'It's all circumstantial, you know.'

'I know.'

'In fact, I'd term it a bit of a long shot. In fact, Izzy Borg's death could well be an accident, as I've told you. Friedland – OK, no argument ... the bugger didn't stab himself. But Adelson ... You said yourself Klankiwitch reckons it was heart failure.'

'Induced by ...?'

'I don't know and neither do you. You've got one murder you seem hell bent on mekkin' three ...'

'Er, four actually. I'm counting the chap who was found dead at the foot of an escalator in Bethnal Green Station last August. He was a rabbi too.'

'And now you've got a list of suspects that reads like ...'

'*Who's Who?*' said Troy holding up the fat red book.

'Zackly. *Who's* bloody *Who.*'

'Does that bother you?'

'Don't be daft, lad. We're the Yard, we haven't tugged the forelock since the days of Sherlock Holmes and that thick copper – what was his name?'

'LeStrade.'

'Right. LeStrade. I'm not bothered a jot or tittle if you suspect a toff, I'm not bothered if you nick one.'

'But?'

'Do you really want to go up against Carsington again?'

In 1936, when Onions and Troy had first met, Troy had fallen foul of Lord Carsington, had suspected him of complicity in a crime, risked all to confront him with it and been firmly put in his place. Onions had smoothed things out, had reprimanded Troy, and rewarded him with a promise. A promise he had kept last September when he had finally claimed him for the Yard.

'I'll tell you now,' Onions went on, 'it could look like a vendetta.'

'It isn't. It's got nothing to do with any previous case. He was named in that letter to the *Post*. He is as much a suspect as any other person named.'

'Being named doesn't make 'em suspects. All it does is make 'em undesirables in the eyes of a bunch of cranky old rabbis.'

'Who are now dying like flies.'

'Don't exaggerate. It doesn't help. Just answer me this, if you get to see any of these nobs and toffs . . . Carsington . . .'

'Redburn, Trench and Lockett.'

'. . . What are you going to say to them? I can't begin to imagine what your line of enquiry would be.'

'Neither can I,' said Troy, 'but I'll think of something.'

Onions thought. Lit up another Woodbine from the stub of the last.

'Anyone with four ounces of nous will just show you the door, you know that, don't you?'

Troy said nothing.

'So, let's cut the risk, contain the flames a bit, shall we? Don't talk to Carsington. Only if you draw a total blank with the other three and only after you've come back to me wi' summat that points to Carsington do you talk to him? OK?'

Troy hated this. It was one hand tied behind his back. To disagree was not an option.

§ 168

Onions was right. A simple 'where were you on the night of . . .?' would have any one of the names on his father's list reaching for the telephone and asking for their solicitor. It seemed to Troy that each required a different approach. What that approach might be he did not yet know, but as he made his way to Lockett's office in a building on Malet Street, the first such tactic occurred to him – that Lockett was as likely to be as interested in him as he was in Lockett; that the man, whilst undoubtedly a charlatan, would see himself as some sort of criminologist. Troy had spent a couple of hours in the London Library, had dipped into *The Criminal Skull*. It had been his father's advice, uttered to Troy when he had been a reporter in the mid-Thirties . . . 'Mug up on your man. Not just his *Who's Who* entry, but the worst he has uttered or written and remind yourself that this is your man at his worst. For the worst that can befall you is to find your man "charming" or "intriguing" and then you should silently tell yourself you have read him at his worst.' To read Lockett at his worst meant dipping into *The Case for Race* too. He had given it fifteen minutes and no more. Lockett could not, would not charm him.

He was huge, and he was woolly. Giant's feet. A soft, warm handshake. Grey hair coiling up in wisps like burst springs on an old sofa. Nutbrown eyes smiling at him from behind pince-nez. The bushiest eyebrows he had ever seen. Mr Chips writ large. Indeed, it was a bit like being back at school, in an office stuffed with books, talking to an old duffer spattered with chalk-dust – but Troy had hated school.

'So good of you to call, so good of you.'

As though he had sent for Troy.

'I've been asking Scotland Yard for I-don't-know-how-long to let me study a detective. So good of you to call.'

'Professor Lockett. I'm with the Murder Squad.'

'Capital, capital. Do sit down, Inspector.'

'I'm a sergeant.'

'Sergeant, quite.'

Troy took the proffered chair, found himself facing a large, white china head, patterned like a jigsaw puzzle, with mental and moral qualities marked on the cranium ... *firmness, benevolence, destructiveness.* And next to it on the desk, a fat, black book, *Races of Man: An Index of Nigressence.* What on earth was nigressence?

Lockett remained standing and, much to Troy's annoyance, seemed to be buzzing around behind him.

'I have measured many criminal skulls in my time, as I am sure you will appreciate. I would even go so far as to say I have measured more than either M. Vidocq at the Sureté or the great Lambroso himself. But the point, the point ... as I have been saying in the *Journal of British Criminal Anthropometry* for quite some time ... is that we must also measure the skulls of the police ... ah ... ah ... erm ...'

Troy felt the man's fingertips touch his head above the right ear. It was shocking, but he resisted the impulse to flinch.

'Of course, ideally, one should shave the head ...'

'Professor Lockett, I'm with the Murder Squad.'

'So you said.'

The fingers travelled up the side of his skull, and back down again to rest lightly upon one ear.

'Hmmm ... secretiveness and destructiveness ... in almost equal measure. Would you say you were secretive, Mr Troy?'

His own brother was wont to describe him as 'the most devious little shit in history'.

'No,' Troy lied.

'Destructive?'

'Who would ever admit to that?'

'Hmm ...'

'I'm on the Murder Squad ... and I'm investigating a murder.'

Lockett looked puzzled, busied himself round to his side of the desk. Then the penny dropped.

'You mean ... right now?'

'Yes.'

'You mean that I am part of your investigation?'

'Yes.'

Lockett looked oddly at him – it wasn't his puzzled look, it was something else, and then as the smile spread across his face Troy realised it was excitement.

'Thrilling, simply thrilling!'

Troy took out the letter his father had given him and laid it out on the desk. The pince-nez were pinched back into place. Lockett's eyes

375

scanned the page, then the pince-nez were removed as he stared back at Troy.

'Unbelievable. Simply unbelievable. Somebody wants to lock me up?'

'Actually Professor, it was several somebodies and it was last year.'

Lockett jammed the pince-nez on again.

'I don't recall that the *Post* published this. I'm not a frequent reader of the *Post*, but surely someone would have told me?'

'The *Post* didn't publish it, Professor.'

'I'm sorry. I don't understand.'

And it seemed to Troy that he didn't. He was looking at Lockett and the look on Lockett's face seemed to him to be one of real bewilderment.

'Lock me up? Why would they want to lock me up?'

Troy recalled the pages he had read in *The Case for Race* – on the inferiority of Jews and Negroes, and how this was easily discernible in the alignment of the jaw, the shape of the forehead, indicating as they did a closer proximity to *Cro-Magnon* man than to *Homo sapiens*, and how the Irish were really black men with white skins – and thought there were reasons aplenty to lock the old fool up. But the phrase itself was telling – the man was a fool, or else he was playing Troy for one.

'Professor, where were you on the night of 19 June?'

'I don't know . . . but I'm sure if I were to find my diary . . .'

He was rummaging through a mountain of books and papers now. And he still hadn't asked what murder Troy was investigating.

'Or the 7th of August?'

Lockett was looking at him now. The thrill of being part of a Scotland Yard investigation visibly giving way to apprehension.

'Or the 7th of September?'

The pince-nez were let fall. The eyes met his with a concentration the man had not seemed capable of mustering these last five minutes.

'Everyone knows where they were on September 7th. I was at home, in my Anderson shelter, in my back yard.'

'Alone?'

'I live alone. *Ergo*, I shelter alone. Had anyone asked to be admitted . . .'

A hand gently waving in the air between them.

'. . . But no one did.'

'Reading by torchlight, I suppose?'

'Quite. Sergeant Troy, who has been murdered?'

'People to whom you gave no shelter.'

Lockett looked shocked. He had not missed the meaning of what Troy had said.

'I take it that is a metaphor for my work?'

'It is.'

Troy took back the letter, pushed back the chair.

'Kikes and niggers, Professor Lockett. Kikes and niggers.'

§ 169

Redburn, Sir Michael Charles Clive. 4th Baronet (cr. 1840); *b* 1 September 1882; *Elders* of Charles (d. 1919) and Lavinia, dau. of Viscount Callow. *Educ.* Sherborne; Dartmouth. Served Royal Navy 1900–07 and 1915–19. *Address*: 414 Chesham Place, SW1.

It was too brief. It concealed too much. Concealed that ever since he inherited his father's title and money Redburn had done nothing except indulge himself – one of those indulgences had been to flirt without commitment with every right-wing splinter-group that had been thrown up since the last war. There was scarcely a rent-a-mob for whom he had not spoken, scarcely a race he had not denounced as inferior.

There was what Troy could only think of as a hollow sound when he pulled on the bell at Redburn's house in Chesham Place. The ringing of a bell in quiet emptiness. When no one came to the door after the second ring, he pushed open the letterbox and looked in. The floor between the inner and outer doors was strewn with mail. It looked as though the house had been shut up for weeks. Troy wondered . . . at his age, nearly sixty, Redburn was unlikely to have volunteered for the Navy again.

A door banged open in the area below him, to his right, and a fat housekeeper bustled out from the house next door into the tiny yard below street level.

Troy called down to her, 'I was looking for Sir Michael, I don't suppose you . . .'

'He ain't there.'

'Yes. I can see that. I wondered if you knew where . . .'

'We ain't supposed to talk to no one.'

Troy fumbled in his pocket for his warrant card.

'It's alright, I'm a policeman.'

He held up the card to her stony gaze.

'That's what they all say. I ain't supposed to talk about it. Been told. You'll get me shot, you will.'

The door slammed behind her.

Troy came down the few steps to the pavement, out into the street, to stare up at the windows of the upper floors. Nothing moved. It seemed to him a silly childhood superstition that people watched you from seemingly empty houses as you tried to watch them. Redburn was no more likely to be hiding than he was to have enlisted. What was puzzling was that people like Redburn didn't just vanish either. Or rather people like Redburn, before the war, might vanish to the Continent to avoid a scandal and to drink themselves to death on absinthe, but now, in a land of identity cards, ration books and restricted areas, to vanish was about the hardest trick of all. Even if you chose to impose yourself on relatives in the country you had your mail forwarded and you had to register just to be able to eat.

Troy walked fifty-odd paces, still in the street. Still not quite shaking off the superstition, glancing back at the house. Stepping out into the street put him in the path of a cab which honked at him. He stood on the kerb and watched as the cab disgorged its passenger, and could not believe his luck.

§ 170

Carsington, Richard Piers Corin Frederick Pile (Cleeve-Jones). 3rd Baron *cr.* 1856); *b* 2 Oct. 1895. Formerly Captain, Coldstream Guards. *e s* of Richard, 2nd baron (d. 1931) and Gillian (*neé* Pile), dau. of Frederick, 5th Earl of Ickenham. *Educ*: Harrow; Christchurch. Served Gt. War with Coldstream Guards 1915–17.

Wounded 1917. *m* 1st, 1919, Penelope, dau. of General Horace Hardwick (marr. diss. 1921); 2nd, 1928, Amelia, dau. of Sir Ian Wood (marr. diss. 1932); no issue. *Heir*: Maj-Gen H.R.G. Cleeve-Jones [*b* 1862]. *Recreations*: none. *Clubs*: none. *Address*: 426 Chesham Place, SW1. Carsington Castle, Carsington, Ashbourne, Derbyshire.

While Stan had expressly told him not to approach Lord Carsington, he had said nothing about the possibility of Carsington approaching him.

He was standing by chance between the cab and Carsington's front door. Carsington would have to confront him or walk around him.

Carsington had paid off the cab man, consulted his pocket watch and turned around.

Gazing up at the sky, sunstruck for a moment, not so much as glancing at Troy, he said, 'You surely aren't looking for me?'

'Actually, Lord Carsington, I was looking for Sir Michael Redburn.'

'I am not my brother's keeper, nor am I my neighbour's. But you will find he has been gone a while. Now, if I can be of no further assistance to you ...'

The pocket watch slipped back into his waistcoat pocket. His eyes met Troy's.

'Daniel Shoval.'

'I beg your pardon.'

'Isaiah Borg.'

'What is this, the List of Huntingdonshire Cabmen?'

'Aaron Adelson ... all dead, Lord Carsington.'

Carsington said nothing to this. The list did not produce a flicker of recognition.

'All Jews. All murdered.'

Troy was short. Below regulation height for a London bobby and only accepted onto the force by a waiving of the rules. Carsington was over six feet tall. A lean man, all elbows, knees and nose. He stepped right up to Troy and bent down as though talking calmly but severely to a disobedient child.

'Do you really want to stand on my doorstep and talk to me of dead Jews? Do you really think I give a damn about dead Jews? Do you really think one dead Jew or a million dead Jews would cause me to lose a moment's sleep? Do you really think you want to take me on again, Constable Troy?'

His eyes were blue washed out to grey, and his breath was foul. It was a visage and a proximity to intimidate.

'It's Sergeant Troy now, Lord Carsington.'

Carsington straightened up.

'Dear boy, you positively reek of power. Now, if you'll excuse me, I've more pressing engagements than anything you can possibly have in mind.'

'Lord Carsington . . .'

'Mr Troy, come back with a warrant, then perhaps I'll see you.'

His voice dropped to a hoarse whisper, 'But cross me again, Mr Troy, and it'll be at your own risk.'

§ 171

Trench, Geoffrey Aldous Coker; *b* 16 Jan. 1904. *Twin s* of Aldous and Ethel, dau of Prof. Francis Coker. *Educ*: Eton; Balliol. Rowing blue 1924–5; British Olympic Team, Paris 1924; Member British Himalayan Expedition 1926; 3rd Secretary, HM Embassy Berlin, 1927–8; Conservative MP for Chipping Campden & Moreton-in-Marsh since 1929. *Recreations*: Climbing mountains, rowing, ski-ing, *The Times* crossword. *Address*: 663 South Eaton Place, SW1. Orchard Farm, Chipping Campden, Wilts.

Troy had grown up with twins. Twins intrigued him. He looked down the column for the other twin but found no mention of him.

He decided to tackle Trench in his place of work. It was a short walk – out of Scotland Yard, down the subway, under Westminster Bridge Road, past the duty copper and into the Houses of Parliament.

A secretary showed him to Trench's office. Trench had his head bent over a pile of letters and did not look up – his right hand scribbling out signatures so precise a machine could be doing it.

'Be with you in a trice.'

Troy looked around. The Conservative Party clearly didn't much favour Geoffrey Trench; it showed in the pokiness of the office, the lack of a river view. Those favoured could overlook the terraces and watch the Thames flow by, those not favoured, consigned to the back benches, could gaze out at walls and tarmac. Yet Trench had stormed into the Commons ten or so years ago as a bright young thing, a new-generation Tory – an articulate orator, a hero of the Himalayas. Being stuck on the back benches was a mess of his own making.

Past glories covered the walls. His Everest and Alpine attempts recorded in a dozen framed black and white photographs. His Olympic bronze medal sat on a small pedestal as a paperweight on his desk. Troy sat down to wait. Trench pushed the signed letters aside and looked at Troy oddly, as though recognising him – but Troy was quite certain they'd never met.

Trench leaned back in his chair, locked his fingers behind his head and stretched, still looking quizzically at Troy. Troy wished he'd worked out an approach. But he hadn't.

'I'm from Scotland Yard,' he said lamely.

'Yes – I know. My secretary told me. Inspector Troy?'

'Sergeant Troy.'

'How can I help?'

'An enquiry.'

Troy wished he had not sounded hesitant, wished he had not resorted to copper-speak. Sarcasm rippled through Trench's words.

'A routine matter?' uttered with so many extra syllables as to make each word sound a yard long.

'I wouldn't exactly say . . .'

The hands unlocked, Trench lurched forward with a jerk, his face so much closer to Troy's.

'Don't be coy, Mr Troy. You wouldn't be here on anything you could pass off as routine. You're known. I know who you are. You're Alex Troy's son – the one who defied convention and joined the police force. Did you not know how you rattled London society when you did that? Do think you're invisible? You pounded the beat in the East End and then Stanley Onions recruited you to his whiz-kid team at the Murder Squad. Beating about the bush is a waste of both our time. Why not just tell me what bee is in your bonnet?'

Cards on the table.

'Where were you on the nights of June 19th, August 7th and September 7th?'

Trench paused. Said nothing for almost a minute, then his right hand reached out for the phone. Now, Troy thought, he rings for his solicitor – but the hand landed down on a desk diary and flipped it neatly towards Troy.

'Nothing I do fails to be recorded somewhere. One of the perils of public life. It's all written down, and it's tedious – but it's also a matter of fact. See for yourself.'

Troy opened the diary, read the entries back to Trench.

'June 19th – constituency meeting with your local party workers. August 7th – lunch at your country home with the Lord Lieutenant of Wiltshire. The evening entry is blank . . .'

'I stayed on. A rare opportunity for a quiet evening with a good book. *Uncle Fred in the Springtime*. Ask me anything you like about the plot.'

'September 7th simply says "George and Dorothy".'

'George Kimbrough and his wife. London correspondent of the *New York Times*. Dinner at my house. Until the big raid put paid to it, of course.'

'Were you in a shelter?'

'No. Were you?'

Troy shook his head.

'Thought not. I was up on the roof of my house with a half bottle of brandy, watching. Amazing, absolutely bloody amazing.'

'Alone?'

'Neither of my guests fancied the climb. I've got three-quarters of the way up Everest, after all – George wheezes on the average staircase. When I got down I found they'd nipped out to the Dorchester and sheltered there. So, effectively, I was alone. Which I am quite sure is what you wanted to hear. Now – that was the last answer until you tell me what you want.'

Troy did what he had done with Lockett. Took out the letter and shoved it across the desk to him.

'I'd heard about this. Chap at the *Mail* told me about it. Never got published. I suppose you got yours from the *Post*? If I took tripe like this seriously I'd never sleep. I get stuff like this sent to me all the time. "You should be locked up . . . shot . . . sent to the tower" . . . I'm almost certain one old fool somewhere out in the shires wanted to horsewhip me personally.'

'Half the signatories are dead. Four of them have died in mysterious circumstances since that letter was written.'

'You're being coy again. Mysterious circumstances, my arse. You think they were murdered or you wouldn't be here. You think there's a right-wing death list with half a dozen rabbis' names on it and you're working your way through the people they tried to denounce. Of course, with your simple copper's logic you have managed to tar us all with the same brush. As far as you're concerned we are all the same. But we're not. Redburn is a political loose cannon. And if you want my two penn'orth, he should be locked up. He's drifted from one faction to another for the best part of ten years and ended up an out and out fascist.'

Trench tapped the page with a fingernail, pinging noisily off the paper for emphasis.

'I, in case you hadn't noticed, am a Conservative MP with three general elections and a healthy majority under my arse. I'm not a fascist, whatever you might think, whatever your father might think, and I'm not in any splinter group. I'm a loyal Tory. I just happen to hold certain views on the relation between international finance and Jewish capital. You will not find them much different from the views held by most Conservative MPs – indeed most Conservative Prime Ministers – I just happen to think holding my tongue on the matter is neither intelligent nor patriotic. Lockett ... for God's sake the man's a complete crank. The last practitioner of bumpology. How he holds down a job in a decent university is beyond me.'

Trench scanned the letter again, before handing it back to Troy.

'The rest are dead or locked up, as far as I know.'

'And Lord Carsington? Lord Carsington is at large.'

'If you don't know, you must be the last man in London who doesn't. Carsington is barking. Mad as a hatter. And if you ever quote me as saying that I'll slap a writ on you for slander.'

Of course Troy thought Carsington was mad, but ...

'In what way?'

'Dunno for sure ... but ask yourself this. Why did neither of his marriages last? Why no kids? Why do both ex-wives cling ferociously to the gin bottle? If you ask me, he's potty and he drove them potty too.'

'Do you not think what they might be saying about you?'

'No. And I doubt that you've asked them. Now ... will that be all or are there other murders you'd like to pin on me while you're here?'

§ 172

'What do you think you're playing at lad?'

'I'm sorry, sir, I don't follow . . .'

'I told you that day at the Russian Tea Rooms. Keep off my patch!'

That was the thing about the Branch, the patch was a moveable feast.

'Sir, with all due respect, just spit it out.'

Troy could feel the force of Steerforth's rage quivering down the wire, crackling into the bakelite.

'Spit it out! You cheeky little sod. Spit it out. I'll chew you up and fuckin' spit you out. You're going round London askin' questions where you shouldn't be!'

OK, thought Troy, that was moderate progress, but there remained a vital question.

'Questions about whom?'

Troy could hear the force with which Steerforth held in the explosion. If they were in the same room the man would surely be trying to throttle Troy.

'Redburn, you little bugger! Redburn! Sir Michael Redburn! You've been round to his house. I know you have, so don't fuckin' deny it.'

'I don't deny it. But I didn't get past the door.'

'And you won't.'

'Then what's the problem?'

'The problem is that I've got the bastard in custody. I've had him banged up for weeks. Who do you think I was on to that day at the Tea Rooms?'

OK, time to state the obvious.

'Redburn?'

'Right, smartarse. Redburn. You nearly fucked that up. Don't fuck it up again. Don't go near the house, don't go near his family until the trial's over.'

'What trial?'

Troy sensed a dropped brick, one Steerforth would have a little difficulty picking up.

'He's on trial for treason. You won't be reading about it in the papers,

384

and maybe you never will. It's what they call *in camera*. Classified. A secret.'

'Then I'm glad you haven't told me.'

The explosion forced Troy to hold the receiver away from his ear. Troy was not wholly certain what he was saying, but 'little gobshite', and 'busted back to walking the fuckin' beat' seemed to be prevalent. When he'd stopped Troy said, 'I've an ongoing murder investigation, sir. If you've had Redburn in custody since that day at the Tea Rooms, then he's of no further interest to me, but while you're on the line perhaps you could tell me whether you have any interest in Lord Carsington . . .'

'Stay away from him!'

'. . . Geoffrey Trench . . .'

'Aaaaaaaghhh!'

'. . . Or Charles Lockett?'

Steerforth slammed the phone down.

§ 173

Troy had got home. Rummaged in the dark place under the sink for a bottle of his dad's vintage claret. It had been a shitty day. It was about to get shittier. The telephone rang. He picked it up, held the bottle in his right hand, corkscrew still in cork, and hoped to get rid of whoever it was quickly.

'I have a long-distance call for you from Burnham-on-Crouch, person to person, Frederick Troy.'

'That's me,' said Troy, expecting his old pal Charlie.

But it wasn't.

'Go ahead, caller.'

'It's me, Walter Stilton.'

'Hello, Walter.'

'I got the bollocking of a lifetime today.'

Troy set the bottle down, and prepared to wait.

'Steerforth?'

'Aye. Steerforth.'

'I'm sorry, Walter. It couldn't be helped. It's Murder Squad business now – official. It's out of Steerforth's hands, but I'd no idea he'd take it out on you.'

'I'm used to it.'

Troy waited for the but.

'But ... it won't stop there. I was thinkin' ... put a bit of space between yourself and our Kitty.'

'Walter, do you really think that's necessary?'

'He's a malicious little sod. If you weren't trespassing on his turf at the Russian caff you are now. He's capable of having you watched. If he gets the bit between his teeth, he'll find the manpower and he'll do it.'

'Does he have someone watching Chesham Place?'

'I don't know.'

'Because I intend to ask Onions to put someone there in the morning. It would be a farce if we doubled up. Two coppers watching each other.'

'Like I say, I don't know, and I won't ask. But if any of his blokes see you and Kitty together and Steerforth adds her to his list of coppers he wants vetted ... need I say more?'

'But will she listen to me?'

'I'm her father ... she sure as hell won't listen to me. Hold her at arm's length for a bit. I'm not sayin' dump her – she'd hate that – just find a convenient lie that stops you seeing her till this is over.'

It suited too well. A convenient lie. It was as though some guiding hand was slotting pieces into place for him. Zette and Kitty and a revolving door. Part of him did not wish to do it, just as much of him could not quite believe his luck.

§ 174

Onions had appeared in Troy's office again, puffing on a Woodbine.

'I'm hearing nowt.'

'There's not a lot to tell you.'

'Tell me anyway.'

Onions parked himself by the fireplace, flicking ash into the grate.

Troy told him, omitting the chance encounter with Carsington.

'D'ye mean to see 'em again. Up the ante next time?'

'I'd rather just put a watch on them. I took Lockett by surprise and for some reason Trench was mildly entertained by the whole thing. Next time they'll want their brief in the room. No, I'll stay clear of them, but I want them watched. Anyone could move around like a wraith in an air-raid. It's the perfect cover. The only way to approach this is to put a man on each of their houses.'

Onions pinched the end of his cigarette, dropped it back in the packet for later.

'I can't spare the men for what you're asking. Three watches at once? And on nothing more than a hunch?'

'It's one of them. I know it.'

Onions wasn't having this.

'Like I said – a hunch. It could be any one of them or none of them.'

'I'd plump for Carsington.'

Onions wasn't having this either.

'Only 'cos you've crossed swords with him before. You said yourself ... Lockett might be playing the fool just for you, and Trench is as smooth as they come. Birds off the trees and all that malarkey. He could have got back to London from his constituency in the middle of the night for the June and August dates. Lockett doesn't know where he was on either date. And they've neither of them got anything I'd call a shred of an alibi for the one night we know for certain it's murder.'

'Perhaps Carsington hasn't either?'

'Mebbe, mebbe not.'

'Let me talk to him.'

'No.'

'Then give me Thomson and Gutteridge to watch the houses.'

'I can't do it. I can't justify the resources. Not the pickle we're in now. Every suspicious body the ARP call us out. Like you said an air-raid is perfect cover. Bound to be a few old scores settled. And there's bodies turning up all over the place.'

'Stan ... it's usually me who turns out for them. I'm handling two or three a day right now.'

'Then you've got your hands full, haven't you?'

§175

It was raining. After another imperious summons to Stanhope Place, mercifully spared sex-in-the-park – 'rain stopped play', as he thought of it – another raid banging down around them, the blackout tightly drawn – Troy sat up in bed with a pencil and paper by the light of a reading lamp.

Zette woke.

'What are you doing?'

'Taking a leaf out of your book. I'm trying to perceive a pattern in the numbers.'

'What numbers?'

'The dates of the killings.'

'And can you?'

'No. 29, 19, 7 and 7. Meaningless to me.'

Zette stretched out an arm languidly and took the sheet from him. Yawned. Rubbed with a fist at one eye and read with the other.

'There's a pattern alright. As for meaning . . .'

'A pattern?'

'School Matric Maths, Troy!'

'I was more of a Latin scholar.'

'God, this is so elementary. They're all prime numbers. They cannot be divided by any other number but themselves and one.'

'They can't?'

'Try it. Find something that goes into 29 without leaving a few over. 21, on the other hand, is divisible by 7 and 3; 25 by . . . do you see?'

'Yes. I can see it now. But why do you say it's meaningless.'

'For God's sake Troy . . . if I thought numbers meant something *per se* I'd have signed up for my father's gobbledegook classes years ago. "Three, five, seven, a quickstep into heaven." It's a pattern. Possibly a random one. Any meaning is a matter of our own interpretation . . . our own projection.'

'Then let me project this. According to you there is something . . . perfect – I can think of no other word – something "perfect" about a prime number. Something imperfect about fractions. Supposing this chap only goes out to kill on nights that are prime numbers? Supposing only prime numbers meet his sense of perfection?'

'Supposing he only goes out wearing odd sock? It doesn't mean anything except to him. Maybe he's just a nutter?'

'Oh,' said Troy. 'He's that alright, I'm quite sure he's that.'

§ 176

They sat at the same oilclothed table in the back room of Nader's house, drinking tea again.

Nader said, 'It's been over a fortnight now. The Luftwaffe haven't missed a night. How long before Eastenders accept being bombed as a way of life?'

'Do you think they're that sanguine?'

'No, but they'll say they are. "England can take it." But how much death can any community take? I attend a funeral every day now.'

'I look at bodies every day.'

'You could say that was inherent in the nature of both our occupations. You and I deal in death, in mortality and immortality.'

Troy could not agree with the last part of this. In his experience the dead stayed dead, but he was delighted that Nader had given him the introduction to the pitch he wanted to make – common ground between them was a godsend.

'Do you not think we might be alike in other ways?'

'Such as?'

'We're roughly the same height. Your hair and eyes are the same colour.'

'But,' said Nader, running a finger raspily down the side of his face, 'I have a beard and you don't.'

Troy placed a small paper parcel on the table and unwrapped it. He took the contents in his fingers and held it to his chin, fingertips pressed to his cheekbones, just below the ears. Nader laughed out loud.

'A false beard, Mr Troy? Where did you get that? In a joke shop?'

'As a matter of fact, I did. The one in Holborn. I bought the spirit gum at the same time.'

'You mean you intend to masquerade as me?'

'Lend me your hat and jacket and we'll see. I have an idea of when our man might strike again. I've been able to come up with a set of likely dates. I can't be certain of any of them, of course – but I am certain the next victim will be a rabbi and that you are next on the list.'

'You don't think your "man", as you put it, will know my father is in hospital?'

'Unlikely. Or are you saying I should dress as him rather than you?'

'We couldn't pad you enough, Mr Troy. You'd have to gain four stones. And I haven't yet said I'll let you play me. That is what you intend, isn't it? To dress as me, and lie in wait?'

'Pretty much.'

'Such a risk. This man has killed four men.'

'So far the worst attack has been with a kitchen knife. I think I can handle that, and of course I'll be expecting him. None of the others were.'

Nader was thinking. Troy did not want Nader to think. He wanted him simply to agree.

'I can't help thinking that it's like trading your life for mine. I couldn't agree to that.'

'It would only be that if I died. I've no intention of dying.'

'Suppose I am, suppose I remain, the bait, and you watch over me?'

'I couldn't agree to that.'

Nader thought again.

'Tell me.'

'We meet here, early evening tomorrow. Discreetly. I won't leave my car outside. I'll come in the back, and you should leave by the back. You have somewhere you could go, I take it?'

'I should think I'm related to half Stepney. I have more aunts than I have fingers to count them.'

'When the raid starts, and that's *when* not *if*, I think, I'll go over to the synagogue and pretend to be clearing up. If I'm right ... something will happen before midnight. If nothing happens by the time of the all-clear, I'll come back here, put my feet up and see you at breakfast.'

'And then?'

'We try again. As I said, I can't really be sure when – but I do know it's you next.'

'You know, I think I just felt someone walk over my grave. Very well. Tomorrow. The 23rd. And after that?'

'The 29th.'

'And the significance?'

Troy didn't want to explain – it felt, for all his confidence in his theory, just a bit silly – so he didn't.

Nader pulled open the drawer in the kitchen table.

'You forgot one thing . . . hair, eyes, height, beard . . . glasses. Take my spares.'

Troy opened the case, slipped them on. Little wire-rimmed spectacles with thick lenses. The world swam. He felt what it must be like to be a goldfish.

'As you are clearly not short-sighted, Mr Troy, I suggest you pull them down to the end of your nose and peer over them. There's not much else you can do. But you'll never pass for me or my father without them.'

§ 177

On the morning of the 24th Nader nudged Troy awake with a cup of tea and a bowl of porridge.

'If you were expecting bacon and eggs you've come to the wrong hotel. What happened?'

Troy sipped at the tea and said, 'Nothing. Not a sausage.'

'You won't get those here either.'

§ 178

'You are an odd mixture, Billy. You profess to be a gut Tory, yet you never applied to be British and hence never received the right to vote as a gut Tory. You are a pillar of the East End Tailors . . . yet you admit to throwing bricks at policemen and you boast of cheating the taxman at every turn. All in all, I do not know what to believe . . . except to ask . . . who are you, Billy Jacks? Do *you* know?'

'Maxie, you can blather all you want, you ain't gonna make me British – been there, done that – and you ain't gonna make me no pinko neither.'

'Billy – am I right in summing up your philosphy as "look after number one"?'

'You should know, you used it to take the piss out of me often enough.'

'And mine can be summed up in much the same words . . .'

'Yeah. Right.'

'No . . . truly it can . . . just hear me out. Looking after oneself requires interdependence. A notion of the common good. I can sum it up in the words of some revolutionary or another – one of the Americans, I think . . . Franklin or Jefferson perhaps – when they said, "We must all hang together, or, most assuredly, we shall all hang separately".'

'Hang. That's like a joke, is it?'

'It is called a pun . . . one word, two meanings.'

'Hang together as in stick together. Like all for one and one for all?'

'Exactly.'

And Drax knew from the look on Billy's face that he had at last sown the seeds of doubt, but Jacks being Jacks he would undoubtedly change the subject now.

Billy stood up, hands stuffed into his trouser pockets, counting change or playing with his balls. Scuffing the floorboards with his feet – the recalcitrant in the playground.

'Me and Hummer get out in a day or two. Trench told us today. John Bull needs tailors. My daughter wrote to our local MP, he got on to the Ministry of Supply. They wrote to the War Office, the War Office wrote to the Home Office . . . and they rang Trench. Trench is only too glad to see the back of me. So we're out . . . back to the old sewing machine. Uniforms for the boys.'

'John Bull? Suddenly you're British?'

'What? Me? Billy Bull? I should Chippin' Campden.'

More scuffing the floorboards, more playing with his balls.

'It will be cold in London,' Drax said. 'Almost autumn after all. Will you give Josef my fur coat? He is so thin I fear there is no fat to keep him warm.'

The coat was hanging on the back of the door.

Billy ran his fingers down the sleeve.

'It's seen better days.'

'All the same, I would be grateful if you would give it to him. I doubt I shall have need of it.'

Missing the point entirely, Billy said, 'What and have him go round Stepney looking like the skinny man's Bud Flanagan?'

Hummel did not miss the point. It reminded him of inheriting his father's coat, and that reminded him of losing his father's coat on Kristallnacht. He accepted the coat and thanked Drax profusely, knowing they would never meet again.

'You would, of course . . .' said Drax, stating the obvious, 'be safer here. London is bombed every night now.'

'It's where I belong, Max.'

'Really, Josef. So soon? And Billy where does he belong? And our absent leader, Herr Troy. Wandering Jews the both of them.'

'One of them a Jew who knows nothing but Stepney and the other no Jew at all.'

'Nevertheless, you take my point.'

'Indeed I do, Max. But it is not a matter of where they belong, merely of when.'

§ 179

As soon as the glue dried under his beard, Troy perched Nader's spare specs on the end of his nose and crossed the road to the Heaven's Gate Synagogue. The air-raid was well under way, the boom of bombs ripping through the air from the docks on the Isle of Dogs, and the street was deserted.

He had decided the last time to make himself useful. It was not yet dusk, but the light within seemed to change little with the time of day. Murky by day – by night the holes in the roof let in moonlight shafts, the reflected glow of London burning, and the interior of the synagogue was a perpetual half-light. Troy sorted debris, built piles of what was salvageable and what he thought was not. The trick, he had decided, was to do it quietly, to always have one ear cocked to the background sound, to filter the sound of mayhem for the one sound that mattered – and almost always to have something in his hand which could be used to fend off an assailant. If needs be, he'd bash his brains out with a 2-by-4 or the ornamental brass base of an oil lamp.

Planes passed directly overhead just about midnight. The growl and grumble of a big cat. It was the re-creation of the fears of childhood, alone in a dark place, the sounds of chaos bursting in the sky above and the knowledge of something, someone terrible just around the corner. For a moment he could feel himself as he was aged seven. He stopped, sat on an intact pew and waited. Heard the bombing start up again a mile or more to the west in the City of London. He felt lucky, relieved. Bombs were not like lightning, they could and probably did strike twice. Looking at Heaven's Gate it was, all the same, difficult not to think that the worst had already happened.

At half past two the all-clear sounded. The streets would fill now. It might be that his suspect was out there somewhere, but far more likely that he wasn't.

He went back to Nader's house, peeled off the beard and slept. He woke around six-thirty to find Nader bumbling around in his kitchen.

'Are we downhearted?' Nader said, grinning, slyly parodic.

'You bet,' said Troy.

§ 180

Wednesday, 2 October 1940

'I've phoned you before. I called you Sunday evening. Lindfors stood me up, I rather thought we could have got together!'

'I was working.'

'More dead Jews?

'The same dead Jews. I put your theory to the test.'

'Eh?'

'I've been staking out Heaven's Gate. Nader is my age and my height. We swapped jackets, I stuck on a fake beard with spirit gum, and I bumbled around a synagogue in half-darkness, trying to look as though I knew what I was doing.'

'You mean you used yourself as bait?'

'I suppose I do.'

'Were you armed?'

'Of course not.'

'Troy, there are times I think you're an idiot.'

'Nothing happened. Nothing happened on the 23rd either. And if you're right, nothing will now until the third.'

'What do you mean?'

'I can't do this every night. I haven't the resources. But I can wangle the shifts and the pattern of work enough to cope with the prime numbers. If it isn't the right theory I'm stuffed because I can't get my boss or Nader to take it seriously enough. But I told Nader I'd be back on the third.'

'Why the third?'

'Next prime number.'

'Troy, you blithering idiot – you missed 1, which was the next prime number, and the next after that is 2!'

'You never said anything about even numbers, I thought they were all odd?'

'Just think for a moment, Troy. A number only divisible by itself and one must include both one and two. Two is the only even prime number. And October 2nd is the next prime date!'

'Oh shit. That's today.'

§

Under moonlight,
infectious moonlight,
a madman dances,
chanting numbers,
one, two, three, five, seven, eleven.
Smeared in excrement,
naked as nativity,
smeared in his own blood,
wailing like a dog in pain,
throat bared to heaven,
mouth the perfect O,

face tilted to night,
eyes wide open,
eyes tight shut,
a razor in his hand,
Lord Carsington dances . . .
Eleven, seven, five, three, two . . . one . . .

§ 181

The raid had started just before 9 p.m. Troy had moved rubble around for a couple of hours, and was feeling the pointlessness of the pretence, and the irritation and foolishness of a fake beard.

Part of his mind told him he had been foolish in the first place to seize on a theory handed to him by Zette as the only pattern perceivable in a chain of numbers. Part of his mind told him that a pattern as odd, as stripped of meaning as this might well be the fixation of a nutcase. Then the rest of his mind told him he was losing concentration and that that was precursor to losing the battle.

The bigger battle raged overhead. Closer than the previous two nights – bombs raining down within half a mile to either side. Great, dull whumpfs taking out whole streets of Shadwell or Bethnal Green.

Any sane man would be in a shelter. But as Trench had made disturbingly clear to him, there were people like Troy and Trench who would never go into a shelter – men, and they weren't all men, too fascinated with the wonder and the risk to want to miss it.

The moon was waning. In a week's time he'd have to stop this farce – too little light would be coming in through the gaping holes in the roof. The interior of the synagogue would be black as pitch.

It was close to midnight now. German planes directly overhead. The City of London about to cop it again. Troy had let his rules slip. He was staring up through a hole in the roof and had nothing that might serve as a weapon in hand.

Out of nowhere there were hands at his throat, a voice and bad breath in his face.

'You bloody fool! What do you think you're playing at?'

Troy caught him with a left hook to the cheek, knocked his hat off, sent him reeling away – and at a couple of paces distance realised this was far too small a man to be his man, and that it was Steerforth. Steerforth angry, Steerforth in a rage, Steerforth spitting fire.

'What did I –'

A hand seized Steerforth by the hair, and another passed quickly and surgically across his throat. The razor slit from ear to ear. A fountain of blood shot three feet into the air in spurt and splat. Steerforth crumpled and his life gushed to nothing in the dust and dirt.

Troy stared at Zette, still clutching the open razor, still staring down at the twitching corpse. Feet and hands shaking like a man in a fit of palsy. Head nodding with every spurt of blood as though jerked on a string.

'Oh my God, Zette. What have you done?'

Now she looked at Troy.

'"An eye for an eye",' she said so softly he could hardly hear her.

'Oh God, Zette. He didn't kill your father.'

It was as though he'd slapped her.

'He didn't? Then who did?'

And she turned to follow Troy's gaze to the far side of the synagogue, to the street entrance, to the tall man, half hidden in the darkness, in and out of moon beams, walking slowly towards them with a revolver in his hand.

'I rather think he did,' Troy said.

Troy had not counted on a gun. A gun was almost the last thing he'd expected. He had not handled a gun since basic training. He hated guns. He wished he had one now.

He backed off slowly, blocking Zette's body with his own, and as they backed off the man approached Steerforth's body and stopped as though unwilling to step over it or step in blood.

He looked down at the corpse. Spent now. Now he raised his arm, now he levelled the gun, now he was within range.

Looking down the barrel of a gun, Troy had one vain hope, that the floor might open up and swallow this bastard, whoever he was.

And it did.

A high explosive burst in the street outside, caved in the east wall, set the solid floor rippling like the liquid surface of a pond, and then the floor opened up and swallowed him. A single shot, a single scream. The floor buckled, split and splintered – and he and the late Mr Steerforth vanished into the pit below.

'Run!' said Troy.

'Where?'

'Back,' said Troy.

'Back where? There's no way out. It's all coming down on us.'

He seized Zette by the hand and ran for the back of the synagogue, towards the open doors of the ark.

'Get in.'

'What?'

'It's the most solid thing in here, and it's the only chance we have.'

He bundled her into the velvet box and, as the roof gave way, he saw a silver shower of little thermos flasks tumble into the pit, then what was left of the roof fell in, the incendiaries ignited and a sheet of blue-white flame shot up from below like the roar of a dyspeptic dragon. He drew the doors shut. Fireproof, Nader had said, but he doubted Nader knew how fiercely magnesium burnt.

'It's pitch dark in here, we could suffocate!'

'No,' he said. 'No we won't, there are airbricks in the back. We have a chance.'

'A chance?'

'You're the one that deals in mathematical probabilities.'

'Then we'll probably die together. All my life I have fantasized about with whom I might live not with whom I might die.'

A crash to deafen them both as the west wall fell in, bouncing rubble off the oak doors – entombing them within the ark.

'Change the subject,' Troy said when his ears stopped ringing.

§ 182

All the way out of London Hummel had read – nose deep into a J.B. Priestley novel. Coming into London, he watched with fresh eyes as London absorbed Nature. Villages turned to suburbs, suburbs to soot-caked cuttings carving their way into London's clay from West Hampstead to Agar Town. Ploughed fields turned to streets, copses and knolls to half glimpsed houses rushing by. London wrapped the green world in her grey winding sheet – a green thought in a grey shade – moss crept across the corrugated roofs of factories, willow-herb sprouted on embankments, and incongruous rows of flag irises and autumn cabbages gathered dust by the trackside in Cricklewood – buddleia, its purple blossom spent, dry and raggy on the stone ramparts. Into the deep, dark maw of a blackened St Pancras station. Jonah swallowed by a whale. In utter contrast to June, the station was almost deserted ... 'the pulse of London low and inaudible'.

'Shouldn't have any problem getting a cab. Eh?' Billy said.

All Hummel had was his carpet bag with a single change of clothes, his German-English/English-German dictionary, his portrait and Drax's old fur coat.

'Can you manage without me?'

'Wot?'

'I ... I would prefer to walk.'

'Walk? Hummer, it's four miles. Maybe five.'

'All the same, I would like to walk.'

'Air-raids. There might be an air-raid.'

'Almost certainly.'

'OK, suit yerself. Kettle'll be on when you get home.'

Hummel smiled at the word.

'*Ja*, Billy. Home.'

It was like the descent into a dream. The descent from a dream. He would never be sure which. All his life, it seemed to Hummel that he had dreamt of Vienna. And that was all that remained of Vienna – a dream. But now there was London. As the ack-ack tore up the evening sky at the first sight of German bombers, a new dream opened up for him.

§ 183

Zette slept.

Troy heard the all-clear sound. Saw daylight at the end of the tiny tunnels of the airbrick. Heard sounds in the street. Called out. No one responded.

A day passed.

Having no choice, they pissed where they lay.

Zette slept.

A new raid began at a new dusk.

What was left of the synagogue shook to another high explosive. Dust and rubble coming down on them, a piece of the ark's roof glanced off Zette's head and she passed out mid-sentence . . .

'If we ever −'

Troy moved her head to the airbrick, pressed her face against it, felt for the wound, wiped away a streak of blood, breathed clean air, waited for the dust to settle, saw night fall.

Zette slept.

Troy slept.

Troy awoke to the sound of banging. Streaks of light in the airbrick. A furry creature at his throat. He flinched and scrabbled. Mouse or rat? Then he realised it was the fake beard that had slipped off.

Banging directly on the ark doors. He tapped back with his fist.

A voice said, 'Hold on. We're digging.'

As if he could do anything else but hold on.

He shook Zette. She woke groggily, complained of the pain in her head, the cramp in her legs, wrapped herself around him.

'They're digging us out,' Troy said.

'How long . . . how long have we been here?'

'About thirty-two hours, I think. I've seen dawn twice.'

Blinding light as the doors slid back, and a voice said 'Gotcher!'

Many hands were grappling to take his. There was George Bonham and Kolankiewicz and Elishah Nader and Walter Stilton and Billy Jacks and a big-eared bloke in a fur coat looking like the skinny man's Bud Flanagan.

'Ach, so,' said Hummel. '*Der andere* Troy.'

§ 184

Troy staggered out onto dust and rubble, shielding his eyes from the light and trying to see. Why was it so bright? And then he saw. There was nothing left of Heaven's Gate. Nothing left but the brick ark from which they crawled. Nothing overhead but the bright blue, cloud-dappled sky with a nip of English autumn in the air.

Zette slipped. Troy caught her in his arms. Found he could not lift her. She passed out again.

'Zette, Zette!'

Her eyes had closed, and the cut in her head opened up again.

Bonham said, ''Ere – let me take her.'

And scooped her up in one giant's paw.

Walter Stilton took his arm.

'Steady, lad. You've been banged up nigh on two days. Bound to be a bit woozy.'

'Walter? Walter!'

'Aye, it's me, lad.'

'I . . . I need your car.'

Troy lurched off across the rubble, got five paces towards Stilton's Riley before Stilton restrained him.

'Goin' somewhere, were you? Don't be daft. Come on now, you're in no fit state . . .'

'Chesham Place . . . got to . . .'

'You want to go to Chesham Place?'

'I have to go to Chesham Place.'

'OK. I'll drive you.'

Stilton dumped him down in the passenger seat. Troy leaned back and closed his eyes. At the sound of the engine turning over, he opened them, looked out through the windscreen. There on the edge of the site, hands stuffed in the pockets of her police tunic, three bold stripes upon her arm, pale and sad, stood Kitty Stilton.

§ 185

'Are we there?'

'Almost,' Stilton said. 'We're parked round the corner. You put your head on the block if you like. I'd rather not be seen, for all I know Steerforth might have a bloke watching Redburn's house . . .'

'He hasn't.'

'. . . And Carsington's.'

'He hasn't, Walter. If he had, things might never have got this far.'

'Maybe . . . all the same, just one bloke watching. You watch your step, if Steerforth . . .'

Troy wasn't listening any more. This wasn't the time to tell Walter that Steerforth had watched the house in person. That he had followed Carsington in person all the way to Heaven's Gate. This wasn't the time to tell Walter Steerforth was dead. There'd never be a time to tell Walter Steerforth was dead.

Troy all but leapt from the car. His own energy amazed him. Dead on his feet, and feeling he could kick the door in if he had to.

A housekeeper in her seventies answered, frail and stooped but defiant.

'The master's not at 'ome.'

Troy held up his warrant card and pushed past her, through the inner doors and into the hall.

'Carsington!'

He looked up the stairwell, iron railings wrapped around him in Piranesi loops all the way to the clouded skylight in the roof.

'Carsington!'

And the stairs fed back his own voice to him in a diminishing echo . . . 'Carsington, Carsington, Carsington.'

'I told yer. The master's not home. He ain't been home all night. I ain't seen him since Wednesday morning. We getting ready to call the p'lice!'

Troy could still hear his own voice. Waited for silence, for silence was his answer. The only answer he wanted to hear. Lord Carsington was not at 'ome. Lord Carsington never would be at 'ome. Lord Carsington was underneath a hundred tons of rubble at Heaven's Gate.

He caught sight of himself in a full-length mirror. He had not stopped to think what he looked like. Now he could see himself as Carsington's housekeeper surely saw him. His jacket – Nader's jacket – was ripped at the shoulder and his trousers at the knee. His hair was white with dust, the knuckles of both hands were bleeding. Standing next to him was a big, grim-faced man.

'Freddie?'

Troy looked at Onions' reflection, then turned to look at the man himself.

'He's dead. It was Carsington.'

'Freddie.'

'I told you it was Carsington.'

'Come with me, now. That's an order.'

'It was Carsington!'

'Outside now!'

They sat in Onions' car.

'Kolankiewicz called me. Said you were fit to do your nut.'

'I'll be fine.'

'Fine? For God's sake, man. You've been buried alive for the best part of two days!'

'I'll be OK.'

'OK, my arse. I'm taking you to hospital.'

'No ... if you have to take me somewhere, take me home.'

'Home?'

'I've broken no bones. It's just cuts and bruises.'

Onions started the car. When they rounded the corner Stilton had gone.

'Kolankiewicz says they took the woman to the London Hospital. Head injuries or summat.'

Troy said nothing.

Onions said, 'You going to tell me who she is and what she was doing there?'

'She's Izzy Borg's daughter. And I don't know what she was doing there.'

'I don't believe you. Try telling me what happened.'

Troy told him. Told him everything except Steerforth.

By the time Onions pulled up his car in St Martin's Lane he was saying, 'You took a stupid risk.'

And Troy was saying as little as possible. He was wondering if they would dig for the body. It would take precious resources. The job of rescue squads was to dig for the living. Would Onions ask for Heaven's Gate to be dug out for the dead?

'It's Carsington down there. You know damn well it is.'

'But you say you never saw his face? Just that he was a big bugger.'

'They're all big buggers. Trench and Carsington six foot or so, Lockett more like six four. But . . . Carsington's missing. I think that says it all.'

'Aye. Missing. He might be back. So . . . I've stuck a jack at Chesham Place . . . all the discretion of Primo Carnera at a midgets' reunion . . . but he's got his orders. I told him. Anything, anything at all, and he comes to me first. Now get inside, get cleaned up and get your head down.'

Suddenly everything Onions was saying became real and the strength seemed to seep out of him and puddle at his feet.

He pushed the door open.

'I'll be in tomorrow.'

Onions said, 'You're on sick leave. Don't bother coming in tomorrow.'

'Stan, I have to follow . . .'

'I'll do the following. Right now I've got Kolankiewicz telling me to put you on sick leave. And for once I agree with the bugger.'

'I have leads to follow. I cannot take leave now.'

Onions said, 'Go to bed. I'll be round tomorrow. It ought to be open and shut. As you said, the bugger's missing. I think that says it all.'

'Is this your way of telling me I was right all along?'

'It's my way of saying if you still want a job in Murder, do what you're bloody well told.'

§ 186

Troy called the London Hospital. Miss Borg had suffered concussion, but was recovering well and would be discharged in a day or two.

He sloughed off his clothes, found the gas was working, ran a meagre bath off the Ascot heater and fell asleep in it.

In the evening Kolankiewicz called on him in the middle of the air-raid.

'I need to give you the once-over.'

'Be my guest.'

Kolankiewicz examined his head, listened to his heart, said, 'OK, smartyarse, so you're immortal. Now . . . you got anything you want to tell me?'

Troy said nothing.

Kolankiewicz said, 'Troy, be a *mensch*. I hate to see you grow up . . .'

'Grow up what?'

'Hard . . . cynical.'

'Secretive, destructive?'

'That too.'

Troy said nothing.

§ 187

In the morning Onions appeared on his doorstep.

'Tell me,' Troy said.

'Stick the kettle on,' Onions said.

Precious time wasted.

Onions sat with his cup of char. Stringing out his moment. Troy could have strangled him.

'They've found Carsington's body.'

Long swill of hot tea. Eye to eye pause.

'They dug down?'

Onions was shaking his head.

'No. They found Carsington's body. In the Bridal Suite of the Empire Hotel in Brighton.'

'What?'

'Bridal Suite. In front of the French windows. Bollock naked. Covered in blood and shit. Cut his own throat.'

For a while neither of them said anything.

Then Onions said, 'It was his fifty-fifth birthday, by the bye. If you think numbers mean anything, that is. If you ask me . . . barking. Completely bloody barking. I nipped down to Brighton. Saw the manager of the Empire. Seems Carsington had booked the room half a dozen times over the last couple of years. Every time it was the same. They'd find a room you'd have to clean with a hose ... blood and shit all over the place. He'd bung 'em twenty-five quid to clean up the mess and keep their gobs shut.'

And Troy said, 'Then it's got to be one of the others.'

Onions was shaking his head.

'Lockett's been in the Radcliffe Hospital in Oxford since Sunday night. Bit of a do at his old college. A bit too much vintage port. Silly sod got himself run over in the blackout. Happens all the time. We've lost more people to road accidents than to bombs.'

'Trench?'

Onions was shaking his head.

'Enlisted Wednesday morning. Been at Camberley barracks ever since.'

'Enlisted?!?'

'Happen it was summat you said to him? Whatever. Conscience finally got to him, and he decided to put his patriotism on the line.'

'I don't bloody believe this.'

'You'd better. It's kosher. Oxford coppers checked out Lockett, I drove to Camberley and interviewed Trench meself.'

'Then ... then ...'

Troy stopped himself saying 'who's in the pit?' The last thing he wanted was to encourage Onions to have it dug out.

Onions finished his tea. Got up to leave.

'Don't feel foolish.'

Troy didn't.

'You were right. I was wrong. You got the bastard. He's dead. That's all that matters. Digging down's a waste of time. Sooner or later we'll have a list of missing persons to work from and one name'll stick out like a sore thumb.'

On the doorstep Onions glanced at the sky – Indian summer, hints of autumn – turned back with one last thought tripping off his tongue.

'Speaking of missing persons. Ernie Steerforth's missis phoned in and reported him missing.'

Troy hoped he looked blank, blank or startled.

'Missing? When?'

'Wednesday night. Silly bugger. Out in an air-raid.'

If Onions suspected a thing it wasn't showing in his face.

'Back to Murder, eh?'

It was as though he'd uttered his motto, à propos of nothing much.

'Quite,' said Troy. 'You said yourself only a few weeks ago, murder doesn't stop just because there's a war on. In fact, it gets worse.'

'Aye . . . and so does the illegitimate birth rate, so I figure we're about even on life and death.'

Had Onions just made a joke? Onions hardly ever made jokes.

'Come to think of it, I reckon we've gone sex mad as a nation. The Commissioner's getting reports from beat bobbies of people shagging in Hyde Park in broad daylight. Would you believe it?'

'It wouldn't be broad daylight if it weren't for Double Summertime.'

'So it's OK to shag in the park as long as it's dark, is that it?'

Troy said nothing.

If Onions suspected a thing it wasn't showing in his face.

He gave Troy one of his rare smiles, blue eyes lit up, told him he was pleased with him, 'by and large', and set off down the alley to St Martin's Lane. He passed Troy's mother coming the other way – but as Superintendent Onions and Lady Troy had never met, neither recognised the other.

§ 188

'At a time like this, Frederick, you should come home, you should be at home.'

It was like being met at the nursery gates, aged four.

'How did you find out?'

'That nice Mr Onions telephoned me. One day you must introduce me.'

Troy gave in. He hadn't the energy to argue with his mother.

In the cab, crossing Euston Road, she said, 'You rest. Then lunch. Then you rest some more.'

His father was out. Troy stretched out on the chaise longue in the old man's study, feeling decidedly unsleepy. The next thing he knew someone was shaking him by the leg.

'Freddie?'

Troy opened his eyes.

It was a big bloke in RAF blue.

'Lunch.'

It was his brother, Rod. He'd never seen him in uniform. Never imagined him in uniform.

'Lunch. I have a forty-eight-hour leave, and some people I'd like you to meet.'

Rod held out a hand and hoisted Troy to his feet.

'Lunch?'

'Yes. With friends. A reunion. Sort of.'

Troy followed him into the dining room. Three other men of varying shapes, sizes and ages were gathered there.

'Let me introduce you. My little brother Freddie . . . this is . . .'

A stout bloke with a sour expression and a rogue's twinkle in his eyes.

'We met,' said Billy Jacks. 'Me and Constable Troy go back a ways, don't we, young Fred?'

A skinny bloke with lugholes like the handles on the Football Association cup.

'Josef Hummel,' said Hummel. 'Tailor of Stepney Green.'

A dapper bloke in late middle-age, riven with dignity.

'Viktor Rosen. I play ze joanna.'

Everyone except Troy laughed at this.

'Where d'you learn that?' asked Jacks.

'From you, Billy. I ascribe all my bad habits to several weeks sharing a room with you.'

'I get it,' Troy said. 'You were all in the same camp.'

'All in the same room,' sighed Rosen.

'So it's the Heaven's Gate Internment Camp Reunion?'

'Nah, mate. We none of us got within a mile of heaven,' Jacks said. 'This is . . . the Stinkin' Jews Reunion.'

Lady Troy seemed almost to have stripped her country home to provide this off-the-ration feast. Chickens had been slaughtered, potatoes unearthed, brassicas ripped bare.

Rod poured wine for them all, a Puligny-Montrachet '34. Herr Rosen rolled it around his palate, Billy Jacks pulled a face and asked if there was any pale ale and Troy and Hummel knocked it back pleasurably . . . and over lunch and a good bottle Troy learnt in snatches of the life they had led these last few months.

The dessert wine was more to Billy's taste, Troy thought – Chateau d'Yquem 1898. He glugged it like Vimto.

'Ninety-eight. Year I was born,' he said approvingly.

And for a moment, in the mind's eye, Troy could see the list of names, with Billy's name and birthdate upon it, that he and Stilton had used to round up these men. And it seemed a lifetime ago, and he was pleased to see that it seemed that way to Jacks too.

At the end of the meal Lady Troy came in and said, 'Herr Rosen . . . before you leave, we have a Steinway in the red room. I wonder if you would be so kind . . .?'

It was just the touch Rosen needed, the continental charm that was the antidote to a long summer spent with a rough diamond like Billy Jacks. He pressed her hand to his lips and said, 'My dear lady, lead me to it. To tickle ze ivories would give me such pleasure.'

They all followed to the red room.

Troy heard Jacks mutter, 'He's takin' the piss, ain't he?'

Rosen played Debussy's 'Estampes', 'Pagodes', 'La Soirée dans Grenade', 'Jardins sous la Pluie'. Played them far, far better than Troy had ever played them. It was a quarter hour of heaven. Troy closed his eyes, and let the music splash down onto him. A round of gentle applause made him open his eyes, to find his father sitting next to him.

Afterwards, on the doorstep Hummel asked, 'Are we to do this every year?'

'Don't see why not,' Rod said beaming and slightly pissed.

'Yeah. Why not?' said Jacks, belligerent with bonhomie.

Rod and Troy watched them walk to the end of Church Row. Jacks turned, cupped his hands to his lips and yelled.

'Chippin' bloody Campden, eh, 'Ampstead?'

Rod yelled 'Chipping Campden' back.

Troy looked at him as though he thought him mad.

'Every year?' he said softly.

'Oh yes. Friends for life. It's the sort of thing creates ties, bonds . . . that sort of thing.'

'To be free you must first belong.'

'Eh?'

'That's what you wrote to me in a letter about two months ago.'

'I did? Well . . . I was right.'

'And of course, to *betray* you must first belong.'

Rod thought about this.

'Y'know, *brer*,' he said at last, 'you've grown awfully cynical since we last met. I am almost tempted to ask what has happened to you, but I won't. Instead I shall nip back inside and have a bit of a chat with that cheery old soul we call "Dad".'

§ 189

Days later Troy could still hear Rosen's performance in the mind's ear. He lifted the lid on his Bösendorfer upright, unused since the day the shifters had lugged it into his parlour, and played the first chords of 'Pagodes'. He was embarrassingly bad.

Only when he'd finished, limped to the end, was he aware of someone standing in the doorway.

Kitty tossed his front door key down onto the carpet.

'You're a sod, Fred. A right sod.'

'You going to tell me why?'

'My dad says you and that Borg woman was wrapped around each other like lovers.'

'We were sheltering from the raid, Kitty.'

'No! Like lovers was wot dad said, and I saw you with me own eyes when the two of you came out. You was like lovers! What was she doin' there in the first place?'

'I can't tell you that.'

'Can't or won't? You've been givin 'er one, 'aven't you?'

Troy said nothing. It would have been more accurate he thought to say that Zette had been giving him one, but neither answer could possibly please.

Kitty came right up to him, bent down to him still perched upon the piano stool.

'You gonna 'ave to choose. Who's it to be? Her or me? Do I pick up that key or do I just bugger off? Who do you want, Troy?'

'I want you both.'

The sigh was enormous, as loud it seemed as any bomb he'd heard lately and a thousand times softer.

'Oh, Troy. You sod. You complete and utter sod.'

In the doorway, all but thrown over her shoulder, 'Me mum was right.

She told me that day you come to dinner. "Stick to your own kind, Kitty." That's what she told me.'

§ 190

On the following Monday, passing Stilton in the corridors of Scotland Yard, Troy said 'Hello Walter.'

Stilton said, 'Call me Inspector Stilton, lad.'

§ 191

He lifted the lid on the Bösendorfer again and tormented himself with Debussy.

History repeated itself. Another woman standing in his doorway – wearing what he thought of as her travel suit, the neat Chanel two-piece in black that she had worn on the overnight sleeper from Paris to Monte Carlo.

'I've come to say goodbye.'

'Goodbye?'

'I have a new job.'

'You do? Where?'

'Initially at Columbia University in New York. After that wherever it takes me.'

'That sounds ... marvellous.'

'Einstein read my last paper ... asked that I be ... I think "recruited" is the word. I'm splitting atoms again. This time for real, not just in theory.'

'Sounds like a blast.'

'If it works, Troy, it'll be the biggest blast in history.'

'More numbers?'

'It's always numbers.'

He was being dumped, and he knew it. 'Don't make plans', she had told him, and instead he had built castles in the air, plan upon plan. He wanted to tell her this, but every iota of intelligence told him not to bother.

'What numbers did I recite to conjure you up as my own personal golem?'

Zette said, '9, 8, 6.'

'Meaning?'

'Body heat, Troy.'

She kissed him on the lips.

She walked out of the door and down the alley.

He never saw her again.

§ 192

It had taken him too long to do this. Partly because he had forgotten, partly because he was fighting shy of it. But it was time Troy got in touch with Nader again. Time he returned his jacket. He'd take it round to him, let him pick his own tailor for the repairs and the cleaning – the East End was full of tailors after all – and offer to pick up the bill.

'Have you called before?' Nader said on the doorstep. 'I have been away. My father is well enough to be moved and we have found a family in Essex to take him in. I have only been back an hour or so.'

'No. I have been . . . a bit busy. But I have your jacket here.'

He held it up.

'I think it's ready to be relegated to gardening and decorating.'

Nader beckoned him inside. Stuck the kettle on.

'You know what happened, I take it?'

'Oh yes. My would-be-assassin is buried under what remains of Heaven's Gate. By the bye, which of your suspects was it?'

Now Troy was face to face with the moment he had tried so hard to put off.

'None of them. I've no idea who's down there. Some Jew-hater. Some nutcase obsessed with "the Controversy of Zion".'

'The what?'

'It was left at the scene, at Friedland's murder. A bible open at Isaiah . . . a list of plagues and disasters and the Controversy of Zion. Can't remember the chapter.'

'Nor I, and that's a professional failing, isn't it?'

'We may never know who it was.'

'Perhaps when we dig out?'

Troy shook his head.

'I saw a cartload of incendiaries fall into the pit. Magnesium burning will melt through steel. I'd be amazed if there's anything more than charred bone.'

Nader shrugged. Began to go through the pockets of his jacket.

'So long as he's dead, eh? Ah . . . I have them. My spare specs. The jacket I could afford to lose, not the specs. And . . .'

He had one hand in the right inside pocket.

'. . . You must be left-handed, Mr Troy, and this must be yours.'

Onto the oilclothed table Nader placed a cut-throat razor, a tortoiseshell sheath folded over a stained steel blade. Troy had no idea it was in the jacket. He had no idea he'd taken it off Zette. But he must have done. The copper's instinct to seize the murder weapon. And the stains – the stains were Chief Inspector Steerforth's blood.

After tea, and promises that they would keep in touch, even though they both knew they would break them, Troy took a walk down by the Thames at Wapping Pier Head, in the shadow of Tower Bridge, and flung the razor as far out into the river as he could. It was still well short of dusk and already the bombers were swarming up the Thames.

§ 193

What Became of Them

Alex Troy died in the autumn of 1943.

Winston Churchill was voted out of office in 1945. He declined a dukedom, and while he was Prime Minister once more from 1951 to 1955 he was never so influential in public life again.

Wolfgang Stahl vanished during a Berlin air raid in April 1941.

Reinhard Heydrich was assassinated by the Czech Resistance in May 1942.

Josef Trager, much against his own expectations, made lance-corporal before his career as a soldier ended. It ended, as for so many, with his death. He was one of the lucky ones who escaped encirclement by Russian troops at Stalingrad, and one of the unlucky ones to be trapped in the retreat by a Russian winter that touched forty below. Forty below what does not matter, it is the point at which Fahrenheit and Centigrade meet. Winter kills. His uniform proved inadequate. Hitler had never made proper winter provision for his troops, and Trager had taken to wearing the trousers from the suit Hummel had made for him under his uniform. To defecate required him to drop both pairs. And that is how he died in the January of 1943 – frozen into a squat, arse-naked, with his German grey trousers and his Austrian blue serge bunched around his knees. His last reported words were 'Oh shit!'

Josef Hummel became a British citizen, opened his own shop in the West End of London, and with the lifting of clothes rationing became established as one of London's most sought-after tailors. Recognising the 1960s youth-quake for what it was he opened a shop in Carnaby Street in 1964, offering the latest fashions for the young, which soon became a nationwide chain under the name 'Vienna Joe's Rags'n'Riches', almost always referred to simply as 'Vienna Joe's'. He retired in 1977 at the age of sixty-nine and moved to Eastbourne, where he still lives aged ninety-six, and where he studies for his doctorate in philosophy at the Open University. 'Vienna Joe's' became part of the legend of Swingin' London, and is widely believed to be the origin of the name chosen by the British rock band Vinegar Joe, but as with so many legends in popular music, this is probably apocryphal.

Hugh Greene was appointed Director-General of the BBC in 1960.

Oskar Siebert never went home. Released in March 1941, he served throughout the war in the Pioneer Corps. After the war he applied for British Citizenship and qualified as a barrister. He achieved brief but pleasing fame as a member of the defence team in the political show trial Regina v. Oz, 1971.

Billy Jacks was elected Labour MP for Tower Hamlets in 1950. Always a rebel he never made it off the back benches and proved an irritant to every Labour leader from Attlee to Wilson. He spoke memorably and movingly against the invasion of Suez, was a frequent Aldermaston marcher, and in the 1960s he campaigned vigorously for CND and against the war in Viet Nam. He was also a regular guest on the BBC Home Service radio programme *Any Questions*, and was widely regarded as the authentic voice of working-class London. Jacks remained on good terms with Rod Troy (himself a Labour MP from 1945), although they moved further apart politically with every year that passed. He died suddenly in 1968. There has been a petition to the Mayor of London requesting a blue plaque to be placed on the building where his shop once stood and talk of a statue. The former seems likely, the latter does not.

Max Drax died at Heaven's Gate, Port Erin, I.O.M., in November 1940, still a prisoner of the British.

Kurt Schwitters was released in November 1941. His greatest creation, his Hanover 'Merzbau', was destroyed in an RAF raid. He died in Ambleside in 1948.

Somewhere in Rod Troy's attic, in the house he inherited from his father in Church Row, there is a small brown attaché case, reinforced at the corners, bearing the labels of hotels in Stuttgart and Paris, containing all the possessions of the late Professor Klemper who died on Derby Station in 1940. Amongst them is a memoir of his time in Oranienburg Concentration Camp. A time there was when Rod had considered seeking out any living relative of Professor Klemper and returning the case. The impossibility of this ruled it out. More times there were when Rod considered seeking a publisher for the manuscript – but once the case was consigned to the attic by his wife, in the new year of 1946, Rod forgot about the manuscript and scarcely remembers it even now.

Arthur Kornfeld gave up mathematics, physics, and his Cambridge fellowship to found a London publishing house in the late 1940s. As all London publishers seemed to him to come in pairs, Eyre & Spottiswoode, Weidenfeld & Nicolson, Chatto & Windus, although he found it hard to believe there'd ever been anyone called Windus, he named his after his old mentor, Drax. Drax & Kornfeld survived for forty-three years, publishing quirky, poorly selling but often well-reviewed books, until they were bought out by the aforementioned Weidenfeld & Nicolson, shortly before they in turn were bought out by Orion. Arthur retained his editorial position and is often to be found wandering the corridors at St Martin's Lane lost between lunch and literature. Had Rod Troy offered him Klemper's manuscript in all probability he would have published it.

Elishah Nader emigrated to Israel in 1974 and was crushed to death by an Israeli tank while protesting at the demolition of Palestinian houses in 1992.

In 1975 Zette Borg, by then in her late-sixties, shared the Nobel Prize for Physics with two other physicists for her work on superconductivity, experiments approaching absolute zero, and papers that pointed to the development of the Bose-Einstein Condensate, a condition attained some twenty years later at temperatures only a few billionths of a degree above absolute zero. At such temperatures, Einstein had hypothesised the inversion of atomic waves and the merging of atomic identities into a single entity. Absolute zero (0 deg. Kelvin, −273.15 Centigrade) is a theoretical condition and is unattainable. Her former lover, Frederick Troy, having little or no grasp of physics, regarded all this as merely metaphor.

§

Historical Note

Yes ... there were internment camps on the Isle of Man ... no, there was no all-male camp as far south as Port Erin.

There is no synagogue resembling Heaven's Gate or Elohim in the East End of London – indeed such is the paucity of synagogues these days that I based both buildings on the Eldridge Street Synagogue on New York's Lower East Side. Just around the corner from Eldridge Street is a former synagogue, as tiny as any still standing in London, which was once known as 'Gates of Heaven'.

Why this topic now? Well, I think we have lived these last few years in a world dominated by a man to whom the rest of the world, other than those from his own green acres in Texas, are just 'kikes and niggers'. A man who cannot even pronounce the name 'Iraq'. If you will substitute 'towelhead' or 'ayrab' for kike and nigger ... it doesn't alter the concept one jot.

A hit list drawn up by a British fascist of critics to be bumped off or dealt with? Of course, I made it up ... until ... towards the end of writing this book I stumbled across a reference to just this kind of list in the wartime diaries of Frances Partridge, a friend of whom was revealed to be on Sir Oswald Mosley's 'hit' list after writing to the *Daily Telegraph* urging Mosley's arrest.

The only point at which I think I have displaced a real figure with a fictional one is that, of course, Freud was rescued from Vienna by Professor Ernest Jones, subsequently Freud's biographer; and himself the subject of a recent biography by Brenda Meddox. (Anyone who wants a straightforwardly factual account of Freud leaving Vienna should turn to Jones's book – anyone who wants one more bizarre and dramatic than mine should turn to *The End of the World News* by Anthony Burgess.) Many of the minor characters in this novel were real – Cazalet, Ciano *et al* – many more are made up ...

I'm deliberately vague about the date of publication of *Moses and Monotheism* (it was, loosely, the summer of 1939) and, whilst Freud was criticised widely for choosing that subject, at that time, to the best of my knowledge, the Board of Deputies never wrote as one body to any national newspaper.

Red Vienna is a slight misnomer and could more accurately be used to describe the Vienna of the early 1930s than the city Hitler seized.

Coming at the war for the third time I was keen not to return to the same sources. Apart from Frances Partridge (Hogarth Press, 1978), the most interesting books on the subject I discovered were the dispatches of Ernie Pyle (McBride, 1941), the diaries of Joan Wyndham (Heinemann, 1985), *Home Front* by E.S. Turner, who died while I was writing this book (Michael Joseph, 1961) and *The Making of an Englishman* by Fred Uhlman (Gollancz, 1960). Uhlman was a refugee who became a well-known North London painter – he died only about twenty years ago. On pp. 201–3 Uhlman offers a celebration of Englishness that I suspect only an immigrant could make ... I used chunks of it in a speech by Viktor Rosen (pp. 297–9) as I cannot better it.

Acknowledgements aplenty . . .

Gordon Chaplin
Sarah Teale
Cosima Dannoritzer
John Fagan
Sarah Burkinshaw
Chris Greene
Clare Alexander
Justin Gowers
Francine Brody
Linda Shockley
David Cantor
Meredith Chambers
Ingrid Kurnig
Richard Donnenberg
Sue Freathy
and
Anna Hervé